Kellie grew up in Nebraska, where her love of reading and writing was cultivated by her grandmother. The two of them passed books back and forth all the time. Her grandmother wrote for the local newspaper and also wrote stories from her childhood. Kellie started writing stories as a child, dreaming of someday writing a book.

Kellie currently lives in Wisconsin with her husband of 30 years, Dan. They have three grown children, Aric, Aaron and Alyssa. They also have three grandchildren with one more on the way.

Kellie enjoys cross-stitching, reading, writing, traveling to see family, and outdoor activities with her husband such as kayaking and fishing.

Kellie Mickelsen

MIA AMATA

AUSTIN MACAULEY PUBLISHERS™

LONDON • CAMBRIDGE • NEW YORK • SHARJAH

Ordering Information
Quantity sales: Special discounts are available on quantity purchases by corporations, associations, and others. For details, contact the publisher at the address below.

Publisher's Cataloging-in-Publication data
Mickelsen, Kellie
Mia Amata

ISBN 9798889107279 (Paperback)
ISBN 9798889107309 (ePub e-book)

Library of Congress Control Number: 2024910688

www.austinmacauley.com/us

First Published 2024
Austin Macauley Publishers LLC
40 Wall Street, 33rd Floor, Suite 3302
New York, NY 10005
USA

mail-usa@austinmacauley.com
+1 (646) 5125767

Dan – My best friend, my husband, thank you for always being there for me and telling me I can when I didn't think that I could. I love you more every day!

Aric, Aaron and Alyssa – Thank you three for letting me bounce my ideas off you and offering advice. A mother couldn't ask for three more fantastic kids or be prouder than I am. I love you all!

My friends – You all know who you are, I would like to thank you all for being my cheerleaders and encouraging me to see my dream to fruition. Thank you!

Chapter 1

I used to believe in love at first glance, but the past five years have shown me that it is a complete myth. Now I consider love at first glance the biggest line of bull I've ever heard. In fact, I don't believe love exists. I will never let my heart overrule my common sense and brain ever again if I am ever given the chance to, I mean. If things continue the way they are right now, I will not be around to see my next birthday let alone have the chance to make decisions about future relationships.

Five years ago, I met the man of my dreams, or so I thought. He turned out to be the stuff of my nightmares. An ongoing nightmare that I cannot seem to escape—ever. He has his hands tightly around my throat and squeezes the life out of me more and more every day. I have nowhere to turn, no one to trust. My main thought on a daily basis is whether I should end this myself or wait for him to end it for me.

These are the thoughts that run through my head as I shower this morning. It would be so easy to just grab the razor and let my life drain out of my body through slits on my wrists. This seemed like it would be so much less painful than waiting for him to kill me. I look down at my body, and I see the scars and the bruises in various stages of healing all over my trunk. This morning is different than all the other times.

I look up at the mirror and see the brand-new bruises on my face. For the first time in five years, he lost control and hit my face, more than once. Tears fall as I look at the black eye and the fat lip, the cut on the forehead. What is next? Does he stop using his fists and grab a knife? A gun? My gaze falls again on the razor, and I reach for it, stopping just inches from it. Why? Why can't I do it? Why am I so willing to let him be the one to kill me instead of taking control of the situation—the only thing I could have control of?

The alarm goes off, and I automatically reach out, shutting the water off. I grabbed a towel and shut the alarm off. I move out of habit now, knowing that if I don't follow his plan for the day, I will suffer for it later. I put on the clothes that he laid out for me, jeans, T-shirt, a bra, panties, which are not the usual 'around the home' clothes he would put out for me if I am staying home, so he must need me to run some errands. This both terrifies and thrills me. I never get to leave the house so whenever I am given the chance, I am excited to do so. It also terrifies me as I know how my face looks.

I look at the counter in the bathroom and see that he has set out some makeup for me. He never lets me wear makeup, so I am guessing he wants me to use it to hide my face. I apply the makeup to the best of my ability, considering I am not sure how to wear it anymore. Also, there is no way to completely hide what he has done to my face.

I leave the bathroom and head to the office to look at THE LIST. That is the way I see it in my head when he refers to it. 'Damn it, Megan! What did THE LIST say you were supposed to do today?' or 'Did you even read THE LIST today? Are you stupid and couldn't understand what THE LIST said?'

I hate THE LIST as much as I hate him. I turn toward the whiteboard with THE LIST on it and grab a marker. I check off the shower, makeup, dressed. I put the marker down and read what I was supposed to do with my day. I see that it does involve me leaving the house, he wrote a grocery list; the list and the money for the groceries are on the board under a magnet. I haven't gotten groceries in a long time. He decided he would do it, another thing taken away from me to keep me trapped in this house.

I took the grocery list and the money, walking out of the office to head to the front door. The office is his, the only thing I am allowed to do in there is look at THE LIST. A new alarm goes off on my phone. I look at it, it says go to the store. I have to leave now or I'm in trouble. One of his methods of control is to set alarms on my phone indicating when I am supposed to start or stop each item on the list.

I head to the front door, knowing he will check the cameras later to make sure I am leaving at the time he expects me to. Next to the front door, on the stand, sits my purse, the car keys, and a pair of socks, while on the floor next to the stand are my shoes. I sit down on the bench, putting on my socks and shoes. When I stood back up, I noticed a pair of sunglasses sitting in my purse.

He thinks of everything, how considerate I think wryly. I leave the house, climb into the car, checking the phone to see how long he has given me to get groceries. I also check the GPS to see which store he has me going to. Turning on the car, I back out of the driveway.

***

I pulled into the parking lot of the grocery store 20 minutes later and parked. Climbing out of the car I am suddenly struck with dizziness and nausea; I manage to turn toward the front of the car before I throw up. When I finished, I leaned against the driver's door, sliding to the ground as I was too dizzy to stay standing. I put my head between my knees and breathe deeply when I hear a voice asking me if I am OK. I can't speak yet, so I give a slight shake of my head, just focusing on breathing. I hear the rustle of sacks, then become aware of someone sitting on the ground next to me.

"Here, honey, let me help you," a woman said.

I feel a cool, damp paper towel on the back of my neck. It feels so nice, and I am so grateful that I started crying. This one little gesture of caring has shocked me so much I can't stop crying.

"There, there, it's OK. If you think you can, try a sip of water," she said, slipping a cold bottle of water into my hands. I take a sip, finally starting to get a grip on my emotions.

"Thank you," I say so quietly that she has to strain to hear me. Forgetting what my face looks like, not realizing I had taken the sunglasses off during vomiting, I look at her. She lets out an audible gasp. It was only then that I remembered what I look like. I turned away quickly, looking for the glasses.

She grabbed my hands and said, "No, dear, don't look at me again."

Hesitantly, I did so. She takes the cool, damp paper towel, wiping my face with it. I close my eyes, letting her do so, noticing how tender and comforting this feels.

"I don't know what happened," I said. "I got out of the car. Suddenly, I felt sick and dizzy. It just hit me so fast. Must be a flu bug or something." She just keeps wiping my face, listening to me, then feels my forehead.

"I don't think so," she replied. "You don't seem to have a fever. How are you feeling now?"

I considered it for a couple minutes before I replied. The nausea was still there a little, yet the dizziness was gone. My face and body hurt terribly from last night, but I told her I was feeling better. I started to get up, but she stopped me, telling me to take it slow.

I shook my head, I really had to get going, I had to be home soon with the groceries, and I still had to do the shopping. She stands up with me, helping me. Suddenly, I realized we were not alone. There is a young woman standing close by, watching. I hide my face, looking for the sunglasses again. I finally see them, pick them up, putting them back on.

"I think you need to come with me," the lady said. I looked at her, wondering what she was talking about. "Is this your car?" she asked, nodding at the one behind me. I nodded yes. "OK. This is what you are going to do," she said, taking charge all of a sudden, "Put everything you have back in the car—your purse, your sunglasses, the keys, any money, everything."

I didn't understand why she was telling me all this. I said, "You don't understand, I have to get the groceries and go home. If I don't..." I let the thought trail off. I didn't need to finish it, she did it for me.

"If you don't, he will beat you again, won't he? I am offering you help to get away from him. Right now. Isn't that what you really want? You don't really want to go back home to him, do you? To face this again tonight or tomorrow?" she asked.

"Mom," the other woman said, "if we are going to do this we need to go— now. Before people..."

"I know," the lady replied. "Put everything back in the car and come with me. Now."

In a state of shock, I did what she said. I put everything, including the phone, my purse that held my only ID, the money, the list, all back in the car. As I was doing so, she was telling me what to do next, speaking quickly.

"I am parked four rows to the right, red van. Don't follow us exactly, go down a few cars, then work your way back to the van on the passenger side. My daughter and I will go now and put our things in the back while you are doing all this. Then walk over there and jump in the back seat, but on the floor so no cameras can see you leaving the parking lot with us. Hurry!"

Not knowing exactly why, I did what she said. Maybe it was because she was the first person to treat me with kindness in a long time. Maybe it was the fact that she offered me a way out, even though I didn't know what she was thinking she could do to help me. I think it was mainly that my two other options were so horrible that whatever she could offer couldn't be as bad. I worked my way down the parking lot, past their van, then back toward them where the door stood open welcoming me in.

"Just dive in, I'll close the door behind you automatically." I did and lay on the floor. She closed the door and drove away—hopefully to my freedom and a better option from death which seemed like my only way out this morning.

Chapter 2

As I was lying on the floor, the lady driving started talking to me. "OK, honey, I know this is probably scary for you, but we honestly just want to help you. My name is Lauren, and this is my daughter, Eva. I am offering you what someone offered me several years ago—the chance at a new life, a new start away from the man who is abusing you. If someone had not given me that option, Eva and I would not be here today. Any time I get the chance to pay it forward, I do so," she was talking while negotiating the traffic. "We only ask two things from you in return."

Here it comes, I thought to myself, *some proposition*. Here is where I learned exactly how big of a mistake I made trusting two total strangers. I look at the van doors, wondering if I could unlock them and jump out fast enough to get away.

Lauren continued to speak. "Someday down the road when you are safe, no longer in fear for your life, you pay it forward if you are able to. That is not something we would expect of you for years. In fact, you are only the fourth person I have helped in the 19 years since someone helped me. Secondly, most importantly, you have to keep everything you see, hear, and learn about us a complete secret or you will endanger our lives." She stopped talking while she maneuvered the van around a couple of cars.

"Right now, I imagine you are terrified that he will find you. So are we. If he finds you, we will be out there in the public eye. I only tell you this as I need you to understand the risk we are taking. Just in case they caught us helping you in the parking lot on a security camera, we are going to make a couple of stops. I know it isn't very comfortable lying on the floor back there, but this is to help you I promise," she explained as she was stopped at a stoplight.

"We had a couple of errands that we were going to run today, so I am not going to stray from what we would normally do today," Lauren said. "One of the errands was to renew the plates on the van, so I am going to the courthouse, where I will park in the view of the camera. I need you to stay hidden, do not look out any windows at all. I want the cameras to show what appears to be an empty vehicle. Pull that blanket on the back seat over you, hiding you from view even more. When we are done here, we will go to one of the drugstores and do the same there. Do you understand the importance of staying hidden? Not only will he find you, but you put us in danger also as there is someone looking for us out there too."

Even though I was in a state of shock, I was able to take in everything she said. Someone did this to her, too? This is not what I had expected to hear, in a weak voice I replied, "I understand. I won't put you or your daughter in danger although I don't think you understand how much danger you are in just by helping me. You need to know, my husband is a cop." I hear both of them gasp.

Lauren said, "Well then, that makes going to the courthouse the perfect cover. Do you think he will be there today?"

"Chances are pretty good he will be. He is at work today, the police station is adjacent to the courthouse. His name is…"

"No! Don't tell me his name," Lauren declared. "I don't want to be looking for him. If I were to see him, my face could betray that I know who he is—that would be dangerous for us all."

I understood what she was saying, so I didn't tell them Allen's name or give them a description of him. I grabbed the blanket, covering up with it, making sure I didn't show anywhere. I also grabbed a couple of their bags off the seat, placing them over top of me.

Eva looked back, saying, "That is perfect, I can't see you at all."

Lauren said, "Great. Now, don't tell us your name either, I am sure I will learn it at some point from the news, but if someone asks me about you, I don't want to show recognition when your name is mentioned."

"Instead, while you are waiting for us to run errands, think of what you would like to be called instead, making it something similar to your real name, so you will get used to it quickly, but different enough to not ring bells when it is heard. That is the name that you will give to Eva and me when we get to the house."

At that point, we pulled into the parking lot at the courthouse, and she parked the van, but before they got out, she said, "I know you are scared, but you need to trust us. I also know I am asking a lot of you, trust is probably hard for you. You have nothing to lose by putting your trust in us right now. I am going to do my best to help you," she reached for the door handle. "Stay hidden, we will be back in a few minutes."

"I promise."

With that, Lauren and Eva left the van, shutting the doors. I heard the doors lock. *Scared?* I thought. Scared did not explain how I was feeling at that moment. Scared was an understatement.

Terrified was an understatement. I lay there hiding, waiting, knowing that the door to the van could fly open at any minute, and he would drag me out of the van. I tried to think about the situation, did I have anything to fear from these two women? Could I trust them?

The conclusion came to me easily. I didn't have a choice. I had to trust them. The fact that they were putting their lives at risk for me, that this mom was putting her daughter's life at risk FOR ME, is finally what made the conclusion obvious. Who would do that? What daughter would be OK with her mom doing this? I wondered if Eva experienced what her mom went through, remembered it and so did this for that reason.

I remembered that Lauren said they had helped four people before this, I wondered how that went. Were they successful? I was going to take a risk to trust these two people with my life. It was at this point I heard the doors unlock and open. I never said a word as Lauren and Eva climbed into the van, buckling up, chatting like a normal mother and daughter probably running errands together. The doors closed, the van started, and soon, we began moving. As we pulled out of the parking lot, Lauren asked, "Are you OK back there?"

"Yes," I replied. "I don't know how to thank you both for what you are doing. I am sorry I don't know how to act or what to say, I am not sure I even believe that this is all real." There was a moment of silence, and then, to my surprise, Eva answered me.

"I'm sure that this morning when you were getting up, showering, eating breakfast—whatever your morning routine is—the last thing you were thinking about was getting away. I'm sure you were thinking about what you could do to make sure that you didn't get hit again. I remember hearing the horror stories about my dad and what he did to Mom. I read the newspaper articles. Mom shared her journals with me. I vowed that I would help anyone I could get out of that situation if I had the chance." Eva paused. "You don't need to thank us; Mom and I have discussed this many times."

"We know the risks we are taking. This morning when we both saw your face, we knew, without even speaking, that we needed to help you. We already care about you, wanting to help you, so that you can have a future. All I want from you is a promise that you will never give up, no matter what. My mother is my world. I will protect her at all costs, even if it means kicking you out. If you can abide by what we ask you, keep us a secret from anyone going forward, I will help you to no end."

I was crying in the back as I listened to this young lady—a girl no longer seemed appropriate to describe her—her words held so much meaning that I would never forget them.

"Eva," I said as I pulled the blanket away from my face enough, so I was not muffled, "I don't know what life holds for me right now, I'm trying to wrap my mind around all of this. I will promise you that no matter what happens to me, I will never give you and your mom up to protect myself. What you have already done for me is more than anyone has ever done for me in my entire life. I have a lot to take in, but that promise I can make to you without hesitation."

"Thank you," Eva said.

I saw her look at her mother and smile. I pulled the blanket back over my head as we pulled into yet another parking lot, going through the same routine as we did at the courthouse. This time when they came out and unlocked the doors, they opened the back doors, putting some more sacks in, including on top of me, yet gentle enough that it did not bother me. We started driving again.

Lauren said, "OK, I think that is good enough, we finished the errands we had originally set out to do today. We need you to stay hidden for just a little longer, we are going back to our house now. When we get there, I will pull into the garage, closing the garage door, and then we will be able to get you out of the van without anyone seeing. There are no windows in the garage, no chance of your being seen in there."

"We do have to be careful when we go into the house though, the less people that know you are there, the better. We have a basement with a bedroom, small kitchen, and full bathroom, which is where we will have you go once we get into the house. It will be like a small apartment for you. Do you think you can stay down there, stay hidden?"

I affirmed that I could do that, after all, none of our neighbors ever saw me anyway. I could easily pretend not to exist, having lived that way for years.

"Perfect. Just remember, this is not permanent. We will eventually get you out of town, to a safe place where you can start over, but for the time being, we need to keep you hidden."

We pulled into the garage; the garage door closed.

Eva turned toward me, "It's OK, you can uncover now." I pulled the blanket back, sat up, moved the sacks back on the seat, then I climbed out of the van.

Lauren walked up to me, saying, "I know you don't know me, but I would like to give you a hug—unless it would make you feel uncomfortable, I will understand." I told her it was OK. She gave me a gentle hug. She then said, "We are going to do whatever we can to make you safe, I promise."

I just nodded, as more tears came. Lauren released me, and I turned, grabbing sacks from the van to help carry in their purchases.

We walked into the house; the garage door led into a hallway. Eva walked into the main part of the house, but Lauren walked in, stopping in the hallway. She turned as I shut the garage door and told me, "The doors right there are where the washer and dryer are. You should be able to come up and use them when needed without being seen from the outside although you might want to wait until one of us is home, in case someone comes to the door and can hear the noise." I nodded to her as I took in the doors she was pointing at.

"This door," Lauren stated as she pointed to a door a little further in, on the opposite side, "leads to the basement. Eva is checking the windows in the other rooms, but we should be good to head straight down there."

At that point, Eva came back to the hallway, nodding at her mom. She opened the door that Lauren said led to the basement. We headed down the stairs. At the bottom of the stairs was a small living area with an eat-in kitchen. It was comfortably furnished, and even though the furniture was not brand-new, it was very pleasing to the eye.

Lauren walked across to the door on the other side of the room and opened it. "This is your bedroom." She nodded at the room. I walked into it, finding another very comfortable room with what was secondhand furniture but very lovely and peaceful looking.

"Over here, you have a full bathroom," Eva said, pointing at another door. I was overwhelmed once again, unable to stop them, the tears flowed.

I looked at Lauren, "I don't know what to say, how to express what I am feeling right now.”

Lauren smiled, “Well, it isn’t much, but I hope you will feel at home here for the time being.”

I shook my head, “It is lovely. So comfortable and peaceful. I am… extremely grateful for what you are doing for me.”

Lauren took my hands into hers, “You are welcome here with all our hearts. This will be your home until we can make other arrangements. We will discuss that later. Let’s go out to the kitchen, I’ll show you a few things.”

We walked out into the kitchen area, and she showed me a well-stocked pantry of canned goods and boxed goods, explaining, “We keep this kitchen well-stocked as we never know when someone will be using it. We keep an eye on expiration dates and use things upstairs as needed.”

She opened the refrigerator, which to my surprise was somewhat stocked also. “These are cold items that have longer expiration dates on them, we come down and get them when we use ours up, replacing them as we go.”

I observed the items in the refrigerator, “Milk and eggs?”

Eva looked at her mom and laughed. “Well,” she said, “those are new. I told Mom a couple of days ago. I felt we needed to buy extra of those types of items, putting them down here. I guess you could say I had a feeling.”

Lauren laughed, “The last time she had a feeling like that was when we helped the last person. So I listened, and we stocked up. Use what you want/need, let us know if there is something else you want or need, and we will pick it up for you.”

She walked over to the table and sat down. She motioned for me to join her while Eva took another seat. She looked intently at me, saying “I think we should discuss a couple of things now, and then we will let you get settled in and rest. First off, what name did you decide on, so I know what to call you?”

“Mattie,” I said.

“OK, Mattie it is. So you know our names. We would like to keep things on a first-name basis if that is OK with you?”

I nodded, I understood. The less I know the better off they will be if I am found.

“Thank you for understanding. Not being rude, we would prefer you to not wander around upstairs where you can see personal items, not only because the less you know about our private lives, but when you go upstairs you run the risk of being seen. Doing laundry is safe, you can’t be seen there from the windows."

Again, I nodded, "I am good with that. It really does feel safe down here."

It was Lauren's turn to nod. Eva said, "There is a variety of clothing in the bedroom closet, a variety of sizes that we have collected here and there. Some are brand-new, picked up on sale. Others are nice items we picked up at garage sales or at thrift stores. I think one of the first things you should do is go change clothes, bringing us what you have on, so we can dispose of them, in case he remembers what you were wearing today when you left home."

I said, "He will know exactly what I was wearing, as he picks my clothes out every day." I got up and walked toward the bedroom, but not before I saw the glance exchanged between Eva and her mom.

I closed the bedroom door behind me, took all my clothes off, including my bra and panties, putting them in a pile on the end of the bed. I opened the closet door, seeing that there were a lot of clothes in there. I stared at them for the longest time, it was like my mind froze. I had no idea what to wear, what size I was, what would even look good together. I opened a drawer in the closet to find a variety of underwear, bras, and socks. Another drawer yielded shorts and another pants. I was clueless. I backed away, sliding to the floor, crying. I couldn't control the sobs. I heard a slight knock on the door.

Eva opened the door a crack, "Mattie, can I come in?" I nodded yes, and she walked in, closing the door behind her. She reached into the closet and pulled out a robe. "Here, let's put this on for the moment." She reached out and took my hand, helping me up. As I slipped into the robe, she saw all the bruises and scars all over my body. "Oh, Mattie, I'm so sorry he did that to you."

She handed me some Kleenex, and I wiped my eyes and blew my nose. I motioned to the closet. saying, "I don't know what to wear."

Eva seemed to take that in stride and said, "Well, what size are you? We can start there."

I looked at her with a blank stare.

"You don't know what size you wear?" she asked.

I shook my head. She walked over to the clothes on the bed and looked through them for size tags. Finding nothing, she put them down and walked back over to me. "OK, I think you are about the same size as me, so let's start with something else. What is your favorite color?"

I had to think about that for a little bit, as I hadn't thought about my favorite anything for a long time. No one cared about what my favorite things were. "Any color?" I asked meekly.

Eva nodded, smiling gently at me. She watched me as I searched my mind for a color I liked.

"Blue," I said, "like the sky."

"Perfect!" Eva said. She went into the closet and pointed to a section. "These clothes here should be the ones that would probably fit you the best. Let's see what we have here." She went through the clothes and pulled out a blue dress, the color of the sky. "What do you think of this?"

I nodded, "It's very pretty."

"I think it will look great on you, matches your eyes. Now, let's see if we can find some undergarments for you to wear." She pointed to more drawers that held things that she thought would fit me and pulled out a bra and panties set that were pretty blue also. She set all the clothes on the bed and said "Try these on. I'll go back out with Mom. Let me know if you need anything else." She walked out and shut the door behind her.

I picked up the bra and panties and looked at them closely. They were nothing like what I was used to. They were pretty and soft, not the more revealing sort that I was required to wear for Allen. I stood up and dropped the robe onto the bed, trying them on. They were very comfortable, fitting me almost perfectly.

I then put the dress on. Looking in the mirror, I was surprised at the results. It was a soft summer dress with spaghetti straps. It changed what I felt like completely. I felt pretty, even though I knew with the bruising and cuts I was anything but pretty. I turned to leave the room, noticing that Eva had taken all the clothes I had been wearing, including the shoes, with her when she left the room earlier. I opened the door, shyly walking back out to the kitchen table where I sat down again.

"Oh, honey," Lauren said, "you look lovely."

"Thank you," I said shyly to both of them.

"Of course! That dress looks so nice on you," replied Lauren. "Now, we need to discuss a couple other things before we can let you get settled. I work a full-time job at a medical clinic where I am a nurse. I work for a fantastic female doctor. The first thing I would like to do is have her come to check you over." She could see how nervous that made me. Lauren stated, "She will do this very privately, nothing will be put on a medical record—anywhere. We need to make sure you are OK."

I could see the sense of this, yet I was still scared. I nodded my assent after seeing the common sense of it.

"Good. I will call her to ask her to come over tonight. She is here a lot, we are best friends, so no one will think anything of her coming over. Then, after we make sure you are OK, we will let things lay low for a couple of days, keeping an eye on the news while we work on a plan for your future. We will not rush that unless the news is showing us a reason to hurry you to a new location. You have a TV down here, so you can watch it during the day while I'm at work and Eva is at school."

"Please just watch the volume and noise level. We don't have neighbors very close, but there is the possibility that a mailman or occasional delivery driver dropping off a package might hear something. We will keep the door closed at the top of the stairs for your privacy, but that should also help with the noise level. We will not intrude on your privacy, always knocking when we need to see you. You can lock the door if it makes you feel safer. Please let us know if you need anything at all."

With that, both Lauren and Eva got up, gave me quick hugs, then went up the stairs.

After the door closed, I just sat there and looked around at my new home, at least for the time being. Looking up at the door at the top of the basement stairs, I went up and quietly locked it, feeling silly but a little safer. I was lost, trying to decide what to do next. There was no LIST, no rules, no fists dictating what to do. I try to think of this as a good thing, but the problem is—I have no idea what to do.

I looked at the clock and saw that it was almost lunchtime, but I really was not that hungry. Even if I was hungry, I had no idea what to cook without THE LIST telling me. I was a good cook, I thought, being able to make a lot of things without having to follow a recipe, but not being told what to cook was overwhelming for me.

My stomach was still a bit upset, so I finally thought I would get myself something to drink, maybe see if there were any crackers. I found some saltines, poured a glass of milk, and walked over to the couch—even though this would never have been allowed with Allen, my husband. Food was only eaten at the table. This felt like my first act of defiance although truthfully that would have been when I didn't get the groceries.

I sat down on the couch, looking at the TV. I was never allowed to watch TV unless he was home, even then I definitely had no say so in what we watched. Here I am in a nice little apartment, all by myself, not only is there a TV here in the living room, but there is a smaller one in the bedroom! What can I watch on two TVs? What is there to watch on one? I looked at the remote lying there, feeling overwhelmed again, and I decided to ignore it.

Looking around, I saw that there was a small bookcase over to the side of the room. This caught my attention, so I got up with the intention of looking at the books. There was a wide variety of books, I picked one that seemed interesting and took it back over to the couch. I sat down, opened the book, grabbed a cracker, and started reading.

Chapter 3

As I sat there reading, eating a couple crackers, upstairs Lauren and Eva were fixing themselves a small lunch, discussing their new house guest. "Mom," Eva said quietly, "her body is so badly beaten and scarred, I would be surprised if she doesn't have internal bleeding or broken ribs."

Lauren looked at Eva, "Really?"

Eva nodded, "I have never seen anything like that before, even with the other ladies we helped."

They never mentioned names, not because they didn't care but because they didn't want to ever slip up at the wrong time for everyone's safety. Lauren picked up her phone.

"Can you watch our soup please?" she asked. "I'm going to call Audra to see if she can come over later today."

Eva took over at the stove and Lauren picked up her phone and made the call. "Hey, Audra. Eva and I were wondering if you were free sometime today to come over?"

Eva stirred the soup and watched her mom on the phone.

"Yes, we were really hoping you could today. We have a new kitten we want you to meet." Lauren stated after a brief pause.

This was a phrase that had been agreed upon a long time ago to indicate they had a person who needed help. Eva knew that her mom's friend would not hesitate now. As if confirming what Eva thought, she heard Lauren say, "That's great Audra, we will see you in about an hour." She put the phone down, and they both quietly got their lunch on the table and sat down to eat it.

"She couldn't even pick out anything to wear from the closet," Eva said quietly.

"Didn't she see anything she liked?" her mom asked.

"She doesn't know what she likes. She didn't know what size she was wearing. I checked her clothes to try to see what size, all the tags were cut out of all her clothes. I asked her what her favorite color was, she didn't even know that. She had to think about it."

Lauren looked at her daughter in shock. She said, "I have heard a lot of things, but this man sounds like the worst type of monster. I'm sure there is a lot more that we can't even imagine. That poor woman. I think we made the right decision today." Eva nodded her agreement as they got up and cleaned up from lunch.

As they finished cleaning, the doorbell rang. Lauren looked at her phone and saw that Audra was there. "Well, here we go. Let's pray that Mattie is OK." She went to the door and opened it. "Hi, Audra. Come on in."

Audra walked in, giving Lauren and Eva a hug. Lauren closed the door, turning toward Audra she said, "Thank you for coming, Audra. Let's have a seat in here first, we will tell you what we know before taking you to see her."

They all took a seat; Audra placed a bag on the floor next to her. Lauren filled her in on how they came across Mattie in the parking lot and the steps they took to bring her home with them. Eva described the episode in the bedroom, describing all of the bruising and scarring she witnessed.

Audra was shaking her head in disbelief. "I've seen a lot of abused women, but this sounds like an extreme case. I'm really concerned that if she has internal bleeding, we may not be able to take care of her here."

"We can't take her to the hospital, he will definitely find her there. I haven't turned the news on yet to see if he has reported her missing, I am hoping we have some time before that happens. I am really hoping that we can nurse her back to health here while we make plans for her relocation." Lauren commented.

"Do you have any thoughts on that yet?" Audra asked.

Lauren shook her head, "I don't. I need to reach out to a couple of people yet to see what is available."

Audra nodded, "She understands what you are doing for her, understands the danger you two are in right?"

Eva spoke up, "Yes, she understands. She has agreed to do everything we ask for our protection. Honestly, I don't think she could do anything without permission at this point. I get the feeling that he had so much control over her that she had to have his permission for everything she did, so much so that I think it is possible she may have a difficult time adjusting to a normal life."

"Do we know how long she has been going through this abuse?" Audra asked.

Lauren shook her head. "We haven't questioned her very much; I feel like she is in shock right now. The fact that she has been rescued, in combination with probably being terrified that she is going to be found and forced to go back to him, is a lot for her to take in. I would say her most recent beating was last night from the looks of her face."

Audra stood up, "Well, let's meet her and see if she will let me give her an examination. I will do whatever I can to try to nurse her back to health here."

Eva said, "I'm going to stay up here and do some homework. Let me know if you need me."

Lauren nodded, "She seems to have a good rapport with you, so we may need you to come down to help keep her calm, but it may be good not to have all of us converging on her. If she is comfortable with Audra, I may come back upstairs to give them privacy. We will let her dictate who she wants around or if she even wants anybody at all." Audra and Lauren head to the basement door and knock.

I heard the knock on the door and sat up, instantly afraid. I had been lying down reading, making my way a fourth of the way through the book already. I had forgotten how much I loved to read. I haven't been allowed to read for five years. I took a couple deep breaths; I knew it was probably Lauren or Eva. I went up and unlocked the door, pulling it open.

"Come in," I said, my heart beating fast in fear. Lauren came in, with another lady who was carrying a bag. I backed away a little bit, which did not go unnoticed by either of the women and then followed them down the stairs.

Lauren said, "Hi, Mattie. This is my best friend, the doctor I spoke to you about earlier, Audra. She would like to talk to you, maybe do an exam to make sure you are OK. Can we sit down?" I tried to relax and let go of the fear, nodding my head. They walked to the kitchen table. Audra set the bag she was carrying on the table, turning toward me.

"Hi, Mattie. It is so nice to meet you. Can we just visit a little bit? Get to know each other a little?"

Again, I nodded my head, feeling stupid, for some reason I couldn't speak. We all took seats at the kitchen table, I found myself staring at my hands, unable to look at either of the women.

Not put off by my apparent inability to look her in the face, Audra started talking to me. "Lauren and Eva filled me in on how they met you this morning, how you came to be here with them before we came down here." I flinched, remembering the parking lot incident. "I was wondering if you would feel OK with answering some questions for me. I would like to ask some questions, ones that could be hard for you to answer. We will take our time, if you don't want to answer that is fine. Just understand that the more I know about you and your situation, the better I can help you. Is that OK?"

I glanced up at Lauren and then toward the stairs. Lauren seemed to read thoughts. She offered, "Would you like me to go up and send Eva down?" For some reason that I couldn't fathom, I nodded my head. "Not a problem," Lauren smiled at me, "I will go get her."

She went up the stairs, and within a couple of minutes, Eva came down. She walked straight to me, sitting next to me at the table. I nodded, feeling so much gratitude toward her at that moment. She sat down, I reached for her hand, not knowing why exactly. I felt like I needed her strength and courage, to see if I could draw my own strength and courage from her. I glanced up at Eva, she smiled at me.

"Ready Mattie?" Audra asked.

Taking a deep breath, I managed to finally find my voice. "Yes, I think so," I said.

"Perfect. Just remember, we can stop any time you want to. If there is something you do not want to answer or talk about, all you have to do is just say so. Let's start off with something easy, how old are you?"

Even this simple question took me a couple minutes to think of the answer. I had to think back to my last birthday party and then calculate how old I would be today. "Twenty-three."

Audra nodded, not displaying any signs that she noticed I had to calculate my own age. "It is obvious to all of us that you have been abused by someone. I assume it is a man. Was he your husband?"

"Yes," I said.

"How long have you been married?" Audra asked.

"Five years," I stated after another brief period of calculation.

Audra nodded. "That means you were 18 when you got married. When did the abuse start? When was the first time he hit you?"

I couldn't help it, but I started to cry again. "On our wedding night." Eva gave my hand a little squeeze for encouragement and support. "I knocked over a glass of champagne at our reception. When we got to our hotel that night he called me a clumsy cow, hitting me in the stomach. He had never shown even a hint of a temper before."

"That is not unusual, happens that way all the time," Audra stated. "Women never see the abusive side of the man until they are living with him. How often did the beatings occur?"

"At first, it wasn't very often, maybe just every couple of weeks or so, with one or two punches to my back or stomach. Probably within six months or so it started to become a lot more often. Soon he would find things on a daily basis where he claimed I failed to meet his expectations."

Quietly, Audra asked, "You didn't have any family, friends, or coworkers you could turn to? He isolated you from everyone didn't he?"

I nodded. "I have no family. He wouldn't let me work, moved me away from any friends I had."

Audra replied. "That is typical of most abusers, they want to have total control over their victims. I am not going to ask you to go into further details about the past and bring up all the bad memories that I am sure are fresh in your mind. What I really need to know about are the details about the last time he beat you. I can see by the bruising and swelling on your face that it was very recent."

Again, I nodded. "Last night. It was different than all the times before."

"Different how?" Audra asked encouragingly.

"It was the first time he hit me in the face. Usually, the beatings were more controlled. He only hit me in places where the bruises and cuts could easily be hidden by clothes. But last night…" I trailed off.

"He lost control?" Audra asked.

I nodded, "Yes. It seemed like, I don't know like he couldn't seem to be able to regain control of himself again."

Audra looked at Eva. "I think you and your mom found Mattie just in time." Looking at me she said, "I believe he would probably have killed you soon, the beatings would have continued to get worse over time. Mattie, your decision to trust Eva and Lauren is probably the most important decision of your life." I just sat there, staring at my hands. I had actually been expecting, actually waiting for him to kill me for a long time. The thought that my life was safe now was hard for me to wrap my head around, I didn't believe it yet. Something in me knew for a fact that if he didn't kill me in a few days, I would kill myself.

I knew I would never be free of him.

"Mattie?" Audra asked. I looked up at her, coming back to the present. "I'd like to give you a physical examination to make sure you do not have any serious injuries. Would that be OK with you? There will be nothing written down or recorded in any way, so there will be no paper trail at all."

"Yes," I said after a few minutes. "I suppose that would be fine. I haven't actually seen a doctor since I was a little girl."

"We will go slow, take our time. I will explain what I am doing every step of the way. Do you want Eva to stay?" Audra asked.

I thought about it. I was nervous enough to have one person see the results of all the beatings, I didn't think I could handle two. "Can we do the exam in the bedroom while she waits out here?"

Both Audra and Eva said that would be fine, so Audra and I went into the bedroom after she got her bag off the table.

In the bedroom, Audra requested that I take my dress off, and put the robe on. As I was doing that, she got her stethoscope along with some other things out of her bag, lying them on a clean blue chuck pad she brought as well.

"When you are ready, just have a seat on the end of the bed. I'll start by just listening to your heart and lungs and then check your pulse and temperature," she instructed.

I tied the sash on the robe and sat down on the side of the bed. Audra took my temperature and pulse and commented that those looked good. She put on her stethoscope, asked me to take some deep breaths, listening carefully and then said I could breathe regularly as she continued to listen with her stethoscope. She examined my face closely, pressing as gently as she could, feeling for broken bones.

"Your heart and lungs sound good. Your face looks worse, probably feels worse, than it actually is. I don't detect any broken bones. The swelling and bruising should go away in a few days. Now, if you would lay back, I'll listen to your stomach and check for abdominal injuries. I need to open the robe to look at your bruises and wounds." I nodded and lay down.

After she finished the exam, she told me to go ahead and get dressed again. She cleaned up all of her things by putting everything back in her bag. She threw away the trash, washed her hands and then reached back into her bag, pulling out a box.

"Mattie, have a seat, let's chat for a couple minutes." I did as she said, and she sat down. "Mattie, you probably do have some internal bleeding, but I do not think it isn't very bad. I think with some rest and fluids, you will heal up just fine. I would like you to stay on bed rest for a couple of days. You can get up, shower, use the bathroom, and fix something to eat, but other than that no heavy lifting. I would like you to do the rest of your time either in bed or relaxing on the couch."

"Oh, OK," I agreed.

"There are symptoms that I want you to watch for, worsening pain in your abdomen, fever, basically anything out of the normal for you. If something like that occurs, let Lauren and Eva know, they will contact me. This is important, I will review this with them also. I think one of them needs to stay in the home with you at all times," Audra stated.

She looked at me intently before she went on. "There is one other thing I need to talk to you about. This could be a difficult subject for you. Mattie, could you be pregnant?"

I stared at her in stunned silence. Pregnant? A baby? Without even thinking about it, my hands went to my stomach. "I don't think so," I said.

"When was your last period?" she asked.

I looked at her, trying to remember. "I don't know. I'm not regular at all."

Audra nodded, "All the trauma you have been through—the stress, the anxiety, all the emotions—I am not surprised that you are not regular. I have a pregnancy test here; I would like you to take it. If it is positive, then we need to do some further testing to make sure the baby is healthy in order to let you make decisions regarding what you want to do. The nausea and the dizziness you had could be related to the injuries you sustained; I believe you probably have a concussion. There is also the chance it could be pregnancy-related. I feel we need to make sure."

She held out the box containing the pregnancy test. I looked at it for a minute, then reached out and took it. She explained how to do the test, so I went into the bathroom.

When I came out, Audra and I moved into the living room where Eva sat, waiting. I automatically walked over to where she was, sitting down next to her. She took my hand, looking at me with concern. "Mattie?" Audra asked. "Can I call Lauren down to talk about the examination and explain what we need to do?"

I nodded my head and Eva squeezed my hand, "It will be OK," Eva said.

I didn't say anything. For some reason, Eva made me feel safe. The fact that this young woman I didn't even know could make me feel that way surprises me. Maybe it is her confidence, her maturity. Whatever it is, I am glad that she is here with me. Audra went up the stairs and opened the door, calling for Lauren to join us. They were both soon back downstairs, sitting across from Eva and me.

"I wanted to speak to you both about things that Mattie and I discussed. She has given me permission to share with you," Audra began. "I gave Mattie as thorough an exam as I was able to here without the full benefits of in a hospital or clinic setting. I don't feel that we need x-rays as luckily, she does not seem to have any broken bones."

Lauren said, "That is a relief."

"Yes, it is," Audra nodded. "I do believe she has some internal bleeding in her abdomen which is not severe. I have instructed her that I would like her to be on bedrest for a couple of days. I have gone over warning signs with her, I'll do so with both of you also. If at all possible, I would like someone to be here with her, at least in the house, until I can see her again in a day or so. Would that be possible?" Both Eva and Lauren nodded, indicating that would not be a problem for them.

"Great. I will make arrangements to come back soon. There is one other thing we may need to discuss, but I need to check the test results." With that, Audra got up and walked into the bedroom. Lauren and Eva looked questioningly at each other and me, but I couldn't bring myself to meet their gazes.

Audra was only gone a few seconds. When she came back out, she knelt in front of me, took both my hands, and then said, "Mattie, the test is positive."

Chapter 4

Positive? I stared at her dumbfounded. After all these years with no pregnancies, I'm pregnant now? I didn't say anything, but it was a huge source of anger with Allen that I never seemed to be able to give him a child. Now I'm pregnant with his baby, and he has no idea. I can't speak. I can't think. "Mattie, do you understand? You are pregnant." Audra repeated.

I slowly nod my head as tears start to fall. I had been beaten many times for not being able to give Allen a son. He blamed me constantly.

Audra sat back down, stating, "I need to go get some equipment and come back. I want to listen to the baby's heartbeat and see if I can do an ultrasound. Then you will know how the baby is and can start to decide what you want to do with your future."

Again, I just nodded. Allen's baby. What am I going to do now? Do I have to go back to him?

"For now, please get comfortable, lay down, and get some rest. Bedrest is what you need right now more than anything. I'll go upstairs and talk to Lauren and Eva about what we need to watch for and let them know what restrictions you should follow for the next couple of days."

I stood up, as did Audra. She gently put her hands on my shoulders. "Listen, Mattie, we are here for you. I know you will have a hard time going forward, learning to trust total strangers, and letting them take care of you, but that is exactly what we are going to do. If you need or want anything, all you have to do is ask. If you need to be left alone for a while, we will respect that. Going forward you are in charge of your own life, we are only here to help you get to where you are confident in that, confident in knowing what you want to do."

She gently pulled me in for a hug, out of habit I stiffened, so she let go. I wasn't ready for hugs yet, she seemed to realize that. It wasn't that I didn't want the hug, I didn't know how to react to someone being that close to me without getting hurt.

"It's OK Mattie," Audra said, seeming to know exactly what I was thinking.

I turned and started walking to the bedroom, yet could feel their eyes on my back. I stopped and slowly turned around to look at them all.

"I'm sorry that I don't know how to express my feelings right now, I hope to be able to sort things out in my head, learn to trust my heart again and get better at expressing myself. I do want to say thank you, I really do appreciate everything you are doing for me. I understand the risk that you all are taking by helping me."

Lauren spoke up, "Oh, honey, we completely understand that you will need time to learn who you are as a person, to figure out everything. Right now, let's just focus on your health, let the rest come as it may. Take things one day at a time."

I gave her a small smile of gratitude, went into the bedroom to change clothes, and crawl into bed. I managed to find a cute pajama set and a tank top with capri bottoms and put them on. They were a perfect fit. I looked at the bed, the TV, trying to decide what I wanted to do, sleep, watch TV, or go get the book to read some more. For some reason, this decision seemed like one of the toughest ones yet.

Why can't I make such a simple decision like this without worrying about the consequences? Why—because I have never been allowed to make any type of decision for myself. The realization that I could pick what I wanted to do, not what I had to do—with the exception of the doctor's orders of bed rest of course—was good in one way, yet bad in another. Good because it was part of my new freedom and bad because even though I could make decisions for myself, I didn't know how to make them.

I stood there a while longer, staring at the bed when I made the first decision of my newfound freedom—even though it was a minor decision it felt good. I decided I was not going to choose one, I was going to pick them all! I walked out to the living room, hesitating a moment, I went and locked the door to the upstairs again. Feeling safer with it locked, I picked up the book I had been reading earlier to take it with me into the bedroom. Climbing into bed, I grabbed the TV remote and turned on the TV. This was a little overwhelming, I was fascinated by the options available to me, spending a long time flicking through channels watching a little of this show, a little of that show.

There were so many channels to choose from that did not involve sports or the types of shows Allen forced me to watch. I think I went through all the channels three or four times before finding a channel that had craft shows on it. Turning down the volume a little bit, I lay back to watch for a few minutes. The current show was a lady teaching basic sewing skills. For some reason, I found this very interesting, soon forgetting the book and intently watching the show.

I did some sewing a few years ago out of necessity, mending clothes because I had no choice, but it was something I didn't know how to do other than that. She made it look so easy, making something from a few pieces of material and thread looked fun. It seemed like practical knowledge that someone should have.

The afternoon wore on, I found myself drifting off into a nice nap with the TV playing more craft shows. Another first for me, I was able to sleep without dreaming or being on the edge, waiting to be woken up for a beating or made to do something.

***

When I woke up an hour and a half later, it took me a few minutes to realize where I was. I had a moment of panic, thinking that I didn't make it home in time with the groceries. I was trying to calm down when I heard a knock on the door. Audra called my name, asking if she could come down.

"Just a minute," I called out to her, muting the TV. I get up, heading out to the stairs. I went up and unlocked the door, letting her in. We made our way down the stairs, pausing in the living area.

"Can we go in the bedroom?" Audra asked. "I brought the ultrasound machine with me." Nodding, I led the way, sitting down on the edge of the bed. She was carrying her bag from earlier along with a couple of others. She put the bags down, taking a seat in the chair.

"How are you feeling?" she asked.

"I feel better. I just took a nap; didn't realize I was so tired." I answered.

"You will probably need a lot of rest, that is exactly what your body needs to heal right now." She glanced at the TV, "I love this channel! Do you do any crafting?"

I shook my head, looking down in shame, "I wasn't allowed to do anything that I wanted to do."

"Mattie, look at me please." I looked at her slowly, she was smiling warmly at me. "You have nothing to be ashamed of—at all." Again, I was surprised by her warmth and understanding. How did she seem to know exactly what I was thinking or feeling at times?

She went on, "It will take time for you to get past that, I understand that, but I just want to put it out there that you have done nothing wrong." I nodded, not knowing what to say. She looked back at the TV and said, "I love to craft, and so does Lauren, so if you see anything that interests you maybe we can help you get started with some crafts."

"Really?" I asked. "That would be great."

"Sure, especially when you have to be on bed rest it would help you to pass the time. Something to fight boredom," she smiled.

"Thank you," I said smiling back.

She looked down at the bags at her feet, saying, "I brought a couple things with me." She reaches for the bags, pulling them closer to her chair. "When talking with Eva and Lauren before I left earlier, we decided that you should have a cell phone. I picked one up for you, it is what they call a prepaid phone. Your name is not associated with it, but you have the ability to text message and make calls. We programmed our three numbers into it for you already, so if you need anything or we want to come down, to see you, we can text each other easily."

She handed me the phone with the instruction booklet, which I was glad to have because I did not know much about cell phones. Allen had programmed the one he allowed me to use, so I had no clue how to use them beyond the things he showed me. I didn't want to admit there was yet something else I was clueless about.

"Thank you," I replied, taking them from her and laying them on the bedside table next to me.

"I don't think I need to warn you about calling anybody other than the three of us with it. Calling anyone you know from your past life with it is too dangerous," she said sternly.

"I have no one to call. Even if there was, I would not have the numbers to call them," I replied.

She nodded. "This will make it easier for me to check in on you to see how you are feeling between visits or let you reach out to any of us if you start not feeling well. The next thing I brought was the portable ultrasound machine from the office. I would like to do an ultrasound and see how the baby is doing and see if we can figure out how far along you are. I also brought some pregnancy and baby books for you to read if you would like.”

She pulled the books out, setting them on the bedside table also. I glanced at them, not sure yet how I felt about them. I haven’t given the pregnancy much thought yet, mainly because it didn’t feel real yet, I didn’t know how I felt about it. I think Audra knew that which is why she placed them there with little fanfare, then went straight back to her bag, pulling out the ultrasound machine.

“So the way this works, I will put some gel on your abdominal area, then put this wand on your abdomen. I will then be able to see a picture on the screen here and take measurements to see how big the baby is. I can also see how well the baby is developing. It should be painless for both of you.” She looks at me seriously.

“I say ‘should be’ because I know you have areas of bruising, so there may be a little pain if I go over an area with significant bruising. I do want to see if I can check on any internal bleeding. It should feel like pushing on a bruise, maybe a bit more painful depending on the severity of the damage he did to you. Any questions?”

It all seemed pretty straightforward; I really didn’t have any questions at this point, so I told her no. “Shall we proceed then?” she asked.

“Yes, let’s do it,” I told her.

“Good. I’ll explain more as I go, if you have any questions or if a spot is a lot more tender, and you want me to stop just let me know.” I nodded my understanding.

She pulled out a tube of gel and a couple of blue pads. She went into the bathroom and brought out a warm wet washcloth, which she handed to me.

“To start with, I need you to pull your top up a little bit and your pants down just a little, so I have access to your abdominal area.” I did as she asked, and then she tucked the blue pads in both the shirt and pants, explaining this was just to keep the gel off my clothes.

She picked up the gel and opened the tube, saying to me with a smile, “No matter how much I try to warm this up beforehand, it is always cold by the time I put it on. Just a warning, the gel will be cold.” She put a significant amount on my abdomen and then put the tube aside. Picking up the wand, she turned on the machine and made a couple of adjustments to the screen that she sat on the bedside table, putting the wand on my belly. She spread the gel around as she moved the wand around, using some pressure to get a decent picture she explained. I had been watching her move the wand around, not looking at the screen, for several minutes in silence.

"Mattie," she said. I looked up at her. "Look at the screen."

I turn, looking at the screen, staring at the image there. "This is your baby. You won't be able to see much, you are pretty early in your pregnancy," Audra pointed to a small area on the screen. As we watched, a little movement could be seen. She moved the wand a little bit so that on the screen a tiny little flicker could be seen. "You can barely see it, but this is the baby's heartbeat. We can try to hear it if you would like."

I nodded, not taking my eyes off the screen. She turned up the volume so that a fast beat could be heard. "It sounds fast, but that is typical for a baby." While she was pointing things out to me, she was also taking measurements. I was transfixed by the image on the screen, and once again, tears started down my cheek.

She took all the measurements she needed, explaining what I was looking at during the whole process. She then asked me if I wanted a picture of the baby.

"You can do that?" I asked.

She smiled, and a few minutes later she was handing me a picture of the baby. I stared at it in amazement. Audra went about cleaning the ultrasound machine and putting things away. She took the warm washcloth, gently washing the gel off of my abdomen. She threw the blue pads away; I pulled my clothes back into position. When she was done putting everything away, she sat back down, smiling at me.

"First off, the internal bleeding I could see is very minimal, you should heal up from that in a few days with the bed rest. No long-term issues from that at all," Audra explained. "Secondly, from all the measurements I took today, I would say you are about six weeks pregnant."

I looked at her in surprise, "That's a little over a month. Is the baby… OK? Healthy?" I asked.

"The baby seems perfectly fine and looks very healthy. Everything seems fine with your pregnancy." She reached into the bags that she brought with her, pulling out a bottle of pills. "These are prenatal vitamins. I want you to take one a day. If you have any problem with these pills, sometimes they can make you feel sick to your stomach, we can try something different like a chewable or a gummy. It is important for both you and the baby that you take these daily. Taking them with food may help with stomach issues."

I took the bottle from her, telling her I would be sure to start them today.

"I know this is all so new for you, Mattie, once it sinks in that you are pregnant, we can discuss what you want to do about the baby. You have options that I will just mention now, we can discuss them in more depth if you would like. You could have the baby, keep the baby, raise it yourself. You can have the baby, giving it up for adoption. We do have enough time that you can terminate the pregnancy." I had been looking at her as she spoke.

"I'm keeping my baby," I say, surprising myself. The words were out of my mouth before I even thought about all the options. I knew in my heart this was what I wanted.

Audra smiled at me, "Are you sure?"

"I know that my future is uncertain, that today is only the first day I've been away from him. Seeing the baby on ultrasound made her real to me. I want to be her mom." I looked down at the picture of my baby.

"Her? It is too early to see the sex of the baby on ultrasound." Audra said, laughing.

"It's a girl. I know it is," I said, smiling down at the picture in my hands.

Chapter 5

Audra packed up her medical bag, leaving me lying in bed, encouraging me to eat with the reminder that I was now eating for two. I asked her not to tell Eva and Lauren anything about the ultrasound, but to send them down, so I can show them the picture and tell them my decision.

"Mattie?" I heard Eva call from the top of the stairs.

"Yes, come on down," I called back. A couple of minutes later Eva and Lauren walk into the bedroom.

Lauren said, "Audra said you wanted to see us?"

I nodded, asking them to sit down. I took a deep breath, then said, "Audra did the ultrasound, the internal bleeding is very minimal. I will be OK in a few days."

"That is great!" Lauren exclaimed.

I smiled at both of them. "Yes, as long as I follow doctor's orders I'll be fine in no time. She also checked on the baby, I am six weeks pregnant. Baby is fine, seems healthy."

"Thank goodness!" Both Eva and Lauren were smiling at me and seemed very happy for me.

"Audra told me my options, raising the baby, adoption, or abortion. She wanted me to take my time deciding what I wanted to do, but I made my mind up already."

Eva and Lauren exchanged glances and Lauren said, "Are you sure you are ready to make any decision so quickly? You have plenty of time to decide."

"I know," I replied. "Until I saw the baby, MY baby, on the ultrasound I hadn't even given the pregnancy another thought. It didn't seem real. I saw my baby; the heartbeat and I knew at that instant I wanted this baby. I want to be her mom!"

"It's a girl?" Eva asked.

I laughed, "Well, Audra said it is too soon to show that on the ultrasound, but I just know she is a girl." I pulled out the picture from the ultrasound, handing it to Eva.

"Oh, wow! That is so amazing!" she exclaimed, passing the picture to Lauren.

Lauren looked at the picture and started crying. "Oh, Mattie, I know the timing is not perfect for you, but I am so happy for you."

Pretty soon, all three of us were crying, yet laughing about the timing of the babies. I looked at these two ladies who had risked everything for me. I told them "This is the first time in over five years that I have been happy. If you two had not found me today, both this baby and I probably would not have a future." This started the tears going again. They finally told me I should find something to eat and then get some more rest. I agreed. They went upstairs, shutting the door behind them. I waited a couple of minutes, then went up the stairs, locking the door, still feeling foolish. They probably had a key and could come down regardless, but it made me feel a little less scared.

I went out to the kitchen. For the first time today, I actually was hungry. I had the opportunity to eat anything I wanted. I opened the pantry, looking around. "Baby Girl," I said, running my hand over my abdomen, "what are you hungry for?"

Soup sounded kind of good although it didn't really seem like exactly what I wanted. I went to the refrigerator and opened the freezer. It was well-stocked with cuts of meat, which would take time to thaw out. I was getting too hungry to wait that long. Pulling out a box, I saw that it was a frozen pizza. That sounded good, so I closed the freezer.

I followed the instructions on the box, it had been a long time since I made a frozen pizza—Allen always demanded homemade meals. Pretty soon I was sitting at the table eating pizza, drinking a glass of milk. When I had finished eating, I took my prenatal vitamin, leaving the bottle on the table as a reminder to take it when I eat tomorrow. I put the leftovers away and washed up my few dishes, leaving them in the dish rack to dry. All of a sudden, I felt exhausted, I also felt the need to watch some news, to see if my disappearance had been reported yet.

I brushed my teeth, then crawled into bed, found the local news station, and shut the lights off. I watched the top news stories, not seeing anything about me on there, so I browsed the channels for something to watch. I settled on a movie that looked interesting and turned the sound down really low, but pretty soon I was sound asleep.

Chapter 6

Upstairs, while I was eating my pizza, Eva and Lauren were having their supper, discussing my situation. "The baby changes things don't it, Mom?"

"It really does. I think we need to move more urgently to get her to a safe, new life before she gets too far along. I need to make phone calls tonight to get things going."

"Do you have any ideas yet?"

Lauren replied, "No, not yet. Hopefully, our contacts will have some thoughts."

Eva said, "I may have an idea. Now that there is a baby involved, maybe she can do something where she can work from home. There are a lot of opportunities now that allow people to make an income from home working remotely."

"That is a fantastic idea, Eva," her mom said. "I'll bring it up tonight on the phone calls. I really do believe that we need to get a plan set in motion that can be started soon. We need to get her to safety as soon as we can."

Eva nodded her agreement. "Go make the phone calls, Mom, I'll clean up from supper."

"Thank you, honey." Lauren gave her a hug and left the room to go to her office. She closed the door behind her although Eva helped her with this, in order to keep her daughter safe, she did not want her involved in all of the arrangements.

"Hello?" a female voice said on the phone.

"Hi, it's me."

"One moment," the female said, "let me see if he is available."

Lauren waited on the phone for a few minutes when a male finally came on and said "Hey, we haven't heard from you in a while."

"I know, things have been very quiet here. I do have a situation now." Lauren stated.

"Give me the basics," he said.

"She is 23, abused severely for five years by her husband who is a cop. She is approximately six weeks pregnant. Cannot be moved for a couple of days to recover from her last beating, but should be moved soon, before she gets too far along in her pregnancy. She wants to keep the baby."

"Husband is a cop? Anything on the news yet?"

"No," Lauren said. "I expect that it will be tomorrow unless he is trying to hide something."

"Give me details on how this situation occurred, so I know what we are dealing with," he said.

"I found her throwing up, almost passing out in the grocery store parking lot this morning. Her face was badly bruised, it was obvious she was in an abusive relationship. I had her put her purse, which contained all her ID, a grocery list, car keys, cell phone, and money back in the car. We, my daughter and I, left her there and walked to my van. We put my groceries in the back, climbed in, and opened the door on the passenger side back seat."

"She walked down a couple rows of vehicles, crossed over, then back to my van out of view of any cameras of the store. She got to my van, climbed in, and lay down on the back floor. I auto-shut the door behind her. She covered up with a blanket, pulled a couple of bags of groceries on top of her, and hid. We then drove to the courthouse, where her husband actually could have been and then made another stop at the drugstore."

"She stayed hidden at all stops. She did not come out from under the blanket until we pulled into my garage, shutting the garage door. From there, she was able to go into the basement apartment in my home, having not been seen by any neighbors."

"Good. So her car will be found in the parking lot of the store with all of her stuff in it. I can work from there. Do you have any thoughts about where to go from here?"

"Nothing other than my daughter mentioned that maybe we can get her a job where she works remotely from home since she is pregnant. Maybe something she can start here if she will be here for an extended period of time and then can move with her, so she has a source of income when she moves."

The man on the other end replied, "I can definitely work with that. I have a couple of contacts that I have worked with recently that can probably help with that. Do you know if she has any skills that will help?"

Lauren sighed, "I really doubt it. She has not had any sort of life for five years."

"Shouldn't be a problem," he replied. "I will work on getting her some funds to move on, a job, along with a mode of transportation. Call me back tomorrow for an update." There was a click on the line and Lauren put the phone down on her desk.

Lauren sat at her desk staring at her computer for a few minutes. She picked up her phone again, making another call. "Hello?" another female voice replied.

"It's me," Lauren said. "I need a favor."

"Yes?" was the reply.

"There is a missing person case. The car left in the grocery store parking lot today. Can you keep me posted on the situation?"

"I can do that," the female voice replied. "Nothing yet."

"Thank you," Lauren replied, ending the call. There were no more calls she could make at this time, so she took her cell phone and left the office.

Eva was in her room, studying. Lauren knocked quietly on her door. "Come in," Eva said.

"I don't want to disrupt your studies, but we should probably talk about a schedule for the next few days that would allow one of us to be here with Mattie."

"Don't worry about it, Mom, I have it covered already," Eva replied. "I have arranged with my professors to do my studies at home for the next couple of days. This is an easy thing for me since Covid."

Lauren walked to her daughter and gave her a hug. "Are you sure?" she asked.

"I'm sure, Mom. There seems to be a trust between Mattie and me. It just makes sense for me to be the one to stay home. I just told my professors that I pulled a muscle, and the doctor stated would take a day or two of rest before I can attend classes in person. They stated they are fine with that as long as I attend online and keep up with homework. You need to be able to go to work. I will text Audra and see if she can help with a note for school stating I pulled a muscle that I can submit to the dean."

Lauren gave Eva another hug, "I love you, honey. I'm sure Audra can help with that. You may have to go in for an appointment to make it legit, but I think that is a great solution. I know that Mattie is more comfortable with you than me. Also, you can study at home, but I can't work at home."

Eva hugged her back. "I love you too, Mom. This just made sense to me. I am happy to be able to help Mattie through this process. I couldn't help much the last time since I was so young then, but I like the fact that I can do something this time that actually means something and will hopefully make a difference for Mattie."

Lauren was so touched by Eva's passion for helping Mattie that she couldn't speak. She turned, walking out, to her bedroom. She was tired, it had been a long day.

Chapter 7

I woke up at 4:30 am out of habit. I sat up in bed thinking I needed to get up and make breakfast. That was the one thing that I did every day that was never put on the daily LIST. I fixed breakfast while he made THE LIST. I got to where I had perfected his breakfast during the time he made THE LIST which meant the beatings that I suffered were never over his breakfast.

He wanted the same thing every day at the same time. I did have an alarm set for 4:45 every morning, but I never allowed it to go off, always waking up before it went off. The first beating of the day would occur if he heard my alarm because that meant I was lazy. I have been 'lucky' in the fact that this beating had not occurred in four years. I realized that I did not have to make breakfast for him today, so I tried to lie down and go back to sleep.

After about 45 minutes, I decided sleep was not going to happen right now. I figured I would go out to find some breakfast for myself. In the kitchen, I found some cereal in the pantry that sounded really good. I was never allowed to eat cereal, I was always made to eat Allen's favorite breakfast, eggs, sausage, toast, orange juice, and coffee every morning. I poured some cereal in a bowl and added the milk, eating this while I brewed a pot of coffee.

I thought about Allen's favorite breakfast. I realized I did not really like sausage. Over-easy eggs actually made me want to throw up. I preferred bacon over sausage. If I had to eat eggs, I would want them scrambled with no sign of runny eggs at all.

Thinking about this further, I would almost rather have toast or cereal than eggs of any type. I felt like coming to this realization was another step to realizing I was a person with likes and dislikes with the ability to decide for myself what I wanted rather than going with what someone else liked. I also realized I have a long way to go, to learn what I liked, what I am capable of doing for myself and now, this baby. I have a wide range of emotions going through me this morning. I am terrified that he will find me, killing the baby and me.

I am thrilled that I am going to be a mom to a baby girl—even though that hasn't been determined yet. I am also afraid to trust that what anyone tells me is the truth. I love this baby already and was surprised by exactly how much I love her. I haven't loved or been loved for years, if ever.

The coffee finished brewing, I washed up my cereal bowl and spoon, poured myself a cup of coffee, taking it to the couch with me. Audra stated that bed rest was a term that didn't necessarily mean I had to be in bed, I could lay on the couch and rest. I lay down on the couch with the coffee on the table within reach, grabbing the TV remote. I turned on the TV, going to the local news channel to see what was in the headlines. When the channel came into focus, I saw my face staring back at me. "In the local news today, a decorated detective's wife has gone missing, and the search has begun for clues as to what happened to her."

I got up and ran into the bedroom. I grabbed the cell phone, sending a text to both Eva and Lauren begging them to please come downstairs. I went back out to the living room, taking the phone with me. The news lady continued, "The officer came home from his normal daily shift to find that his wife was not home. He immediately called his supervisor stating that this was completely out of the normal for his wife, indicating that something must have happened to her."

The news report went to a video of him stating, "She had a couple of errands that she was going to run today, but she should have been home before I got home from work. I am very worried about her because she always lets me know what her plans are for the day. We keep in touch throughout the day as we are able. Please, if you know anything about Megan's disappearance, call us and let us know. I just want my wife to come home safely. Megan, if you can hear this, I love you. Stay strong, we will find you and bring you home."

I heard a knock on the door, which startled me at first. I hurried up the stairs and unlocked the door, letting Eva or Lauren in.

"Are you OK?" Lauren asked.

"I'm on the news," I stated. We hurried down the stairs to watch more news. The picture returned to me; we exchanged glances, all of us sitting down to watch. When the news went on to another story, I muted the TV, saying, "I need to leave today. You heard him; he will find me." I was almost in a state of pure panic.

Eva grabbed my hand. "Mattie, listen." She was calm, which helped me to calm down a little. "We knew this would happen. If we try to move you right away, we run the risk of being found out, putting all of us in danger. We are confident that we have covered our trail so that they will not find you here. They haven't even found your car yet. You need to try to trust us. I know that's difficult for you, but you have no choice right now. We are all you have."

Eva's words did what they were intended to do. I felt calmer and able to breathe again.

"They will find the car soon since he was the one who sent you to the store. They probably have already been there, looking for video or witnesses to what might have happened," Lauren said. "Eva and I did not touch your car at all, so our prints won't be on it. Hopefully, when they do find it, they will get the impression you were kidnapped, mugged, or something. You are still safe here." I didn't say what everyone was thinking, 'for now', but felt better overall. "We will keep up with the news and our actions will be based on what is reported on a daily basis."

I felt better and was even able to apologize for waking them up. "Don't worry about waking us up," Eva said. "We all need to keep up with the news. Just know that we are working on a solution for you already."

We sat, watching the news a bit longer, but it repeated the things from earlier, so it was decided that we should all try and get a bit more sleep. I needed sleep to heal, Lauren needed sleep to go to work, Eva needed sleep to do her schoolwork. I felt awful that my situation was depriving them of the sleep they needed to continue their normal routine, they both reassured me that they had made the decision to help me and that I had nothing to feel guilty or awful about.

Lauren and Eva gave me gentle, brief hugs before heading back up the stairs to try and get more rest. I followed them up the stairs, locking the door behind them again. I decided to try to go back to bed too. I shut the TV off and then the lights and headed back to bed. This was so out of the norm for me, I never slept past 4:30 am prior.

I was tired, so I curled back up into bed and turned the TV on in the bedroom to a channel that was playing a movie. I don't know why but leaving the TV on seemed to help me sleep. Within minutes, I was asleep although it was restless this time. The dreams came, I couldn't escape them, but I also did not remember them when I finally woke up again.

When I opened my eyes again, I rolled over, glancing at the alarm clock on the bedside table. I was stunned to see that it was 9:00 in the morning. I was never able to sleep this late with Allen, so it was really a surprise that I had slept so long. The TV was still on, I grabbed the remote, searching through the channels to find something that caught my attention. I ended up on the channel I found the day before that showed crafts.

I stopped there, putting the remote aside. This particular show was teaching how to crochet an Afghan. I thought this was great. The ability to handmake a beautiful blanket that would keep a loved one warm greatly appealed to me. Maybe I can make my baby girl a blanket to wrap her up in after she is born. I thought I would ask Audra or Lauren to teach me how to crochet.

I watched the show for a little while, then decided I wanted a shower. I picked out some clean clothes, hoping I made some good choices that would look good together and then went into the bathroom. I found new shampoo and conditioner, along with body wash, then enjoyed a nice warm shower. This was the first time in a long time that I did not have to worry about how long I took in the shower, no alarm was going to go off telling me my shower time was over.

The only thing that motivated me today to not be in there too long was the fact I did not want to use up all the hot water for the others in the house. It felt really good to be cleaned up and wearing fresh clothes. I don't think I could handle staying in pajamas for bed rest all the time.

Since I had breakfast super early, I thought I would go see if there was something I could have for a snack. Yet another thing that I was not allowed to do with Allen, snack or just eat without permission. I wondered, as I picked out a banana from the other fruit in the pantry, how long would I be this way, thinking that I could never do this or do that before. Would I ever get to the point where I didn't care anymore about that type of thing? I didn't think that it would ever be completely gone, but I certainly hoped I could get to the point where this was not a constant thought in the back of my mind.

I ate the banana, washed up and then headed back to bed to be the good patient Audra expected of me. I climbed onto the bed, picking up the book I started reading from where I left off the day prior. After about 45 minutes or so, I hear the cell phone on the table next to me alert me to a text message. I picked it up, seeing that there was a text from Eva asking if she could come see me. I replied yes. I'd be right there to let her in.

Letting Eva in, I asked if she minded if we sat in the bedroom. "No, not at all. How are you feeling now? Were you able to get some rest?"

I smiled at her, "Yes, I managed to fall back asleep, waking up around 9:00 am. It felt nice to be able to rest."

"That's great," Eva replied as she sat down in one of the chairs in the bedroom. "I gave Mom an idea last night, she asked me to talk to you about it to see what you think."

"Oh?" I asked, curiosity evident on my face.

"I'm not sure if you know everything that is involved with getting you to a safe place, there are actually a lot of people involved, a lot of pieces that need to fall into place. One part of that will be helping you with a job because you will need to have an income."

"That makes sense. I really haven't had a chance to think about anything. Now, with the baby, I'm not sure how I will be able to find work," I said. "I don't know how I will be able to get a job, I have very little work history, nothing at all in the last five years."

"I'm not trying to stress you out about an income. Let me explain a bit of what happens here. As I said, Mom and I are only a small part of this picture. We have… contacts let's call them, that we reach out to that help us make you a new life. You will be getting a new identity made for you by one of our contacts. That contact also helps get you a job with other contacts we have."

"Oh, wow. That sounds complicated," I replied. "I wondered how you and your mom thought you would be able to help me, I had no idea that there were people out there that did this type of thing for people like me."

"It can be complicated; everyone keeps their identity secret. I guess that came about years ago when a contact was murdered by the husband of someone they were trying to help get to a safe place. Since then, it is safer for all involved this way." Eva said, "Anyway, I came up with an idea as far as the job for you that I think will be perfect for your situation. How would you feel about a job working from home? There are a lot of companies that will let you work remotely. Our contact states that he does have the ability to set you up with that if you would like."

"That really sounds like a great idea. I don't have very many skills. I took a few college courses before I got married, but I quit going—I should say was forced to quit.”

“That shouldn’t be a problem. Can you type at all?” Eva asked.

This was something that I could do. Allen made me do a lot of his reports for him and made me type up letters and other things during our marriage. “Oh yes, I can type about 60 wpm. I also have some very basic computer skills.” I stated.

“That is great, that will help a lot. I am sure that whatever job our contact manages to find for you will train you. A lot of companies with remote workers supply the equipment needed to work for them.”

I thought about this for a few minutes. How perfect would it be if I could work from home? Not only would it be great with the baby on the way, but it would also keep me out of the public eye a lot, so the chance of being recognized would be smaller. I looked at Eva, “I love that idea, it sounds ideal. I could stay out of the public eye easier.”

“Perfect! I think it will be great. We can’t promise where you will end up living. In fact, Mom and I won’t even know where you end up. It all depends on our contacts and their contacts to find a place that will be safe for you. The other thing we need to talk about is we need to change your appearance a little bit. How would you feel about a hairstyle change, including a different color?”

“Yes! I would love something new.”

Eva smiled at my enthusiasm. “We have a local contact that we will reach out to today to see when she can come over. She specializes in helping people change their appearance. She is one contact that we see face-to-face, but we still don’t share names with her. Unfortunately, now that you are on the news we need to try and get things going. We will need to get you some place safe soon.”

“Has there been more on the news about me?” I asked worriedly.

“They found your car; police are viewing this as a kidnapping now. Your husband is supposed to go on TV later with a plea for your safe return.”

“This I have to see,” I said, “it is a little ironic that I am safer now than if I return to him—even though he claims he wants me ‘home safe’.”

“So true,” Eva said. “We plan to keep you safe here. I’ll leave you alone now, I have some schoolwork to do for my classes today. I’ll text you when our contact will be here to give you a new look.”

“Thanks, Eva.” She reached out, gave my hand a little squeeze, then turned to leave the room.

"Eva?" I called to her. She turned and looked at me, "I was wondering if I could get some yarn and a crochet hook?"

"Sure! I didn't know you could crochet."

"Well, I can't yet, but I saw a show on it. It looked like something I would love to learn."

"I'm sure Mom has plenty of supplies. I think she might even have a book that shows you the different stitches and how to do them. She would be happy to loan it to you I bet. I'll check with her; we will get you some starter supplies." She turned, walking out.

After locking up after Eva left, I turned on the TV, thinking I would watch more crafting shows to pass the time. I thought about the changes Eva mentioned and the fact that I might be able to learn how to crochet. I felt a sense of excitement that I had never felt before. A baby, new job, new look, new life. Do I dare let myself get excited? Can I dream of a future that will be happy? I decided that I was not going to let myself get my hopes up too much because there were a lot of things that had to fall into place before I was even safe.

I spent the rest of the morning watching some craft shows, sort of tossing and turning in the bed. I shut the TV off at lunchtime, heading out to the kitchen to find something for lunch. I opened the refrigerator, pulling out the leftover pizza. I remembered how much I used to love pizza, even like cold leftover pizza. I grabbed a piece and decided I wanted to spend the afternoon on the couch.

I poured a glass of milk and took it with the cold pizza to the couch. I had brought the book out with me, so I read while I enjoyed my lunch. I finished the pizza and washed up my dishes when I heard the cell phone text alert go off. I walked back over to the couch picking up the phone to read the text message. It was from Eva again, simply stating 'Hair appt 6:00 tonight'.

I sent a simple message back "Great!" Feeling a little tired, I moved back into the bedroom, taking the book and the cell phone with me. I crawled back into bed, read for a little while longer then closed my eyes for a nap.

Chapter 8

Upstairs, Eva was in her room logged into her college courses working away. It was hard for her to concentrate, her mind wanted to wander down the stairs to Mattie. Even though they knew her real name now, they were not going to use it because Mattie needed to get used to being called something else. She shook her head, trying to refocus her attention on her current class. Eva is in her second year of college.

She took extra classes her senior year of high school and during the summers, so she could get a lot of the basic classes out of the way. She still hasn't decided completely on what her major was, but she was leaning toward social work or criminal justice. She really wanted to do what they were doing for Mattie somehow on a full-time basis. She was not exactly sure how to proceed with her college career in the best way to be able to help people in the way she wanted to. She liked the social work idea, but she also wanted to be able to make enough of a living financially to be able to help.

If she went into law, she could do her job as a lawyer, but on the side help those who need it secretly. The sort of help they are offering Mattie has to be done so carefully, so quietly as not only Mattie is in danger, but Eva and her mother are in danger for helping her. If her husband found out about Eva and Lauren, he could harm them trying to find out where she is.

Eva had talked to her mother about this before. They have contacts they reach out to for help, but they do not know these people on a personal level. It is safer for all involved to maintain low-key identities with others. Eva isn't even sure how it works, but she really wants to figure out a way that she can be someone that others contact to help people out. Lauren doesn't know how it works either.

They have often wondered if, when Eva is ready to take on responsibility, they could reach out to their contact and see if he could help her get set up as someone who is able to help people. In the meantime, Eva was going to keep her grades up and work hard to finish school early.

Eva worked tirelessly on her studies until her last class for the day was over. She stretched in her chair, looking at the clock. It was 4:30, she had time to start supper for her mom. She closed her laptop and headed into the kitchen, pulling ingredients out of the refrigerator to make some pasta and a salad. Most nights she was home about the same time as her mom.

They either made supper together or took turns cooking. Since she was home today, she was more than happy to cook supper for her mom who worked hard to support the two of them. Eva had a part-time job, but she worked mainly weekends unless her boss called her to see if she could cover a shift during the week when someone called in. Her mom would not let her help pay any of the household bills, insisting that she put her money into savings for her future. While in college she honestly was not earning a lot of money, but she felt bad that her mom refused to let her help out.

Her mom has done so much for her and gave her a good life, the best she could, given the circumstances, and she wanted to help her mom out. This was another reason why she was leaning toward becoming a lawyer, she hoped she could earn enough money to take care of her mother. She would love to take her mom on some extended trips and vacations and do the things they always talked about. They had gone on vacations, but they were small and not too far away.

Eva had a wonderful childhood; she loved the time spent with her mom. She certainly did not harbor any ill feelings that they lived a modest lifestyle. She just wanted to take care of her mom in the best way possible and give her things to make her life easier. Lord knows she did not have an easy life.

***

Lauren's childhood was very difficult. Her father was an alcoholic who gambled most of his paychecks away. Her mother worked outside the home, trying to make ends meet, leaving Lauren home alone a lot with the next-door neighbor to check in on her and make sure she was OK. The neighbor was a single woman with three kids of her own who made sure that Lauren was fed and clean, but she was always looking for the next great love of her life. Unfortunately, the men she dated were not that nice, most were abusive or lazy. She seemed to always be in new relationships.

When Lauren was five, the summer before she was to start kindergarten, the neighbor's newest love interest volunteered to check on Lauren. Lauren was a pretty little girl, with long blonde curly hair and blue eyes. She was also very smart, her mom taught her at a young age things that she should do and not do when she was home alone. Her mom was a good mother and loved Lauren very much, but due to her husband's addictions she had no choice but to work. She thought she was leaving her daughter in the safe hands of the neighbor.

The neighbor accepted her boyfriend's offer to check on Lauren as she had to take her three kids over to their father's house for their weekend visit with him and was running late. The boyfriend went into Lauren's family's apartment shortly after the neighbor left with the boys. Lauren was playing with her dolls in her bedroom at that time.

Lauren doesn't share many details with Eva about what happened next, Eva thinks her mom didn't remember everything that happened to her, but she knows that the boyfriend sexually and physically abused Lauren. When the neighbor came home, she found the apartment door wide open and a battered little girl lying on her bedroom floor. Horrified, she called the police and ambulance, then called Lauren's mother. Lauren was taken to the hospital where she spent a few weeks recovering from her injuries. During the time that she was in the hospital, her mother had to go to court to prove that she was a fit mother.

Her mother was able to provide several witnesses to her character and prove that she was a good mother. The judge did demand that Lauren's father be brought into court. Her father would disappear for days on end, drinking, gambling and not supporting his family. In a highly unprecedented ruling, the judge told the father to stop drinking and gambling and take care of his family, or he would send him to jail for as long as he could.

Lauren's mother told the judge that she did not feel like she could stay married to him, and the judge agreed. They went through a divorce, but Lauren's father finally sobered up, worked hard, and paid Lauren's mother alimony and child support which allowed her mom to take care of Lauren.

Lauren recovered from her injuries. With the help of a therapist, she was able to start kindergarten on time. Her mother was able to return to work at a job that allowed her to work during school hours and be home when Lauren was home.

During the summer months, she could afford to send her to a decent daycare. Her father remained sober but did not spend any time with Lauren. She never saw him until years later. Not only did he stay sober, but he stayed up to date with alimony and child support, probably more out of fear of going to jail.

Lauren's mother raised her alone until Lauren's senior year of high school. That year, her mother was killed on her way home from work in a car accident. Lauren was devastated. She and her mom were extremely close, all they had in the world was each other. The only other family she had was her father, so she was sent to live with him.

He was an uncaring father, who seemed to blame Lauren for his lot in life. He made it very clear that he expected her to clean the house, do the laundry, and cook his meals for him. Other than that, he really had nothing to do with her. He treated her like she was the dirt on his shoes.

Toward the end of her senior year, Lauren met her future husband. He was the new kid in town. He immediately showed interest in Lauren. He asked her out, and she accepted. They were constantly together after that, seeming to be the perfect couple. No one knew that he was already abusing her, she kept it a secret.

They married right after high school; Lauren was pregnant with Eva at that point. The relationship got worse right after they married. He was the typical fly off the handle and hit her abuser, then begged for forgiveness later, promising it would never happen again, claiming that she drove him to it.

One day, Lauren was preparing to cook supper, and she realized she was out of a key ingredient. She grabbed her purse and headed on foot to the grocery store a few blocks away, figuring she would be able to make it back before her husband got home. She ended up buying a few more things they needed that were on sale, struggling to carry it all home.

The owner of the store, seeing her struggle with all the groceries, came out, offering to give her a ride home. She accepted the kind offer, having known the owner for years. Soon they were pulling up in front of her house. He helped her get the groceries in, then she walked back outside with him to tell him goodbye, thanking him again for the ride when her husband pulled up.

The grocery store owner got in his car to drive away but stopped when he saw Lauren's husband strike her with his fist, making her fall to the ground. As he climbed back out of his car, he could hear Lauren's husband yelling at her as he continued beating her. The grocery store owner ran over to try to stop him but was struck down himself. He was much older than her husband.

Her husband continued to beat him while he lay on the ground. When he was sure the man wouldn't get up to interfere again, he turned his attention back to Lauren, but she was not lying there anymore. When he had his back turned, she ran into the house to call the cops. He figured that was where she had gone, so he went in after her.

Knowing that he would eventually come in looking for her, she made the call, left the phone off the hook, and then ran out the back door. She snuck back around to the front of the house. Seeing that her husband had gone into the house, she knew she should get away, but she couldn't leave the grocery store owner lying on the ground. She ran over to where he was lying, horrified to see that he had been beaten so badly.

He was still alive but unconscious. She took his hand and tried to tell him that help was on the way, but before she knew it her husband had her hair by the handful and was pulling her back away from the old man. Luckily the police showed up, managing to get her away from her husband.

It was at the police station when she went to give her statement that a police officer gave her the tiny piece of paper that saved her life. He was taking her into a room where she would give her statement when he handed her the piece of paper, whispering to her. "Don't look at that until you get home. Don't share it with anyone. It will save your life." He turned, walking out of the room.

She slipped it into her pocket, thinking that it was probably a good lawyer recommendation or something. She gave her statement and went home, remembering the paper later that evening. Pulling it out of her pocket she saw it was a phone number, nothing else. She called the number, and the rest is history.

Her husband was charged with assault on the grocery store owner and her, but only given a short jail term of one year. She was gone the day after the trial with only the clothes on her back. Thanks to that police officer she began a new life and has been paying it forward every chance she gets.

***

Eva was in the kitchen making supper for her mother when Lauren walked in the door. "What a lovely surprise Eva." Lauren said, "It smells wonderful in here." Lauren walked over to her daughter and gave her a hug.

55

"How was your day?" Eva asked her.

"It was good. Not a lot of drama going on, and the patients were great. Did you manage to get your classes done today?" she asked Eva.

Eva nodded. "I talked to Mattie about things today too. I think she is excited about the new look she will be getting tonight. She also seems to be very agreeable to a position that allows her to work at home."

"That's wonderful. Speaking of that, I need to go check in to see what the progress is on her situation. After that, I will come help you finish up supper."

"Sounds good," Eva said.

Lauren went into her office, closing the door behind her. She called the number. "Checking in," she stated. She waited while she was connected to another contact.

"I have some news," the man on the phone said. "I was able to get her a place to live. I am working on finalizing the deal. We have a small 2-bedroom house for her."

"That is great," Lauren said. "So she has a house to rent. Any news on a job?"

"She will own the house outright," the man on the phone said. "It was donated by a previous contact. The job is almost completed. I have her being set up as a legal transcriptionist. Have a few more details to work out on that too, but the equipment will be set up for her in the house."

"That sounds great. She actually does have typing and some computer skills. It should work perfectly. When are we planning on moving her? She is hot news here now." Lauren was worried about this.

"I will know more tomorrow, but I think we can move her in a couple days, probably Friday if that is agreeable. Do you think you can safely drive her to a location where she can then continue on by herself?"

"Yes, I will make it work. I'll check in tomorrow for more details." With that, they hung up. Lauren was very nervous about this one. Mattie's husband is a cop, actually a detective. They are running a huge risk, but it was one she knew they had no choice about. She left the office, going out to help Eva finish up supper.

Chapter 9

I woke up from my nap feeling well-rested. I had not slept so much in years. I really was starting to feel better although my body was still sore from all the beatings it had. I lay there, wondering if there would be long-term effects from being abused. I had no idea if I ever had any broken bones because going to the hospital or doctor was never a possibility for me.

I decided that there was nothing I could do about that right now, so I rolled over, looking at the clock. I was surprised to see that I slept the afternoon away! I decided to find something to eat for supper, as I was going to be getting my makeover soon. I was really looking forward to that. I have been forced to keep the same hairstyle the whole time I was with Allen. I was not allowed to cut or color my hair. It was very long now. I usually braided it or put it up in some way.

I went out to the kitchen, deciding today to have a bowl of soup. I found a can of beef stew in the pantry, heating it up on the stove. I took it, along with a few crackers, to the couch. I wanted to sit down to watch some news.

I figured I had better see what was going on, plus Eva had said that my husband was going to be on tonight making a plea for my 'safe' return. I turned the TV on, watching the end of a show right before the news. There was a knock at the door, so I went up and unlocked it, finding Eva and Lauren waiting, so I invited them in.

"We didn't mean to bother you while you ate, but we figured you would be watching the news. Thought you might like a little company?" Lauren stated.

"I would like that," I said. "Please sit down."

Eva sat next to me, while Lauren sat on the other couch, saying. "Don't let us stop you from eating. You need to keep your strength up."

I nodded, taking another bite when the news came on. Turns out I was the top news story again. There was my face staring out at us. I had no recent picture taken of me, so the picture they were showing was from our honeymoon.

The news anchor recapped the story of my disappearance and then stated there have been some new developments. They talked about how my car had been found, but it was not in the parking lot of the grocery store where we left it. Apparently, someone saw my keys and purse lying on the seat with the doors unlocked and stole the car.

The thief drove the car to a neighboring town and then used the money he found in my purse to buy some alcohol. He then proceeded to get drunk and attempted to run from the police when they tried to pull him over for suspicion of drunk driving. A car chase started, then the police soon realized that this was the car of a missing person after running the plates. Thinking that maybe I was in the car with the thief, they backed off hoping he would slow down.

They wanted to avoid an accident if at all possible. They followed at a safe distance, calling on the state police to help. The man panicked when he saw even more police cars, even though they were not closing in on him. He picked up speed, missed a curve in the road, missed a bridge, and landed in the river.

They went live to the scene where a reporter interviewed a state patrol officer. According to him, they had not been able to get to the car as the river in that area was deep with a very fast current, as it was currently at flood stage due to recent storms. They were waiting for a special dive team to arrive even though enough time had passed that the driver and I were assumed dead, drowned in the river. In the background, I could see my husband standing there staring out at the swirling water.

Another police officer took him by the arm, turning him away. The emotion on his face was one that I was used to seeing. He was angry. There were no tears of sadness, no signs of mourning my death. He was angry that I had escaped him, even though it was through death that I had.

Lauren and Eva looked at each other, then looked at me. "This is great," Lauren exclaimed. I looked at Lauren, but I knew what she meant by that. If I was dead, the police would stop looking for me.

The state patrol officer was talking about how they would do their best to search for the car to recover the bodies, but he stated that they may never find the bodies. The search wouldn't start until the next morning, it was too dangerous for them to dive at night. I reached out without looking, and Eva took my hand.

"I'm free," I said. "I can't believe it. I am finally free."

"Believe it," Eva stated, squeezing my hand. "They will search for you for a few days, but I think it is over."

"We can't get careless though," warned Lauren. "You can't be seen. We still need to give you a makeover, get you out of here. We also cannot assume that he will believe you are dead. Obviously, we know they will not find your body. Who knows if he will accept the fact that you are dead or if he will continue to look for you?"

What she was saying made a lot of sense. Knowing my husband, unless he had absolute proof I was dead, he would not believe it.

"Let's hope they can't find the driver either." I glanced at Eva. She said, "If they find his body but not yours, he will figure you were never in the car to begin with."

I took my bowl and spoon to the kitchen, washing up the dishes. I knew Eva and Lauren were right. I can't let myself get too comfortable, cannot let my guard down. I need to get out of here, I need to start a new life somewhere else. WE—I corrected myself. There were two of us now that needed to go.

The doorbell rang at that point. Eva ran up to answer it. She returned back in a few minutes with a slightly older woman who had a couple of bags with her.

"This is the young lady that needs a new look," Lauren said, not saying names.

"Nice to meet you," she said, sticking out her hand.

I shook it in return, "Nice to meet you also. Thank you for doing this for me."

"I'm happy to help. Let's have a seat and talk about what changes we should make." Eva and Lauren said they were going to head back upstairs and would come see me when I was done. "Can I take a look at your hair?" I nodded. She undid the braid, brushing out my long hair and running her fingers through my hair. I had long blonde hair, not super thick but not fine either. "You have lovely hair, but you do have some split ends that we should take care of to start with." She sat back down across the table from me.

"I haven't had a haircut in over five years," I stated. My hair was down to my waist, and I usually wore it in a braid to keep it under control.

She nodded, "I could tell it had been a long time, but it does look like you have taken very good care of it otherwise. So let's talk length. I'm thinking we go shoulder length or shorter. What are you thinking?"

"I want to go really short," I replied.

"I think you would look really nice with a shortcut, like a pixie cut. It would frame your face nicely. What about color? How do you feel about becoming a brunette?" I told her I approved, and she clapped her hands together, "Perfect! Let's get started!"

She worked away, cutting my hair off, giving me a short pixie cut, then coloring it brunette. She gave me a piece of paper with the color information on it so that I could keep it up wherever I went. She took me to the mirror to show me the finished style. "What do you think?" she asked.

"I love it!" I exclaimed. "My head feels so light now, this will be so easy to take care of."

"It looks great on you," she said. "Now let's have a seat to discuss makeup and how to use it to make you look a little different." We discussed the different ways to use it to make myself appear older or younger without drawing a lot of attention to myself. Lastly, we discussed some other ways that I could change my appearance, just slightly. She explained to me that, as part of what she does to help people, she was trained in a couple of other things that we could do to make small changes to my appearance.

She could do piercings and small quick tattoos. Things that could be done quickly. I didn't have pierced ears, so we double-pierced them and put one up at the top of my right ear, which she stated is a popular trend. She also gave me a tiny tattoo behind my ear. We decided on a butterfly, which was a symbol of new beginnings.

She sat back and looked me over. She seemed satisfied; she took me back over to the mirror. I stared at my reflection, hardly able to recognize who was looking back at me. I looked older, but only by a couple of years. I turned to her, "I love it! I can hardly recognize myself. Thank you so much!"

She smiled at me, "You are very welcome. Best of luck to you." She grabbed all her things, leaving me some makeup and a few pairs of earrings. She also gave me instructions on how to care for everything. She headed up the stairs, opening the door, "I'll send Lauren and Eva down to see the new you." A couple of minutes later, Eva and her mom came down the stairs. They stopped when they saw me, staring at the new me.

"What do you think?" I asked them, taking a slow turn to give them the full effect.

"Wow!" Eva exclaimed. "You look great! I hardly recognize you."

"I agree. Not that you weren't pretty before, but you are stunning!" Lauren stated.

"Thank you," I said shyly. "I feel so different. I feel like I have changed a lot in two days."

"You definitely have," Lauren stated, "you will have a lot of hard days ahead of you. You are getting stronger both physically and mentally, but there will definitely be days when you feel like you have lost ground. You need to remember that you are a strong person, you can change your circumstances. You are your own boss, not a prisoner anymore."

"I know I have a long road in front of me, but for the first time in years, I feel like I do have a choice, that I have a chance at a good life. I want that so much, yet it is so hard for me to make even the simplest everyday decisions for myself."

Eva took my hand, leading me to the couch. "We have some news about your future. Can we sit down and chat for a bit?" Sitting down, Lauren and Eva told me about the job that was being lined up for me. "That sounds like a great situation for me," I remarked, "since most of the typing I did for Allen was all legal-related."

"There is more good news for you, regarding your living situation. Our contacts have found you a house. They are working on your fake IDs, including a deed to the house. You will own the house outright."

"How is that even possible? I don't understand, your contacts bought me a house?"

"Not exactly, one of the contacts recently gave the house to our… group I guess you could say, to give to someone that really needs a safe place to live. You fit the guidelines that the person outlined for who should get the house. It is all yours, free of charge. Although going forward you will be financially responsible for all the household bills, maintenance, taxes, etc." explained Lauren.

I sat in shock, trying to absorb all of this information. I will have my own house! This was more than I could have ever hoped for. Every minute of every day since these two wonderful women rescued me my life has gotten better. I feel now that I have been blessed somehow to be this lucky. We chatted a little bit more although they said they didn't know the exact details—it would be something I would learn that they would not be privy to, again for all of our safety.

Lauren told me that she had asked Audra to come over tonight, so they could discuss how soon I could travel, with all the new developments, it was felt that the sooner I could start my new life, the better off we all would be. There was some more planning that was needed, so we needed to come up with a set time frame. She then took a picture of me with her phone, to send to the contact, so I could get proper IDs with my new name on them. This was all happening so fast, but I felt so ready to get my new life started.

The doorbell rang. Lauren went up to answer it. She soon came back with Audra. Audra gave me a hug, then sat down on the couch with Lauren. "You look great Mattie." She observed. "Besides the new makeover, you look well-rested, like you are feeling better."

"I am," I stated. "I have been following the doctor's orders, getting a lot of rest."

"Good, I'm glad. Lauren and Eva said that everything is in the works for you to be moved soon." Lauren had specifically told me not to give Audra details, other than that I need to move ASAP, to keep other information between the three of us, again for the safety of all involved.

"Yes, I guess it depends on when you say I can go," Audra stated she wanted to give me a quick exam before we made that decision, so we went into the bedroom. We came back out after the exam, taking our seats again.

Audra looked at Lauren, "She is doing a lot better, but I would like her to rest for two more days if possible. Today is Tuesday, I would say she can plan on leaving on Friday."

"That will be perfect," Lauren stated. "We have a few things to finish up before everything is finalized, then she will be set."

I looked at them, "I will never see any of you again, will I?"

"I'm afraid not," Lauren said. "None of us can risk that."

I nodded, I understood, but I couldn't stop the tears. "I will miss you all. I won't know anybody there. I'm terrified about starting over from scratch. I have a lot to learn. I am so grateful to you all. I don't know how I will ever find words enough to thank you for all you have done for me."

"Just live your life, be happy. As I have mentioned before, if you get the chance to pay it forward someday to someone else in need, please do so," Lauren said.

We sat there, chatting for a little bit about what the future could possibly look like for me. Lauren and Eva told me there was a small backpack in the closet in the bedroom I could use, giving me permission to take whatever clothes, bathroom items, etc. that I felt I needed. Audra said she needed to get going but promised to stop on Thursday to see me before I left for one last quick checkup. I thanked her, giving her a hug, which was starting to feel more natural at least with these three women.

***

Lauren walked Audra out but came back down with a box in her hands. "Eva told me that you would like to learn to crochet, so I have a surprise for you."

Eva stood up, "We have another surprise for you too, I'll be right back."

Eva went up the stairs, while Lauren came to sit next to me. She handed me the box, curiously I opened it up. Inside was a tote bag. I took it out, finding to my delight that it held a book with instructions on all the different crochet stitches, along with easy patterns for beginners. There was also some yarn in pastel colors with some crochet hooks of different sizes.

"I thought you could make a baby blanket after you learn the basics. The tan yarn is for practicing with. Crocheting is fairly simple, I think you can teach yourself, but tomorrow night when I get home from work if you need some help just let me know. I can come to spend some time with you to go over things and answer your questions."

"Thank you, Lauren," I said. "I can't wait to start!"

Eva walked downstairs with a present. It was wrapped in baby shower paper. She sat down, handing me the gift. "This is from Mom and I," she said.

"You both have given me so much that I can never repay. You really didn't need to do anymore."

"This was fun," Lauren said. "I enjoyed shopping for this gift for you." She had gone on her lunch break to shop for the gift, at Eva's suggestion.

"I can't remember anyone ever giving me a gift. I mean we received wedding gifts, but I don't think I have ever gotten a gift for just me before." I took off the wrapping paper and opening the box. Inside was another tote bag. I pulled it out, seeing that it was a diaper bag.

Inside the diaper bag were diapers, pacifiers, blankets, baby clothes, and a few other practical items I would need for the baby. "This is so sweet and thoughtful," I exclaimed. "Look at how cute these are!" I was holding up an outfit with a pair of little socks.

We examined everything in the diaper bag, talking about babies. I thanked both women for the gifts. They headed back upstairs. After locking the door behind them again, I packed everything back into the diaper bag. I took both bags into the bedroom with me, tucking the diaper bag into the closet next to the backpack I would be using.

I took the craft tote with me to the bed, making myself comfortable in bed. I opened the instruction book, thumbing through it, reading sections here and there. I found a pattern for a baby blanket that looked reasonably easy to make. I took out the tan yarn with the appropriate-sized crochet hook for the blanket pattern, then practiced the stitches until I felt comfortable with them. I then picked out the color I wanted to start with, choosing a pretty yellow, then began to make the blanket.

I sat there, crocheting with the TV on and a movie playing quietly. Pretty soon I started to feel drowsy, I was making pretty good headway on the blanket, but I figured I better get some sleep. I tucked everything away in the tote, setting it aside. I brushed my teeth and crawled back into bed, leaving the TV on. I could get very used to this life, nice, quiet and… safe.

Chapter 10

I slept pretty well in spite of the fact I had a couple of dreams that were unsettling. I imagine this will be a normal occurrence for me for quite a long time. I decided that I wouldn't dwell on them, there was no benefit in rehashing the past, and it would serve no purpose. I knew it was easier to say that than do it, but for my own sanity, for my future, I needed to try to look forward not behind. If I let the past control my future, it would be like letting him control my life still. It was time that I took that control back.

I climbed out of bed and went in, running myself a bath. It felt good to soak for a bit, I was still sore from the last couple of beatings, but definitely feeling better. The warm bath water seemed to help a lot. I soaked for a while until I decided I was hungry. Finishing off in the shower, washing my hair—which did not take nearly as much shampoo or conditioner as it had when it was long—then got out.

I looked in the closet and found a pair of shorts with a cute T-shirt to wear. I was rather tired of wearing pajamas and was ready to be dressed, like I was ready to face the day. I figured I would spend the day on the couch instead of in the bed—although I would not rule out the possibility of a nap this afternoon. I knew I needed to get rest today and tomorrow before I travel on Friday. I would rest and definitely do some crocheting today. Tomorrow I will pack for leaving.

I made some toast and coffee, then sat down to watch the news. I was not the top news story this morning although I was still a hot topic. The state police stated that they were unable to find the bodies of the thief/kidnapper or me. They were claiming we were considered dead, ruling the case closed. They showed a video of my husband leaving the police station with his head down, the perfect picture of a mourning husband.

I knew that he was not mourning my death, he was furious that I had escaped his control—no matter how I did it. I hoped that he would accept the state police's decision and stop looking for me. A part of me suspected that he wouldn't although I couldn't see how he would proceed with looking for me. There did not seem to be any way that he could find out that I was alive or where I was. Part of me also knows that he is a cop, not just any cop but a well-decorated homicide detective.

I washed my breakfast dishes up, turning the TV to a different channel. Sitting on the couch, I picked up the blanket I was making for the baby and started working on it again. I was really pleased with the way it was going. It looked like the one in the instruction book, maybe not as neat, but it was definitely easy to see the pattern starting to take shape. The yarn Lauren and Eva gave me was so soft, it was going to make a nice baby blanket.

While I crocheted, I thought about the little house that I would have. I know I haven't seen it yet, but I was already very excited to have it. I was told it was a 2-bedroom house, nothing more. I thought about coffee on the porch or the deck—if there was one—or just in the yard, watching the sunset or sunrise. I thought about the second bedroom, about the nursery I would create in there. I was starting to believe that I actually had a future that was going to be good, yet it was hard to believe that in two days this would actually be happening.

I vowed to take it easy today, following Audra's orders of rest. Tomorrow I will do some laundry and start getting things packed for Friday. I didn't know what the plan was for Friday, but I wanted to be ready to go. I made a mental note to ask Lauren about taking a few food items from the pantry with me.

I was wondering about groceries, small things that I would need right away. I have absolutely no money. Maybe I can ask Lauren for a small loan to get me by although I don't know how I could repay it when we would not be able to stay in contact after I leave.

I sat crocheting on the baby blanket for most of the morning while listening to different TV shows or movies. I was making great progress on the blanket; I have to admit it looked fairly good for the first attempt. Hopefully, the baby would love it regardless of the little mistakes it may have.

I took a break at lunchtime and made myself a grilled cheese sandwich with a bowl of soup. After cleaning up from lunch, I decided I would go try to take a nap. Audra stressed that I would need to rest up as much as possible to let my body heal, to regain strength. I had to be strong for both me and the baby when we made the trip to our new home. I still didn't know the details such as how I was traveling or if someone was taking me.

Hopefully, we will have a plan soon. I wished that Lauren and Eva could drive me there, but I didn't think that would happen as I was pretty sure that they couldn't know exactly where I ended up. As I lay in bed, snuggling up under the blanket, I let myself, again, think that maybe I would have a decent future. I dozed off dreaming of a future that was, as of yet, not certain.

Chapter 11

Lauren and Eva went about their day as normal on Wednesday. Audra thought that it would be OK for Mattie to be left alone—she was doing very well, and she had the cell phone—so Eva went to school and Lauren went to work. They always found it difficult not to be able to share what was going on with their close friends. Obviously, Audra knew, she was Lauren's best friend, but they couldn't share what they were doing with anyone else.

Lauren couldn't share everything with Audra, but she did know that Lauren had done this before, so they did share the knowledge to a certain extent. Eva faced harder difficulties with not being able to share anything with her best friends at school. They both had to go on with their days as if nothing was going on.

Lauren was at work, having just roomed a patient for Audra when the receptionist came back, telling her there was a detective there who would like to talk to her. "Me?" Lauren asked. "Did he say what it was about?"

"Yes, he asked for you. He didn't say anything other than he wanted to ask you a couple of questions."

"OK," Lauren stated, feeling Audra glancing at her briefly. "Can you show him into the conference room and let him know I will be right there?"

"Sure," the receptionist turned away. Lauren didn't want to look like there was anything wrong. So she walked over to Audra and told her about the patient she had just roomed, giving her the details she needed before she went to see the patient. She put her laptop down at her station, asking a coworker to room the next patient if she wasn't back in time. She went to the conference room. She walked into the room to see a man standing by the windows, looking out. "Can I help you?" she asked.

He turned toward her, Lauren realized that this was Mattie's husband, recognizing him from the news reports. "My name is Detective Allen Davis. I was hoping to ask you a few questions if I could."

"Of course, would you like to sit down?" She tried to keep her face from showing that she recognized this was Allen, Mattie's husband.

He took a seat and pulled out a notebook from his jacket pocket. "You are Lauren Mitchell, correct?"

"Yes, I am," she replied.

"Do you drive a red van?"

"I do. What is this about, Detective? Has something happened to my van?" she asked.

"No, not at all. I'm just following up on leads on a missing person report. Were you at the grocery store Monday morning?"

"Yes. I had Monday off, so my daughter and I did a few errands in the morning. Picking up groceries was one of the errands."

"Did you happen to notice this car sitting in the parking lot?" He pulled a picture out of his pocket. Lauren took it, looking at it.

"I'm not sure. It might have been there, but I really didn't pay attention to cars."

He took the picture back, pulling a different photo out. "How about this woman, did you see her?"

This brought Lauren a moment of fear. Did they catch her and Eva on a camera in the parking lot helping Mattie? If she lied to him, if he had video evidence that she talked to Mattie in the parking lot they would be in a lot of trouble. "No, I'm sorry. I don't recall seeing her. I recognize her from the TV though, she is missing, isn't she?"

"Yes," Allen said. "You were identified on the camera in the store as being there that day. We are questioning everyone that we are able to identify as being at the store during the time frame she disappeared."

Lauren was watching him while he spoke. He was not showing any signs of emotion. He never identified himself as Mattie's husband. You would think that he was devastated that she was gone. He was acting like he was just a detective investigating the case of a stranger. So cold, callous even. "I'm sorry, I don't remember seeing her there."

"Where did you go from the store?" Allen asked.

"Let's see," Lauren thought, "oh yes, we went to the courthouse to renew the plates on my van, then stopped at the drug store to pick up a prescription for my daughter's allergies. After that, we went home."

"What is your daughter's name?" he asked.

"Eva," Lauren stated.

"I would like to talk to her if possible."

"That is up to her, but I don't think she would have a problem speaking with you. She is in class right now at the university."

Allen asked Lauren a couple more questions, then said, "Here is my card. If you remember seeing anything or have anything you think might help, no matter how insignificant it may seem, please give me a call."

"I will, Detective," Lauren wondered how much she could push the subject. "Detective?" He had gotten up and was headed to the door, but he turned to her "I was just wondering, I saw a news report that said she was thought to have been killed. Is it normal policy to keep investigating after the missing person has been ruled dead?"

For a moment or two, Lauren thought she had gone too far, she could see the cold anger in his eyes briefly. "Her body was not recovered. We are just covering all the bases before closing the case completely." With that, he turned and walked out the door.

Lauren knew she needed to just get up and go right back to work, like it was no big deal so that others did not become suspicious. She wished she could call Eva to warn her that Allen was on his way to question her, but she couldn't risk being overheard by others in the office. Lauren and Eva had discussed this type of situation many times, so she believed that Eva would be able to handle the situation smoothly. It would be better if it appeared like Eva was not expecting Allen's visit.

***

Eva was on her way to the library after class to do some research for a paper she had to write for one of her classes. She was walking with a couple of her friends. They were discussing the class they just left and the next assignment for it. When they got close to the library, one of the friends went on to a different class while Eva and her remaining friend headed into the library.

They found a table near some windows, sat down, taking out their laptops, discussing the assignment for the paper. They discussed several possible ideas, bouncing ideas back and forth. Finally, they both settled on what they wanted to write about and started to do some research on their laptops. They sat in silence for about an hour, taking notes and making a list of references they wanted to look at in more depth.

"Excuse me," a male voice said. Both girls looked up to see a guy standing at the end of their table.

"Can we help you?" Eva's friend asked. It was obvious she thought he was very attractive, trying to flirt with him.

"I'm looking for Eva Mitchell." Not showing the slightest bit of interest in Eva's friend.

Eva and her friend glanced at each other. Eva looked at him, "Who are you?"

"I'm Detective Allen Davis. Are you Eva?" Eva had recognized him, but she managed to hide that from him.

"Yes, I am."

"I'd like to ask you a couple of questions if I could." Eva's friend was looking at Eva with a questioning look, still disappointed that the detective wasn't interested in her.

"Questions about what?" Eva asked.

"I'm investigating a missing person case," Allen stated. "I just need a few minutes of your time."

"Have a seat," Eva stated. "This is my friend. Is it OK if she stays here?"

Allen pulled a chair out from the table and sat down. "That's fine with me."

He proceeded to ask Eva the same questions he had asked her mom earlier, showing her the same pictures. Eva pretty much answered the same as her mom had done. He handed her his card, asking her to call him if she thought of something. She agreed to do so. She watched him walk away, then pretended to lose interest going back to her research. Her friend shrugged her shoulders, deciding not to think anything of it, and went back to her report also.

They worked on their reports for another hour until the librarian came around to let them know the library was closing in a few minutes. They gathered up their stuff and walked out to the parking lot. They chatted for a little bit by their cars, then climbed into their cars to drive home. On the way home, Eva wondered if Detective Davis had talked to her mom. She had wanted to text or call her, but that might have made her friend suspicious.

She watched for cars as she drove home that could possibly be following her, but she never saw anything that made her suspicious. She arrived home shortly after her mother did. She took her backpack to her room and heard her mom in the kitchen getting supper started. She joined her mom in the kitchen and sat down at the table, telling her mom about the detective questioning her at the library.

Lauren told her daughter that he had questioned her at work as well. They compared notes, both agreed that they had handled the situation well and that Allen did not seem suspicious that they knew anything at all. They then discussed whether they should share the information with Mattie or keep it quiet.

"What do we gain by telling her that we talked to her husband today?" Eva asked. "I think that she would become super stressed, and she doesn't need that."

"I agree," Lauren said. "But is it fair to her to not tell her? I am thinking that maybe I will call Audra and ask her opinion of it."

"That is a good idea," Eva commented, "But I do feel it would cause her a lot of stress for no reason. If he believed us, then he would not think twice about us. Not to mention that she will probably be on her way the day after tomorrow."

"I know," Lauren sighed. "I am torn between telling her because she has a right to know or protecting her from this."

"Exactly. I do understand your point."

Lauren's phone rang. "It's Audra," she told Eva.

Eva stood up, taking over at the stove for her mom while she walked to her office to answer the phone. Lauren taking these types of calls in her office was protocol for these situations. Lauren and Eva shared almost everything, but if there were things that it was better that only one of them knew, in order to keep the other safe, then these conversations were held in private.

Eva set the table, pulling supper off the stove. Soon Lauren was back. Eva looked at her questioningly. Lauren explained that Audra felt it would be in Mattie's best interest to not share the interviews unless she asked. They should use their best judgment. They sat down to eat supper, agreeing not to tell Mattie unless absolutely necessary.

Eva then asked Lauren when they expected to learn more about the plan to get Mattie to safety. Lauren said she would call their contact this evening after supper to see if there were definite plans yet. They chatted for the rest of the meal about their day. Lauren told Eva about a funny incident that happened at work. Eva shared the new research paper she was working on and how excited she was about it.

She thought it was a very interesting topic. Pretty soon, they cleaned up from supper, Eva stated she needed to work on some homework for her classes the next day. Lauren went back to her office to call their contact. Before she called, she grabbed a sheet of blank paper and a pen, so she could take notes. Taking notes was necessary to keep details straight, but she knew they also had to be careful.

She knew better than to write on a tablet as what was written could show up on the page below by shading over it with a pencil. By taking a single piece of paper, they could burn it or flush it; then the evidence of it would be gone. In order to know the details of where to go and what time they needed to make all this happen, she had to take some notes. Once she had the details of the plans, she left her office, heading to Eva's room. Eva was sitting at her desk and working on her laptop.

"Eva?" Lauren said from the doorway. Eva looked up at her mom.

"Hey, Mom, did you find out the plan?"

"Yes, I'm going to go discuss the plan with Mattie, want to join us?" Eva nodded, standing up. She followed her mom to the basement door and Lauren knocked. Pretty soon they heard Mattie unlock the door.

"Come in," Mattie said, letting them by her. They all proceeded down, taking seats in the living room.

Chapter 12

I had a very relaxing day, taking a nap after lunch, I woke up feeling more refreshed and then worked some more on the baby blanket. After an hour or two, my eyes felt a little tired, so I took a break from crocheting. I cooked a small meal for supper consisting of a potato and a small steak, with some corn. Once I was done eating and had everything cleaned up again, I lay on the couch, turning the TV on. I wanted to crochet some more but felt my eyes needed a break.

I was almost halfway done with the blanket; I had plenty of time to finish it before the baby made her entrance into the world. I scrolled through the guide on the TV, deciding to watch a cooking competition show. It looked like an interesting, fun show. I was enjoying the show when Lauren and Eva knocked at the door. I muted the TV and then headed up to unlock the door. Lauren and Eva sat down with me in the living room.

"I love this show," Lauren stated. "It is a lot of fun to watch them compete, but you can also pick up tips."

I nodded, "It has been interesting."

Eva asked, "How was your day? Are you going stir crazy shut in here all day yet?"

I smiled at her. "Oh, not at all! Look at what I have been working on!" I pulled out the baby Afghan from the tote bag at my feet. Lauren and Eva both looked at it, commenting on how nice of a job I was doing with it.

"You caught on very quick!" Lauren stated. "You are a natural!"

Eva nodded in agreement, "You've got a lot done on it since last night. It looks great!"

"Thank you," I said. "It was pretty easy to catch on to the stitches. The pattern is one of the simpler ones in the book you gave me. I should be able to finish it in plenty of time before the baby arrives."

"I would say so," Lauren replied.

I put the blanket back in the tote, looking at Lauren and Eva. "I'm sure you didn't come down here to talk about my crocheting. Is there more news?"

"I do," Lauren said. "I have the plans for getting you to safety."

I sat more upright on the couch. "Am I leaving Friday?"

Lauren nodded, "That is the goal, to get you out of here, on your way early Friday morning."

Emotions flowed through me, fear, because, in a couple of days, I would be on my own, fending for myself. Then a sense of excitement hit me when I realized that I would be starting my new life. "So… what's the plan?"

Lauren started telling Eva and me the plan. "We will be letting everyone know we are going away for the weekend, just a little mother/daughter trip. Not out of the ordinary for us, we do this occasionally. We will hide you in the back of the van, probably hidden from view by our suitcases. We are to drive to a VRBO home with a two-car garage, pulling into the garage."

"Once in the garage, we will close the garage door. You will then transfer to a car that is waiting for you. In the car, there will be everything you need to start your life over. The paperwork for the house, the car, your new identity, bank information, credit cards, cash. There will also be a new cell phone."

"Your new destination will be programmed into the GPS system in the car. Depending on how far you will actually have to travel, you might probably have to stop for a night or two along the way, but that will be up to you. You will have enough cash and credit on your credit cards to get a motel room, plus everything you need for groceries and household items."

"What about the job?" I asked. I wanted to be able to support myself, even though I was super appreciative of all they were doing for me.

"Your home office will be set up for you already in your new home. You will find information about your job when you get there. You have a week to get settled in, then you will start training for the job. It will all be laid out in the paperwork you will find in your new office. You will have a decent, well-paying, full-time job that will be able to support yourself and your baby well."

"It is an independent contractor position, which will enable you to work when you can, take care of the baby, not having to find daycare unless you want to. You can work your own hours. As long as you get 40 hours a week, they won't mind what your hours are. They do want a rough idea of the hours you want to work, but they work with single mothers who need to raise their children. Health insurance has also been purchased for you, as that is not a benefit of your job. All information will either be in the car or in your home office."

"That all sounds great," I said. "I really don't know how I can thank you all enough. I seriously thought that I had no way out other than dying. Every morning I considered taking my own life because I didn't see a way out. I thank God for bringing you both into my life and helping me as you have."

Both women wiped away tears, but it was Lauren who spoke up. "Just live a good life, raise that baby well."

I wiped away tears of my own, "I wish we could stay in contact. I feel like you are family. I will miss you."

"We will miss you too," Eva stated. "While we can't stay in contact, we will be happy thinking about you living a good life, a better life, in your new home."

We talked a little bit more about the plans for my start to my new life, and then Eva and Lauren left me to get some rest. They needed to make their own plans for the weekend trip. Eva had classes on Friday, and Lauren had work, so they both had to make arrangements to free themselves up for the trip. Lauren's boss was Audra, so she was sure it would not be a problem.

I shut everything off in the living room, heading into the bedroom to get ready for bed, thinking I would watch some TV in bed. I knew I had some things to get ready tomorrow to leave Friday. I brushed my teeth and crawled into bed, pulling the blankets up over my shoulders. I turned on the TV to a movie that caught my attention but turned the volume down pretty low.

I lay there, not paying attention to the movie, but thinking about what I needed to do tomorrow to get ready for Friday. I made a mental list in my head of things I needed to pack and how to make myself comfortable in the back end of Lauren's van for the trip to the VRBO home. As I went over plans in my mind, I started to drift off to sleep.

I woke up a few hours later to the TV still playing a different movie than what I fell asleep to. I was tired but found myself tossing and turning, trying to go back to sleep. For some reason, my mind was racing. I kept going over the plan for Friday's escape running through my mind. It really seemed like it would work out perfectly.

Allen thought I was dead, at least I hoped he believed that. The state police declared me as having died in the river, so I felt that no one was really looking for me anymore. Yet I was not willing to risk everything by sitting up in the van where I could be spotted at any time. Not being able to fall asleep right away, I picked up one of the baby books Audra had left for me, thumbing through it, reading portions that caught my eye. Eventually, I was able to put the book aside and fall asleep, but it was still a restless night for me.

I woke several times throughout the night, would look at the clock, realize it was super early and then roll over to go back to sleep. Finally, at 6:00 am I gave up, getting out of bed. I showered and got dressed.

After breakfast and a cup of coffee, I went into the bedroom. I pulled out the diaper bag and the backpack I was to use for the few things I would be taking with me. I got the laundry ready to wash, carrying it out to the living room, knowing I would wait to do it until later this evening when Eva and Lauren were home. I went back into the bedroom, picking out a few more items of clothing, some personal items such as toothbrush, toothpaste, brush, shampoo, and conditioner.

The backpack was mostly packed, just needed the few items of clothing that I was going to wash to put in there, that would suffice. I took the tote with the baby blanket in it out to the living room, sitting down to pass some time crocheting. About mid-morning, I felt sleepy, so I curled up on the couch and fell asleep.

Time seemed to go so slow. I spent my time napping, crocheting, reading, and watching crafting shows on TV. I sent a text message to Eva, asking if she was home yet at about 4:30 that afternoon. She replied that she was. After learning that the washer and dryer were free, I carried the laundry basket up the stairs to the laundry area. Eva came into the hallway with me, and we chatted a little bit about our day.

Eva had made arrangements for the next day with her professors, so she could miss her classes. Her friends agreed to share their notes with her. She planned on taking her laptop with her and work on her research paper over the weekend, but she stated it was no problem for her to miss the day. Her professors knew her dedication to her classes, so were a little bit surprised that she was going to miss a day but felt that she needed to get away for a weekend as she worked really hard all the time. With the laundry going, Eva promised to let her know when the washer was finished by text message, I went back downstairs to find some supper.

When I had finished the laundry, I packed it in the backpack and then cleaned up my supper dishes. There was a knock at the door. Having not locked the door this time, I called for whoever it was to come on in, Lauren and Eva came down the stairs. We sat down around the table to discuss the plans for the next morning. We had a rather strict schedule to adhere to, needing to leave by 6:00 am at the latest. "I'm all packed, except for the couple of things I will need tonight and in the morning," I said.

"Good," Lauren replied. "Did you make sure to take everything you need?"

I nodded, "Yes, I believe so. I might take a little snack food for the trip if that is OK with you."

"I think that is a good idea," said Lauren. "We should have plenty of room for whatever you need. If anybody were to look, it would just look like things we need for a weekend away. I will lay a couple of quilts and pillows down for you in the back to lay on, then we will pack things around you. Hopefully, you will be comfortable, I know it isn't the ideal way to travel, but it is for the best right now."

"It will be fine; I will have a couple of snacks with me. I don't know if I will have room, but I can take the book I am reading and hopefully pass some of the time that way."

"We will be able to talk to you," Eva said. "It will just look like Mom, and I are conversing as we drive. I think you should be able to hear us just fine."

"That will be nice. Hopefully, I won't get very claustrophobic that way."

Lauren looked worried, "Are you claustrophobic?"

"Yes, but I will be fine."

"Are you sure?" Eva asked.

"Yes, I will. I am determined not to let anything stop our proceeding tomorrow." I could tell they were concerned, but they seemed to be reassured by my determination. We discussed the details for a while longer, and then Eva and Lauren went upstairs to do some last-minute things before the trip tomorrow. I went into the pantry and found a plain cloth grocery bag that I used to pack a few food items in.

I included some quick-fix things like soup so that when I got to wherever I was going I wouldn't need to go grocery shopping right away. I included a couple of pieces of fresh fruit on top of the bag, along with a couple empty Ziplock bags for any trash, then put it on the kitchen table.

I went into the bedroom, gathering the diaper bag and the craft tote bag, into which I packed the baby books, along with the book I was currently reading. I took these two bags out to the table also. I left the clothes backpack in the bedroom so that I could add my last-minute items to it in the morning. It was still early, but knowing that I probably wouldn't sleep well, along with the fact that I had to get up early, I decided to lie down in bed to watch some movies. I turned the volume down so that I could hear it, but also so that I could sleep should I get drowsy. The first movie was over with, and the second one was about midway through it before I finally dozed off.

***

It was another restless night, as I thought it would be, I spent it more or less napping while I watched parts of movies. I woke up at about 4:30 am, deciding to get up. I showered, packed the rest of the items I would need into the backpack and carried it out to the table, along with the cell phone.

My stomach was a little upset, but I knew I should try to eat something. I made some toast, grabbed a banana, poured a glass of milk, and sat down at the table to eat. At about 4:45 am, Lauren sent a text message asking if I was ready. I replied that I was, quickly washed up the few dishes I had used, brushed my teeth—ready or not, it was time.

Lauren and Eva came down. We gathered up my bags and headed to the garage. The back gate of the van was open, so we walked back there. They had lay down a few blankets and pillows for me to lay on. I climbed in and was able to get comfortable—as comfortable as I could.

I had the book and a couple snacks along with bottled water. They packed my bags next to me, then their suitcases. They piled blankets and pillows over top of me but left my head uncovered for the time being. Lauren told me that if they felt I should cover my head they would let me know, then just pull one of the pillows or blankets over top. I could look out the window this way which definitely should help with my claustrophobia.

Lauren and Eva looked over the way they had packed everything in. I actually had a little bit of room, so I could change positions as needed yet remain hidden. They were satisfied with the way things looked from all angles and then closed the gate. I heard them climb into the front seat, start the van. Shortly afterward, we were backing out of the garage and headed to my new life.

Chapter 13

I was fairly comfortable lying in the back of the van, the ability to change my position a little bit helped. The three of us chatted back and forth about a variety of things until I dozed off for a while. I woke up later to hear music playing on the radio, wondering how long I had been asleep. I had given Lauren's cell phone back because they were going to dispose of it the first chance they got. I really had no way of knowing what time it was. "Mattie?" Lauren asked.

"Yes?"

"I need to stop for gas, so I need you to cover your head for a little bit."

"OK," I replied, doing as she asked. I heard the blinker and felt her slow to turn into a gas station. She stopped the van. I heard both doors open, and they got out, leaving me alone in the van. They were only gone for a few minutes, then we were back on the road again. I dozed off again but was awakened after a while by Eva calling my name.

"Yes?"

"We will be at the VRBO house in about 10 minutes."

"Great," I replied. I was relieved that we were going to be able to get out of the vehicle soon. I needed to use the bathroom and stretch a little bit. "What time is it?"

"It's one o'clock in the afternoon," Lauren said. I was surprised to find out how much time had passed; I must have slept for several hours. A few minutes later I felt the van slow, and heard the blinker turn on.

As the van came to a stop, Eva said, "I have to go in the house to open the garage, so hang on a few more minutes." I heard her get out. Shortly afterward, I heard a garage door opening up. Lauren pulled the van into the garage; I heard the garage door shut as she turned off the van. Lauren got out of the van, coming around to the back with Eva. They unpacked all the bags from around me and then helped me climb out. I stood, stretching, getting my legs limbered up a bit before trying to walk.

"There is a bathroom right inside, and you won't be seen going there." Eva pointed to the door to the house.

"Thank you," I replied, walking into the house.

By the time I came back out to the garage, they had my bags sitting on the floor next to an SUV that had to have been mine. "We didn't want to touch the car, just in case."

I understood what they meant, if I had an accident, stopped, and my car was examined in any depth they didn't want their prints anywhere on it. I noticed they had used a towel to pick up my bags. The SUV was a fairly new one, a pretty dark blue. I am not a car nut, but it seemed very new. It was a Chevy Traverse and looked like it would get very good gas mileage. I went around to the back, opened the hatch, putting my bags in. I turned to Eva and Lauren, with tears in all of our eyes, we gave each other hugs, saying our goodbyes.

They went into the house, standing just inside the door, so they could open the garage door for me. I climbed into the car and found an envelope under the passenger seat. I looked through the envelope, finding my new set of IDs, Social Security card included, two credit cards, a new cell phone, ownership papers for the car, along with the deed for the house. The key fob was there for the car. I also found a set of keys that I assumed were for the house.

There were also papers for a security system that had been installed in the house with the code to disarm it when I got there. I pulled out another envelope, in it was a large amount of cash. A quick count of the money showed $5,000 in various bills. I put some in my pocket, thinking it would be enough for gas and food along the way, even though I had no idea what things cost now. I also put my driver's license with one credit card in my pocket.

Everything else I tucked back into the envelope, putting it back under the seat for now. I didn't see any map or directions to the house, but there was one post-it note that only said 'GPS' on it, so I figured that the destination was already programmed into the car's system. I turned the SUV on and waved to Lauren and Eva. They opened the garage door. I looked at the map on the screen of the car, it was giving me directions. I backed out of the garage and was soon on the way to my new home.

According to the GPS, my new home was another 20 hours away. I decided to drive as far as I could, then stop for the night. I felt really well-rested at this point, with the naps I took in the back of the van. I checked over the car's interior, noted the low mileage on it, and was impressed. It would be a very reliable car for me and the baby, very low maintenance, and hopefully not cost a lot for gas.

Right now, I have a full tank of gas. I had to drive on the interstate, which I had never done before but had been in the car when Allen drove, so I wasn't too nervous. Once I got onto the interstate, I set the cruise control and found a radio station to listen to. I enjoyed the music and the changing scenery as I drove along. I drove for several hours before I felt like I needed to make a stop.

I pulled off of the interstate, stopped at a gas station where I topped off the gas tank, used the restrooms, and bought myself a large cup of coffee. I went back out to the SUV, got into the hatch, pulling out an apple and a granola bar. I climbed back in and started out back on the interstate. I enjoyed the apple, wrapping the core up in the paper from the granola bar, the two items making me feel full for now, giving me some energy. I sipped my coffee as I drove on into the night.

The traffic thinned on the interstate as the night wore on. The large trucks were pulled off for a few hours of rest before they continued on their way. I felt wide awake, so I kept driving. I finally stopped at about 9:30, deciding I should probably get a decent night's sleep before I continued on. The sign said I was in Sidney, Nebraska. I found a nice motel for the night, asking for a wake-up call at 5:30 the following morning.

***

I actually woke up the next morning and was showered before the wake-up call came. I loaded my backpack back in the SUV and drove to a gas station to top off the tank. I then found a coffee shop that was open, went through their drive-through to get some coffee and a breakfast sandwich, then I was back on Interstate 80.

According to the GPS, I had 13 hours of drive time to get to my new home. I couldn't wait. I planned to stop only as I needed, getting gas and food and using the restroom. Looking at the GPS again, it looked like I would travel clear through Nebraska before eventually starting north. Having never been out of Nevada, I was curious to see what Nebraska would be like. As the day wore on, I saw fields of corn and pastures with cows and horses. There were a lot of smaller towns along the way. I drove through some larger towns, Lincoln and Omaha, then crossed into Iowa. Once I hit Des Moines, Iowa, I turned and headed north.

The rest of the trip was uneventful. Iowa was a lot like Nebraska, with fields of corn and pastures of cows. Huge wind turbines could be seen in several fields boarding the interstate. I continued to stop only as I needed to. I did know that it would be nice to be in my own home, off the road, and able to eat a home-cooked meal. One can only tolerate eating fast food for so long. Thankfully I had the foresight to pack some fruit and granola bars, which helped keep the fast food purchases to a minimum.

Finally, at about 8:30 pm, I came upon a town of about 3,000 people. I drove through the town, to the north side of the town where I turned west on a small, paved road with a mailbox at the corner. This apparently was my driveway. It led back into a group of trees, curved to the north, and then back to the west. I could see water through the trees, so I knew I was close.

Around the final curve, there was the house. I stopped the car in the driveway in front of the garage, just sitting there looking at it. It looked perfect. It had an attached one-car garage. It was a one-story blue house with a front porch. There was a swing on the porch.

Glancing up at the sun visor, there was a garage door opener. I hit the button; the garage door opened. I pulled the SUV into the garage, which held a snow shovel, snow blower, rake, lawnmower, along with a few other tools. I closed the garage door, shutting the SUV off. I went straight to the door that connected the garage to the house, using the key from the envelope to get in.

Inside the door was the keypad for the alarm system, which was beeping for the code. I put in the code that disarmed it, making a mental note to change the code to something only I would know. Walking into the house, I looked around. The door leads into a mud room/laundry area with a washer and dryer in it. That led into the kitchen. It was a cute kitchen with an open concept in the living area. It was apparent that the house had been recently updated with new appliances, countertops, and paint. I loved it.

Everything was white except for the blue backsplash and the granite countertop was white with splashes of gray and blue in it. I walked into the living area. At the east end was the door that led out to the front porch with big picture windows. The east end of the kitchen had a little eat-in breakfast nook with bench seats.

To the south end of the living room was a fireplace with a large TV hung above it. There was a sectional couch in the living room and a built-in bookcase to the left of the fireplace. To the right was a doorway that led to a hallway. The west side of the living room had floor-to-ceiling windows with French doors that led out onto a huge deck.

The view took my breath away. I went out onto the deck, which had a gas grill and some lounge chairs, and I walked to the rail. The yard sloped down a little bit, and there was a path that led down to a pier. I went down the stairs of the deck to the path and followed it down. The ground leveled out about halfway down to a firepit with more chairs around it.

I continued down the path, standing on the pier in no time. I walked out onto the pier, looking in amazement at the lake. The water was so clear you could see the bottom. You could watch the fish swim by. I even saw a small turtle swimming by.

It was not a huge lake, definitely not one that huge boats would probably be on. Following the curve of the shoreline, I could only see a handful of piers. I could see a walking path going either way from the path I had followed down to the pier. I thought I would take a walk on it soon. The view was gorgeous, I sat on the bench on the pier, enjoying the scene for a few minutes.

I went up to the house and went back inside. I went down the hallway, finding to the left a full bath, past that a little bit was a door on the right. I opened the door to find the master bedroom. It had huge floor-to-ceiling windows with a door that went out on the deck also.

There was a huge walk-in closet. The master bathroom was very nice. It had a soaking tub beside a shower. There was a king-sized bed in the bedroom with built-in bookcases on either side of the headboard.

I went back out to the hallway, investigating the next door on the left which was a small linen closet. At the end of the hall was one more bedroom. It was smaller, but still a nice size with a walk-in closet. It had windows on both outside walls. It had been fixed up as a nursery.

It had a crib, rocking chair, and changing table, with a built-in bookcase next to the closet door. I sat down in the rocking chair, I was crying. The house was perfect, I loved every inch of it. I couldn't believe it was mine. I wished that I could call Lauren and Eva to let them know I made it. I wanted to tell them how perfect the house was.

There was one more door that I hadn't checked out yet, so I walked back out into the hallway and headed toward the kitchen. In the corner of the kitchen was a door that I opened, discovering it led down into the basement. I went down the stairs.

The walk-out basement was fully finished. It was one large room, with a half bath and a closet at one end. It was set up as an office on one end with a play area on the other end. I would be able to work yet have the baby down here with me. There were windows, again on the west side, that looked out to the lake with a door that led out to a small patio area under the deck.

In the office area, there was a desk that had a computer set up on it with a landline telephone. There was a filing cabinet in the corner, a printer on a printer stand against the wall behind the desk. On the shelves below the printer were extra paper and ink for the printer. There was also a shredder next to the printer stand.

I went around the desk, opening drawers to find pens, paper, staples, stapler—pretty much anything I would need to run a business from home. Hung on the walls were a bulletin board, a white board, and some hanging wall files. Lying next to the keyboard was a file folder. I opened it to find paperwork pertaining to the new job that I was to start the following week. I closed it for now, vowing to come down soon to read through it.

The playroom side had playful rugs on the floor. There was a toy box and a bookcase. The walls on the playroom side were painted with fun storybook scenes. I was amazed at the work that someone had done to make this place perfect for me. Maybe it hadn't been done exactly for me, but they had gone through a lot of work to make it suitable for either a single mother or a small family.

It was perfect. I was starting to feel at home here already. At first, the huge windows made me nervous, but there were blackout drapes that I could close at night if I felt the need to. I tried the door to the patio. It was locked, which was fine with me. I turned, going back up the stairs.

I went out to the car, carrying my few bags into the house. Once back inside, I reset the code for the alarm and then armed it. I put the few groceries away and found that the pantry was reasonably well-stocked with canned goods, a few boxed goods. There were a few items in the freezer.

I would probably need to go to the store for a few things like milk and butter in the next day or so, but I could get by for now on what was here. I opened each cupboard to examine what was there. From what I could see, there was very little I would need to buy as far as pots and pans or dishes. I would work on a list of things that I need to pick up when I venture into town.

I took my craft tote into the living room, setting it on the coffee table. I then carried my backpack into the master bedroom, putting my few items of clothing away. The linen closet was well-stocked with towels and extra bedding for my bed. I would need to pick up bedding for the crib and other baby items, but I had plenty of time to do that. I took the diaper bag into the nursery, putting the few items it contained away.

Within a few minutes, I was unpacked. I looked at the alarm clock on the bedside table. It was 9:30 at night. I was exhausted, having driven so many miles the last two days. I made sure all the doors were locked, pulled the blackout drapes, changed into pajamas, and crawled into the bed. I was soon fast asleep.

Chapter 14

On my first night in my new home, I slept soundly. I was exhausted from the trip here, but I also felt like I was truly home. I woke up on Sunday morning, feeling refreshed, ready to do the few things that I needed to get done. After dressing, I had breakfast and coffee out on the back deck, looking out over the lake. It was such a peaceful morning. I decided to go for a walk on the path.

After I washed up my breakfast dishes, I went back out on the deck, armed the alarm, locking the doors behind me. I put the keys in my pocket, heading down the path.

When I got to the path, I decided to go north. It followed the shore of the lake around. I was enjoying the quiet walk when I glanced up to see a tiny black dog running straight at me. It was obviously a Labrador puppy. It stopped at my feet, wagging its tail, and barked at me.

I reached down with my hand and let it sniff me. He immediately started to lick my hand. "Can I pick you up?" I asked the puppy. He seemed to understand, wagging his tail and putting his paws up on my leg. I picked him up. He wiggled around, lying his head on my shoulder, letting me pet him. "Where did you come from little fella?" I asked.

He lifted his head, licked my cheek, then nestled his head in the crook of my arm and went to sleep. I was not sure what to do but figured someone was missing this little guy, so I continued to walk down the path some more. Pretty soon I hear a male's voice calling, "Lucky!" I froze, terror hitting me out of the blue. I took some deep breaths, probably just the owner of this little puppy.

"Is that your name little one? Lucky?" I said softly to the puppy I was holding. He let out a little snore as I continued to walk. Pretty soon I saw two men walking toward me, leading an identical black puppy on a leash. "I think I found Lucky," I said.

The man walking the identical puppy, looked at the sleeping one in my arms, smiling. "The little guy is an escape artist I swear. Slipped right out of his collar and took off down the path. Thank you for catching him. He can be hard to rein in." I glanced at the other man, it was obvious they were brothers, to find him looking intently at me with the most gorgeous blue eyes I have ever seen. I tore my eyes away from him and looked back to the other man.

"It was no trouble, he actually came right up to me, begging me to pick him up. Then he promptly fell asleep."

The guy seemed a bit surprised, "Really? He rarely lets anyone hold him or goes to anyone. Even my fiancé has trouble picking him up. Now his twin sister, Lady, is different. She likes everyone to give her attention and will bug you for it."

I laughed. "They are adorable."

"Adorable but a handful!" He pulled a collar out of his pocket, putting it on Lucky. He then hooked a leash to it, saying "Well, thanks again for bringing him back." I put Lucky on the ground, and he turned toward me, paws up on my legs again, whining. "My name is Josh." He said, holding his hand out. "This is my little brother, Jacob." He nodded toward the other guy.

"Mattie," I said, hesitating briefly before shaking his hand. Jacob smiled at me as he shook my hand.

"I haven't seen you around here before, are you visiting family?" Josh asked.

"I just moved into the house just south of here."

"That's great. My fiancé, Randy, and I are your neighbors to the north. If there is anything you need just let us know."

"Thank you," I said.

"We'd better get these two back home. Nice meeting you."

"You too," I said, starting to turn away, but hesitating. Josh was already headed back toward his house, having a difficult time getting Lucky to go with him. Lucky kept looking at me and whining. I smiled, such a cute little puppy.

"It was very nice to meet you, Mattie," Jacob said before turning to follow his brother. "I hope to see you again soon."

I felt lost in those blue eyes of his, but was able to say, "Nice to meet you too, Jacob." I turned and walked home.

***

When I got back home, I made a shopping list of things I needed, walking around the house and getting ideas. It was a fairly extensive list, and although I knew I had the money to buy all the things on it today, I felt that I should divide it up into two or three shopping trips, in order not to draw a lot of attention to someone new to town buying a ton of things. The less attention I got the better. I decided I would pick up the groceries, then I needed a purse and wallet, some odds and ends like that for right now. Clothing for myself could wait until the next trip.

I found trash bags, some cleaning supplies, so there really wasn't much I needed. There were small containers of laundry detergent and softener, so I would pick up some of that. I put some of the cash along with one of the credit cards in my pocket. I also put my driver's license in my pocket. Later today when I got home, I would start reading through the paperwork in the manilla envelope that had been left in the car for me more in-depth to see what all was in there.

I folded my list, walked out to the garage, and hit the button on the wall of the garage to open the garage door. As the door opened, in ran Lucky. He came running up to me, demanding I pick him up. "Lucky! What are you doing here you naughty puppy? Did you escape again?"

I walked out of the garage door, looking around to see if I could see Josh, Jacob, or Randy, Josh's fiancé around. There was no one. I opened the car door and climbed in with him. "Come on," I told Lucky. "Let's take you home."

He looked up at me from the passenger seat of the car, curling up he went to sleep. "I must be boring; you seem to fall asleep around me." I chuckled as I pulled out of the garage and headed out to see if I could find Lucky's home. I drove out to the main road and then turned north. I didn't have to go far when I spotted a driveway that I assumed was theirs. I turned, following it up to the house. Josh and Jacob were standing outside with a woman, whom I assumed was Randy. They watched me pull up and get out of the car.

"I think I have something of yours," I told them smiling. They looked at each other, then back at me, a confused look in their eyes. I walked around to the passenger door, opened it and reached in picking up Lucky.

"Lucky! How did you get out?" Randy exclaimed. She came down, trying to take him from me, but Lucky seemed to try to get away from her, burrowing down into my arms to hide. "He really likes you apparently!" Randy laughed. She took him, saying, "You must be Mattie. Josh told me you found Lucky earlier when he got away. I'm Randy."

"Nice to meet you," I said. "Yes, this time when I opened the garage door, there he was sitting there waiting for me." I laughed.

Josh replied, "I swear he was in the fenced-in backyard. He must have dug a hole or something. I'm sorry you had to bring him here."

"It was no problem; I was headed into town to pick up a few groceries." Jacob was standing there, looking at me intently. I looked back at him, his staring unnerved me, so I headed back to the driver's side of my car.

"Well, thank you for bringing him by. Let me give you our phone numbers in case the little rascal gets away again, you can just call us, and we will come to get him." Randy went into the house with Lucky, who looked over her shoulder at me, whining.

Jacob noticed Lucky's reaction, saying, "I think you have an admirer." The look he gave me made me feel like he was not referring to Lucky.

I laughed nervously, "He is a cute little guy."

Randy came back out and handed me a slip of paper. "Cute but ornery!" she said. "Text us later, so we have your number. I included Jacob's number there, in case you can't reach us. If you need anything just holler!"

"Thank you," I replied. "I'd better get going." I climbed back into my car and started to turn around to head into town. I caught a glimpse of Lucky looking out the window at me. He looked so sad. I made a mental note to buy both Lucky and Lady a couple of dog toys while I was in town. I noticed Jacob was watching me drive away too, then he turned to follow Josh and Randy inside.

Chapter 15

My first stop in town was at the local shopping center. I went in, grabbed a cart, and headed up and down the aisles looking for the things I needed. I found a purse with a matching wallet that I liked and found some toys for Lucky and Lady. I picked up a few other items and then headed to the checkout. I paid for my items, went out to load them in my car, heading next to the grocery store.

I bought the few groceries I needed, loaded them in the car, and then decided to drive around the town a little bit before heading home to see what was around. It looked like a nice town, the businesses all looked like they were doing well, and the homes were mostly nicely kept. I made note of some stores I wanted to check out eventually, then drove home.

Once home, I unloaded everything from the car, putting things away. I left the dog toys on the counter, made a pitcher of iced tea, and took a glass of tea out to the deck. I took the purse, wallet, envelope containing the papers, and the cash out with me. I loaded the IDs, cash, and credit cards into the wallet. I then put the wallet, the keys, some small items I purchased like Kleenex, hand lotion, Chapstick, notepad, pen, fingernail clippers, just little things I thought would be handy, in my purse.

I came across Randy, Josh, and Jacob's cell phone numbers when pulling the cards out of my pocket, so I sent all of them a text message from my phone, so they would have my phone number. They seemed like nice people. Maybe we could be friends although I knew I had to be careful about what I told them.

Josh responded with a simple, "Hey, let us know if you need anything or if Lucky shows up there." Randy asked if I had any difficulty finding what I needed in town. I replied no that I had found everything I needed for the moment. She replied back saying there is a larger town about an hour north of here that has some bigger stores, so if I needed something I couldn't find locally to let her know, and she could recommend some place there. I thanked her, telling her I might take her up on that soon.

Jacob didn't reply as quickly, but when he did, I had to take a minute. "Hey, Mattie," his message started. "It was really nice to meet you today. Let me know if you need anything." I read the message, then I sent back, "Thank you. It was nice to meet you too."

I put the cell phone down. I wasn't sure what to think about Jacob, the way he looked so intensely at me made me uneasy. I decided not to worry about him, I probably wouldn't even see him very much.

I started reading through the paperwork in the envelope that was left for me in the car. The papers showing ownership of the house and car were in there. There was also an envelope from a bank that I had seen in town. I opened it up, finding a debit card along with a deposit slip for an account in my name.

According to the deposit slip, there was another $5000 in my account. I couldn't believe that people who didn't even know me were so generous. I thought about adding the rest of the cash to what was in the account, but I decided against it for now. I would keep it in an inside pocket in my purse in case for the moment, in case I needed to make a getaway.

The information for the two credit cards was in the envelope also, showing the credit line on both along with the dates the payments would be due. I vowed not to use them too much unless I absolutely had to. I took my purse and the paperwork back into the house and put them on the table. I would take the paperwork down to the office later and file it away.

I went back out to the porch, sitting down, drinking my tea, and looking out at the lake. There was a pair of loons swimming out there, diving for food. I watched them for a while, then realized that one of them had a baby on its back. While I watched, I heard a small bark. I looked down to see a black ball of fur running up the steps to my deck.

"Lucky!" I laughed. "What are you doing here?" He ran over to me, and I picked him up. He gave me a couple of licks, then curled up in my lap. He didn't go to sleep, but he seemed very content lying there. I picked up the cell phone, sending a message to Randy. "I have an ornery little puppy sitting here with me on my back deck!"

A couple minutes later she replied, "Oh my gosh! I am so sorry! We will walk over and get him in a couple of minutes."

"No problem, he seems pretty content right now." I put the phone down, stroking Lucky's fur while watching the loons out in the lake.

As I looked out over the lake, stroking Lucky's fur, I felt completely at peace and happy. About 10 minutes later, I see Randy, Josh, and Jacob coming through the trees. I waved at them and motioned for them to come on up. They joined me on the deck, I invited them to sit down. They did, looking at Lucky lying there in my lap. Jacob was looking at me, I couldn't bring myself to meet his gaze.

"I hope he hasn't been a bother," Randy said.

"Not at all. He showed up, I picked him up. He instantly fell asleep and has laid here ever since."

"He seems quite content," Josh said, looking at Randy.

"Yes, he does," Randy said.

Jacob, who had sat in the chair next to me, reached over and scratched Lucky on the top of his head. "Looks like he belongs here." Jacob's closeness to me unnerved me. I could smell his cologne; he was so close.

"We actually were talking on the walk over here. We think that you should keep Lucky," Josh said.

"Oh, I can't take your dog away from you!" I said.

"You would be doing us a favor actually," Josh said. "We only wanted one dog, but we couldn't bring ourselves to separate the siblings from each other. It is obvious that Lucky is happier here with you than with us since he comes straight here whenever he gets loose."

"Who could blame him," Jacob said quietly, looking at me.

"I don't know," I replied, trying to keep my calm with Jacob so near. I looked down at Lucky lying in my lap. He was looking up at me as if begging me to let him stay. "What do you think Lucky? Do you want to live with me?" He promptly sat up and licked my check, as if he understood exactly what I had said and was voicing his opinion. The four of us laughed.

Randy said, "Well, I guess that is that."

Josh added, "I'll run home and get you some of his dog food, along with his dishes. Also, his dog bed. I'll be right back."

"I'll go with you," Randy said. "I need to check on supper."

He headed down the steps. Randy laid a leash on the table. "He really looks happy here." Randy observed before she headed down the steps behind Josh.

"He does look happy," Jacob said, not making any move to get up.

"I always wanted a dog but never got around to getting one. He seems like a sweet little guy." I was so nervous at being left alone with Jacob, I hoped that Josh and Randy wouldn't be gone too long.

Jacob laughed, "Well, if you didn't agree to take him, Josh or Randy would be here every half an hour or so picking him up to take him home."

I laughed, asking, "What about Lady? Won't she miss him?"

"I don't think so, besides, they live close enough that you should be able to get them together often for play dates. She will get more attention at home this way," Jacob said.

We chatted a little bit about the puppies, while Lucky slept in my lap. I finally got my nerve up to glance at Jacob.

Jacob looked back at me, those blue eyes locking with mine.

"Would you like a glass of iced tea?" I asked.

"No," Jacob said, "I'm good, thanks."

I blushed, looking away. I found it difficult to make small conversations with him.

Jacob leaned closer, "They say that a dog is the best judge of character in humans. Lucky seems to love you already."

Nervously I stroked Lucky's head. "I have to admit, he has captured my heart too."

Jacob laughed. "Well, he is very smart, look at how often he escaped." We both laughed at that.

I sat silently for a couple of minutes, looking down at Lucky sleeping in my lap. I didn't know what to say to Jacob.

"Mattie?" Jacob asked. "Is that short for something? Matilda? Madeline?"

I looked up at him. Our eyes met and again, I felt the intensity of his blue eyes on mine. "No, I'm just Mattie."

"You don't seem like a Mattie. What's your full name?"

I hesitated. "Mattie Irene Austin." I kept my middle name, just to make remembering it easy.

"You don't seem like an Irene either," he said thoughtfully.

"Who exactly do I seem like?" I didn't know where this was going. Could he have picked up on the fact that Mattie is not my real name? Socializing and small talk were not things I knew how to do very well.

"I think you are a… Mia Amata. That's what I'm going to call you. Mia Amata." He asked me a few more questions, changing the subject before I could ask him why he was calling me Mia Amata.

Thankfully it wasn't long until Randy and Josh came around the side of the house. They had driven back over, parking out front, so they walked around the side of the house.

"We drove over. Turns out with the dog bed, dishes, and food, there was a lot more to carry than I thought." Josh said as they came up the steps to the deck and sat down. They brought Lady with them, so Lucky woke up and the two of them ran down in the yard, playing and chasing bugs. Jacob and Josh got up, walking down the steps to keep an eye on the puppies as they played.

Randy and I stayed on the deck, watching as the guys played with the puppies. Randy commented on the lovely house I had, and I thanked her. "Is it just you here?" she asked.

"Yes, just me." I didn't offer more information than that.

"Well, it's a good thing you have Lucky then! He will be a great companion and guard dog. They are very loyal dogs. Do you work around here?" Randy asked.

I shook my head, "I start a new job a week from tomorrow. I'll be working at home."

"Oh, that's nice! I envy you that. What kind of job is it?"

"I'll be transcribing legal documents, court cases, and things like that."

"Sounds very interesting."

"Do you work?" I asked Randy.

She nodded her head, "Yes, I work at a dentist office in town. I'm a dental hygienist. Josh runs his own business, building houses."

"Is there much house building going on here in town?" I asked.

"There are quite a lot of houses being built actually. People leave lake life as they get older, wanting to live closer to doctors and stores. Younger people want to live on lakes. He sometimes travels a few hours away to build when it is slow here. In fact, he is leaving Monday for a job site about eight hours away, so he will just stay there during the week."

"Hence, the reason we got the pups, so I would have companionship, maybe a guard dog while he is away. He worries about me a lot when he has to be gone for days at a time, and I miss him a lot." She seemed sad at the thought of his leaving Monday. I liked Randy a lot. She seemed very easygoing, and I was hoping she would become a friend.

"Maybe we can get together a couple of times while he is away, make the time go a bit faster for you," I suggested.

"I'd like that," she said. "Josh is from here, but I just moved down here recently and still haven't made a lot of friends yet. Between moving and the new job, I've not had a lot of time to socialize. It would be nice to have a friend so close by."

"Sounds like we are in the same boat," I replied. "You three are the only people I've met. It will be great to get to know you both better." We smiled at each other and continued to chat while the guys played with the puppies. Pretty soon Jacob and Josh joined us back on the deck, along with the puppies. Lucky came straight to me, so I picked him up, letting him rest in my lap. Jacob took the seat next to me, Josh sitting next to Randy.

Randy looked at Josh, saying "Mattie and I are going to get together a couple times this week while you are gone."

"That's great," he said taking her hand in his. "What do you have planned?"

"Well, nothing yet, but maybe supper out one night."

"I'd grill for us too," I said.

"Sounds like you ladies will have a good time." He looked at Randy, "Maybe you won't miss me at all."

"I'll miss you terribly," She smiled at him. I watched their interaction with each other and could see how much they loved each other and how happy they were. I glanced at Jacob, to find out he was watching me. We all chatted a little bit, I asked if they wanted to stay for supper.

"We would, but unfortunately we have a family dinner tonight," Josh said.

"Oh, do you have much family around here?" I asked.

"My parents live close. My sister and her husband live an hour away. Jacob lives about 20 minutes away. We try to get together a couple of times a month at least."

"That's nice," I said. Lucky let out a snore from my lap, and we all laughed.

"They are really nice people," Randy said. "Josh doesn't know it, but I'm marrying him only for his family."

Josh laughed, "I can probably live with that." We all laughed. "We should probably get going. Where do you want me to put everything?" he asked.

"I'll open the garage door, and you can bring it in through there." I sat Lucky down, and we all entered the house.

"This is a gorgeous house!" Randy exclaimed.

"Thank you," I said. "I am in love with it."

"I can see why," she said.

Josh was looking around, "Looks like a good solid house. If you ever need any repairs or anything, give me a call. If I can't do it myself, I can recommend people."

"Thanks, I will keep that in mind." I walked them to the garage door, and we went out that way, retrieving Lucky's items from Josh's truck. We left the bucket of dog food in the mud room, and they set everything else on the table. They turned to leave when Randy surprised me, giving me a hug. I hugged her back.

"I am so glad you are here," she said. "I think we are going to be great friends."

"I think so too," I said.

Josh smiled and then walked out with his arm around Randy. Jacob hesitated a moment, then said, "Bye Mia Amata," then followed the others out to the car. I waved goodbye as they drove off, shutting the garage door behind them.

I shut the door, turning to see Lucky sitting there looking at me. "Well, boy," I said. "It's just you and I now. I should have asked if you were housetrained." My cell phone went off, it was as if Randy read my mind, "BTW L is trained."

"Good to know," I sent back. I filled his food and water dishes, putting them in the mud room where he could get to them easily. I took his dog bed into the living room, putting it on the floor in front of the fireplace. Lucky was following me around the house, watching every move I made. I went back into the kitchen, made another pitcher of tea, and put it in the refrigerator. I realized that I had skipped lunch, so figured I would fix myself an early supper. "What sounds good for supper Lucky?"

Lucky barked at me.

"I agree. A hamburger does sound good." I got the fixings out to make myself a hamburger and started cooking the burger. On a plate, I put a bun with a piece of cheddar cheese. I put a bit of ketchup on that and grabbed a bag of chips out of the pantry. I put a few on my plate and then put the bag away.

Pretty soon my hamburger was done, and I put it on the bun. I sat down at the table and ate my supper.

Before I finished, my cell phone chirped. I looked to see a new text message from Jacob. "Welcome to the area Mia Amata. Hope to see you again."

I wasn't sure how to feel about his texting me like that. There was something about Jacob, I couldn't place my finger on it, but I felt uneasy. I debated about replying to his text message but decided not to. I didn't feel like I should encourage him too much.

Lucky went back to his food dish and ate his supper, while I washed up the dishes by hand, even though there was a dishwasher, putting them away. I then went into the living room. I armed the alarm system and then sat down with the remote. Lucky sat at my feet, looking at me, whining. "I really shouldn't let you on the couch you know," I said looking at him. "That is probably a bad habit to get into."

He tilted his head to one side and looked at me.

"Stop that, no fair! No sad puppy eyes."

He tilted his head to the other side and gave me the same look.

"OK OK! Get up here." I patted the couch next to me, he jumped up lying his head on my lap. I laughed and stroked his head. We sat like that, watching a movie on TV. When the movie was over, I stretched, looking down at Lucky. "I'm tired, boy. I think I will take a nice bath and turn in."

He jumped down, sitting there looking at me expectantly.

"I'd swear, it's almost like you can understand everything I say to you. It's uncanny."

I got up, shutting all the lights off. I checked the alarm again. I had closed all the drapes when it got dark. I headed to the bedroom with Lucky following behind, not letting me out of his sight. I ran the bath water, putting my clothes in the hamper. I got my pajamas out and lay them on the bed. I climbed into the tub, letting out a huge sigh. I turned up the hot water a little bit, letting it run for a little while longer. Lucky lay on the floor where he could keep an eye on me.

After my bath, I crawled into bed. Lucky sat on the floor looking at me again, whining. "Seriously?" I laughed as I looked at him. He put his paws on the side of the bed, begging me to let him up. "I guess the bed is big enough for both of us." I spread a small blanket on the other side of the bed and said,

"All right, get up here." He leaped onto the bed, almost not making it with his puppy legs. He immediately lay down on the blanket I put down for him. I shut the lamp off, rolling over on my side, stroking his head. He gave my hand a quick lick. Pretty soon we both were sound asleep.

***

I slept soundly, getting up once during the night to let Lucky out when he whined. He was such a good puppy, letting me know he needed to go out and then going right back to sleep. We had no reason to get up super early the next day, so we lazed in bed until mid-morning. Finally, my stomach and Lucky's bladder demanded that we get up. I left Lucky outside, leaving the door open to the deck, while I went into the kitchen to make a cup of coffee.

I took my coffee, along with some toast I made, out on the deck, watching Lucky chase butterflies, then a squirrel who sat in the tree chattering at him. As I sat there drinking my coffee, I heard a voice hollering my name. Randy was coming up the path with Lady. I waved at her, motioning her to join me on the deck.

"Morning," I said as she joined me on the deck.

"Good morning," she said. "Hope I'm not imposing."

"Not at all. There is coffee in the kitchen if you would like a cup." I offered.

"Oh, that sounds wonderful. Thank you." She went into the kitchen, poured a cup of coffee, then came back out and joined me. "Lady and I like to go for a walk in the mornings before I go to work. I thought we would walk in this direction and say hi if you were up."

"I'm glad you did. We are just sitting out here enjoying the morning. It is so beautiful here."

"It really is. I'm not from here, I moved here a couple of months ago after Josh asked me to marry him. I have come to love it here."

"So, you and Josh are my neighbors to the north. Jacob lives reasonably close Josh said. He isn't married?" I asked, trying to seem like I was just making conversation and not trying to pry information about Jacob out of Randy.

"Yes, that is right. Jacob rents a small house about 20 minutes away. He isn't married. Their sister, Janet, and her husband, Jack, live about an hour away. Nora and Donald, their parents, live just a few minutes away. They try to get together every weekend, if possible." Randy sipped her coffee.

"Sounds like a close-knit family," I commented.

"They really are. They are all so nice, I feel lucky that I am going to be part of the family. They already treat me as if I am family. You would like them," she looked at me out of the corner of her eye.

Taking a sip of my coffee, I asked, "Do you work today?"

"Yes, I should probably get going in fact," She stood up. "Would you like to come over for supper tonight?"

I smiled at her, "Thanks for the offer, but I really can't tonight. Let's plan some night this week though. I would love to have a girl's night with you soon."

"Sounds good, I'll text you later, and we can work out the details." I stood up with her, picking up our coffee cups. She went down the steps to the backyard, taking Lady with her, they headed up the path toward her house. She waved at me before I lost sight of her in the trees, I waved back.

***

After washing up the dishes, I went down into the basement, with Lucky following me down there. I sat at the desk, reviewing all the information for the new job I would be starting in a week. I used the login information in the folder to login in to the computer, where I was instructed to change the password. I checked the email that I was set up with, replied back to some emails from my supervisor and then checked out the programs I needed for work. I set up the company chat as instructed, sending my supervisor a chat message stating it was done.

She replied back right away, said she was glad to meet me and was looking forward to working with me the following Monday. I told her I was excited to start. She asked if I would have time to read over some account information and protocols before Monday, which would make my training go much faster. I told her I would have plenty of time, so she said she would send the information over. I watched for the documents, printed them out, putting them in one of the 3-ring binders that I had found in one of the drawers on the desk.

I spent the rest of the morning going over the information in detail, asking a couple of questions and making some notes as I went along. My supervisor advised me to keep track of the time spent reviewing the information, putting it on my timesheet on the computer, so I would get paid for it. I could consider it part of my paid training.

I took a break at lunchtime, making myself a sandwich. Lucky and I went outside on the deck. Lucky went down, running around in the yard, while I ate my sandwich, watching him, laughing at his playing with a butterfly, smelling the wildflowers. I was surprised that he never ran off, he never got too far away from me at all. He kept a very close eye on me, stopping to check on me every so often.

My cell phone chirped, alerting me to a text message. Randy sent a text asking how my day was going if I would be free Wednesday evening for supper. I replied back to let her know Wednesday sounded good. We texted back and forth a couple of times, then she went back to work after we set up a time for her to come pick me up.

I stood up to go back inside. Lucky ran up the stairs and was at my side in an instant. We went back inside, washed up the lunch dishes, then I went back down into the office to do some more studying of the information for the account I would be working on starting Monday. After reviewing the information for a couple of hours, I recorded my hours on the time sheet and then went upstairs to do a few things for myself.

I sat down at the kitchen table with my purse. I reviewed the instruction booklet on my cell phone, trying to familiarize myself with the things I could do with it. After playing around with the smartphone for a bit, I took out a notepad and pen. Using my phone, I looked for the name of an OB/GYN doctor.

I would need to get established with one soon. My bruises were almost all gone, no one seemed to notice them last night thanks to the makeup tricks I had been shown. I knew I would have to come up with a story for the scars on my body, so I figured a car accident would probably work.

As to the father of the baby, if asked, it was someone I had been involved with but found out he was married, so I moved here to make a new start. I thought that would cover the bases. I researched some doctors, finding one that seemed like she would be great. Her reviews were really good, people talked about how caring she was. I called the office and spoke with the receptionist, stating that I was new to the area and was about six to seven weeks pregnant.

She took the new insurance information work had provided for me. We set up an appointment on Friday of this week. She asked me if there was some place where they could get my medical records from. I told her that I have not been to a doctor for years, so I don't have any records. She didn't seem like that was a huge problem, then repeated my appointment time for me.

I added it to the calendar on my phone. I figured when I met the new doctor Friday I could ask her for pediatrician recommendations, I had plenty of time for that. I would also need a regular doctor for when I wasn't pregnant, for other health visits. I had time for that too, maybe the OB doctor could make recommendations for that also. I could ask Randy Wednesday night at supper for some vet recommendations also.

I then searched for local clothing stores. I will need some maternity clothes soon. I also couldn't wait to buy some baby clothes, figuring I would start with some basics until I knew what sex the baby was. I wrote down some local stores. Wednesday night, I would tell Randy that I was pregnant, to see if she had some ideas where I could shop.

I researched the town, looking to see what was available for other businesses, such things as restaurants and stores. I made notes, then just browsed a map of the area to try and get more familiar with the town. There were a lot of lakes and parks with hiking paths. There seemed to be a lot of things to do around here as far as outdoor activities. From what I am learning—both on my drive around town yesterday and my research online—I felt I could really love living here.

I noticed the time. I decided Lucky and I would go for a walk down to the mailbox. I doubted I would have anything, but I should check and empty out any junk mail. I grabbed the leash, just in case. I didn't want to risk him running out into the road and getting struck by a car.

"Come on, boy. Let's go for a walk." He seemed excited, so we walked out the front door. I armed the alarm behind me, then we headed down the driveway. Lucky stayed close to me but was not willing to risk anything, I hooked him up to the leash when we got close to the mailbox.

As expected, the only thing in the mailbox was a flyer from the local hardware store. We turned back. When I thought it was safe, I unhooked Lucky from the leash. He stayed close to me but sometimes would chase a bee or butterfly. He never did get far away from me.

Going back into the house, I took out my notepad again. I glanced through the flyer, and it gave me a few ideas I wanted to try for the house. I made another list and grabbed my purse and car keys. "I'll be back, Lucky. You behave while I'm gone."

He barked, wagged his tail, then promptly went and lay down in his dog bed, watching me. I shook my head in amazement, he really seemed to understand me.

I drove into town, stopping at the hardware store. I picked up some shelving, screws, hooks, nails, a hammer, and an impact driver with extra drill bits, things the salesman recommended that I would need for my projects.

From the hardware store, I went to the local nursery/greenhouse to pick out some plants. There I spoke to a saleswoman who helped me find plants that would thrive where I wanted to place them. She also recommended soil and plant food and helped me pick out planters. She advised me on the care of all the different plants I purchased. She gave me a business card for the greenhouse, telling me to call if I had any questions.

My last stop was at a little home decor store that caught my attention the day before when I was driving around. This time, I told the saleslady I would just like to browse, as I wasn't sure what I was exactly looking for. I wanted some decor that would add color here and there.

I liked the white walls and cupboards, but it seemed pretty stark. I found a beautiful blue bowl that would go on the island. I found a matching vase and votive candle holders for a centerpiece on the dining room table. I picked up a runner for the breakfast nook table and some bookends for the built-ins by the fireplace in the living room.

I was done shopping but was hungry, so I decided to stop at an Italian restaurant on the way home. "Welcome!" A man's voice boomed as I walked in the door. "I am Sal, welcome to our restaurant!" I instantly liked Sal—he was everything one would expect when picturing an Italian.

"Thank you," I smiled at him.

"A table for one?" I nodded. "A lovely vision like you dining alone? I will give you our best table. Louisa!" Sal called back. "Louisa!" His booming voice could be heard throughout the whole restaurant. "I'm coming old man," boomed a woman's voice from the kitchen, almost as loud as her husband. "Who is this lovely young lady?"

"My name is Mattie," I said, shaking her hand.

"Give her our best table Louisa. We will cook her the best Italian meal she has ever had!"

"She is a vision, eh Sal? Eating alone, such a waste of all that beauty is it not Sal?" Before he could answer her, she went on, "Come! Come! Your table is ready for you. I will seat you."

She started to lead me into the dining room. She took me back to a small table in the back, next to a large window overlooking a lake. It was a beautiful view. "Sit, sit," she said. The table was set with two settings, right next to each other instead of across the table. I sat down, while she took the second place setting away. "You are new here, no?"

"Well," I hesitated, nervous about sharing things with strangers. "Yes, I just moved here a few days ago."

"You have plenty of time to find a man here," Louisa predicted in typical Italian fashion.

"I'm not really looking," I explained.

"Oh, but you will. The men, they will be after you like crazy!"

Just then we heard Sal's booming voice, "Jacob! It's about time you paid your uncle Sal and aunt Louisa a visit. Louisa! Our Jacob is here."

"That man," Louisa said, shaking her head, but it was obvious she adored Sal. She hurried over after handing me a menu.

"Uncle Sal, Aunt Louisa!" I looked over to see Jacob standing there. I instantly looked at the menu, hoping he wouldn't notice me. I could hear the three of them chatting by the entrance.

"Jacob! It has been too long." Louisa chided him.

"Sorry Aunt Louisa, I've been busy lately."

"Too busy to come see your family?" Louisa scolded.

"Louisa," Sal boomed, "quit harassing the boy, show him to a table!"

Having made my mind up on what I wanted to order, I lay down the menu, looking out the window at the lake. I waited for the waitress to come take my order.

"Mia?" I heard Jacob ask. Steeling myself, I turned to look at him.

"Hi, Jacob," I said.

"You know our Jacob?" Before either of us could reply, "Sit! Sit!" Louisa was pushing Jacob to sit on a chair at my table.

She looked at us, then gave a huge smile, "I bring you your drinks then take your order." She walked off, calling to Sal as she went.

Jacob looked at me apologetically. "Sorry about that. They are the typical Italian family. I can ask for my own table if you want me to."

I watched Sal and Louisa working together, "I like them. It's OK, I would hate to upset Louisa." I really didn't want him to sit at my table, he made me nervous and anxious, but I didn't want to be rude.

He asked what I would like to eat, I told him what I had decided to order. Pretty soon Louisa was back with our drinks, ready to take our order. I ordered the pasta primavera, while Jacob ordered shrimp Fra d iavolo.

I looked around the restaurant, which was busy, but I noticed that the tables closest to ours were not being used. This did little to help my anxiety, but I was in a public place and a loud cry for help would get attention. That realization helped me to calm down.

"Sal and Louisa are making sure we aren't disturbed. Sorry, they like to play matchmaker for me." He took a drink of his soda.

I laughed a little. "Do they do that a lot?"

"Yes, they do. They think it is a shame that I am still not married."

Louisa showed up with our meals at that point. "You're not getting any younger Jacob. You could do worse than this lovely young lady." She said this all matter-of-factly and then walked away.

I was stunned, didn't know how to reply to that. Jacob seemed nervous, picking up his fork and playing with the shrimp on his plate.

Deciding to ignore Louisa's statement, I picked up my fork and started eating. We ate in awkward silence for a few minutes, then started a casual conversation.

"How's your pasta?" he asked.

"It's very good."

"This is the best Italian in the state," he declared.

I laughed. "So you have tried every Italian restaurant in the state of Minnesota?"

"No. There was no reason to look any further than this one." He smiled.

I smiled back, "Uncle Sal and Aunt Louisa. You don't look Italian to me."

"We aren't actually related. Dad and Sal served in the Army together. They have been through a lot together and refer to each other as brothers. He has always been Uncle Sal to us kids," he explained. "He was the best man at Dad's wedding to Mom and was there the night they met. Dad was there when Sal met Louisa and best man at their wedding."

"That explains a lot. Sal and Louisa definitely look Italian, but you don't."

"What about you? Do you have any siblings? Are your parents still alive?" he asked.

This was something I didn't have to lie about; I just wouldn't tell him about the exact names from my past. "I don't know who my parents are, or if I even have siblings."

"You don't?"

"No. I was abandoned in a trash bin when I was a newborn. A policeman walking by heard my cry and took me to a local hospital."

"Oh, Mattie," he said, "I am so sorry."

"It's OK, I came to terms with it a long time ago." I smiled at him.

"Mattie?" Jacob said.

I looked at him, "Yes?"

"Why are you here?" he asked.

I smiled sadly at him. "I needed a new start."

"From what? Am I prying? Did I overstep?" he asked.

"No," I sighed. "It's fine. I made the mistake of getting involved with the wrong man."

"Wrong how?" Jacob frowned.

"He was charming and told me all the right things. There were signs that something was wrong from the beginning, but he lured me in. I was naive and young. I believed I was in love with him. Then suddenly, he didn't want anything to do with me. Turns out he was already married with two kids. I was so stupid." I felt terrible telling him the lie, but I still had to protect myself, the baby. I glanced at Jacob who seemed angry.

"You made a mistake, that doesn't mean you were stupid. Men like that are pigs. Did you tell his wife?" he asked.

"No, I thought I would, but decided against it. I didn't want to destroy his kids' home life. I decided to start over some place new so that we wouldn't risk running into each other ever again. That is why I am here," I replied.

"You were used by a man who didn't deserve someone like you. I admire you for not ruining the jerk's marriage when you could. That says a lot for your character."

We finished our meal in silence. Louisa came back, asking if we would like dessert. I told her no; I was too full. The meal was fantastic. I told her I was ready for my bill, I needed to get going.

"Your meal is on the house!" Louisa declared. I tried to protest, trying to talk her into letting me pay for my meal. "You make our Jacob smile. He is falling for you. Anyone who makes Jacob happy, we welcome any time. Just like your mama and papa eh Jacob? Love at first sight!" She took our plates and walked off, again leaving me speechless. She was good at that. I looked at Jacob.

"Don't try to argue with her," he stated, "full-blooded Italians always win." Standing up, he walked me out to my car.

Hesitantly, I said, "Thank you for walking me to my car. I had a nice time."

He smiled, "Even though we were rather forced together?"

"Yes, even though it wasn't up to us."

"I had a good time too Mia Amata," Jacob said. He watched me climb in my car, then turned and went to his truck.

***

Once I was home, I unloaded the plants, pots, and soil, leaving them in the garage. I took the rest of the items in the house. I washed up the bowl, vase, and candle holders, then put them out as I had planned. The pop of color it added was nice. I needed more decor, but I was pleased with my purchases so far.

I took Lucky outside, walking down to the pier with him. He played around for a while. My cell phone in my pocket went off. I pulled it out seeing a message from Jacob. "I had a nice time tonight, Mia. Thank you for the company." I debated about responding but decided I didn't want to be rude, so I decided to be honest. "I had a nice time too." Lucky and I headed back up to the house where we relaxed watching a movie, then headed to bed. Lucky sleeping on his blanket next to me.

I woke up stretching. I lay on the bed, petting Lucky who was lying on his blanket next to me, remembering supper with Jacob. It had turned into a good night. Lucky gave a little whine, so I got up, throwing a robe on. The coffee was already done, so I poured a cup, and Lucky and I went outside on the deck. He ran down to take care of business, then chased a squirrel around a tree. Pretty soon I hear someone holler "Hello!" Randy and Lady walked over again. I waved at her, and she came on up.

"I hope you don't mind; I just had the urge to come visit with you before work," Randy said when she walked up the steps.

"Not at all. Help yourself to some coffee. Creamer in the refrigerator."

She went into the kitchen and came back out with a cup, looking at me suspiciously. "When did you go to Sal's? I saw the leftovers in the refrigerator."

I blushed. "Last night."

"Oh? With whom?"

"No one. I stopped in after shopping for some plants and decor for the house. Why would you think I went with someone? I don't know anybody here except for you."

"I was just curious, it's Jacob's favorite restaurant."

"Oh?" I said, but I blushed bright red.

All of a sudden Randy let out a little squeal. "You had a date with Jacob last night!" I smiled but shook my head.

"Not exactly. I stopped in there by myself, he showed up a few minutes later."

"So what happened?"

"When Louisa realized we knew each other she sat him at my table, then said since I make Jacob smile, and he is falling for me, my meal was on the house."

Randy laughed, "I knew it! I knew there was something between you two. I could sense a change in Jacob from the moment he met you. He kept asking us questions about you, trying to be all innocent about it."

"Slow down. It was just a chance meeting. Not a date."

"If Louisa said it, it must be true! Jacob is falling for you!" Randy stated.

"He doesn't even know me. You're imagining things," I said.

"He has talked about you often since meeting you. There is a family history of love at first sight!"

"You believe in love at first sight?"

Randy became completely serious. "I do. When you meet Donald and Nora, you will too. I'd better get going and head to work. We still on for tomorrow night?"

"Of course, I'll see you tomorrow morning for coffee."

She grinned, "You do make great coffee. Oh, when are you seeing Jacob again?" She stood up and walked to the stairs.

I blushed again; I couldn't help it. "I'm not. We have no plans."

Her grin got even bigger, not sure how, but it really did. "You will. I'd bet money on it. I'll text you later." She winked and ran down the steps, calling for Lady.

My cell phone went off. It was a text from Jacob again, "Morning Mia Amata. I hope you have a good day."

I replied back, "Thank you. You too."

Lucky and I went inside. I threw some things in the crockpot for chicken and rice and mixed up some dough for some homemade rolls. I let that sit to rise, cleaned up, and went down to the office, Lucky at my heels.

I spent my day reviewing things for my new job, I really wanted to be prepared for work on Monday. I also had some things that I wanted to do around the house, so after lunch, I worked around the house doing some light cleaning and repotting the plants I bought. I had some issues with the rail planters I purchased, so I sent Josh a text just to ask his opinion. He didn't offer me any advice, instead he said he asked Jacob to stop by to help me out.

I finished all my chores early, checked on supper, and decided I had time to soak in the tub. I took the book I was still working on with me and enjoyed a nice long soak with Lucky lying on the floor next to the tub. While I was in the tub, Jacob sent a text stating he would swing by after work to help me. It seemed like we were constantly being thrown together, whether we liked it or not.

After my bath, I threw on shorts and a V-neck shirt. I went into the kitchen and put the rolls in the oven, having kneaded the dough earlier and letting it rise again. I grabbed ingredients for a salad and started chopping up the vegetables for it. Once that was done, I made a homemade vinaigrette, putting that in the refrigerator until it was time to eat. Everything was almost done, so I decided to take Lucky out before Jacob got there. I stood at the rail watching Lucky run around, chasing some bug I couldn't see from here. I heard Jacob knock on the door, so I went inside, leaving the door open for Lucky.

I opened the door. Jacob was wearing shorts and a tank, showing his tan body. "Hey, Mia Amata." He smiled.

"Hey back." I moved to the side to let him in. I closed the door behind him. "Thank you for stopping by. It wasn't urgent."

"It's not a problem. Josh said you had some planters you needed to set out, but there was a problem?" he asked.

"Yes, the planters I bought don't seem to want to fit, even though I took measurements with me when I bought them."

"Where are they? I will take a look." I showed him to the back deck. "You lifted these to the rails?" he asked.

Confused, I said, "Yes. I carried them from the garage, then tried setting them on the railings."

He shook his head. "You should have asked for help. I would have been happy to lift these for you." Feeling a little insulted, I retorted, "I'm perfectly able to carry things. I just need help mounting them to the railings."

"Sorry," he replied, "I didn't mean anything. I'm sure you are capable. Let me see if I can figure out what the problem is."

"It's OK. I need to do some work on the front porch. Let me know if you need anything." I went out to the front, setting up a ladder, so I could hang the potted plants from the roof overhang between the posts. I went to the garage, getting my hanging plants, carrying them to the front porch. I climbed up the ladder to place the hook for the first plant. I reached up with the drill in hand to make the first hole. All of a sudden, a wave of dizziness hit me, and I found myself falling from the ladder. I cried out, unable to catch myself, landing on my back on the floor of the front porch. I lay there trying to catch my breath, but blacked out, unable to fight it.

I came to with Jacob kneeling next to me, calling my name. "Please, answer me."

"I'm OK." I tried to sit up.

"Lay still," he demanded, "the ambulance is on the way."

"I'm fine. I don't need an ambulance."

"Mia, you fell off a ladder and were unconscious. You need to get checked out. You scared the hell out of me."

"I'm sorry," I said weakly, closing my eyes, drifting to sleep.

"Mia Amata, stay with me. You have nothing to apologize for. Come on baby, don't leave me." Jacob was very anxious.

I barely caught what he said, but I tried to open my eyes. "My baby. Is she OK?" I asked drowsily.

Jacob was confused, "Lucky? He is fine. I put him in the house."

I shook my head, "No. My baby. I'm pregnant. Please. Is my baby OK?" I started drifting off. I started to shiver.

"You and the baby will be fine, just lay still. Hang on, I'll grab a blanket." He ran into the living room, coming back with a throw from the couch and covered me up. "Stay with me baby, please don't leave me."

The ambulance soon arrived, and I was loaded onto a gurney. They told Jacob to follow the ambulance in his truck. He ran into the house, shut the oven off, grabbing my purse for my insurance card, then followed us to the local hospital.

Once at the ER, the doctor came out to talk to Jacob. I was drowsy, it was difficult to get information from me. Jacob explained what happened and also told him that I was pregnant, but he didn't know how far along I was. The doctor asked a few more questions and then went back into the examination room.

About two hours later, the doctor came out to get Jacob, bringing him into the room where I was sitting on the side of the bed. "Hi," I said quietly.

"Are you OK?"

"I'm fine. The doctor says I have a slight concussion, but otherwise, I'm OK. I'm so sorry to cause so much trouble for you."

"Please stop apologizing. I'm just so relieved you are OK."

"I need to bother you for one more thing. Can you give me a ride home?" I asked. The doctor was listening to our conversation.

"Mr. Vance. I need someone to keep an eye on her tonight. She should be fine, but with a concussion there could be issues that arise in the first 24 hours. Do you think you can arrange that?"

"Yes, I'll keep an eye on her, make sure she is OK." I tried to protest but the doctor threatened to admit me if I didn't agree. I finally gave up. The doctor went over all the signs and symptoms to watch for, saying to wake me up every couple of hours to check on me.

I stood up to leave, Jacob wrapped my throw around me and led me out the door. He kept his arm around me, helping me into his truck, making sure I got seat belted OK. We drove in silence for a while. "Mia, are you sure you're OK?"

"Yes, I'm sure. I am so sorry for causing you so much trouble."

"Mia, stop that. You are no trouble. You just scared the hell out of me. What happened?" he asked.

I took a deep breath. "I'm pregnant Jacob. I climbed the ladder, reached up to use the drill, and felt dizzy. Evidently, I passed out and fell."

Jacob was silent for a while. "You aren't hurt? You and the baby are OK?"

"The doctor said I might be sore for a couple of days, I have a slight headache, but the baby and I are OK."

We pulled into my driveway; Jacob shut the truck off. We sat there in silence for a couple of minutes. "What the hell were you doing on a ladder?" He seemed so angry, I cringed away from him, against the passenger door, getting as far from him as I could. I worked on unbuckling my seatbelt, getting ready to flee.

Quietly, I said, "I'm pregnant, not incapable of doing my chores." I got the seatbelt unbuckled.

"Yes. You are pregnant. You have no reason to be on a ladder."

I didn't reply. I opened the door to the truck and climbed out, heading to the house. I heard Jacob close the truck door, following me to the house. Lucky welcomed me happily when I walked in. "Hey, boy," I scratched his head, then let him outside. I followed him out, standing at the rail as he ran down into the yard. Jacob came out on the deck.

"Mia Amata," he said, grabbing my arm. I pulled away, frightened.

"Please don't grab me," I said.

"I'm sorry. I won't hurt you. I am just trying to understand what happened. What is going on?"

"What more is there to understand? The man I was involved with previously didn't want anything to do with me when he found out I was pregnant. I am here, alone. I am trying to figure out my life."

"Do you know how much you scared me tonight? Had something happened to you, I don't know what I would have done."

I looked at him confused. "Why do you care? You don't know me." Lucky came back up the steps, I led the way back inside the house. Jacob stayed on the deck for a couple more minutes, then followed me in. I went into the kitchen, checking the rolls and the food in the crockpot. The rolls were done, but cold. The chicken and rice was done, still hot. I looked at Jacob. "I'm sure you are hungry, the least I can do is feed you for all the trouble I've caused you."

Jacob rubbed his face, tired. "Mia, you aren't any trouble. Let me help you."

"Just have a seat at the table, I've got this under control."

Jacob washed his hands, then sat down at the table, watching me as I pulled the rolls out of the oven. I tossed the salad and added the vinaigrette, setting it on the table along with a plate of rolls. I grabbed the chicken and rice, putting that on the table too. I poured us some iced tea, then joined Jacob.

"I have to admit, this smells wonderful. Did you make all of this from scratch?" He looked impressed as I nodded.

Conversation between the two of us was difficult as we ate supper. We avoided the elephant in the room.

I really didn't feel good, my stomach was nauseous, and my head hurt. Jacob told me about his job, he worked as a game warden and really loved what he was doing. "I grew up in the outdoors practically, always bringing home stray animals, hunting and fishing. It just seemed the right course for me to take."

"Can it be dangerous?" I asked.

"Yes, honestly it can. I deal with hunters and poachers; you never know how they are going to respond to you. For the most part, they are decent people who make a mistake."

"Do you carry a gun?" I looked at him, concerned.

"Yes, I do. I've never had to fire it except to put a hurt animal out of their misery. Most of the time I take animals to local shelters or vets to try to get them help, so they can be released back to the wild. I even have some room at my place where I can keep a couple animals from time to time, having vets come out to help me nurse them back to health."

"Sounds like you really enjoy what you do." I smiled at him.

"I really do. Not only do I get to help animals and the environment, but I also get to teach people. I'm up for a promotion, I've been working hard for it. I should know in the next couple of weeks if I get it."

"I'm sure you will, you really seem to have a passion for what you do." We stood up. He insisted I go rest on the couch; he would clean up supper for me. When he finished, he walked over to where I was resting.

"Do you feel like a walk down to the pier?" he asked, "It's a beautiful evening out there."

"Fresh air sounds nice."

We walked outside with Lucky at my side. We walked down, taking a seat on the pier bench. After a few minutes of silence, Jacob spoke up. "Mia Amata, explain to me what is going on with you?"

"I've already explained Jacob. There is nothing more to say. What do you feel you need to know? Better yet, why do you feel you need to know?"

Jacob thought for a couple minutes, "I guess you don't owe me any explanation. You asked me why I care. I do care Mia Amata. I can't explain it, but there is something about you that has captured my heart. I've never felt this way before about anyone."

I was quiet, not knowing how to respond. "Jacob," I hesitated.

"Don't Mia. Please don't say anything. I just want to get to know you better."

I didn't say anything for a little bit. Then I sighed. "I don't understand, but what do you want to know about me?"

"You said you didn't know your family. Let's start there. Were you adopted?" he asked.

"No, I grew up in foster homes. Some were good, some were horrible. I ran away from the last one at the age of 16 after…" I trailed off. I hadn't thought about that for a long time. I had buried that memory because of the trauma I had been dealing with in the years after that.

"After?" he asked softly.

"After my foster father raped me," I said, hiding my face from him in shame.

"Mia Amata, look at me," he said. I couldn't raise my face, he reached over, taking my chin gently in his fingers, pulling my face up to look at him. "Never hide your face in shame. You did nothing wrong. What he did was not your fault. Do you understand that?" I nodded as tears fell. He wiped my tears away. "I am sorry you had such a rough life. I wish I could have protected you from all that pain you suffered."

I brushed more tears away. "I hadn't thought about that in years. I survived." Right at that point Lucky came running past us and jumped into the lake, splashing both of us. "Lucky!" We both cried out, laughing.

We sat, talking. Lucky soon tired of running around and came to lay beside me on the pier. I was getting cold, but I didn't want the night to end, talking to Jacob felt good, once I let go of my fears. He noticed that I shivered though, and he promptly stood up, pulling me to my feet also.

"You're cold, and it's getting late, let's go back to the house." We made our way back to the house. Once inside, he shut the door behind us. "Listen, Mia, I'm glad you are OK. You scared the hell out of me. Promise me no more ladders? I'll hang things for you tomorrow. I promised the doctor I would keep an eye on you tonight. If you have a blanket and pillow, I'll lay out here. He said to wake you up every two hours, I don't want to scare you every time I check on you."

"I'll be fine. You can go home if you want."

"No, I'm not going to risk that. The doctor explained to me what could go wrong. I'm staying. Maybe I can take one couch, you the other, that way I can keep a close eye on you."

I thought about it for a few minutes. I was so tired, I just wanted to sleep in my own bed. As much as the idea scared me, it seemed like the best option. Shaking my head, I said, "No. I have a king-sized bed. You just as well lay in there if you insist on staying. I'm so tired I want to sleep in my bed."

"Are you sure? I don't want to make you uncomfortable."

He already had, but once again, I was finding I had to put my trust in a stranger. "Give me a few minutes, I'll let you know when you can come in." I walked away, heading to the bedroom with Lucky by my side. I changed into capri pants and tank pajamas. I walked back out to get Lucky's dog bed, looking at Jacob. "OK, you can come in." I took Lucky's dog bed and lay it on the floor at the end of the bed. Lucky lay right down, not seeming to protest that he couldn't lay on the bed. I climbed into bed, pulling the blanket up and getting comfortable. I faced away from Jacob, but I could hear him getting undressed and then felt him crawl into bed on the other side.

"Mia Amata," Jacob said quietly.

"Hmmm?" I murmured, almost asleep already.

"Sleep well."

***

Jacob kept his promise to the doctor, waking me every two hours to check on me. I woke up on my own about 4:30 in the morning, found that I was lying on Jacob's shoulder, his arm around me. It took me a few minutes to realize what was going on. I tried to move away from him, but at first, his arm tightened around me. I froze and then slowly managed to get out of his grasp. I got out of bed, heading into the bathroom. My head hurt, but my stomach was feeling somewhat better. I went out into the living room, and let Lucky outside, watching him from inside the door.

"Mia?" I heard Jacob call.

"Out here."

He came out a minute or two later, pulling his shirt on. "How are you feeling?"

"I'm fine. Thank you for everything. I'm sorry that you have had to do all this for me." I looked at him.

"You need to stop apologizing. You are not inconveniencing me at all. I am happy to help you. I have to leave now, to take a shower then get to work. Will you be OK?"

"Yes, I will be fine."

"I'll stop by after work tonight to hang those planters for you if that works for you."

"I have plans with Randy tonight, we are going out to eat."

He smiled. "Have a good time. How about Thursday night? Or are you busy that night too?"

"I'll have to check my social calendar," I said with a little smile. "Thursday night will be fine. I really do appreciate your help."

"Six o'clock Thursday," Jacob said.

"I'll see you then," I replied.

He reached out, running his fingers over my cheek, "Bye Mia Amata."

I closed the door behind him and leaned against it myself.

I climbed back into bed to get some more rest; this time Lucky was lying back on his blanket next to me. My phone went off. "I'm glad you are OK. I'll see you Thursday night."

I smiled and sent a reply of 'Thank you'.

Chapter 16

I was awakened later that morning by another text from Jacob. "Morning Mia. How are you feeling."

I replied, "I'm fine. See you tomorrow."

The day went as usual, Randy joined me for coffee in the morning, and we finalized our plans for the evening, she would pick me up at about 5:00 when she was off work. I did some more studying of protocols and processes for the new job on Monday and was pretty ready for the training. Spent some time sunning on the deck for a little bit while Lucky ran around. I was getting a pretty nice tan, which I felt looked good on me. Having been locked in the house for five years made me look really pale.

I was all dressed, ready for supper out with Randy a little early, so I took Lucky out back again, letting him run around the yard for a little bit, wearing off some puppy energy. I walked down to the pier, sitting on the bench for a little bit. The loons were back swimming, diving for food for the baby. I enjoyed watching them. Lucky soon got tired of running around the yard, came and lay down at my feet. We sat there for a little while, losing track of time. I heard Randy holler from the backyard by the house. I stood up, waving at her.

"Hey," she said as she walked onto the pier. "You didn't answer the door, so I figured you were out here." She gave me a hug, then we sat back down on the bench.

"Yes, I'm just enjoying the gorgeous view with Lucky here," Randy said hi to Lucky, scratching him behind the ears. "Sorry about that," I said. "I meant to be back up to the house before you got here. Nature interfered."

Randy laughed, "Yeah, it has a way of doing that. I love it here. I could get lost for hours just sitting outside enjoying nature." I agreed. We sat in quiet for a few moments watching the loons on the lake. I turned to Randy, "I'm ready to go if you are."

"I am," Randy said. "I'm going to take you to my favorite restaurant in town."

"Sounds good," I replied as we walked back up to the house. We went in through the French doors with Lucky at our heels.

"Before we go," I said, "would you like a tour of the house?"

"I was hoping you would ask!" Randy exclaimed.

I first took her down to the basement, showing her the office with the play area. She looked around, exclaiming it to be adorable, but kind of giving the play area a funny look. I then took her back upstairs, showing her the master, then down the hall to the nursery. She walked into the nursery and stopped, turning to me in surprise.

"Are you pregnant?" she asked. I nodded my head, and she came over to me and gave me a hug. "That is so wonderful! I am so happy for you… it is happy right?" I laughed, assuring her it was a happy occasion. She linked her arm to mine, leading me out. "Let's go for supper. Then you can tell me whatever details you want. I am so excited for you."

We gave Lucky some scratches, I told him to go lie down. He lay down in his bed as we walked out the front door. I set the alarm before joining Randy at her car. She had a questioning look on her face, which I decided to ignore. I opened the passenger door, saying said, "Let's go, I'm hungry!"

While Randy drove us into town, we chatted about her job and my job. We talked about how Josh was doing. She pulled into the parking lot of a tiny little pub. I glanced at her, and she said, "Don't judge it by its appearance. It doesn't look like much, but you will be surprised by how good the food is. It is also very reasonable pricewise."

I looked at the small pub and said, "If you say so."

"I do," she replied with a smile. We climbed out of the car and walked into the pub. It looked like what some people refer to as a 'dive bar'. Randy was welcomed by a lady behind the bar. She introduced her to me as Marie, asking her if they had a table for us.

The lady said, "For you, any time." She pointed to a small table toward the back, and we made our way to it. The place was pretty small, but almost all the tables were full. We sat down at our table. Soon the waitress brought us menus, taking our drink orders. I glanced at the menu and then up at Randy in surprise.

She smiled, "I told you not to judge by the looks of the place." The menu had items that you wouldn't find in a 'dive bar'. Chicken alfredo, steaks, shrimp. It was the menu of a higher quality restaurant with prices that didn't seem possible. The waitress came back with our drinks, taking our food order. "The food here is fantastic. Marie and her husband, Leo, own the restaurant. Leo is the cook. You will love it. So… how far along are you?"

"I'm about seven weeks along. Still pretty early."

"That is so exciting. Am I prying too much if I ask about the father?"

I shook my head, "Not much to tell. I was involved with a man who turned out to be married. When he found out I was pregnant, he wanted nothing to do with me."

"What a jerk!" Randy said.

"He is. I could have gone to his wife and told her, but they have kids together, which I found out after he dumped me. She deserves to know, but I couldn't do that to their kids. So I moved away, starting a new life here. Just me and my baby."

"Well, I, for one," Randy said, "am happy you did so."

"Me too," I smiled at her. "So I was wondering, I need to go shopping for some maternity clothes, baby things, maybe a few household things. Would you go shopping with me? Recommend a few places?"

"Oh, I would love to! We could go to the city. When would you like to go?"

"I know I have time before the baby gets here, so there will probably be more than one shopping trip, but I start work Monday, so I was hoping to go during the week, or if you can't get away maybe Saturday?"

"We are closed on Fridays; we could go then?" Randy said.

"That would work if you don't mind that we go after my doctor's appointment. I am meeting my new OB/GYN early Friday."

"Perfect!" Randy exclaimed. "How about I pick you up and take you to your appointment? I don't mind waiting in the waiting room for you. Then we can go from there shopping."

"You really don't mind?" I asked.

Randy answered, "I really don't. It sounds like a fun day."

"Then that sounds perfect!"

We finished our meal chatting about the shopping trip on Friday, discussing things that I would need for the baby. The topic then changed to Randy and Josh. I asked if they had set a wedding date yet.

"No, not yet." Randy smiled. "I really want an outdoor wedding, small, on a lakeshore somewhere. Josh's family really wants us to get married in their church. Josh wants to make me happy, but he also wants his family to approve of our plans, so for his sake, I am thinking of the church."

"I bet that they will love the wedding no matter where it happens. As long as Josh is happy, they will be happy. Could you have the wedding at a lakeshore and then the reception at the church? Would that be work?" I asked.

"That might be a possibility." Randy looked thoughtful. "I'll have to look into that. They do have a nice area for the reception at the church. Also, the minister will be the one doing the ceremony. Surely, he would do a service somewhere else for a member of his church."

We talked about the other possibilities and what plans she has made as far as her dress and flowers. "We haven't really done any planning yet, have only been engaged three months at this point."

"We could look Friday at some dresses if you want. Just to get an idea. Unless you are planning a trip with your bridesmaids or family," I suggested.

"If we have time, I would love to do some browsing. I haven't decided who is going to be in the wedding party, but I'm sure when I am ready to buy it there will be a few people that will go with me. I kind of want everyone to be surprised by the dress, but I also want someone else's opinion, so I don't buy something I think I look good in, yet it turns out I actually don't!" She laughed.

"You will look great in whatever you pick. You have the perfect figure to wear pretty much any style dress." We paid our check and left the pub. "You were right, that place is great. The food was really good. I'll have to come back." I told Randy.

"Maybe we can make it our regular spot and go there often. Girls' night out!" suggested Randy.

"That would be a lot of fun," I said, "I think if we go every week I'll be as big as a house! Maybe every other week or something. I would love a regular girl's night though. Maybe we could do weekly and go someplace different once in a while."

"I think that would be fun!" Randy said. "We will work something out. I am so glad you moved here."

"Me too," I smiled back at her.

Thursday was spent with a little bit of time reviewing things for work and going on a walk with Lucky—all after Randy and I had our morning coffee together. It was becoming a daily occurrence that we had coffee on the deck together every morning. I really enjoyed Randy's company, and it felt so natural with her. She was quickly becoming my best friend, I felt like I might be able to trust her. I didn't share my true story with her. I could never share that part of my past with her as it would put her in danger. We also texted each other throughout the day, laughing like schoolgirls over some things. I was starting to feel secure and safe in my new life, but I doubted I would ever let my guard down, too many lives hang in the balance if I do.

Jacob was coming over tonight at 6. I had offered to cook for him, it was the least I could do since he was helping me out.

Jacob knocked on the door, pretty much right on time. I opened the door. "Hey, Mia," he said smiling.

"Hi," I said, letting him in.

"Hey, Lucky," Jacob scratched his head, looking at me. "I'll get the planters on the deck rails for you, then hang your planter basket on the front porch."

"Jacob," I said as he walked to the doors to the back deck. He turned, looking at me. "I appreciate your help. I'm sorry to have to take up your time. I'm sure you have more important things to do or someplace else you would rather be."

He paused with his hand on the door handle, 'Mia Amata' clearly considering what he wanted to say. "There is no place I would rather be." He went out on the deck to work on the planters.

I watched Jacob as he went to work, pondering what he meant. I shrugged it off and went to the kitchen to start supper for us. I got the hamburger patties ready, then went out to start the grill. Jacob finished the two planters while I was out there.

"There you go. It just took a little bit of extra hardware to get these to stay on your rails. They do look nice there."

"Thank you. I love them. They really do look nice. I hope burgers are good for supper."

"Sounds good," he replied. He headed around the front to hang the baskets, I went back into the kitchen to work on supper. I was pulling the burgers off the grill when Jacob came into the house.

"All done," he said.

"Perfect timing. Supper is done too." I smiled at him. I put everything on the table while he washed up, then we sat down to eat.

"Did you and Randy have a good time last night?"

"Yes, she is super nice, a lot of fun. We seem to get along really well."

He nodded. "She is great. Josh is a lucky man."

"They really do seem happy together. She misses him a lot when he is gone."

"What about you?" he asked, looking at me.

"What do you mean? Do I miss Josh?" I was confused.

His intense blue eyes were staring into mine like he was trying to read my mind. "No. Do you miss the father of the baby?"

I shook my head. "No, I haven't given him much thought really."

We finished eating, and Jacob insisted on helping me clean up. "It's pretty early," he noted. "How about we go to a pub, maybe play some pool, listen to some music?"

I hesitated, "I don't know. You don't have to keep an eye on me anymore. I'm fine. It's OK if you want to leave."

"Mia Amata," he said, reaching out and taking my hand. It was all I could do to not yank my hand away. "I'm not asking out of obligation. I think it would be fun, I like spending time with you." I still was hesitant. "I won't hurt you, Mia Amata."

Finally, I nodded, "I don't know how to play pool though." He said he would enjoy teaching me.

Trying to pick something to wear to the pub turned out to be a little bit of a challenge. I wasn't showing a lot, but the only pair of jeans I had were getting a bit snug. There was no way I could wear them all night and remain comfortable. I finally grabbed the short skirt and a different T-shirt, along with the only lightweight jacket I had. Looking in the mirror, I thought I looked OK. I had my sandals on, completing the outfit with some hoop earrings.

I got Lucky all set for the evening with food and water. When I walked out to the front porch where Jacob was waiting, he gave a low whistle, "You look great," he said.

I smiled shyly, "Thanks."

He walked me around to the passenger side, helping me into his truck. He closed the door, walking back around to the driver's side.

We had a nice time at the pub. He said hi to a couple of friends, giving them a brief introduction, but not moving to sit with them. I thought that was a little odd, but didn't question it, figuring he wanted to sit by the pool table, so we could play. He taught me how to play pool, he did seem to enjoy teaching me.

After a couple of games, we sat in our booth talking.

"We could join your friends if you really want to, I don't mind."

"Hell no," Jacob said. "I won't subject you to them. Plus, they are all sitting over there jealous that I am here with the most beautiful woman in town."

"I seriously doubt that!"

"Just wait, tomorrow, maybe even later tonight I will start getting tons of text messages asking me who you are and what are you doing with me. Some will even have the nerve to ask for your number." As if to prove his point, one of the new guys who came in while we were playing pool walked over.

"Hey, Jacob, how are you?" he asked, sticking out his hand.

"I'm good," he shook the man's hand. "Tyler, this is Mattie. Mattie, Tyler."

"Nice to meet you," I said.

"Same," Tyler said, looking at me. "I haven't seen you around here before."

"I'm new to town, haven't been here very long."

Tyler nodded, wanting to say more, but Jacob spoke up first. "Hey, if you don't mind Tyler, Mattie and I were having a conversation, I'll catch up with you later."

"Oh, sure, just wanted to say hi. Nice to meet you, Mattie. Catch you later Jacob." He walked back over to the bar, and immediately, the other guys were leaning over asking questions.

"See what I mean? They are great guys, don't get me wrong, but any one of them would love to have your phone number right now. I'm trying to eliminate the competition." Jacob smiled at me.

"Competition for what?"

Jacob looked at me, "For you."

A slow song came on the jukebox right then. "Dance with me?" He stood up and held out his hand. Somewhat taken aback, I took his hand, letting him lead me onto the dance floor where three other couples were dancing. He took me in his arms, and I lost all train of thought. It was like the entire bar was swallowed up by a hole in the ground. Nobody else existed except for this man who had me in his arms. I felt confused and anxious. What was going on here?

Soon the song ended, and another one started. Someone tapped Jacob on the shoulder. It was Tyler. "Mind if I cut in?"

Jacob tensed up; I could feel the tension in his arms. "That's up to Mattie," he said.

I had no desire to dance with Tyler. I looked at him, "Oh, I'm sorry, but we were just leaving." Jacob led me off the dance floor, and I grabbed my purse. I caught a glimpse of Tyler joining his buddies at the bar.

They were all laughing, punching him in the shoulder.

We got to Jacob's truck; he walked me to the passenger door. Before he opened the door for me, he said, "You could have danced with him if you wanted to." He was looking at me intently, those blue eyes felt like they could see to the bottom of my soul.

"I know."

He moved a little closer. "Why didn't you?" still looking at me.

"I didn't want to."

He leaned down like he was going to kiss me. "Why?" he said softly.

I had no answer, I looked down. He put his fingers under my chin, tipping my head up to look at him. "Mia Amata, look at me. Can I kiss you?" I nodded, not understanding exactly why I did. He started kissing me gently, I'd never been kissed like that before. I reached my arms up around his neck, and he put his arms around my waist, pulling me closer. He moved his lips down my neck while he slid his hands down to my hips. All of a sudden, he pulled back, "Damn Mia. You take my breath away."

I stood there breathless, not sure what really just happened.

He helped me in the truck. He stood there with the door open. "You may not believe me, but I am falling for you, Mia Amata." He leaned in, kissed me again, then shut the door, taking me home.

Chapter 17

Friday came around and Randy picked me up early Friday to take me to my OB/GYN appointment. She went in with me, taking a seat while I checked in with the receptionist for my appointment. I sat down next to her; we chatted a little bit about our plans for the day when we finished here. I didn't have to wait long until they called my name. I went back with the nurse who took my history, got my vitals, and then left me alone to wait for the doctor to come in. Soon there was a knock on the door. A young woman walked in. "Mattie?" she asked.

"Yes," I said.

"Nice to meet you. I'm Dr. Amanda Lee." I shook her hand. She sat down at the desk next to me. "I understand you had a positive pregnancy test."

"Yes," I replied. "By my calculations, I think I am about seven weeks along."

"You haven't seen any doctor yet?" she asked.

"No, I was in the process of moving here, didn't have a chance to. I figured I would establish care here once I moved."

Dr. Lee nodded. "Makes sense. So what I would like to do is get some history from you first, then we will do an examination, obtain an ultrasound to check dates." She stood up and listened to my heart and lungs. She then asked me to lay back. She asked me to pull up my top to do an abdominal exam. She hesitated momentarily, then asked, "How did you get the scars and bruises?"

I told her about the minor car accident, the story that I came up with. "Did you see a doctor for that? Go to the emergency room?"

"No, I didn't. I didn't have insurance at the time. I really felt fine overall. A few aches and pains from the accident, but otherwise I felt fine."

"You should have been checked out. You could have had some internal injuries."

"I know, but I couldn't afford to pay out of pocket for the medical bills."

Dr. Lee did her exam and then had me sit up. "I think you are pretty spot on regarding how far along you are, but I'll go get the ultrasound machine to do a check to make sure. I'll be right back."

Leaving the room and returning shortly with the ultrasound. She explained what would take place to me. I acted like I didn't know anything about it. Once the ultrasound was completed, the doctor told me my estimate was pretty spot on, I was about seven weeks along.

She printed some pictures of the baby for me and then had me get down from the examination table and taken a seat in a chair. We reviewed the normal pregnancy course, discussing my approximate delivery date. The doctor answered all of my questions, saying she would be happy to take on my care.

I told her I would like for her to be my new OB/GYN, asking her if she could recommend a pediatrician and family practice doctor. "I certainly can," she replied. She gave me a list of names. One of them was Dr. James Lee, who was a primary care physician. I looked at her questioningly.

She smiled, "Yes, he is my husband. I can't recommend him over the others for the sake of ethics. You will have to make that decision for yourself. Make an appointment with him and a couple of the others and decide for yourself. I feel that any of those would be good choices for your care."

I thanked her for the recommendations but knew that I would probably go to her husband to care for my baby and myself. I was impressed with Dr. Lee. She put me completely at ease, didn't pry too much into the past and concentrated more on the baby and the future. We chatted a little longer about what I could expect and what her protocol was for future appointments. Dr. Lee walked me out, taking me up to the appointment desk, letting them know she wanted to see me back in one month with lab work prior.

I made the appointment and then walked out to the waiting area where Randy sat waiting for me. She got up as I walked out. We walked out to her car. "How was the appointment?" she asked as we climbed into her car. I told her about Dr. Lee and the appointment and what would happen going forward. We chatted about the list of doctors she had given me as recommendations.

Randy said, "Her husband is my doctor. He is awesome. He would actually take care of both you and the baby if you felt comfortable with not having a pediatrician."

"I would be fine with that. It would be nice having the same doctor taking care of both of us, like his wife is doing right now."

We chatted about things as Randy drove us to the city an hour away. Our first stop was a clothing store that had maternity clothes. I tried on a few things and picked out a few cute outfits that I thought would tide me over the next couple of months. Randy and I decided that we would make another trip later on during my pregnancy if I needed additional clothing. I also picked out some warmer clothes, including a coat as there would be snow on the ground before I gave birth.

We then went to a baby store where we had a lot of fun picking out a few outfits. I also picked up some crib sheets, a blanket, and some other odds and ends that I would need. I also purchased a car seat and stroller that all worked together, knowing that the car seat would be an immediate need when the baby was born. I looked at baby monitors and decided to do some more research on those before I purchased one.

After the baby store, we stopped for lunch in the food court at the mall we were shopping in. I went for a piece of pizza while Randy went for Chinese. We met in the middle, talking about our finds, the things that I would need eventually. There were a lot of things out there that were supposed to make things easier for a parent, but some of them didn't seem necessary to me. We discussed the need for a bassinet, but I wasn't sure that one was needed.

The nursery was close to my bedroom, and I felt that the baby needed to sleep in her own room. Also, with the right baby monitor, there should be no issues with having the baby in the crib from the beginning. I decided I would think about it, as I could see the benefits of one, especially if it could be moved from room to room, but I felt the baby would outgrow it pretty quickly, so I didn't feel it was a wise use of money.

When we finished lunch, we browsed some other stores, including a bridal store where Randy picked up some brochures and looked at a few dresses. We were told the best thing would be to make an appointment when she was ready to seriously shop for a dress, they would be better able to help her find the perfect dress. Randy agreed to do so.

Our next stop was a home store. We browsed around, discussing all the different decor for my home. I picked out some wall decor that I really liked. I found some nursery wall decor that I thought would be perfect for the nursery.

We walked around the mall, making small purchases here and there. I bought a new pair of shoes, some slip-on tennis shoes. After all, I only had one pair of shoes at this point. I also purchased a pair of black flats that would look cute with some of the new outfits I bought, but yet would be comfortable should my feet swell with pregnancy. We finally left the mall and started driving home.

"That was fun," Randy stated, "but I am worn out."

I laughed, "I am too. I was able to check a lot of things off my list today, and for those I didn't I have some ideas of what I do want. We will probably have to make another trip in a month or so."

"I'm game!" Randy said, "Maybe, on that trip, I will have an appointment to look for a wedding dress too."

"That would be fun," I said.

We talked about the purchases we made today, most of them mine, and how the nursery was going to look cute with the decor I bought for it today.

"I really need more home decor," I told Randy. "I really don't have much as far as decorations go."

"Well, you bought enough books to fill some of those shelves next to the fireplace!" she said.

I laughed, "Yes, I haven't read in a long time, so there were a lot of books that caught my eye. I could have bought a lot more had you not dragged me out of there."

"I didn't think we could fit much more into my car! With the baby car seat and stroller, all the clothes, shoes, decor, and books, I'm surprised my car can move and that we have room for us in it! Should have borrowed Josh or Jacob's truck."

We laughed and joked the rest of the way home. We finally pulled into the driveway at my house. I unlocked the door, letting Lucky out to take care of some business. He ran around a bit while we started to carry things into the house. A set of car lights came around the curve and Josh pulled up in his truck. Randy squealed, running to give him a hug as he climbed out of his truck. "I thought you couldn't make it this weekend."

He hugged her in return, "It just worked out that I could make it back. I have to go back Sunday night, so I am there first thing Monday morning, but I wanted to see you."

I carried a couple of bags into the house, letting them have this moment alone. Lucky went into the house with me. I gave him some fresh water and food before I headed back outside to get more of my bags from Randy's car. While I was getting the water for Lucky, Randy and Josh came into the house, carrying the big things that I had purchased that day.

"Hey, Mattie," Josh said. "Randy told me about the baby, congratulations!"

"Thank you," I said smiling at the couple. "Thanks for helping me carry my stuff in too."

"No problem. Where do you want us to put the stroller and the car seat?"

"Back in the nursery if you don't mind."

"Not at all," he said, following Randy down the hall to the nursery. We got all of my packages carried in, just depositing them on the couch. I looked at Randy and Josh and said, "I would invite you to stay for something to drink, but I can tell you two want to go home and be alone."

Randy blushed, while Josh said, "Are we that obvious?"

I laughed, "Yes. I know how much Randy missed you while you were gone. Get out of here you two. I'll talk to you later."

Randy gave me a hug, and they left. I shut the door, arming the alarm system. I was a little hungry, so I made a sandwich and started to go through my purchases for the day. I knew I would wash all the bedding and clothing I got for the baby before using them, but for the time being, I just took off the tags, putting the items in the nursery in the hamper. I laid out the décor, so I could decide where I wanted to hang the items.

I put the books on the shelves next to the fireplace. I took all the tags off the clothes I bought for myself, putting those in the hamper to wash this weekend. I could still wear most of the clothes I got from Eva and Lauren, but I could tell that in a couple more weeks I would probably need to move into maternity clothes.

After supper was done, I cleaned up the kitchen. I then got the hammer and nails to hang the decor I had picked out. I got the step stool and got ready to climb on it to start hanging decor when someone knocked on the door.

Thinking maybe I left a bag in Randy's car, I went to the door and pulled it open. It was Jacob. "Hey, Mia."

"Hey," I said as I let him in. He noticed I had a hammer in my hand.

"What are you doing?" he asked, walking into the living room.

"I was going to hang some things on the walls. I wasn't expecting company."

He smiled. "Josh sent me a text letting me know he was home for the weekend and mentioned that Randy just dropped you off. I hope you don't mind I came by unannounced."

I hesitated, "No, I'm just in the middle of something."

He saw the step stool and all the decor lying around. He looked at me. "You weren't getting up on that stool to hang things, were you?"

"Well, of course, I was. How else can I reach where I want to put them?"

He reached out and took the hammer from me. "Mia Amata, promise me you won't climb on any stools or ladders. If you were to fall again…" he trailed off.

"I'm pregnant Jacob, not an invalid."

"I know that. You fell once already, if you fall again, it could end badly. If something happened to you." He looked at me so intently that I promised him I wouldn't do any ladder-climbing or stand on any stepstools. "Good. Now tell me where you want things hung."

It took a little while, but we finally got everything hung and positioned to my liking. Jacob put the tools away, while I looked around at my home. I was happy with the way the house looked. It felt more like home every day. There were moments when I could hardly believe that I was free. It had only been a couple of weeks, but I felt so at home here, so happy. I had new friends, a loyal dog, a home, and a baby on the way, what more could I ask for?

Jacob came back in from the garage. "What's next?"

"I was just going to watch some TV and work on the baby blanket I'm making."

"Can I keep you company for a while?"

"Won't you be bored?"

"Is that your way of telling me you want me to leave?" He tried to look so sad, I couldn't help but laugh.

"Of course not."

We picked out a movie, sitting on the couch together. I crocheted for a while until my eyes were tired. The baby blanket was coming along nicely. I wasn't sure how much time I could dedicate to it when I started working on Monday, but I vowed that I would try to do a little every night, even just a few rows.

I had plenty of time to finish it before the baby came as long as I dedicated time to it on a regular basis. I crocheted until the end of the movie, then put it away.

"You are talented," observed Jacob. "That blanket is cute."

"Thanks, my first attempt at crocheting. The next movie looked interesting, want to stay? I'll pop us some popcorn?" Surprising both myself and Jacob by asking, I think.

"Sounds wonderful," he smiled at me. "As long as I am not ruining your evening."

I shook my head, "I'm glad you are here." I meant it too. I enjoyed his company tonight.

Popcorn was popped, I turned the lights down, sitting back down by Jacob, so we could share. He put his arm around me, and we settled in to watch the next movie. When the popcorn was finished, I covered up with a blanket from the back of the couch.

We both dozed off, and the next thing I knew Lucky was whining to be let outside. I sat up and looked at the clock, realizing it was three o'clock in the morning. Jacob didn't stir, as quietly as I could, I took Lucky outside.

I stood outside on the deck, shivering, while I waited for Lucky. Jacob came out, wrapping a blanket around me. We stood there in silence until Lucky came running back up the steps. Going back inside, Jacob looked at me. "I should go."

"No, Jacob. It's too late. You can stay here tonight."

"Thank you. Do you have a pillow and blanket I can use on the couch?"

"Yes, I'll be right back." I soon came back out with a blanket and pillow for him.

"Thank you," He looked at me intently, then leaned over and kissed me softly. "Good night, Mia Amata."

"Night, Jacob." I went to the bedroom, and as quietly as I could I locked the bedroom door, wondering why Jacob was here and why I was letting this happen.

***

The next morning, Jacob and I were enjoying coffee on the deck watching Lucky run around in the yard playing when we heard Josh and Randy hollering from down by the lake. Lady ran up, greeting me as usual, then ran down to play with her brother in the yard. I waved at Randy and Josh; they headed up toward the deck to join me.

I looked at Jacob, he looked back. "I'm sorry."

"For what?" I asked, confused.

"They are going to think I spent the night."

"Well, you did," I replied.

"You know what I mean." Jacob smiled back at me.

"I do, but it was perfectly innocent. There is nothing to hide."

"No, but I don't want anyone to draw the wrong conclusions if it would bother you."

"I'll be fine Jacob. Besides, it could be fun seeing them try to resist asking questions."

Jacob laughed, "Yes, that would be fun."

"Coffee's fresh," I said as they joined us on the deck. I saw the look of surprise when they saw Jacob sitting there with me. "Help yourself. There are some fresh baked cinnamon rolls on the counter too."

"Count me in!" Josh exclaimed as he went into the house. When he passed Jacob, he gave him a fist bump, which I raised an eyebrow to.

Randy laughed. The exchange between brothers and my raised eyebrow not escaping her. "I had better go in and make sure he doesn't eat the whole batch!" She followed him in, and they soon came back out with a roll and a cup of coffee each. They sat down on the deck, and we chatted easily while they ate, and we all drank our coffee. Josh went back inside for a second roll, bringing the coffee pot out to refill our cups.

He sat down, "These rolls are fantastic!"

"Thanks. I enjoy baking. Cinnamon rolls sounded really good today."

Randy added, "I'm surprised you found the time to make them," she smiled as Josh almost choked on his roll. She added hurriedly, "You will have to give me the recipe! They are fantastic."

"I can't, I don't have a recipe. I just threw them together."

Randy looked at me in surprise. "Really?" I nodded. "I wish I could do that. I mean after I make something enough times I can usually get to where I don't need the recipe, but I'm not good at throwing ingredients together to make something this good."

"I've always been able to make things without a recipe. If it is a new item, I may look it up to see what is in it, but then I never follow the recipe. I don't know, it just seems to come easily to me." We sat there for a while longer discussing our plans for the weekend. I invited them to come back that night, stating that I would cook supper for all of us, then maybe we could watch a movie, which they accepted. We talked about what sounded good, all three of them stated together Italian, so I said I would make lasagna.

"Well," Josh said, "we had better get our day going, have some errands to run and things to do around the house today."

We all stood up, taking our dishes into the house, Lady and Lucky following us in. Randy offered to wash the dishes, but I refused. I wrapped up a few cinnamon rolls for them which Josh was more than happy to take home with him. They left, but not before I saw Josh give Jacob another fist bump. I was washing up the dishes and cleaning up the kitchen. Jacob took my trash out for me. I checked the cupboards to make sure I had everything I needed to make lasagna with garlic bread for supper.

Jacob and I sat down on the couch together when I finished the dishes. "What was all that about?" I asked him.

He feigned innocence, "All what?"

"All the fist bumps with Josh," I said.

"It's a guy thing. He knows I spent the night here last night; it was his way of saying way to go."

"But nothing happened!"

"I know, I'll make sure he knows that too. It just didn't seem an appropriate time to bring up the fact we haven't had sex yet."

"Yet?" I looked at him. I felt uncomfortable with the way the conversation was going.

"If it bothers you that much, I can call him right now. I don't want to do anything to hurt you."

He looked so distressed at the thought I was upset with him; I couldn't figure out what was happening there. "Jacob," I started, but he didn't let me finish.

He sighed, "Honestly, I know he will bring it up later, and I will tell him that we fell asleep watching movies and that nothing happened. I would never lie about that just to make myself look like I…"

"Got lucky?" I asked.

"Exactly. Josh knows that too. We are super close; we share a lot with each other. He is honestly probably just happy for me."

"Happy why?"

"Because I finally found someone." He got up and walked away, heading to the bathroom, before I could respond to that. I sat there stunned. Jacob kept saying things like that. I had no idea what he thought was happening here and how to handle whatever this was. Jacob walked out, heading to the front door. "I should run home. I need to shower and run to the store for a few things for the week. Can I pick up anything for you?"

"No, I have everything I need here. Unless you all want something besides tea, water, or milk to drink. I don't have any alcohol around here."

We walked to the door. "We don't need alcohol, whatever you have here will be fine. I'll grab some soda, just in case." When we reached the front door, he turned toward me. "Would it be OK if I come back early? Before Josh and Randy get here? I think we should talk."

I hesitated, then nodded. "I may be busy with supper."

"That won't bother me, we can talk while you cook."

"You can come back whatever time you'd like. I'll be here doing some things around the house and cooking."

He leaned down and kissed me. "Love you," he turned and walked out before I had a chance to reply. I shut the door, once more stunned. I wasn't sure what to think. I stood there a couple of minutes, then shook my head, needing to get some things done before they all came back for supper that night.

First, I gathered up my laundry throwing it in the washing machine. I then went back to my bedroom, grabbed my empty backpack, and picked out some items to put in it. I had been thinking that if I needed to run, I should have a go bag that if able I could just grab and leave. I put the rest of the $5000 cash in there, knowing that I had the checking account along with the credit cards, plus starting Monday I would be making money I could live off of.

I put an extra set of car keys in there, some clothes, things that I could wear pregnant or not. I decided that I would keep the diaper bag packed at all times, so I could just grab that for the baby. I thought maybe I should sit down and figure out an escape plan in detail, maybe even two, but for right now having bags ready to go would suffice.

I walked into the nursery and started packing the diaper bag. Once the baby is born, I would pack it with one or two bottles and a can of formula, whatever I would need until I could get some place. Both bags were packed. I took them out to store them together in the linen closet. I will work on a bigger plan soon. I didn't want to put it off too long, otherwise it may be too late.

I went to the laundry area, taking the clothes from the washer, and putting them in the dryer. I did some light cleaning, then went down to the office to do some more studying on the protocols for work on Monday. I felt like I had a good grasp on them, but I wanted to make sure I was prepared. Lucky was following me around while I was doing chores around the house, and I wondered how I would be able to take him and the baby if we needed to make an escape. I figured the way he followed me everywhere it wouldn't be a problem; he would get in the car with me without hesitation but keeping him quiet could be an issue.

I decided I would pack some dog food, bottles of water, and extra dishes into a bag. This was turning into a lot that I needed to grab if I had to make a run for it. I would have to figure out another way. Some way I can just grab the baby and the dog and go. This would take some thinking. I vowed to sit down soon and figure out a better plan.

When I left Laurie and Eva, they had given me a phone number. No name, just the number. This was a number for me to contact if I needed help again or if I was able to help someone else. I had it in my wallet, but I wanted to try to memorize it so that it was not found. I wanted to make notes on things, but if I did, I would have to destroy all evidence of them or make sure to take them with me.

Making an escape plan that can be discovered would obviously not be a good thing. I tried to focus on the plans for work, but my mind kept wandering. I gave up and went back upstairs. I got a glass of ice water, taking Lucky outside. I walked down to the pier, and he ran around and explored, but never got too far away from me. I went down, sitting on the bench on the pier. Lucky soon brought me a stick.

"What's up? Want to play fetch?" He wagged his tail at me and gave a bark. I flung the stick out into the water watching as he jumped in after it. He swam out, got it, then swam back to the shore like he had been doing this for years. "Oh boy," I told Lucky. "I'm going to have to give you a bath when we go back in the house!" He dropped the stick at my feet, barked, and wagged his tail.

I threw it again, watching as he dove after it. We played fetch for a while until it was apparent that he was tired. I let him lay at my feet, hoping he would dry off a bit before we went back into the house. I would give him a bath, but I would rather he not be sopping wet when we went back in. He was soon dozing in the sunshine while I enjoyed the view.

I glanced at my watch after a bit, finally deciding we had been out long enough. I needed to go in, give Lucky his bath, then start the lasagna. I stood up, and Lucky was immediately up and alert. We walked back up to the house, Lucky running around and chasing dragonflies or butterflies.

Once in the house, I ran bath water for Lucky, and he readily hopped in the tub when I told him to. I gave him his bath, which he actually seemed to enjoy. I managed to get him all rinsed and clean, drying him the best I could.

Once finished with his bath, I went to the kitchen, pulling out the ingredients to make the lasagna.

I got the lasagna all put together, then put it in the oven to cook. I then got the garlic bread all ready, setting it aside to put in the oven soon. I washed up the dishes from making the lasagna and put them away. I then set the table for the four of us when the phone rang. It was Randy.

"Hey, Randy," I said.

"Hi, there! Hey, I was wondering if there was anything that we can bring for tonight."

"I didn't plan anything for dessert, so if you have a chance to grab something that would be great."

"Josh is running into town here in a few minutes, I will have him pick something up. Any special requests?" she asked.

"I'm good with anything chocolate," I laughed.

"We have to be sisters," she laughed. "I love chocolate. We will see you soon."

I went around the house, doing some straightening and light cleaning, not that the house really needed it.

I sat down, relaxing until it was time to put the garlic bread in the oven.

I couldn't find much to watch, so I shut the TV off, going to take a quick shower. When I was dressed, I heard a knock at the door. It was Jacob, carrying a sack with some soda in it. He walked into the kitchen and put the soda in the refrigerator. Once he was done, he turned to me, where I had been leaning against the counter across from the sink.

"Hey, Mia." He smiled at me.

"Hey," I said. "I need to work on supper. Make yourself at home."

After assuring him there wasn't anything he could really help me with, I motioned him to the couch, telling him to find something to watch. Instead, he pulled out a stool at the bar. "I would rather talk to you."

I was putting the garlic bread in the oven. When I leaned over to do so, the shirt I was wearing slipped off my shoulder.

"Wow, how did you get that bruise on your back? It's huge. Are you OK?"

I froze, then regained my composure, continuing to close the oven door. "I'm fine," I said, "I was in a minor car accident. Nothing to worry about."

He was looking at me, the amount of concern in his eyes really surprised me. "You're sure you are OK?"

"Yes, I'm fine." He seemed reassured.

After a few minutes of silence, Jacob asked, "You seem quiet today, is something wrong?"

Hesitating, "I don't know Jacob. I'm… confused."

"About what?"

I wasn't sure what to say or how to bring up the subject. Finally, I sighed, deciding to just dive in headfirst. "You. Me. This… whatever is going on here."

Jacob nodded his head. "What do you think is going on here?"

"I don't know. You have hinted around before, but earlier today when you were leaving…" I trailed off.

"I said 'love you' when I left. Did that bother you?" He was watching me closely.

I looked at him, "I don't know what to say."

"Can you deny that you feel something for me?" He dared me.

"I do feel something for you. I'm not ready to call it love. In fact, I'm not sure that love even exists."

Jacob said, "I know it does. I see it with my parents, with my sister and her husband. We both see it with Josh and Randy." He stood up, coming around to where I was standing, turning me to face him. "I know it sounds crazy, but I think I fell in love with you the moment I saw you."

I stared at the countertop, my mind going in 20 different directions at once. "Mia Amata?" he whispered. I looked at him, he leaned in and kissed me, so tenderly that I thought I would faint. I knew I should pull away, but I couldn't. He finally pulled back, staring into my eyes. "Say something," he pleaded.

"Oh, Jacob," I cried. "You don't know me at all. How can you say you love me?"

"I don't know, but I haven't been able to stop thinking about you since the moment I saw you. I realize we don't know each other very well. We can start getting to know each other better."

I pulled away from him. I could sense his disappointment, but I was so confused. I needed to think. He leaned against the counter; I started pulling out the vegetables to make a salad. I was working on the salad when I heard a car pull up outside.

Jacob went to the door, opening it to let Randy and Josh in. Randy and Josh walked into the kitchen, both giving me hugs. "Supper is almost done. Make yourselves at home." Lucky was happy to see Josh and Randy.

Everyone gave him scratches behind his ears, and then he went over and lay down in his dog bed. Randy stayed in the kitchen with me while Josh and Jacob sat down on the couch talking football.

Pretty soon, I told everyone to have a seat at the table, I was ready to pull it out of the oven. "He is so well-behaved now," Josh said, looking at Lucky lying in his dog bed. "How did you do it?"

I shrugged my shoulder, "I really didn't do anything. He just seems to know what to do and when to do it. I haven't had to hook him up to a leash at all. He won't leave my side."

Josh and Randy looked at each other in amazement. Jacob was the one who finally said something. "It was like he waited for you to come along and has dedicated himself to you."

"Maybe," I said. "All I know is he is a very well-behaved dog. I love having him here."

I went to the oven, pulling the lasagna, and garlic bread out of the oven. "That smells fantastic," Randy said. The guys agreed. Randy helped me finish getting the food on the table. Everyone took helpings of salad, lasagna, and garlic bread. We settled down to eat. The conversation was easy and light-hearted.

We had a lot of laughs during the meal, I couldn't remember when I had ever had so much fun, even with the conversation that weighed heavily on my mind. We finished eating, the guys having seconds of the lasagna, declaring it some of the best they had ever had.

"Don't let Sal or Louisa hear you guys say that," Randy said sternly. "They would never forgive you." The guys laughed, begging to be able to take leftovers home with them. I told them I would definitely put some in containers for them if they took Lucky out back for a little bit. They agreed to do so. Randy helped me clean up from supper. While loading the dishwasher, Randy looked at me slyly. "So Jacob spent the night last night?" she asked innocently.

"Yes. We fell asleep on the couch watching a movie, waking up at three am. I wasn't going to let him drive home that late."

"Oh, sure."

"What's that supposed to mean," I asked.

"Nothing!" she said. "You two can't seem to take your eyes off each other. I haven't seen him take an interest in any woman like he has with you."

Josh looked at me as they came back inside from the deck, "Lucky is definitely loyal to you. He took care of business outside, then immediately came up to the door where he could watch you. Pretty soon he was whining to be let in the house."

I scratched Lucky behind the ears. "He is pretty easy to love. He has definitely become a good companion for me."

"I'm glad that he has a good home," Randy said.

"Does anyone want dessert now, or should we wait a little bit?" I asked.

Everyone groaned. "I'm so full," Jacob said. Randy and Josh voiced their agreement with him.

"OK, so we will wait for a bit. What would you all like to do now? Should we find a movie to watch?"

"That sounds great. What type of movie do you like?" Jacob asked me. Having not been able to watch much TV over the past five years, I went on with what I have watched since I gained my freedom.

"I like old black and white classic movies the most I guess."

"Really?" Jacob asked. "I've been wanting to watch some older movies, but just haven't yet. Maybe we can find one to watch."

We all sat down on the couches. Josh and Randy sat on the bigger couch, leaving the smaller one for Jacob and me. Randy had a slight smile on her face, so I knew it was deliberate. Jacob and I sat down on the smaller couch.

I turned on the TV. We found TMC where Alfred Hitchcock's The Birds was on. We started to watch it when Randy jumped up, shutting the lights off. "Alfred Hitchcock is better watched in the dark I hear." She sat back down with Josh, and we all settled in to watch the movie. We were all enjoying the movie, chatting about it.

About halfway through it, Jacob and Josh declared they now had room for dessert, so we paused the movie. Jacob and I went to the kitchen, serving up dessert for everyone. I made a pot of coffee. We all enjoyed chocolate cake and coffee while we watched more of the movie. We were pretty soon all quiet, involved in the movie while we finished our cake.

When the movie ended, we pulled up the guide. It turned out to be an Alfred Hitchcock marathon night, so while we waited for the next one to start, Randy and Josh cleaned up our dessert dishes, to their insistence. We discussed how much we enjoyed The Birds and were looking forward to the next one starting.

Lucky decided at that time to join us on the couch. He lay down next to me with his head in my lap. I stroked his head and Jacob commented, "I have never seen a dog-owner relationship like yours before. He is definitely devoted to you."

Randy laughed, "Yes, he was definitely a good escape artist to get here to you."

"Yet, now that he is here with you, he hasn't run away once," Jacob said.

I paused, "No, he hasn't. He never wanders away from me." Jacob reached across me to scratch Lucky's head, purposedly making sure we touched in the process.

"I bet he would defend you against any danger. You probably have a great guard dog here." His face was close to mine, he looked at me. I found myself looking into his eyes and couldn't look away. "I can understand why he would be so devoted," Jacob said quietly so only I could hear. Randy and Josh came back over to the couch, having finished the dishes. Jacob sat back up.

I glanced at Randy and Josh to see if I could read what they were thinking. They didn't appear to give us a second thought. The next movie, Psycho, soon started; we all went quiet as we watched the classic movie. Lucky hopped down, heading to his dog bed, curling up, promptly falling asleep. I pulled the blanket off the back of the couch, covering up with it.

Jacob put his arm around me. I didn't pull away but felt rather anxious and tried to concentrate on the movie. We watched the rest of the movie with his arm around me. Not too long after the movie had started, I heard light snoring from the other couch. I looked over to find both Josh and Randy sleeping. I smiled and looked at Jacob who had also heard them.

He looked at me and smiled back. He leaned close and whispered to me, "Let's go outside on the deck."

I nodded, so we got up quietly, letting the movie play while we went out on the deck, with Lucky joining us. Lucky went down into the yard. I walked to the deck rail, looking out over the backyard. Jacob joined me, putting his arm around me. We stood like that for a couple of minutes, watching Lucky run around. Then Jacob turned toward me, pulling me closer.

"Mia Amata," he said softly. I looked at him. He leaned over and kissed me. He pulled back, "I've been wanting to do that all night."

"Jacob, we need to talk. I can't… I don't know what we are doing. I'm not good enough for you. I'm… terrified." I walked over, sitting down on the top step of the deck, looking out at the yard, watching Lucky.

Jacob sat next to me. "Listen to me. I never want to hear you say you're not good enough for me. You have nothing to be afraid of, I will never hurt you."

I was crying. "I have heard that before, by my foster dad, by my ex—by everyone that ended up doing just that, hurting me."

"I'm not them, you can trust me."

"I don't trust anyone. I don't know how."

"I will help you learn to trust me if you will let me," he said.

"Then there is your family. How would your brother feel about your getting involved with me."

"You mean because of the baby?"

"Yes. Jacob, I'm pregnant with another man's baby. How do you think people will react to that when they realize that we…" I trailed off.

"When they realize what?"

"That we care for each other." I finished.

"Is that true? Mia Amata?" He lifted my chin with his finger. "Do you care for me?"

"Jacob, people are going to think awful things of me. How will you deal with the way others will think about me?" I tried to pull away from him, but he wouldn't let me.

"Mia, please answer me, do you care for me?"

I looked at him, tears in my eyes. "I can't explain it, but I think I do. I'm so confused, we haven't known each other long. People are going to object."

"If you care about me, even just a little, then I don't care what others think about us. All I care about is us." He leaned down, kissing me gently.

"But your family, Jacob. How will your parents and your sister feel when they find out I'm pregnant? Have you considered that? What if they hate me?"

"They will love you; I promise. My family does not judge others. They are not that way. I bet you that Josh has already accepted us being together. It's obvious Randy wants us together."

I smiled, "Yes, she seems to." Jacob kissed me again, this time more passionately. When he finally pulled away, I sighed. "I'm just not sure about a relationship right now. It scares the hell out of me truthfully. I don't want to get hurt or have you be ashamed of me."

"I would never be ashamed of you. I promise I'll never hurt you. I'll prove it if you let me. All I ask is that you give me, give us a chance." We sat quietly, until he finally asked, "Can you do that? Do you want to do that?"

"I think I do want that; I'll try to give us a chance. I hope I don't disappoint you." I started to shiver. We stood back up to go back into the house.

"Can I see you tomorrow?" Jacob asked.

"Yes, that would be nice." We made plans for lunch the following day, then went back into the house, Lucky at our side. The movie was still on. Randy and Josh were still sleeping on the couch. We sat down, I covered up with the blanket as I was cold from being outside. Jacob put his arm around me, pulling me close. We finished the movie, then Jacob whispered to me "I should make sure the old couple get home." We both smiled at this.

He leaned over, kissing me. I put my arms around his neck. He pulled me into his lap, kissing me even more passionately. We heard someone move on the other couch, so we both looked over in that direction.

Randy and Josh were still asleep, but we knew they could wake up at any time.

I could hear Jacob struggle to get his breathing under control. He whispered in my ear, "God Mia Amata, you drive me crazy. I want you so much." I stiffened, he felt it and said, "It's OK, we will take things as slow as you need to." We sat there holding each other, both of us waiting for our breathing to return to normal, when we heard Randy from the other couch.

"Oh my gosh, I'm so sorry we fell asleep." Then she saw us, with me sitting on Jacob's lap with our arms around each other. "Or not," she said, smiling. She shook Josh awake. "Come on honey, let's go home. It's late."

"Sounds good." He saw Jacob and me then, his face breaking into a huge grin. "Don't bother getting up, we will show ourselves out." They grabbed the leftovers from the refrigerator and were out the front door before we could even move.

We looked at each other and broke out laughing. "Well, I think that answers your question about how they would feel about us."

"Yes, I think it does." I stood up, letting Jacob get up. We walked to the door, Jacob holding my hand. Jacob pulled me into his arms at the door, giving me another kiss, this one deep and drawn out. He finally pulled back and said, "I will see you tomorrow." I nodded, not able to speak.

I went back inside and set the alarms for the night. I shut all the lights and TV off and went back to my bedroom as I thought about the night. I felt like my heart skipped a beat when I thought about kissing him. I had vowed not to let my heart run my life again, but it seemed like that was just what I was doing. The last thing I wanted to do was make the same mistakes all over again.

When I compared Allen and Jacob though, there were a lot of differences. There were traits that Allen had shown from the beginning that I was just too naive to understand. He had always been rough around the edges and always seemed to push me to his way of thinking, to agree with him. He was very manipulative.

I know I haven't known Jacob for long, but I did not get the same sense with him, yet I debated that maybe it was too soon to know him that well. I wanted to get to know him better. I think I am starting to care for him. This scared the hell out of me. I finished brushing my teeth. As I was climbing into bed my cell phone went off. It was a text message from Jacob. "Hey, Mia. Thank you for tonight. I had a great time. I can't wait to see you tomorrow."

I replied back, "I had a good time also. Looking forward to tomorrow."

He replied back, "Good night."

"Night," I replied. I curled up with Lucky lying on his blanket on the other side. I lay there for a long time thinking about where this relationship could go, or if it should even go anywhere. I finally fell asleep and, yes, I dreamed about Jacob.

Chapter 18

I woke up and looked at the clock. I was surprised to see it was 9:30 am already. I got up and used the bathroom, opened the curtains, then crawled back into bed. I curled up under the warm blankets, looking out the window. There was a deer in the yard with her baby. I lay there, content to just gaze out the window when my cell phone went off. I rolled over, picking it up. "Morning Mia." the message read. It was from Jacob.

I smiled. "Morning," I replied back. Another text came a couple seconds later, "Can't wait to see you. I'll pick you up at 11:30."

"Perfect," I answered.

After lying there for a little while longer, I got out of bed and took a shower. I put on the blue sundress that Eva had given me and took some care with my makeup and hair. I completed the outfit with what little jewelry I had and my sandals. I looked in the mirror, pleased with what I saw. I had healed up pretty well; the makeup covered what remained of the bruising on my face.

My ribs and abdomen were still a little bruised and sore, but much improved. I went out to the kitchen, making a pot of coffee, and took a cup out on the deck. Lucky ran around the yard playing for a little bit then stopped, coming to lay at my feet. My phone chirped. I looked to see a message from Randy. "Overslept, did I miss coffee?"

"Having it now," I replied.

"Be right over," came her reply.

A few minutes later, Randy was walking up to the porch. "Well, don't you look pretty this morning. You didn't need to get all dressed up for me." She laughed. She went inside to get a cup of coffee and grabbed a cinnamon roll too then came back out.

"Josh still sleeping?" I asked.

"No. He is doing some laundry and getting some things ready to go back to work. He has to leave after lunch." She was clearly sad about his leaving, but she looked at me slyly, "I see you didn't ask about Jacob." She looked at me and raised an eyebrow. "Why do I have a feeling you already know he is up, not to mention exactly what he is doing?"

I smiled. "I do."

Randy smiled back, "Did something happen last night that I missed out on?"

"Yes."

"Spill it, girl! Tell me all you can without the dirty details!"

"Well, let's see. Norman Bates killed a lady in the shower…"

"Mattie!" Randy exclaimed. "Not in the movie! What happened last night between you and Jacob?" I brought her up to date on my relationship with Jacob, leaving out the most personal details of course. I also told her we planned to spend the day together. "I am so excited for you! He is falling head over heels for you!"

"I think you might be right. Oh, Randy, I don't know what to do." I sighed.

"Why?" she asked.

"We really seem to connect, but I just recently got out of a terrible relationship and am pregnant. What man would want something to do with me now?"

"Stop that!" Randy said. "You are a very pretty woman. Not to mention smart, witty, with a fantastic personality. I know I haven't known you for very long, but I feel like you are like a sister to me. What guy wouldn't want to get to know you better? Right now, that is all it is, just two single people attracted to each other going to spend some time together."

I nodded, "Yes, that's true. I guess you are right, we just met Sunday, so nothing to lose right?"

"Exactly!" She exclaimed. "Plus, Jacob is a great guy. I've known him for almost as long as I have known Josh. You two would make a great couple."

"Couple," I said. "I don't know if that is what I am looking for right now."

"Why not? Are you still in love with the father of the baby?" I thought to myself that I just left my husband, but I truthfully had not been in love with him for years, he beat that out of me a long time ago.

I replied honestly, "No, I don't think I ever really loved him. I think it was more that I wanted to be loved. He just flattered me, saying all the right things, making me think it was love. Now I know it wasn't."

"Look," she said, "I'm not pushing you to make a commitment with Jacob at all. All I am saying is why not give it a chance? You deserve to be happy, just as much as he does. If it works out between you two, great. If not, you will end up with another good friend, which is still a win for both of you. Now I'm going to get going before he gets here." We both stood up and took our coffee cups into the kitchen.

She gave me a hug. "Look, just have fun today with Jacob. Don't sweat over it. Let things go where they may."

"I will," I replied.

With that, she turned and left. I washed up the coffee cups. Looking at the clock, I realized that Jacob would be here soon. I fed Lucky, filling his water dish as well. "What do you think about Jacob?" I asked Lucky. Lucky looked up at me, wagging his tail and barking. "Sounds like you approve. I think I'm crazy for even considering the idea after everything. Oh well, I'm not going to worry about that right now. We will just have a good time today." Lucky barked and wagged his tail again.

A few minutes later I heard Jacob's truck pull up to the house, then a knock on the door. I opened the door, letting Jacob in. He walked in, looking at me with those intense blue eyes of his. "You look beautiful," he said, leaning down to kiss me.

When he pulled back, I said, "Thank you. Let me just grab my purse. I'm ready to go."

"Great. Hey, Lucky!" He knelt down, petting Lucky while I went back to my room, grabbing my purse.

I walked back out; he was standing there with Lucky at his side.

"Looks like you have made a friend," I smiled.

"He is a great dog," Jacob said looking down at him.

"I'm ready to go if you are," I said.

"I'm not ready yet," he said. I looked at him questioning, he bent over kissing me again. "Now I am ready." He smiled. I smiled shyly. This was going to take some getting used to. It still made me uneasy. We went out to his pickup. He walked me to the passenger side, opening the door for me. I started to climb in when a wave of dizziness came over me, I would have fallen to the ground had it not been for Jacob catching me.

"Mia Amata!" he cried, looking concerned, "Honey!" He picked me up, gently placing me on the seat of his truck. "Are you OK?"

I took some deep breaths, then nodded. "I'm OK."

"Are you sure? You and the baby are OK?" That surprised me a little bit, he seemed to really be concerned about a baby that wasn't his.

"Yes, the baby and I are fine." I smiled at him. "The doctor explained that sometimes dizziness and nausea can happen during pregnancy. I'm fine now."

He relaxed a little, reached out, and stroked my face. "Are you sure you want to go today?" He kissed me gently.

I smiled at him, "I'm sure. I'm pregnant, not dying."

That got a smile from him. He kissed me again, then shut the door for me. He walked around the truck, climbing into the driver's side. I buckled my seatbelt asking, "So where are you taking me?" I asked.

He smiled, reaching out, taking my hand in his as if it was the most natural thing to do. It felt… nice. "Well, I thought about taking you to a fancy restaurant but changed my mind. Instead, I would like to take you to my most favorite spot where we can have a picnic." He nodded toward the back where he had a blanket with some pillows.

"That sounds lovely, but… um… I don't see any food?"

He laughed, "I called in an order to one of my favorite restaurants, we will stop there to pick the food up. I hope you like fried chicken and potato salad."

"Sounds great," I said.

"Good," Jacob looked at me. "I really want some place private, so we can get to know each other better, I thought a quiet picnic would be better than a noisy restaurant." Pretty soon he pulled into a restaurant parking lot, telling me he would be right back he went in to get our food. He was soon back, putting the food in the backseat. He climbed back in, saying, "I hope bottled water is OK, I didn't know what you would like to drink."

"That's fine, I really don't drink soda. The food smells good. I'm eating for two, so I hope you brought enough!" I replied making him laugh. He pulled out on the street, starting to drive out of town.

"We will be there in about 20 minutes," he said. He reached over, taking my hand again. It felt very natural. "That house right there is where my parents live," he said, nodding to a large two-story house. He drove a little past it, turning off the main road.

"Are we on their property?" I asked.

"Yes, this road leads to my favorite place. Somewhere I grew up, spending a lot of my childhood." We drove along for a few minutes through some trees when we finally came to an opening.

"Oh, Jacob," I exclaimed, "it's beautiful!" Sitting before us was a small cabin with wildflowers around it.

To the north of the cabin was a lake. There was a pier going out over the lake with a small rowboat on the shore next to it. It could have been a painting.

He stopped the truck at the cabin, saying, "Come on, we are almost there."

"This isn't it?" I asked, confused.

"Not quite." He smiled at me, climbing out of the truck. He came around, helping me out of the truck. "Come on," he said, taking my hand. "I'll walk back for the food and stuff in a minute."

He walked me down to the pier, helping me up the steps, walking out to the bench at the end. He was showing me different things, then pointed down at the water. I looked; it was so clear you could watch the fish swimming by, several feet down. "I fish here a lot; fishing is really good. Stay here, give me a minute to get things ready."

I sat down, watching him walk to the rowboat. He did a few things to it, then went to the truck to get the picnic things, putting those in the boat. Walking back to me, he said, "Your chariot awaits Madam." I smiled nervously, taking his outstretched hand.

We walked over to the boat, he helped me in, holding my hand until I was able to take my seat. He was wearing shorts, took his shoes off, putting them in the boat. He pushed the boat out into the water a little, wading in with it. He leaped in the boat smoothly and sat down taking up the oars. He started rowing, we were soon on our way out into the lake. I trailed my hand in the water while I looked around at the scenery.

He turned the boat gradually north, pointing ahead of us. "See that huge pine to the north? The one with the huge nest toward the top?" I shaded my eyes with my hand, looking in the direction he indicated. "Oh, yes I see it."

"That is where we are headed. It's an island that my family owns. That is an eagle's nest, they build there every year." As if on cue, an eagle soared past us, swooping down to the lake. He came back up with a fish in its claws, then flew to the nest on the island.

"Look at him!" I exclaimed. "So beautiful!"

Jacob smiled at me, "You will probably get to see him close up if he stays in the nest long enough."

We continued toward the island with Jacob pointing out things as we went, turtles sunning themselves on a log, a blue heron fishing toward the shore. It was obvious that he was very happy here, very at home. When we were closer to the island, I could see the eagle in his nest eating his fish. Jacob steered the rowboat around to the other side of the island, where there was a beach that he aimed for. He climbed out of the rowboat, pulling it up on the shore. He reached for my hand. When I stood up, he put his hands on my waist lifting me out with ease.

"We swam here all the time as kids." He pointed to a rope that hung from a tree. "We would swing out on that, let go, landing as far out as we could." I smiled at the vision that gave me in my head. He handed me the blankets and pillows. He then grabbed the food and drinks and started leading me up to the beach. "Come on, it's just inshore a little."

We followed a path to a small clearing. There, in the middle was a stream running over a bed of rocks. "There is a natural spring from underground here; the stream leads to the lake."

We followed the stream to a small pond with water that was so clear it seemed almost nonexistent. We both stopped, quietly watching a deer drink out of the pond. She shifted her body so that we could see a little fawn lying in the grass beside her. The deer suddenly looked up, seeing us watching them, but didn't run away. She watched us warily, moving back between us and her fawn, hiding it from view.

We didn't want to disturb her, so we crossed to the other side of the stream, carefully crossing on some rocks sticking out of the water, Jacob holding my hand, so I didn't slip. We slowly walked to the other side of the pond across from the deer and her baby, not wanting to scare them away.

"Here we are," Jacob said, "I thought we could picnic here." He motioned to a huge flat rock, like a small patio at the side of the pond. He set the food down, taking the blankets from me, and he spread them out on the rock. I lay the pillows down on the blankets. I sat down while he brought the food over.

We sat there, enjoying our lunch, watching the deer across the pond. The little fawn had gotten up, running around frolicking in the tall grass closer to the trees. Soon, the deer led her baby into the trees. We finished our meal, talking about the wildlife around here. Jacob lay back on one of the pillows, watching me.

I had my knees pulled up with my arms wrapped around them, looking at the pond with the little fish swimming around. A turtle surfaced on the other side, climbed out on a rock, and sat there in the sun. I watched another small turtle swim after a small fish. I could feel Jacob's eyes on me, but I felt nervous and scared. I was alone with a man I barely knew. What was I thinking? It wasn't necessarily an awkward silence, but I felt that he had something on his mind he wanted to talk to me about.

As if right on cue Jacob quietly said, "Mia, can I ask you something rather personal?"

"You can ask, depending on what it is I'll answer honestly or tell you I'd rather not answer it."

"Fair enough." He hesitated for a minute or two, then asked, "Are you still in love with that guy, the married one?"

"We already discussed that," I said.

"No, we discussed if you missed him. I asked if you still loved him."

I didn't say anything for a moment, then shook my head. "No. I don't think that I ever really loved him. I think I was in love with the idea of being in love, with being loved. I never really felt loved in my life—ever. I was naive."

"Were you with him for a long time?"

"Off and on for about five years." I watched as the turtle in the water caught a little fish to eat. "Probably more off than on."

"You didn't date anyone else that whole time? You just sat around while he was at home with his wife and kids?"

I shook my head. "He was my first and only boyfriend I've ever had. I always waited for him to call. Sooner or later he always did."

Jacob stood up, walking along the edge of the pond until he was almost to the other side. I couldn't make out what he was thinking, he wouldn't look at me. When he finally did, the look was one I hadn't seen to this point, not clearly disgust but close. I got the picture. Standing up, I started packing up the lunch things.

"What are you doing?" Jacob asked, walking back toward me.

I looked at him, "Look, Jacob, I understand. You can take me home now. I get it."

He looked confused, "Get what?"

"That you regret today, are sorry that you are wasting time on me," I said.

"What are you talking about? I don't regret anything."

"You don't?"

"No, why would I?" he exclaimed.

"I'm pregnant with another man's baby, who turned out to be cheating with me. I let him use me for almost five years. I'm not exactly a great catch. You can take me home. We can be friends. I won't hold it against you."

"Stop, Mia. Please, sit down." He took my hand, pulling me down on the blanket next to him. "I don't regret meeting you or spending time with you. I am upset that some pig used you like that and took advantage of you. For some reason, I am drawn to you. I want to protect you. I know we just met. I really want us to spend more time together." I looked at him, he was so sincere that I was finding it hard not to believe him.

"You do? Why would you want to spend time with a woman pregnant with another man's baby?" I asked. "Seriously Jacob, I come with a lot of baggage that you don't need in your life."

He thought for a minute before answering, looking at my hand as he stroked my fingers. "My last relationship was with a woman that I thought I was in love with. I imagined spending the rest of my life with her. She lived in the city; we were about as different as two people could be. There were all sorts of signs there, she always came to my place, claiming it was nice to get out of the city."

"One day, I was driving to the city on business when I saw her. She was with another man. I followed them into a restaurant where I confronted them. That man turned out to be her husband, the father of their child. I ended up breaking up their marriage. He wouldn't forgive her for cheating." He looked away.

"What did she do?" I asked.

"She tried to contact me, saying she was never in love with him, and wanted to make things work for us, but I couldn't trust her. It was much easier letting go of her than I thought it would be had I really been in love with her."

"I'm sorry Jacob," I said softly. "It still had to hurt."

"Hurt my pride," he said smiling. "See, I had been taken in by someone too. My point is almost everybody has baggage. What I feel for you is different."

"Different how?"

Again, he was quiet for a few moments before he answered. "The moment I saw you with Lucky sleeping in your arms, on the path I just knew. Mia Amata, I love you. I have never felt this way before—ever. When we are apart, I feel like I can't breathe. When I am with you—I am so happy, I want to be with you every moment I can. As far as the baby, he…"

I interrupted, "She."

"Oh, is it a girl?"

I smiled, "It hasn't been proven by ultrasound yet, I just know that the baby is a girl."

He smiled back. "OK, then. That baby girl is a part of you. If you allow me to, I know I can love her too."

I sat there in silence again, taking in everything he said. If he was lying to me, he was really good at it. I was still confused, but there was something in me that was telling me I wanted this man in my life.

"Mia Amata?" I looked at him. "Will you let me be a part of your life, and your baby's life?"

"I think I would like that," I replied, "but you have to be patient with me Jacob. Having been recently hurt, trust and love may not come as easily for me as they seem to have for you."

"We can take things as slow as you need," He leaned over, kissing me so tenderly and gently. When the kiss ended, he moved around, sat behind me, and took me into his arms. I leaned back against him. We sat like that talking about ourselves, getting to know each other.

Eventually, he shifted positions, pulling me into his lap. He pulled me tighter to him. I snuggled up to him, feeling warm and safe, for the first time in years. I nuzzled my face into his neck, reaching up to put my arm around his neck. After a little while, he lay me down on the blanket and pulled back a little and then started to kiss me.

Pulling his head back, he looked at me, his eyes partially closed. He stroked my face, kissed me again, then lay his head down beside me. I curled up to him. I could hear his heartbeat, and it seemed to be pounding really hard, just like mine.

I must have dozed off for a little bit in the warmth of his arms. "Mia," he said gently rubbing my arm. Opening my eyes, "Yes?" I asked sleepily.

"It's getting late, we should go."

Rolling onto my back, I looked up at him. "Do we have to?"

He laughed, kissed me, and then sat up. "Yes, we do."

I groaned, sitting up too. We packed up our picnic things, heading back down the path by the stream to the boat. By the time we made it back to his truck, it was 5:00. He took me around to the passenger side, opening and shutting the door for me. I buckled up as he slid behind the steering wheel.

When we started to move, his hand found mine. We talked about the coming week and our jobs. He asked when he could see me again.

"When will you have time?" I asked.

"Tomorrow night," he said, smiling. "If that is OK."

"I think that would be OK," I said. "I'll make you supper."

"You don't need to go to a lot of trouble for me."

"It would be my pleasure. You know, it is early yet," I said, as we pulled up to my house. "Do you want to come in? I can make us some sandwiches or leftover lasagna."

He shut the truck off, "Now that's a deal. Your homemade lasagna is fantastic. Don't tell Sal, but I think it is probably better than his." I laughed as we entered the house with Lucky greeting us inside the door. "Hey, boy," I said. I looked at Jacob. "I need to take Lucky out, then I will get the lasagna warmed up for us."

"I'll join you outside. I'm not in a hurry to eat." We went outside with Lucky. I walked to the deck rail, watching as Lucky chased a squirrel. Jacob came up behind me, wrapping his arms around my waist. I leaned back against him. This felt nice, but I still had an inner argument about if this was the right thing to do. Lucky soon tired of chasing the squirrel, took care of his business, and then came running back up the steps to us. The three of us went back into the house.

"Make yourself at home," I told Jacob. "I'll be right back." I used the bathroom, washing up some before I started cooking. Walking into the kitchen I started the oven. "Turn on the TV if you want."

"I'd rather sit here and talk to you," he said, as he sat on one of the stools at the counter.

I smiled at him. Pulling the lasagna out of the refrigerator, I set it on the counter to warm it a little before sticking it in the oven. I prepared a couple pieces of fresh garlic bread. I put both the lasagna and bread in the oven to heat them up, then pulled the fixings out for a little salad.

"Is there something I can do?" he asked.

"I have this under control, but you could set the table if you don't mind…"

"Sure." He slid off the stool, finding the things easily enough. We worked together quietly, chatting about nothing and everything. It seemed more relaxed, easy, not pressured or stressed than before. Soon, we were sitting down at the table, eating and chatting about the day. He told me stories of staying in the cabin at the lake when he was younger and all the fun they used to have there. We laughed at some of the trouble he and his two siblings used to get into.

"I envy you. You have some great memories of your childhood. Ones you will cherish forever." I smiled at him.

"I do," he replied. "I wish you did. Do you have any happy memories from your childhood?"

"Not really," I said. "I moved from foster home to foster home, never really staying very long in one place, so it made it hard to develop friendships. One foster home though, the lady that ran it introduced me to books. Thanks to her I developed a love of reading. Other than that, there were not a lot of happy moments."

"I'm so sorry," he said. "How did you come out with such a great attitude? A lot of people that have gone through half of what you have such a negative attitude toward life."

We had finished eating, I stood up to clear off the table. He stood up, helping me. Together we loaded the dishwasher, cleaning everything up. I offered him a glass of tea, took one myself. We went to sit down on the couch, automatically sitting on the small couch. "So you never answered my question," he said, smiling.

"What? Oh, yes, my attitude." I smiled. "I guess I do have one good memory, something that probably has a lot to do with my attitude. I ran away from the last foster home at the age of 16, as I told you before. I left with a backpack with a few clothes, a couple books, and what little cash I managed to save from babysitting."

I took a sip of tea, setting the glass down on the coffee table. "I traveled by foot for a few days, hiding when I saw police. The last thing I wanted was to go back to another foster home. I ate what I could find. Sometimes, I'd go into stores to buy something, but I was trying to budget my money very carefully. One day, I was walking when it started raining."

"I had no shelter, jacket. I just kept walking until it was dark out. I came across a farm on the outskirts of a small town. I snuck up to the barn, found a way in, curled up in the hay, and fell asleep. I figured I would get up after a couple of hours of rest, leaving before anyone could find me there. I felt horrible by the time I got there, feverish, and chilled. I woke up two days later."

"Two days?" Jacob asked.

I nodded. "I was no longer in the barn. I woke up in a bed in the farmhouse. The farmer discovered me the next morning. He and his wife managed to me in the house. She took care of me, getting me out of my wet things, tucking me in the bed, and then nursing me back to health."

"They were very kind to me, decent people. They let me stay there until I was well and then invited me to stay there with them full-time, offering me room and board and a little money for helping them on the farm. I told them my story. The farmer's wife cried. I stayed with them and helped them on the farm, taking care of all the animals they had. Probably one of the happiest times of my life."

"What happened? Why did you leave?" Jacob asked, reaching out to stroke my hair.

I frowned, "The couple ended up having some bad luck strike them. The economy went bad, they were losing money on their farm. They ended up selling their animals and most of their equipment. The man suffered a stroke, dying shortly afterward. Their son showed up and moved his mother to live with him."

"I found myself homeless again. He made it clear that he didn't want me anywhere near his mom and thought I was a freeloader no matter how much his mother protested. I packed what little I had into my backpack, hitting the road again. They taught me a lot about how decent people can be and how to respect others."

"They helped me overcome the bitterness that I had from my past. Taught me that if I let my past affect me on a daily basis, then the past wins. I had to choose not to let the past dictate my future. I guess they had a lot more influence on me than I thought they did."

Jacob put his glass on the table next to mine. "What did you do next?" he asked.

"I traveled around, doing odd jobs here and there. Discovered that most people are essentially kind and generous, like the farming couple. I finally found a town and a job that I really liked. Soon, I was able to get a small apartment and started to make a life for myself. I was there until I started over again here."

"Makes the things that happened to me in my life, that I considered awful, seem so… insignificant," Jacob said.

"Don't minimalize the things that happened to you." I smiled at him. "I really believe those things help make us who we are today."

Jacob leaned over and kissed me tenderly. "I am glad you are here now. I hope I can help make some good memories for you." He said quietly as he leaned in, kissing me some more. The kisses started to become more passionate until I finally pulled away.

"I should go." He said breathlessly. I nodded. We stood up and walked to the front door with our arms wrapped around each other.

He turned toward me, took me in his arms, looking me in the eyes. "I had a great time today."

"I did too."

"See you tomorrow night?" he asked.

"Yes." He bent down, kissing me gently. He pulled back, "Night Mia Amata, I love you."

"Night Jacob." I watched him walk out to his truck and then shut the door.

Chapter 19

I woke up to the alarm going off at seven that morning. Shutting it off, I lay there for a few minutes, remembering the day I spent with Jacob. I smiled at the thought that I would see him again that night. I started my new job today, so I got up ready to get going. After showering and getting dressed, I made my coffee, taking it out on the deck as usual.

Lucky ran around the yard, soon barking at his sister, Lady, and Randy. Randy came up the stairs, went in to get coffee, then joined me on the deck. She seemed a little sad this morning. I knew it must be because Josh was gone again "Are you OK?" I asked her.

She sighed, "Yes, I just don't like sleeping alone. I never used to mind it, but now that I have Josh in my life, I hate it. I miss him."

Just then my cell phone chirped. I picked it up off the table between Randy and me, reading the text message from Jacob. "Morning, Mia. I had a great time yesterday. I miss you."

I must have blushed because Randy said "Is that from Jacob? How did things go yesterday?"

I didn't answer right away, as I was replying to Jacob. "I had a good time too." I put the phone down, looking anywhere but at Randy. "It was nice. We went for a picnic and talked."

Randy looked at me suspiciously. "Talked? You are blushing too much for just talking. So tell me what's going on with you two?" I told her about our picnic, and we talked a lot while there. "He must be serious about you," she exclaimed.

"Why do you say that?" I asked.

"Because neither of the guys share that place with anyone unless they are serious about them. Josh never took anybody there except me. I know for a fact that Jacob has never taken anybody there either. What happened next?" she asked.

I told her about the rest of the day, stopping with him helping me clean up from supper, that we continued talking after supper; then he left.

Randy let out a squeal. "You guys will be great together I know it!"

"On the picnic, we agreed to take our time," I said. "I'm terrified of a new relationship."

"Take all the time you need," Randy said. "Sometimes you just know when it is right. I have to go, need to head to work. I'd rather stay here and chat with you though!"

"Me too. I have to get to work soon," I said.

"When are you seeing Jacob again?" Randy asked.

"Tonight," I said, smiling.

"I won't bother you tonight then." She said winking at me. "I am so happy for both of you. I just know you two will be great together." She gave me a hug, then ran down the steps, whistling for Lady. I watched them go when she got to the path leading into the trees she turned and waved. I waved back. Turning, Lucky and I went into the house.

I had enough time to start our supper in the crockpot again, this time it was ribs. I'd let them cook all day in seasonings, then throw them on the grill shortly before we ate. I managed to get the ribs started, cleaned up the kitchen, and then headed down to my office to start work. Lucky followed me down, curling up at my feet as I started my first day. The day started with finishing up some paperwork and then training via a web call. We took a break at 12 for lunch.

I went upstairs, adding a few more ingredients to the ribs, then made a sandwich, taking it out on the deck so Lucky could run around for a little while. The break was soon over so Lucky, and I headed back to the office. Toward the end of the day, the trainer thought I understood the job well enough she let me work alone for the last hour. I sent all my reports directly to her, which was protocol for the first couple of days.

Then, when my work was consistently up to the standards set in the protocol, I would be able to send my work directly to the customer. My trainer received my work and told me she would review it, getting back to me in the morning with feedback. Clocking out, I went upstairs.

I checked on the ribs, deciding to make some mashed potatoes and sweet corn to go with them. I got those started, then sat down to watch a little TV while I waited until time to through the ribs and sweet corn on the grill. Lucky jumped up on the couch next to me. I stroked his head while we watched a cooking show. When the show was about to be over, there was a knock at the door. My heart skipped a beat, I shut the TV off and went to answer it. It was Jacob. He came in, closing the door behind him. "Hi," he said.

"Hi," I said smiling. He leaned over, kissing me.

"Mia Amata," he said. "I couldn't stop thinking about you today." I didn't say anything, I couldn't. "Mia?" he asked. I raised my head to look at him. "Are you OK?"

I smiled, "Yes, I'm fine." I laid my head on his chest; he wrapped me in his arms. We stood like that for a few minutes, until he said, "What's that wonderful smell?"

"Supper," I said.

"Well, it smells great," he said, smiling.

I looked at him. "Are you hungry?"

"Famished," he said. "I worked up an appetite today."

I went into the kitchen. Jacob sat up on a stool at the counter. I felt him staring at me, turning I said, "What?"

He smiled, "You're beautiful."

I shook my head. "No, I'm not."

"Mia Amata," he said, "you are beautiful. I wish I could teach everyone that hurt you, that made you think you were unworthy of being happy, a lesson."

I didn't say anything. My self-worth was almost nil. The fact that Jacob recognized how low it was actually hurt. I started to set the table. He came over to help. I carried the ribs and corn out to the grill; they only needed a couple of minutes there. While they cooked, I finished the mashed potatoes and gravy, sitting those on the table. I went out, pulled the corn and ribs off, and we sat down to eat.

"This smells fantastic," he exclaimed as he picked up his fork. He took a bit, groaning. "And she cooks too, a woman of many talents."

"Thank you," I said smiling. I asked him about his day. He told me about saving a little fawn whose mother had been hit by a car. He took it to a local woman who would raise it on a bottle until it could be released into the wild. We talked about my first day at my new job. I told him all I could, he understood that I couldn't share what the reports were about. I then told him that Randy knew we had been spending time together.

He raised his eyebrows. "How did that happen?" he asked.

"She comes over every morning for coffee. She has a way of worming information out of me." He was quiet. "Is that bad that she knows?" I asked, getting up to clear the remains of our supper off the table.

He laughed as he got up and started helping me. "She is very resourceful. She is great though. I don't mind at all. She will probably tell Josh, but neither of them will tell my parents until we are ready to tell them ourselves. Besides, it is nice to know she will be here for my girlfriend too. I'm glad you are friends."

When he said girlfriend, I dropped the silverware I was carrying into the kitchen on the floor. He picked them up for me, putting them in the dishwasher. "Girlfriend?" I asked, "Is that what I am?" He came up behind me at the sink, putting his arms around my waist. "I hope so. There is nothing I want more right now than to call you, my girlfriend." I turned around in his arms and faced him. "We are supposed to take it slow," I said.

He looked at me, "Are you going to be dating other men?"

"No," I said.

"So you are going to date me exclusively?" he asked.

I could see where he was going, but I wasn't sure I was comfortable putting a title on our relationship. "Yes, Jacob, but…" He didn't let me finish.

"Well, I am not going to be dating anyone but you. We will take things slow, but the terms girlfriend and boyfriend do not mean we are engaged. It just means, at least to me, that we will not be dating other people. Will you be my girlfriend?" I hesitated; he sensed it. "Mia Amata?" He was looking at me worriedly.

"Jacob," I said. "Have you seriously given this relationship thought? I know we have talked about it; I know you say you love me, but have you really thought about it?"

"Yes, I have," he replied.

"What will your parents think when you introduce your pregnant girlfriend to them? They are going to dislike me, think I'm a slut or something." I walked to the window overlooking the deck. He walked over to me. He turned me around to face him, I ducked my head to hide my tears. He pulled me in his arms.

"Oh, Mia. You are not a slut."

I laughed ruefully. "I'm pregnant with another man's baby."

"How many relationships have you had before me?" he asked.

"One."

He laughed. "That's hardly a slut. Listen, Mia Amata, my parents will love you. They will see you as the person you are, not for your past. They will not judge you." He wiped away my tears with his thumb. "What about your friends and other people? They are going to think you knocked me up?"

"So what? Who cares what they think? Besides," he said, raising my chin, so I was looking at him, "I'm OK with them thinking that."

"You are?" I was surprised.

"Definitely, I love kids." He kissed me. "People will see us together and think, 'Look at that happy couple expecting their first baby together'." He kissed me again.

"Jacob," I said.

"Yes?" he said.

"I will be your girlfriend."

"Good," he replied.

It was still early, so we turned on the TV. We were watching a show when a commercial came on for the local hospital, showing their delivery area with a very pregnant woman checking in. I looked at Jacob, "That will be me in a few months, you won't want me then."

"Now what are you talking about?" he asked.

"I'll be fat, not beautiful at all."

He laughed, "I disagree. I think you will be extremely beautiful."

"Really?" Raising an eyebrow, not believing a word he said.

He looked at me, running his hand over my stomach, which was showing just a minimal pregnancy bump. "You have a life growing in you. Your body is amazing in that it provides all that a baby needs for the first few months of its life. What could be more beautiful than that?"

Either this man was turning out to be too good to be true, or I was an even bigger fool than ever before.

Chapter 20

Just as Lucky and I had fallen into a comfortable routine together, Jacob and I soon fell into one too. He came over several nights a week after work for supper, either I cooked or he would bring some takeout. We would go for walks or watch movies, and then he would leave. On the weekends, sometimes, Lucky and I would go to his house for supper, and he would cook for me. He was in a small one-bedroom house he was renting for the time being. Most of the time he would come to my house.

Every Saturday night, we would get together with Josh and Randy either at their house or mine, Jacob's was really too small for us to do much there. We would watch movies, play games, sometimes just have a bonfire out back, and spend the evening laughing and joking.

One Saturday night, everyone was at my house. We were playing a game at the table, laughing and having fun. I got up to get everyone some more tea to drink. I pulled the tea out of the refrigerator, taking it over to the counter when I felt something. I froze and just stood there. Jacob noticed, immediately coming to my side, "Mia Amata? Are you OK?" he asked. Randy and Josh both jumped up too, looking at me worriedly.

"I'm fine," I looked at him. "I think I just felt the baby move." I stood there, still not moving, soon feeling it again. I smiled at Jacob. "It is the baby, she is moving. I can feel it."

He smiled at me, "What does it feel like?" I thought about it for a moment, how should I describe it?

"It feels like… butterflies in your stomach." At this point, I was in my second trimester, 19 weeks along, Jacob and I had been seeing each other for 12 weeks now. Josh had put his arm around Randy, they were smiling at us. Jacob had his hand protectively over my stomach, my hand was over his.

"You two are just so damn adorable," Randy said.

Jacob looked at her, laughing. "Me? Adorable? Why thank you!" We all laughed. He helped me finish getting tea for everyone. When the game was over, we all went out on the deck to get some fresh air, letting the dogs romp around for a little while.

We were sitting there when Josh said, "So when are you two moving in together?"

Randy elbowed him, "Josh!"

"What?" he asked her. "They are together almost all the time when they aren't working. It's obvious that is the next step."

Randy looked at us, "You do have a point. It is obvious to anyone that sees them together how crazy they are about each other."

"Um, guys?" I said. "We are right here you know."

We all laughed. Jacob cleared his throat. "We aren't in any hurry," he said. "I'd move in tomorrow if Mia asked me to, but we have plenty of time." Smiling, I looked at him, appreciative that he wasn't rushing me.

"I haven't even met the rest of your family yet," I said. "They are going to hate me, aren't they?" The three of them laughed. Randy was the one who answered. "No, Mattie. They are going to be crazy about you."

Josh nodded. "They have commented on how happy Jacob has been lately. It will be nice when they finally do meet you, so they can stop hounding Randy and me about what is going on with him."

Randy laughed, "Yes, it will be a huge relief. Really, Mattie, you will love them. They are great."

"Speaking of which," Jacob said, clearing his throat, and looked at me. "I told them I would come to see them tomorrow for lunch that I had someone I wanted them to meet."

"Jacob!" I cried. "Tomorrow? That's not much notice!"

"Well, I knew that if I told you last weekend that we were going tomorrow you would have stewed, worrying about it all week."

Randy shook her head, "Men."

Both Josh and Jacob said "What?" at the same time.

Randy and I looked at each other. We burst out laughing. I looked at Jacob and found he was looking at me, smiling. I moved closer to him, which didn't escape Randy's notice. Randy got up and pulled Josh out of his chair, they walked down to the pier, giving us privacy.

We watched them walk away. Jacob looked at me, then moved to the edge of the chair. "Listen, Mia, I know we agreed to take this slow, if you aren't ready for us to live together, I get it, I won't push. But Mia," He paused. I looked at him questioningly. "I love you; you know that." He pulled a box out of his pocket. He kneeled down, opening the box, "Mia Amata, I want to spend the rest of my life with you. Will you marry me?"

"Jacob," I hesitated. The past three months had been great, we spent a lot of time together, and I was starting to trust him. I enjoyed spending time with him. I knew that I could never legally be his wife, that it wouldn't be fair to him.

"Do you love me, Mia?" he asked, searching my eyes. This man has been so loving and so caring and has been there for me daily since I agreed to be his girlfriend. He was everything I had always wanted, but did I love him? I searched my heart, realizing I really did love Jacob. I don't know how I would handle marrying him, but I did love him. I knew that now.

"Yes, Jacob, I love you." This was the first time I had spoken those words to him. The look of happiness that came across his face brought tears to my eyes.

"Then, Mia Amata, will you marry me?"

"Yes, Jacob, I will marry you."

Jacob let out a whoop, pulling me out of my chair and wrapping his arms around me. Randy and Josh heard him and came running up the steps in time to see him put the ring on my finger and kiss me. Randy squealed in excitement; they both came over congratulating us both. Jacob put his arm around me, we stood around talking for a few minutes.

"Come on Josh, let's go," Randy said, looking at Jacob and me.

"But it's early," he said. "I thought we were going to watch a movie."

Randy smiled, "Do you remember the night we got engaged?"

"Do I ever," Josh said. Then it donned on him what she was referring to. "Oh… yeah. We better go."

"Maybe we can relive that night when we get home."

"Night guys," Josh said as he took Randy's hand, pulling her through the house and out the front door to their car. Jacob and I were laughing as they drove away. Jacob closed the doors behind them. Lucky was curled up in his dog bed on the floor as Jacob and I sat down on the couch. I was looking at the ring on my finger, having never felt this happy in my life. Jacob was watching me. "Happy?" he asked.

"More than I have ever been in my life."

"Me too, Mia Amata." He smiled at me.

"OK, I have to ask, why 'Mia Amata'? You have never explained why you call me that."

"It's Italian," he said. "It means 'my beloved'. From the moment I saw you, you have been Mia Amata to me."

"You did love me from the very first, didn't you?" I asked.

"From the moment I laid eyes on you. You are the most beautiful woman I have ever seen." He leaned over and kissed me. He pulled back, looking me in the eye. "I love you, Mia Amata." He kissed me again, only this time it was so passionate I felt like I would pass out from it.

I slid my arms around his neck, and he pulled me into his lap. I could feel how much he wanted me. He slid his hand around to my breast, teasing me through my shirt. I moaned, straining against his hand. I knew I should probably ask him to leave, but I didn't want to. I wanted him to stay.

We continued to kiss. He ran his hand down, then up under my T-shirt, feeling my breasts through my bra. I pressed my body against him, not wanting him to stop. He slipped my T-shirt over my head, then unhooked my bra, sliding it off. He teased my nipples first with his fingers, then with his lips.

Pulling back, he groaned, lifting his head to look at me. "If I don't leave now, I am going to carry you back to the bedroom. I want to make love to you Mia." I pulled him down for another kiss, not wanting him to stop. He ran his hands down my back, my hips, my thighs, then up between my legs, pressing his fingers against my shorts.

I moaned and pressed his hand with mine. I felt him start to pull away, I deepened the kiss, pressing my hips against him even tighter. He moaned in return, scooping me up in his arms. He shut the light off, carrying me back to my bedroom. He laid me gently on the bed and then lay down beside me. He leaned over me, looking me in the eyes. "Are you sure?" He whispered.

"Yes," I said, pulling his head down toward mine. He lay down beside me on the bed, teasing my nipples, driving me crazy. I slid my hands under his T-shirt, feeling his back and chest, running my hands all over him. He paused long enough to take his shirt off, then leaned back down to kiss me. He ran his hands down to my shorts, sliding them down my hips to my ankles where I kicked them off.

I slid my hands down his back, as his fingers slid between my thighs, and his lips trailed down my neck to my breasts, then continued down my stomach.

He stood up, breathing heavily, watching me as he took the rest of his clothes off. He got back on the bed, but this time he was kissing my thighs, gently spreading my legs.

My breath caught as I felt his tongue, my hands going to his head, and I raised my buttocks off the bed in response. He continued for a few minutes until I thought I wouldn't be able to take it anymore, then he started moving up my body, kissing me all over. He finally got to my lips, kissing me then pulling back to look at me. I looked at him and felt him pressing against me, wanting to enter me. "Mia Amata," he whispered, "I love you, but I will stop if you want me to, I want you to be sure."

I looked at him, tears coming to my eyes. "I love you, Jacob," I whispered. "Please make love to me." He leaned down and kissed me ever so gently, spreading my legs and entering me. I gasped, crying out.

We made love with a passion I never knew existed. It went on for so long that I clawed Jacob's back, crying out for him. We finally collapsed, both of us breathing hard and exhausted, unable to speak. Jacob moved a little to the side, so he wasn't lying right on top of me, but held me, not letting go. "Mia Amata," Jacob finally said.

"Hmmm?" I murmured.

"I'm glad I stayed."

"Me too," I said. "So about moving in?"

He raised his eyebrows, looking at me.

"Can you move in tomorrow?" I asked.

"Yes," and he leaned over, kissing me.

We celebrated our engagement a few times that night, finally falling asleep around two in the morning, exhausted. When I finally opened my eyes, stretching, I looked at the clock. It was 10 a.m. "Jacob?" I said, noticing the empty bed next to me. He comes walking in, carrying a tray.

"Good morning Mrs. Vance," he said.

I laughed. "Not yet." I sat up. He put the tray over my lap on the bed.

"It's not much," he said. "If I know Mom, she would have a huge meal cooked for us, so we had better be able to eat."

"I'm eating for two, that shouldn't be a problem."

"You still eat like a bird. I hope you are getting enough to eat for both of you."

"The doctor says I'm doing just fine. Baby and I are both growing as expected," I said. "Speaking of the doctor, I was wondering if you would like to go with me to my appointment this week? If you can."

"Of course, I will if you want me to. Is there any particular reason why though?" he asked. He sat down on the bed, taking a piece of toast.

"I'm going to have an ultrasound. You would be able to see the baby. We should be able to learn the sex of the baby. You don't have to go, I just thought…"

"Really?" He said cutting me off. "I would love to go."

I smiled at him. We finished off the toast and coffee. He picked up the tray, putting it aside. "What time do we have to be at your parents?" I asked.

He climbed back into bed, pulling me down, "Soon," he said.

We finally pulled ourselves out of bed. He cleaned up our breakfast dishes while I showered. He then took a shower. Pretty soon, it was time to go. I was quiet as we were driving to his parent's house. Jacob asked, "Nervous?"

"Scared stiff," I said.

He took my hand to his lips and kissed it. "Don't be. I promise they will love you." All too soon it seemed like we were pulling into their driveway. Jacob came around, helping me out of the truck. Walking in the front door, Jacob called out, "Mom? Dad? We're here." His mom came out of the kitchen. She was a pretty woman, tall and thin.

"Jacob!" she said. "I'm so glad to see you." She gave him a hug. Behind her, a man came from the back hallway.

"Hey, Dad," Jacob said, giving his dad a hug. "I'd like to introduce you to someone." He took my hand, "Mom, Dad, this is my fiancé, Mattie Austin." His mom and dad looked at each other in surprise. "Mia, this is my dad, Donald, my mom, Nora."

"Fiancé?" his mom asked.

"Yes, I asked her last night, and she said yes." A couple of seconds of silence passed, and I figured this was it; they hated me already. To my surprise, his mother suddenly lit up.

"Congratulations! That is so exciting," she said. It seemed that she was genuinely happy. She gave me a hug while his dad shook Jacob's hand.

"Thank you," I said. His dad gave me a hug also. His mom ushered us into the living room where we all sat down.

"I knew that there had to be a reason why Jacob seemed so much happier lately. Now I know. I am thrilled! How did you meet? Wait, Mattie? Aren't you Randy's friend?"

I smiled. "Yes, I moved into the house south of Randy and Josh. We have become good friends."

Donald said, "So that is how you met Jacob."

Jacob nodded, "Yes. I went walking with Josh and the pups one day. Lucky had gotten away again. Down the path toward us walks Mia, carrying a sleeping puppy in her arms. The rest is history. She hasn't been able to get rid of me since." We laughed. I waited for what he was going to say next. I knew it was coming. I was extremely nervous. We had agreed that we would tell his parents about the baby from the beginning.

"We have something else we want to tell you," Jacob said, taking my hand. "Mia moved here to start a new life. She was in a relationship with a man who she later found out was married." He paused.

Nora said, "Oh, that is awful. I'm so sorry to hear that."

His dad seemed angry. "I will never understand how men can be pigs like that."

Jacob held up his hand, "There is more." He looked at me.

I took a deep breath, continuing the story from there. "I found out he was married after I told him I was having his baby. He told me he didn't want anything to do with me, that he was already married. I thought about telling his wife and drove to their house to do it, but I saw their two kids playing in the yard. I couldn't do it. So instead, I moved here to start over, with my baby."

They looked at me. "I'm pregnant." I held my breath waiting for the outburst and protests about us getting married. Instead, his mom got up, coming over to me. She sat down, pulling me into her arms.

"Oh, my dear, I'm so sorry you went through all of that. I am so glad you are here now." She pulled back, holding my hand in hers.

"You aren't upset that your son wants to marry a woman having another man's baby?"

To my surprise, Donald was the one to speak up. "Biology does not make a father. What makes a man a father has more to do with being there for the mother and the child, regardless of whether he is the biological father or not."

"Exactly," Nora said. "Jacob will make a wonderful father to your baby if you allow him to." I had tears in my eyes at the kindness of these two people I just met. "Oh my! I just realized something," Nora turned, looking at her husband.

They both said at the same time, "We are going to be grandparents!" They were so excited about being grandparents! His mom went over, sitting down again next to her husband, and they hugged each other. Nora turned to us with tears in her eyes. "You two have made us very happy!" she exclaimed. "We are thrilled for the two of you."

"Thank you," Jacob said. A buzzer went off in the kitchen.

Nora stood up, wiping her eyes. "The roast is done. We will eat in a few minutes."

"Can I help?" I asked.

"No," Nora said, "but I would love to have company." Jacob squeezed my hand as I got up, following Nora into the kitchen.

She grabbed some hot pads and opened the oven. She motioned to the small breakfast nook, telling me to have a seat. She pulled the roast out of the oven and set it on the stove. "Is your family excited about the baby?" Nora asked, glancing at me. She started dishing up the roast, potatoes, and carrots into different dishes.

"I don't have any family," I said.

"I'm sorry to hear that, what happened to them?"

"I don't know," I replied. "I was abandoned as a newborn, a policeman found me in a trash bin."

"My God, that is horrible! Did you ever try to find out who your parents were?"

"No. They tossed me out like common household garbage, I never had the desire to look for them. I went from foster home to foster home, until I ran away at 16."

"Oh, Mattie," Nora said with tears in her eyes. "You have had such a rough life. I'm sorry." She walked over to me, taking both of my hands in hers. "But you have family now if you allow us to be."

"That depends," I said. Nora looked at me questioningly. "On whether you let me help you with the food." I smiled at her.

Nora laughed. "You can make the gravy."

"Perfect," I said. Nora and I became fast friends as we worked together getting the meal on the table.

Nora mentioned that she has heard a lot about me from Randy. "Randy adores you," she said.

"Randy is great." I smiled.

"She is. I'm happy that they are getting married. I just wish they would set the date for the wedding soon."

I picked my words carefully. "I think the holdup is they are trying to figure out how to have the wedding they want, yet still please everyone."

"They will never get married if they try to please everyone," Nora said. "Who are they worried won't be happy with their choices?"

"Honestly, I think you and Donald."

"Us? Why are they worried about us?" She turned to look at me.

"Josh thinks you will be disappointed if they don't get married at the church. Randy would like to get married outside. I made the suggestion that maybe they can have the outdoor wedding yet hold the reception at the church." I looked at Nora, hoping I hadn't pushed the boundaries. The last thing I wanted to do was make her upset with Randy. Nora picked up the plate with the roast on it and carried it to the table.

"Of course, we would love them to get married in the church," she said, "but it is their wedding. They should do what they want." She came back into the kitchen. "The pastor at the church will marry them wherever they want. They don't even have to have the reception at the church if they don't want to."

She opened a cupboard, pulling out a gravy boat, handing it to me. She picked up a couple of bowls, carrying them to the table while I poured the gravy into the boat. She walked back in, looking at me. "I'll talk to Randy about it. The only thing that is disappointing me is that they haven't set a date yet." She filled some glasses with ice, taking them to the table. I followed her with the gravy.

"I think that would be good. She thinks a lot of you and Donald."

"We adore her." Nora smiled.

We sat down at the table, passing food around and talking. Nora asked me how I liked the town.

"I haven't explored it too much yet, but I have a couple of little shops that I found that I adore." Nora nodded, "If you need to do some major shopping you need to go to the city really, but there are some cute boutiques downtown." I told her about the shopping trip Randy, and I took into town.

"I'm still looking for decor for the house. I have a few more things I'm looking for, but the house is really coming along."

"Do you have a nursery started?" Nora asked.

I nodded. "I have several things already, a crib, changing table, stroller, and car seat. I have a few baby clothes. There seems to be a lot left I need to get though."

"Do you know what you are having yet?" Donald asked.

Jacob smiled at me, "Mia Amata is positive it is a girl. We go for the ultrasound this week to find out for sure though."

"Mia Amata, that is so sweet." Nora smiled. "Listen, Mattie, what would you think about you, Randy and I going on another shopping trip soon for the baby? Pick up some of those other things you need?"

"I would love that," I said.

"You have to promise to let me buy some things for the baby. I want to start spoiling her already."

I laughed. "Of course, I promise."

"Great! Make a list of things you need yet; we will make a day of it."

Donald looked at Jacob. "Maybe, when they go shopping, you, Josh, and I can go fishing."

"Sounds good," Jacob said. "The fishing season is going to come to an end before we know it…" We finished our lunch, making plans to go soon. We decided to go in a couple of weeks after we checked with Randy and Josh to find out what works best for them.

When we had finished eating, Donald and Jacob insisted that Nora and I go sit while they cleaned up. I watched Donald, it was easy to see where Jacob learned to be so caring and kind. Nora and I sat down to relax.

"Nora," I said, "I know that Jacob and I haven't known each other very long, that this might seem sudden to you, but I love your son very much. He is so kind, generous, and caring. You have raised him to be a wonderful man."

Nora smiled at me, "I take it that Jacob hasn't shared the story of how Donald and I met, has he?"

"Louisa mentioned something about you being married two weeks after you met. Jacob told me a little bit."

"You met Sal and Louisa! I'm sure they didn't hold much back about you and Jacob, did they?"

Smiling, I said, "No, they were pretty clear they thought Jacob took after you and Donald, love at first sight type thing."

"You don't believe in love like that?"

Looking at Jacob as he joined me on the couch, "I didn't until recently.

Some days I am still on the fence, but then there's Jacob." He smiled, taking my hand.

"I didn't think I did either. Then a friend talked me into going to a dance one night when we were in college, our freshman year. We walked in, there were a couple of men dressed in uniform. They were friends of some of the guys that went to the college. Donald and I locked eyes across the room. He made his way over to me and asked me to dance. I said yes. We were married two weeks later."

"Really two weeks later? You never met before that at all?" I said.

Donald, who had joined his wife, shook his head. "Nope. We got married two weeks later and had one month together before I went to my first deployment overseas." He took Nora's hand. "This poor lady set up our new home and went through our first pregnancy without me. She also got her college degree. I couldn't be prouder."

Nora smiled at him. "Look at us now, we will celebrate our 28th wedding anniversary this year." She turned to look at me. "What you said about Jacob, I thank you for that. He has grown into a wonderful man that we are proud of. It is obvious to us, even though we have only seen the two of you together here today, how much in love the two of you are. I don't care how long you two have known each other, whether it be a day, a week, or years. What matters to me is how happy you both are."

Jacob put his arm around me, pulling me close to him. "Mia Amata makes me very happy. I felt something from her the moment I saw her, I can't wait to spend the rest of my life making her happy."

I smiled at him, "I'm very happy also. I didn't think I could ever feel like this. I thought I would never find anyone like Jacob. I basically dragged my feet the entire way."

We sat, visiting until Jacob looked at his watch. "I hate to be cut this short, but we really need to go."

"What's the hurry," Donald asked, as we stood to leave.

"I'm moving in with Mattie today."

"Need some help?" Donald asked.

"Thanks, but no, I don't have a lot of stuff to move since the house was furnished when I rented it."

Nora and Donald walked us to the door.

Nora took my hands, "I am so happy you came today. You are a wonderful addition to our family." She gave me a hug, then hugged Jacob. Donald gave us both hugs too, then they stood waving at us as we climbed in the truck.

Jacob backed out of the driveway. As we turned onto the road back into town, Jacob reached out, taking my hand. "So what do you think of my parents now?"

I smiled at him, "They are great. I really like them."

"They adore you."

"They were so accepting of me and the baby. They are calling her their grandchild," I said amazed. "Does that surprise you?" Jacob asked.

"Yes. For total strangers to be so accepting, welcoming us into their family after just minutes of meeting us, I've never had that before." I thought about it. "I met some when I was younger that showed me most people are decent, but to accept me like that without a second thought…" I grew quiet, lost in thought.

Jacob squeezed my hand, "Are you OK?"

I smiled at him, "Yes. I just got tired, that's all."

"I'll take you home, so you can take a nap while I go get my stuff."

"Are you sure?" I asked, "I could go with you to help."

"No, you should get some rest. It won't take much to get my stuff in the truck. I should be home by supper time."

"Home." I smiled at him.

He smiled back. "I can't wait," he said.

"Me neither." We drove the rest of the way to my house, soon to be ours, in silence, content to just be together. We got to the house; he pulled the truck to a stop. "Do you want me to come in with you?" I leaned over and kissed him. "No, it's fine. Go get your things, hurry back."

"I love you," he said, kissing me again.

"I love you too." I got out of the pickup and went inside. I let Lucky out for a few minutes while I went to change into Jacob's T-shirt, I laid claim to it which he did not mind at all. I let Lucky back in, then went to lie down. I really was tired.

I lay there thinking about how I was lying to Jacob. I did love him, but the thought that I couldn't tell him the truth about my past made me feel sick to my stomach. I agreed to marry him, even though it would never be a legal marriage. How could I go through it? It just didn't seem fair to him. I thought about what would happen if Allen found me, especially if he found out that I was living with another man.

I believed he would kill us both without hesitation, he had threatened to for years. If I was smart, I would pack up and leave. I knew I loved Jacob too much to live without him. I fell asleep finally, but it was a fitful sleep, dreams of Allen and the beatings ran rampant through my head. The beatings in my dreams slowly turned into the last one where he hit my face.

I ran from him. I was running toward Jacob. As I got closer to Jacob, I could hear Allen behind me yelling at me, threatening to kill me. Just before I could reach Jacob, I heard a gunshot and saw Jacob fall to the ground.

I got to Jacob's side and saw the blood coming from the gunshot wound in his chest. "No!" I screamed. Just then Allen grabbed me from behind and said in my ear, "I told you what I would do if you ever left me."

"No!" I cried out again, trying to fight him off.

"Mia!" Jacob said. "Wake up, honey. It's me." My eyes flew open as I cried out again. Jacob had a hold of my arms trying to wake me up. "Mia Amata, it's me." I stopped struggling against him, letting out a sob. Jacob pulled me into his arms, holding me against his chest as I sobbed uncontrollably. "It was just a dream," he said. "You are OK."

"Oh, Jacob," I cried throwing my arms around his neck.

"Shhh," he said, pulling me onto his lap. "It's OK, I'm here." He held me until I finally was able to stop sobbing. "That must have been some dream," he said. "Do you want to tell me about it?"

"I don't remember all of it. What I do remember was awful," I said. "I dreamed that someone shot you in front of me. You were dead."

"I'm fine, Mia. I'm right here," he said. "It was just a dream." I knew he was right, but I also knew it could become a reality. I wiped my tears, sitting back.

"You have perfect timing, as usual," I said. He wiped some final tears from my face, looking at me with concern. "I was carrying a box in the front door when I heard you scream. Scared the hell out of me."

"I'm sorry," I said.

"You don't need to apologize for having a bad dream," he replied. "Are you sure you're OK?"

"Yes, I'm fine," I said as I got out of bed. "I'll go throw some supper on while you bring your things in." I started to walk past him when he reached out, gently grabbing my arm. I stopped, looking at him.

"You're sure you're OK? You were so scared when I was trying to wake you up. I'm worried about you." I could see the concern in his eyes.

I leaned over and kissed him. "Yes, I'm sure. You are right. It was just a dream. Most of it is fading away already."

I hated lying to him, but I had no choice. I went out of the bedroom with him following behind me. I went into the kitchen, and he picked up the box that he dropped when he heard me scream. He took it back to the bedroom. I pulled things out of the fridge, figuring I would throw some burgers on the grill for us.

Leaving the door open, I went outside, starting the grill. Lucky ran down into the yard, barking at a squirrel sitting on a low branch in a tree. I smiled as I watched him for a few minutes, then went inside to get the burgers ready.

Jacob carried in a few more boxes, taking them all back to the bedroom. I carried the burgers outside, putting them on the grill. I checked on Lucky, he decided he had enough of the squirrel, running back up to the house to check on me. We went back inside while I set the table. Jacob came out of the bedroom.

"That's it. I'll have to unpack, but all my stuff is here."

"That's great," I said. "Supper is almost ready. I hope burgers are OK."

"Sounds good," he said. "What can I do to help?"

"Would you go flip the burgers for me?" I asked.

"Sure." I handed him the utensils as he went out to the deck. Lucky followed him out again, probably to look for the squirrel again. I watched as Jacob flipped the burgers and then picked up Lucky's ball, going down the steps to the yard to play with Lucky. I finished setting the table, then took a platter out to the grill for the burgers.

Setting the platter down, I checked the burgers. They needed a few more minutes, so I shut the grill and walked over to the deck rail. I smiled as I watched Lucky and Jacob playing around in the backyard. Jacob and Lucky joined me on the deck. I turned; Jacob took me into his arms.

"You look so sexy," he said, kissing me.

I laughed, "I do? In a T-shirt?"

"In anything. Or nothing." He smiled at me. He kissed me again.

"Our burgers will burn," I said. He groaned, letting go of me. I laughed and went to the grill, pulling the burgers off.

After we had eaten and cleaned up, we spent the rest of the evening unpacking Jacob's belongings and putting them away. Or at least Jacob put them away. I just kept him company at his assistance. I assured him I wouldn't break, but he refused to hear it, insisting that I should just relax and let him take care of everything. It didn't take him long to get everything tucked away where it belonged, taking the flattened boxes out to the garage.

I heard Jacob come back down the hallway where he stopped. He opened the linen closet door, I assumed to get a towel for a shower. The door closed; Jacob continued his way into the bedroom. "Mattie?" I looked up at him to find he had my backpack in one hand and my envelope of cash in the other. "What's this?"

Thinking fast, I decided to go with part of the truth. "That is what I guess you could call my 'go bag'."

"A 'go bag'? Why do you have a 'go bag'? I don't understand."

"It's nothing, Jacob. Growing up like I did, going from foster home to foster home, you learn to keep your bag partially packed with important things. That way you can grab it in a hurry. I guess I put it there out of habit." I smiled at him, "Really, Jacob, I've always had one."

"Oh, Mia," he walks over to sit on the bed next to me. "I'm sorry you had to live like that, but you don't need to anymore."

I nodded, "I know. I've been trying to work my way up to taking the money to the bank to put it in my account. Now that I have my own home, a place I can stay, I think I can get rid of it soon."

Jacob put the money back in the bag, zipping it shut. "I hope you feel safe here like you don't need to run anymore."

Answering 100% truthfully this time, "I'm beginning to, Jacob, it will just take time, but I'm getting there. I know that I was in one place for several years, but for some reason, I didn't feel safe. Maybe because I was renting the house it didn't feel like I was safe."

"I hate that you lived that way." He reached out to stroke my face. "You are safe, Mia Amata, I'm here with you."

I smiled, leaning over and kissing him. "I just need some time. I think it will take a little while to get completely past that feeling that I may have to run because I have had the feeling my entire life. I hope you can understand that be patient with me please."

Kissing me back, "Of course, just remember I'm here for you Mia. I am a bit nervous about having that much cash in the house though.”

“I’ll take it to the bank soon, I promise.”

Chapter 21

We spent the next few days adjusting to each other's normal routines, which did not take much since we had been spending most of our time together anyway. Thursday came. We got up preparing to go to my doctor's appointment together. We were both excited to have the ultrasound to find out whether the baby was a girl or a boy. Once we got to the doctor's office, I checked in. Then we took a seat in the waiting room. There were other couples in there. I realized that they probably thought that Jacob was the father of my baby. I discovered for some reason that didn't bother me as much as I thought it would.

We were soon called back by the nurse, who took my vitals and got us situated into a room. It wasn't long until the doctor entered.

"Hi, Mattie," she said. Then turned to Jacob. "You must be the lucky father."

Before I could say anything, Jacob replied, "Yes. I'm Jacob, Mattie's fiancé." I looked at Jacob in surprise, but he looked at me and smiled.

"Well, it's nice to meet you. How have you been feeling Mattie?" After asking some questions and doing an examination, Dr. Lee said, "Everything seems to be going well. Let's use the ultrasound machine to take a look at the baby."

She got the ultrasound set up and then arranged my clothes. She put the gel on my abdomen and used the wand to locate the baby. It didn't take long for the ultrasound machine to show pictures of the baby. "There's the baby. Heartbeat is good and strong. I'll take a few measurements now to make sure the baby's growth is on target."

Jacob was looking at the screen in amazement. He squeezed my hand, "Look at our baby. That is amazing."

"Baby's growth is right on schedule for a delivery date of February 27." Dr. Lee said. "Do you want to know the sex?"

"Yes," we both said at the same time.

Dr. Lee smiled, "Let me be the first to congratulate you on your baby girl."

Jacob looked at me, "You were right, we are having a daughter." He leaned over and gave me a kiss. Dr. Lee put away the machine after having printed out some pictures for us, telling us she wanted to see us again in a month. On the way out, we stopped at the reception desk to make the next appointment, then were soon on our way.

Jacob drove home, talking all the way about how amazing that was. He looked at me and said, "I hope you don't mind that I said I was the father."

I smiled, "It surprised me, but there is no one I would rather have as the father to my baby."

"I already feel like this is my baby, I love her like my own." He had tears in his eyes.

"How did I get so lucky to meet you?" I said.

"I'm the lucky one," Jacob said. We pulled into the driveway; I was surprised to see vehicles parked in our driveway. Jacob laughed. "Looks like everyone couldn't wait to learn the sex of the baby." He parked the truck, we went through the house to the back deck where we found Randy, Donald, and Nora sitting there waiting. Jacob and I walked to the rail, turning to face them.

"Hey, everyone," I said.

Jacob said, "What's up?" Everyone looked at us in exasperation.

Randy said, "Well, don't keep us in suspense! Is the baby a boy or a girl?" She looked at me. I looked at Jacob.

"Go ahead," I said.

Jacob looked at his family, "Mia and I are having a daughter. Her due date is February 27."

Nora clapped her hands, "Exactly what you thought! I'm so happy for both of you!"

I sat down between Nora and Randy, and the three of us talked baby while Donald got up and walked over to talk to Jacob. I told them that I had been working on the list of things I needed to buy for the baby when we made our shopping trip to the city. Nora and Randy looked at each other, something passing between them that I missed.

"About that," Randy said. "Would you mind if we made it the weekend after next? Josh and I had plans already." I was disappointed to put it off, but I told them that would be fine.

Nora said, "In the meantime, why don't you text us copies of your list, so if we see something on your list, we can pick it up." I told them I would send them the list that evening after I went through it again to make sure I didn't miss something.

Donald turned to Nora, "We had better get going, I have a meeting this afternoon." Nora stood up. Both Donald and Nora gave me a hug and then hugged Jacob. "We are both thrilled for you." They gave Randy hugs and left.

Jacob said, "I need to run to the office for a couple hours, do you mind?"

"Not at all." I had taken the day off. He gave me a kiss, going inside to change clothes. I looked at Randy. "Do you need to run off too?"

She shook her head. "No. My boss is on vacation. She left today and won't be back for two weeks. I'll go in now and then to do paperwork and check messages. The receptionist is working short hours too. When the boss goes on vacation, I have an easy job."

"Great, can you stick around? Maybe help me in the nursery? If you want to that is?" I asked her.

"I'd love to! I can help you finish your baby shopping list too if you would like. Oh, by the way, Nora and I talked about the wedding. She said you told her that the main holdup was we didn't want to upset anyone."

I nodded, "I hope I didn't overstep."

"No, I'm glad you said something to her. We had a really good talk. Josh and I will sit down this weekend to make some plans."

"Speaking of which, stay here, I'll be right back." I got up and went into the house. Jacob was just coming out of the bedroom, dressed in uniform, ready to go to work. He took me in his arms, "I can't tell you how much I would rather stay here with you all day."

"Um… I do like seeing you in uniform," I said, smiling at him.

"Don't tempt me, I won't be able to leave."

I laughed, "Randy is still here." He glanced out the window.

"Tonight then," he kissed me and left for work. I grabbed a book off the shelf and took it back outside.

Sitting back down next to Randy, I handed her the book. "I meant to gift wrap this for you, sorry about that."

"A wedding planner! I have been thinking about getting one. Thank you! This will be very helpful."

"You're welcome," I replied.

"I have a ton of ideas in my head, this will help eliminate the outrageous ideas, bringing to light the ones that will really make the wedding great." We thumbed through it together, discussed different aspects of the book, and tossed around some ideas. Pretty soon we decided we were hungry and went for some lunch. The rest of the afternoon we spent in the nursery and the playroom down in the basement cleaning, putting things away. We finished the list of things I needed and talked about decor for the nursery, now that we knew for sure we were having a baby girl.

"I really don't want everything pink. I just want pastel colors. I was thinking of a baby wild animal theme. I have seen some really cute things out there with baby animals on it."

Randy smiled, "I think Jacob would like that theme also."

I smiled back, "I think so too. You know, he told Dr. Lee that he is the father's baby today."

Randy raised her eyebrows, "He did? How did that make you feel?"

"Oh, Randy," I sighed. "I wish he was the biological father, but I am happy that he feels this baby is his in all the ways that matter." We sat down in the living room.

"Have you two talked about getting married yet?"

"No," I said. "Still wrapping my mind around the fact, he is living here, that we are engaged. Everything has happened so fast."

She nodded. "I understand. Something to consider though, if you get married before the baby is born, the birth certificate will show you as a married couple with the baby having his name. I did a little research and found out that if you two are married, then Jacob will be the baby's legal father."

"Really?" I said.

"Yes, I hope you don't mind my researching it, but I was curious how it would work out. If you wait to get married, Jacob may have to adopt the baby to make it legal."

I thought about it for a few minutes. I knew that our marriage would not be legal. I wanted Jacob to be the father of my baby so badly though, what Randy was saying was very appealing to me. I don't know what would happen if I was found out, but having Jacob's name on the birth certificate would make me so happy. "I don't know, Randy. I don't want to take anything away from your wedding."

Randy smiled, "Please don't worry about that. Our wedding will still be special, as will yours. You still don't look convinced, what else is going through your head?"

I laughed. "Well, I personally love the idea, but what if Jacob isn't ready yet?"

"Ready for what?" Jacob said as he came through the front door. He walked over and gave me a kiss and then sat down. I looked at Randy.

"Now is as good a time as any to talk to him about it. I'll leave the two of you alone." She gave us a quick hug and left.

"What's going on," he said looking at me.

"Well, Randy did some research. She found out that if you and I were married before the baby was born, you would be the baby's legal father." I watched him take in what I said.

"How do you feel about that?" he asked.

"I would love it," I replied, which was the truth. I felt awful to continue to lie to him, I just wanted to make him happy and protect the baby. "What about you? That's asking a lot of you."

"I told you; I already feel like this baby is my daughter. I'd marry you tomorrow if you would agree to it. I say we do it, the sooner the better!"

"Really?" I said.

"Really. Let's look at the calendar right now to pick a date."

"Wow, when you set your mind to something, you run with it don't you?" I said, laughing.

"Yes, I do. I can't wait for you to become Mrs. Jacob Vance." He stood up, "Wait, what about Josh and Randy—will they be OK with us getting married before they do?"

"Randy said they would."

"Great, come on then!" He pulled me up off the couch, we grabbed a calendar, taking it to the table along with a notebook and pen.

"So when would you like to get married?" Jacob asked.

"Before I get too fat. I don't want to waddle down the aisle," I said, laughing.

"So before January?" he asked.

"Definitely. I really don't want to get married with a ton of snow on the ground either," I said thoughtfully.

"So not in December or late November."

"That doesn't leave us much time!" I said, looking at the calendar.

"Nope," Jacob said, "October it is. Weddings usually happen on Saturdays, so which Saturday in October would you like to become Mrs. Vance?"

Looking at the calendar again, "October 28th."

"October 28 it is! We have a wedding date!" We looked at each other and then started laughing.

"Now what?" I asked.

He thought about it for a few minutes. "We need to tell the family. Let's make reservations for Saturday night, invite them all." I hadn't met his sister, Janet, and her husband, Jack yet.

"OK. I'll make the reservations; you call your family." When that was done, we sat back down at the table. "I'm thinking I'll ask Randy to be my bridesmaid."

Jacob nodded, "Obvious choice. I'll ask Josh. Now, where should we get married?"

I thought for a few minutes, "How about here? The backyard is gorgeous overlooking the lake."

"Perfect," he said. "Are you OK with the pastor marrying us?" I nodded. I had met him on a couple of occasions when I went to church with Jacob and his family.

"What's next?" he asked.

"The reception. Since it will just be a small wedding anyway, we can do it here. I can cook something."

"I will agree to the reception here, but I'd like to have it catered. I don't want you to work that day. It is your day. Catering for the small group won't be bad."

I agreed. "I'll ask Randy to help me with the decorations, there won't be too many. Oh, what about clothes? I don't think you guys need to wear tuxes, but it would be nice if you were dressed nice."

"If you want us in tuxes, we will wear them," Jacob said.

"No, I think dress shirts and ties would be enough," I replied.

"What about you?"

"Me?" I said. "Um… maternity clothes I guess." I shrugged. Jacob rolled his eyes. "What?" I said.

"I'm not expecting you to buy an expensive wedding gown, but I think you can find something in a wedding dress if you look around."

"You want me in a wedding dress? With my baby bump?" He leaned over, kissing me.

"Do I need to show you again how sexy I think you are, baby bump and all?" he asked kissing me again.

"Yes," I whispered, "I think you do." We got up, stumbling our way to the bedroom, leaving a trail of clothes in our wake where he showed me exactly what he thought.

Chapter 22

Saturday was here before I knew it, I found myself getting ready for supper with all of Jacob's family, including his sister, Janet, and her husband, Jack. I wasn't as nervous as I thought I would be, I was more excited to share with them that we wanted to get married in October. I had made reservations for us at a restaurant in town, reserving the smaller party room, so we could have privacy.

Jacob was already dressed, ready to go, waiting for me in the living room. He had let Lucky out, now Lucky was lying on the bedroom floor following me with his eyes as I tried on multiple outfits before settling on a new maternity dress that was off the shoulders. I put on some flats, looking at the end result in the mirror. It was obvious that I was pregnant although not too far along. I sighed. I guess I wouldn't be able to hide it any longer.

"Mia Amata," Jacob called. "We need to leave soon."

"I'm ready." I grabbed my purse as I walked out to the living room. Jacob looked up from the football game on TV he had been watching. He picked up the remote, shutting the TV off. "Well, I guess I can't hide the baby bump anymore." I ran my hands over my belly. I looked at Jacob who hadn't stopped staring at me. "What?" I asked, running my hands through my hair. "Do I have a spot on my nose or something?"

He shook his head, got up, and walked over to me. "You look amazing," he said. He kissed me, wrapping his arms around my waist. My arms curled up around his neck, pulling us closer together. The kiss went on, I could feel his reaction.

He groaned, "How much time do we have?"

"Not enough," I said, pulling away. "We need to go."

"I need a cold shower," he said grumpily. I laughed as we walked out to the car.

Everyone was already at the restaurant when we got there, even though we were right on time. "Are we late?" Jacob murmured to me when we walked in, seeing everyone already there.

"No," I whispered. "They are all early." We greeted everyone, Jacob introduced me to Janet, who was a lot like her brothers but looked like Nora and her husband, Jack. Everyone had a drink already, so we all sat down at the table, except for Jacob.

"Thank you all for joining us tonight on such short notice." All eyes were on him as he continued on. "All of you are aware that I asked Mia… Mattie to marry me. All of you also know that she is pregnant. I already feel that the little girl she is carrying is my daughter 100%."

"Randy brought something to our attention, which I then spoke with a lawyer about. If we are married before the baby is born, then the baby is legally my child. So, with that in mind, we have set a wedding date of October 28th."

The congratulations from around the table were thunderous and full of joy. Jacob took my hand, pulling me up. He motioned for them all to quiet down, then looked at me.

"Thank you, everyone," I said. "I can't tell you what it means to me to have you all accept me and the baby into your family like you have. Randy," I turned toward her, "I was wondering if you would do me the honor of being my maid of honor?"

Randy had tears in her eyes. "It would be MY honor. Thank you."

Jacob looked at Josh, "I need a best man, what do you say Josh?"

Josh stood up and gave Jacob a hug, "My pleasure, as long as you will be mine when we get married."

"Of course," Jacob said, pleased. We all sat down, Jacob and I told them the plans we had for the wedding.

Donald raised his glass, "A toast, to the happy couple. Here's to a long happy life together!"

***

The next week went by in a flurry of activity. We both worked during the day and then worked on wedding plans at night. When the following Saturday came, I told Jacob I was going into town. "Want me to come along?" he asked.

"I have an appointment this morning to try on some wedding dresses. If you want to meet me for lunch afterward that would be nice. Then you can go with me to pick out some decorations for the wedding. I might need your help.”

“Sure, sounds good.” I gave him a kiss, then headed into town for my appointment.

I was the only one in the bridal shop when I got there. I was greeted warmly by a stately, older woman.

“You must be Mattie! My name is Karen. Is anybody joining you today?”

“No, it will be just me. I want my dress to be a surprise to everyone.”

“Wonderful! I do love the older traditions, nowadays a lot of times the groom comes with the bride. What did you have in mind, anything in particular?”

“Well, we are getting married in October. I do have a pretty good idea of what I want. The dress I have in mind is simple, yet elegant. I would like it to have half- or full-length sleeves, V-neck in front, maybe down the back, about knee-length in front, longer in the back.”

Karen listened closely. “I think we have a couple of dresses like that. What are you thinking about the waistline?”

I laughed, “Well, I don’t have much of a waist these days, so I was thinking of a higher waistline.” I ran my hands down my stomach.

“Oh, congratulations! I think I have just the dress for you! Have a seat, I will go grab it along with a couple of others just in case.” I sat down, looking around while I waited. She soon came back out with three dresses in plastic bags. She hung them on some hooks where I would be able to see them.

“I’m saving the best for last,” she said smiling at me. “This first one is not as flowy. It hangs straighter. It has beadwork all over—which you didn’t mention, so I don’t know if you want beadwork or not. It has cap sleeves with the V-neck down the front.”

I studied the dress but shook my head. “No, I don’t think so. I don’t think I want that much beadwork. Seems too fancy for our small wedding.”

“No problem,” she said. She moved the dress to a different hook, pulling a second one forward, taking the plastic off it. “This one is a little closer to what I think you are looking for. It is shorter in the front and longer train in the back. It is strapless though. It has a higher waist, covered in lace.”

“This one is pretty; I do like the lace. It is a contender though not what I really had in mind.” She moved it back in front of the other dress.

“If you would like to try it on you definitely can, but here is the one I think is perfect for you.” She pulled the third one out of the bag.

When I saw it, I caught my breath. It was almost exactly what I had in mind. Karen saw the look on my face and said, "I think we found your dress. Let's go try it on." She helped me try it on, then we went back out in front of the full-length mirrors. I looked at myself in the mirrors, the tears started flowing. Karen said quietly, "You are beautiful. Your fiancé will love to see you in this."

The dress was simple, white with Bishop sleeves, an A-line silhouette, V-neck, made of Chiffon, so it had the flow I was looking for. "It's perfect. Exactly what I was looking for. I'll take it."

We discussed some items to go with the dress, veils, and hair pieces. Then Karen helped me change out of the dress. We went to her office to discuss the details. I asked her for a final fitting the day before the wedding for any quick-fixed things that might need to be done, offering to pay her extra.

"That won't be necessary," Karen said, smiling at me. "I would be happy to do that for you, with a pregnancy it is understandable that we may need to make some last-minute adjustments." We worked out all the details, and I paid the deposit for the dress. "I will order it today; it should get here this coming week sometime. Once it gets here, I will have you come in for the first fitting. Try to bring the shoes you are going to wear with you so that we can use them to judge the length better."

Telling Karen I would bring the shoes, thanking her for all of her help. I headed out for lunch with Jacob.

As we ate our lunch, Jacob tried to get out of me what my wedding dress looked like. I smiled, finally telling him he would just have to wait. He mentioned the pastor would like to meet with us some evening this week, I told him to set it up any time. We would be there. After lunch, we went to some craft stores and flower shops, trying to pick out the right decorations for the wedding. We went with fall colors, those flowers being the easiest to find, plus fall is my favorite season. At one of the flower shops, I ordered my bouquet, along with flowers for Randy, Nora, and Janet.

We made one more stop at our favorite restaurant, discussed the food, and made arrangements for the setup and then later cleanup with them. With the small party, we were having we didn't need servers, but we did pick out some nice plates and silverware to dress things up a bit. We arranged for them to set up a larger table than mine so that we could all sit around it comfortably, Jacob and Josh would move furniture a little to make room for it.

When we finished there, Jacob said, "Anywhere else we need to go today? You look tired."

I smiled at him. "I am tired. I believe we are done for today. We got a lot of things checked off our list for the wedding."

"Good," Jacob replied. "I'll take you back to your car, then follow you home."

It was late afternoon when we finally got back home. I changed clothes into a T-shirt and shorts. Jacob did the same. "You should lay down and take a nap." He said, looking at me, concerned.

I shook my head. "I'd rather just get comfortable on the couch with you. I'll have to make supper soon anyway."

"I like the cuddling on the couch, but how about I fix you supper tonight?" Jacob suggested.

"That sounds great." We sat down on the couch, I snuggled up with my head on his chest, his arm around me, while we watched some football.

"Mia, wake up," Jacob said. "Supper is ready, you should eat." I woke up to find I was lying on the couch covered with a blanket.

I stretched, sitting up. "I fell asleep? I'm so sorry."

Jacob laughed. "Nothing to be sorry about, you needed the rest. But you also need food." He took my hand, helped me up, leading me to the table. I could barely keep my eyes open at the table. I ate a few bites, until Jacob finally said, "OK, come on. Let's tuck you in." He took me back to the bedroom, tucking me into bed. He gave me a kiss, then went back out to the living room. I was asleep before he got out the door of the bedroom.

I slept really well, waking up at 3:30 in the morning. I rolled over, curling up on Jacob's shoulder. His arm automatically went around me. "You OK?" he asked sleepily.

"Yes, I'm fine." I leaned over, kissing him.

"Mm mm," he said, kissing me back. He rolled over, so I was now on my back, kissing me again. His hands roamed my body under my shirt, I groaned, straining up against his hands. "Is this, OK?" he asked, as he kissed me again. "I know you were so tired."

I groaned again, "Don't you dare stop now," I whispered. Afterward, we fell back asleep in each other's arms until Jacob's alarm went off in the morning.

***

The week seemed to go by really quickly. We met with the pastor on Tuesday evening and discussed all the arrangements with him for the ceremony. We worked on decorations as we could, some we made by hand, often Randy would join us to help make them in the evenings. I had a fitting for my wedding dress, which seemed to fit almost perfectly with some room for the baby to grow a little bit. Randy found a dress to wear, the guys picked some shirts, ties, and dress slacks to wear. Everything was coming along nicely for the wedding.

Finally, the weekend came for the shopping trip to the city for Nora, Randy, and me to go buy the remainder of the baby things. Jacob was to drive me to Nora's house, then we would leave from there while the guys went fishing. We walked into Nora's house, where both Jacob and I were surprised to find Nora, Donald, Randy, Josh, Janet, and Jack there. "Surprise!" They all yelled when we walked in.

Turns out they put together a small wedding shower and baby shower for Jacob and me. They had taken the list of things I needed for the baby and went shopping without me. There was only one present for the wedding shower, something they had all gone in together on, a honeymoon cruise to Alaska. I looked at Randy in surprise. She was the only one who knew that one day I would love to take a cruise to Alaska. She smiled at me; I gave her a hug. We had a fantastic time spending the day with family.

***

The day of the wedding arrived quickly. I had continuously argued with myself about going through with the wedding. It would never be legal, but I had a new identity, and that person was not married. It didn't make a lot of sense, but I was trying to make it right in my mind. I would lose Jacob if I told him, I didn't think I could handle that.

I had my final fitting of the wedding dress the day before. Jacob had gone to Josh's the night before the wedding while Randy came to stay with me. The furniture had been rearranged to fit the table we needed, plus all the decorations were ready to go. Nora, Donald, Janet, and Jack arrived Saturday morning to help us decorate. They then took charge of the inside of the house for the reception while Randy and I went to my bedroom to get ready.

Things were pretty much ready for the caterers to bring the food later, so everyone else went back to Nora and Donald's to get dressed for the ceremony. A friend of Randy's came over to do our hair and makeup.

Nora and Donald soon came back, Nora knocked on the bedroom door asking if she could come in. Randy and I were not in our dresses yet. We had some time before we needed to put them on.

Nora had a gift bag in her hand. "Oh, Mattie, you look so pretty."

I smiled, "Thank you."

She gave me a hug before sitting down in the chair next to the bed. "Randy and I have some gifts for you. First," she said smiling, "you need something blue." She reached into the bag and pulled out a garter with a blue ribbon running through it. We laughed, I told them it was perfect, and I loved it.

Nora then said, "Next is something borrowed." She reached for the bag, pulling out a box. "This is my first anniversary present from Donald." She handed it to me. I opened it to find a beautiful diamond necklace and earring set. It was simple, yet very elegant.

I had tears in my eyes, "Oh, Nora, it is lovely," I said, giving her a hug. "Thank you so much."

Nora hugged me back, "My pleasure," she said.

Randy cleared her throat, and with a sly look on her face, she said, "Now for something new." She reached under the bed, pulling out a box that she handed to me. I opened the box to find a beautiful, lacy bra and panty set.

"Randy!" I said, laughing.

She laughed, "Well, you bought everything you needed, as far as I could tell. I figured this might be the one thing that you hadn't thought of." We all laughed, I commented on how lovely they were, very pretty.

We heard people talking, taking a look at the clock, Nora said, "Well, it's time you ladies get dressed. The ceremony will be starting soon." She left the room to go out with Donald.

Randy looked at me, "Where's the dress? I can't wait to see it!"

"In the nursery closet," I told her. She went to get it, hanging it up, taking the bag off. "Oh, Mattie," She cried, "it is lovely. I can't wait to see you in it."

Smiling, I said, "One second, Randy, I have a gift for you." I gave her a package, "Thank you for standing up with me today."

She had tears in her eyes as she opened the gift. I had given her a bracelet engraved with the saying, "Not sisters by blood but sisters by heart."

"Oh, Mattie!" she cried, "I love it!" She put it on, giving me a hug.

"You better stop crying, you will ruin your makeup."

She wiped her tears, checked her makeup, then turning to me said, "Let's get you in your dress." She helped me get dressed, I turned around for her to see the full effect. "Mattie," She said, "you are so beautiful. Jacob will agree, I am sure." Randy put her dress on, we made some last-minute touches to our hair and makeup. We peeked out the window, everyone was ready. The music then started.

I turned to look at Randy. "Here we go." She smiled at me, picked up her flowers, and headed to the bedroom door.

Randy led the way, meeting Josh at the French doors leading out to the deck. I watched him take her arm in his, escorting her out on the deck. I then started down the hall myself to the doors. I watched as they met Jacob and parted, going to separate sides. The music changed to the song for me to walk out to.

I took a couple deep breaths, then headed out the door. There was no turning back now. I crossed the deck and down the steps to the yard. I followed the path down. I looked at Jacob, he was not only smiling a huge smile, but he had tears in his eyes.

I walked up, joining him in front of the pastor. He took my hands in his, staring into my eyes, smiling at me. I smiled back, not being able to take my eyes off of him either. He looked so handsome.

As the pastor went through the ceremony, it all seemed like a dream. Soon the pastor was asking me if I take Jacob to be my husband if Jacob would take me to be his wife. We both said 'I do' pretty much before he finished asking us, much to the amusement of the onlookers. We were oblivious, still looking at each other. We exchanged rings, soon the pastor pronounced us man and wife. Jacob was kissing me before the pastor had the chance to say, 'You may kiss the bride'. Everyone laughed.

Soon, Josh tapped Jacob on the shoulder, "Hey, we are all still here you know."

Jacob pulled back, grinning sheepishly at everyone. "Um… Sorry everyone," he said.

We turned to his family; they all came up to congratulate us. We made our way up to the house, Jacob holding my hand tightly in his. He leaned over, whispering, "How long will everyone be here?"

I whispered back, "At least an hour or two."

"I don't know if I can wait to be alone with you that long," he groaned. "You are so beautiful in that dress."

"Wait until you see what I have on under it." I smiled wickedly at him.

He groaned again, "You are torturing me." I laughed as we entered the house.

The catered meal was fantastic. We sat around the table talking and laughing. Many toasts were made.

Jacob's hand rarely left my hand or leg under the table the whole time. Soon we heard the caterers come back to clean up, so we all moved out onto the deck.

Jacob whispered in my ear again, "How can we get rid of everyone?"

"Behave," I said. "They will leave soon."

"Not soon enough for me." I elbowed him in the ribs, turning to talk to everyone some more. Pretty soon the caterers had everything cleaned up and left, so the guys moved our furniture back into place. I sat down on the couch, Jacob noticed that I seemed slightly pale. He came over to me kneeling down in front of me.

"Are you OK?" he asked.

I nodded, "Just felt a little light-headed for a moment, I'm fine."

Nora overheard our conversation and made the decision it was time for everyone to go. She herded everyone out the door, but in a manner that made it look like it was their own decision to go. Once Jacob saw the last one out the door, he shut it, locked it, and then came right back to me. He sat next to me, taking my hand.

Seeing the look of concern on his face, "I'm fine. Probably just all the excitement."

"Are you sure?" I nodded, leaning over to kiss him. He held back a little bit, but the more I persisted the more he relaxed.

He pulled back, "Wait a minute, was that an act to get everyone to leave?" he asked.

I laughed. "No, it wasn't although it did work."

He kissed me again, "Yes, it did." We kissed some more. "Did I tell you how beautiful you look?"

I smiled at him, "Yes, many times."

"You take my breath away." He kissed me again, then pulled back again, "If I remember right, you said something about what you have on under that dress?"

"I did." Standing up, I took his hand, leading him to the bedroom. I pushed him to sit down on the bed, then slipped off my dress. I stood in front of him wearing the new bra and panties.

"Oh, Mrs. Vance," he said thickly, "you are beautiful." He pulled me toward him, ran his hands over my belly, kissing it, and then pulled me down on the bed.

We lay on the bed a little while later, breathless, entangled in each other's arms. "What time is it?" I asked.

Jacob looked at the clock and chuckled, "4:30. Why?"

"I was just thinking, it will be a long night so maybe I'll take a nap." I smiled at him.

"Well, Mrs. Vance, you sound like you have some plans for tonight."

"Maybe," I said as I yawned. He leaned over, kissing me gently.

"Get some rest," he said. "We have all night and tomorrow." He covered me with a blanket and then got up.

Sleepily I asked, "Where are you going?"

"I'll be in the living room. I need some ice water, worked up a thirst." I smiled at that and drifted off to sleep.

I slept soundly for about an hour. I woke up rolling over and stretching. I used the restroom, washed up, and then pulled a box out from under the bed. I pulled the negligee I had bought out, slipping it on over my head. I looked in the mirror, liking the way it fit, although the baby bump was showing, it flowed nicely over my body. I smiled to myself, then headed out of the bedroom.

Jacob was sitting on the couch watching TV. "Hi," I said, yawning as I walked past him to the kitchen. I caught a glimpse of Jacob out of the corner of my eye when I passed by him, his eyes widened. He turned, watching me walk by his eyes following me as I got a glass out of the cupboard filling it with ice water. I walked back to where Jacob was sitting on the couch, taking a seat next to him, "What are you watching?" I asked innocently.

"I don't know," he said, still looking at me.

I noticed Lucky, so I stood back up. "Oh, hey Lucky, come on, I'll take you outside." I walked out on the deck, going to the rail to watch Lucky in the yard. Lucky ran down the steps, into the yard playing. I sensed Jacob coming out on the deck behind me. Soon he slipped his arms around me.

He never said a word and started kissing my neck while his hands ran up my stomach to my breasts and then down to my thighs. I groaned, pressing back against him. He groaned in return, picking me up he took me back inside to the couch, leaving the door open for Lucky. He lay down beside me on the couch, kissing me hungrily this time. I responded just as hungrily in return.

***

I later woke up on the couch, with Jacob sleeping next to me, his arm wrapped around me protectively. Trying not to disturb him, I slipped out from under his arm, going into the kitchen. I was starving. I pulled out some things to make a sandwich, deciding I would make Jacob one, leaving it in the refrigerator for him to eat later.

I ate my sandwich, drank a glass of milk, and then put my dishes in the sink to wash later. I walked quietly back to the bedroom, heading into the master bathroom. Running a warm bubble bath, I climbed in, sighing as the warmth relaxed me.

"Mia Amata?" I heard Jacob call a few minutes later.

"In here," I said. He came into the bathroom, sitting on the edge of the tub. "Hey, beautiful," he said.

"Hi. I made you a sandwich, it is in the fridge."

"Thanks, I'm starving." He went out, bringing the sandwich back in the bathroom, sitting back on the edge of the tub. "Did you eat?" he asked.

I nodded, "I was hungry."

"Good, glad you ate something. How do you feel?"

"Truthfully," I said. "I'm exhausted."

He smiled, "Me too. You wore me out. How about I join you in the tub, wash your back for you, we will relax for a little while, then go to bed."

"Sounds like heaven."

He finished his sandwich, getting undressed he climbed in the tub behind me. I laid back against him, sighing. This was the life I had always dreamed about my entire life. A happy marriage with a baby on the way. Closing my eyes, I relaxed while Jacob rubbed his hands up and down my arms. I started to feel really drowsy.

"Hey," Jacob chuckled. "Don't fall asleep in here. I might have trouble

195

getting you out of here when you're all wet."

"Mmmmm," I said.

"Come on, Mia," he said. "Let's get you to bed." We rinsed off and Jacob helped me out of the tub. After drying off, he led me into the bedroom. "I'll be right back," he said. "I'll go lock up the house."

I slipped on a T-shirt and climbed into bed. Jacob was soon back, climbed in behind me, and pulled me back against him. "I love you, Mrs. Vance," he said.

"I love you, Mr. Vance," I said. We soon drifted off to sleep.

***

We woke up late the next morning. Throwing on a T-shirt and shorts, I made a pot of coffee, taking a cup with me out on the deck and let Lucky run around. Jacob joined me a few minutes later with a cup of coffee, handing me a plate with some toast on it. "You need to eat something," he said.

Thanking him, I munched on the toast while we sat there, enjoying the quiet morning. We discussed the trip we were taking tomorrow, and what time we needed to leave to make our airplane in the morning. Jacob took my hand, "You look tired, babe."

"I feel exhausted, like I could sleep a few more hours," I replied.

"How much packing do you need to do?" he asked.

"I'm all packed, just add some last-minute things in the morning, like my toothbrush and stuff."

"Then when you finish eating your toast, I'm going to tuck you back into bed," he said. I started to protest, but he stopped me. "We have a big day tomorrow with the flight, then the start of the cruise. You will have some jet lag probably."

"You need to get some rest today while you can. I'll run Lucky over to Josh and Randy's house this afternoon. Even if you don't sleep, you can lay there, watching TV, just relaxing. I don't want you to get sick or have anything happen to you or our baby."

"OK," I agreed, "if you will relax with me for a little while. We have something to discuss." He looked at me questioningly but didn't ask. At that point, Lucky came running up the steps, ready to go inside to get a drink. We finished our toast and coffee, so we went back inside the house. Jacob wouldn't let me do the dishes, insisting he would do them later. We went back into the bedroom; I lay down on top of the blankets. Jacob covered me up with a little throw. He sat on the bed next to me.

"What do we need to discuss?" he asked, looking a little worried.

"Don't worry," I replied. "I just think it is time we discuss a name for our daughter, don't you?"

He smiled, "Yes, it probably is time. Do you have any thoughts as to what you would like to name her?"

I do." I looked at him. "After I met you, I came up with a name that has stuck with me. I've tried to think of other names, but I keep coming back to it."

"Sounds like it was meant to be. What is it?"

"Jayden Lee," I replied.

Jacob looked thoughtful, trying it out himself. "Jayden Lee."

"I wanted to name her after you. Jayden is close to Jacob and, well…"

"Lee is my middle name. Are you sure?" he asked.

"Only if you like it. If you don't, we can discuss some other names," I said, watching him.

"Jayden Lee Vance. I love it. I feel honored that you want her to be named after me."

"How could I not want to name her after you? You have accepted her as your own. She should be named after her father." Jacob's eyes welled up; he pulled me close to him.

His voice was hoarse as he said, "Thank you for making me a father, for letting me love you and our little girl." He ran his hand over my belly. His timing was perfect, at that very moment Jayden Lee kicked.

He pulled back, his eyes wide with amazement. "Was that what I think it was?" he asked.

"Yes, it was our daughter," I said, smiling. "I think she approves of her name." As if voicing her agreement, she kicked again.

"Hey, there little girl," Jacob said, rubbing my belly.

Chapter 23

Allen never did accept that his wife, Megan, died in the car accident. He refused to believe it until he saw her dead body in a coffin. That was the only way she could leave him, dead. Oh, he played the part of the grieving widower and took an extended leave from work. His coworkers thought he was mourning, he let them believe it. Told them he might even take a small trip to get away from things for a little while. What he was really doing was looking for his wife.

Allen had been a police officer for 10 years, the last 6 of those spent as a homicide detective. In those years, he made relationships that helped him be highly successful in his job but weren't necessarily sanctioned by the department. He was reaching out to some of those contacts in his search. He looked for information on the thief first, to see if he had done anything like kidnapping in the past. All the reports he had on this guy showed he was a petty thief, taking Megan's car was the biggest thing he ever tried to pull off.

His arrest record showed most shoplifting of alcohol and cigarettes, or small items he could pawn easily for money. What little family he had left said he had a problem with alcohol and had been homeless at the time of the accident. Allen didn't think that this petty thief had the brains or even the desire to kidnap anyone. Allen also didn't find anybody that the thief hung around with that had the brains or would even think about kidnapping someone.

Allen's next step was to reach out to a computer hacker that he knew. This was a kid that he could have arrested for a crime but didn't. The kid was so grateful that in return he would help Allen with cases when he needed him. Grateful or scared, since Allen still held the evidence that would put the hacker away. Either way, Allen didn't care as long as he got the help he wanted when he needed it.

He took his laptop to the kid, telling him he wanted a program that automatically searched the web for keywords or even pictures that were similar to one of Megan. It took him a couple days to figure it out and work out the details. A program looking for keywords was easy, but pictures took a little bit more work. He finally got it up and running, setting it up to run constantly, sending alerts to Allen on leads that he would check out, either eliminate or investigate further. In the few months, since Megan's disappearance, he had investigated almost 50 photos that were close to Megan but turned out not to be her.

During this time, he also gathered equipment he would need when he found her. Night vision goggles, weapons, dark clothing, untraceable smartphones, rope, duct tape, gloves, Army MREs, tent, sleeping bag, cash, and whatever else he thought that he would need. He purchased a car with cash, parking it in a storage unit in the next town over. Everything he needed was already packed in the trunk of that car. He was ready to go on a minute's notice when he found her.

If she was still alive, he would find her, then he would make her pay. He really had believed that she would come back to him on her own, couldn't believe that she didn't. Stupid bitch. She was his, and she knew it. He would never let her go.

The morning that Megan/Mattie left with her new husband on her honeymoon to Alaska, Allen was in his basement looking at a wall that he had covered with maps and photos. His computer was on the desk behind him running the program as normal. Drinking a cup of coffee, he searched the wall looking for the next clue he needed. His computer dinged behind him, another hit from the web search. He took a sip of his coffee as he sat down to check out this one, probably another dead end, but he researched them all.

He pulled up the information. It was a small wedding announcement from a small town newspaper over 1,700 miles away for Mattie Austin and Jacob Vance. He read the announcement in anger. This couldn't be his Megan, she wouldn't be that stupid. At the bottom of the column was a picture of the bride and groom, not a professional photo but one that someone took from their cell phone of the happy couple after the wedding.

The woman in the photo didn't look like Megan at first. Short dark hair and a small tattoo behind her ear, he almost dismissed it. Then he looked at the report produced by the program. It compared all sorts of points and took measurements of ears, the nose, the distance between the eyes, and things that couldn't be changed with makeup or hair color. The report claimed there was a 97% possibility that this was Megan. He cropped and enlarged the picture of her, then printed it. He looked closely at the picture on the computer while it was printing. He looked at her eyes in the blown-up version, and he knew. It was Megan.

He stared at her, gripping his coffee cup. Not only had she left him, but she married someone else, illegally! He stood up, pacing back and forth. She couldn't legally marry; she was still his wife. Mattie Austin? He looked at the photo on the computer again, then clicked back to the one with her new husband. Jacob Vance.

This man was with Allen's wife. He was touching her. Making love to her. He'd kill both of them. He threw his coffee cup hard against the far wall of his office, which shattered when it hit. He paced for a while longer, trying to calm down. He had work to do.

He grabbed the photo from the printer, tacking it to the wall behind his desk. He sat down at the computer, reading the announcement again. According to it, the happy couple went on a honeymoon to Alaska. He clenched his fists. He pulled up the newspaper the announcement had come from and grabbed a pad of paper and a pen.

He started writing down notes. Mattie Austin. Jacob Vance. He added the name of the newspaper, researched it, finding the name of the town it was from. He pulled up Google Maps, plotting out how to get there from where he was. He printed that map, also saving it to his favorites, so he could pull it up in the car. He then grabbed his cell phone and dialed a number. He waited a few minutes, then someone answered.

"It's me," he said. "I need an address." He listened, "Jacob Vance, lives in a town called Moose Lake, Minnesota." He listened a couple minutes longer, then picked up the pen and wrote an address down on the pad. "Thanks," he said and hung up.

He leaned back in his chair, tapping the pen on the paper. He thought for a couple minutes, then printed the announcement including the picture of Megan with her new husband. He put the map, announcement, and pictures in the folder. He grabbed his briefcase, putting the folder in it with the pad of paper and pen. He turned off his laptop, putting it in the briefcase also.

He pulled a set of keys out of his pocket, unlocking the bottom drawer where he pulled out a large envelope. From there, he took out a set of car keys, which he put in his pocket, a smartphone that was untraceable. He took his other cell phone, placing it in the drawer after he shut it off. He put the envelope in the briefcase. The last thing he pulled out of the drawer was a pistol in a holster.

He unsnapped the holster, pulling the gun out. It was a Glock G-series 9 mm, smaller than what he carried as a detective, only about 4 inches tall, 6 inches long. The serial number had been filed off, so it was untraceable. He reached back down into the drawer, pulling out two extra magazines and extra rounds. Each magazine only held six rounds, so he took extra, but he knew he would only need two.

He put the extra magazines and box in the briefcase. He examined the gun, ejected the magazine, put it back in, and then put the gun back in the holster. He put the gun in the briefcase for now, he had some traveling to do before he would need it. He had larger weapons waiting for him in the storage unit. He shut the briefcase and headed up the stairs. He grabbed his jacket and headed out to his car, locking up the house behind him.

Driving to the next town, he turned into a set of buildings containing storage units. He drove slowly through the property, there was no one else around. His unit was one of the last ones on the lot. He unlocked the padlock, pulling up on the door, sliding it open to reveal a car. He took the keys out of his pocket, popping the trunk.

He double-checked that everything he needed was in there before closing the trunk. He backed the car out of the unit and then drove the other car in. He grabbed the briefcase off the front seat. Once he was back outside the unit, he closed the door, replacing the padlock to lock it back up.

He glanced around again, there was still no one around. He climbed into the car and placed the briefcase on the seat, and started to leave the property. He knew the guy that owned this set of storage units had fake security cameras set up, so there should be no one that saw one car drive in and another drive out.

He pulled up the map he had saved and then started heading down the road. The trip would take him around 27 hours. He knew Megan/Mattie and her so-called husband wouldn't be back until next week, so while he wasn't in a hurry he did want to get there before they got back, so he could case the town, their house, come up with a solid plan. He was going to take his time and watch their routine for a while. He wanted to make her suffer. He had all the time in the world.

He drove for several hours, finally stopping for the night at a small roadside motel. It wasn't much, but the room was clean, and I had a shower. He slept soundly, getting up the next morning at dawn. After a shower, I went to a small diner next door, eating a huge breakfast. Soon afterward, he was back on the highway.

He made a phone call. "Hello?" a man said.

"I need some information," Allen said.

There was a pause at the other end. "What kind?"

"I need to know what you can tell me about Moose Lake, Minnesota."

"Taking a vacation?" the man asked.

"Maybe. Just get me the information and send it to my email. I also need information on a Jacob Vance."

"I'll send it later today." Allen hung up.

The email the man would send it to was not traceable to him, the same as the laptop he brought with him.

He would review the information on Moose Lake when he stopped for the night. He figured he would drive a good nine hours today and another nine tomorrow. He drove seven yesterday so that should put him about an hour away from Moose Lake.

He drove all day, stopping only to eat and fuel up the car. He finally stopped for the night at another roadside hotel. Once in his room, he took his laptop out. The email was there, so he reviewed the information for Moose Lake. He took his time, memorizing all the ways into and out of the town, checked out the local businesses, looked for local police and emergency services and anything that he felt would be useful to know.

He then pulled up Google Maps and put in the address of where Megan lived. He wrote notes, there was only one way to her house by road. He would have to rule out that it would be too obvious and easy for him to be caught. He checked out behind her house. It appeared that her house had access to a lake. That may be his way in.

He explored the shores of the lake. There were only a couple of houses on the same side of the lake as Megan's. There was an access road at the south end of the lake that led to a boat ramp, then traveled a little further to a small camping area. From there, it looked like forest land the rest of the way around until it came to the first house. This could be just what he was looking for.

He studied the area more. If he could figure out where to hide his car, he could hike around the lake directly across from Megan's house. With the right scope or binoculars, he could probably see her house, the lake was not that big. He had both in the trunk. There were a couple of things he would need that he did not have. He grabbed the paper and pen, making a small shopping list. He figured he could stop in the Twin Cities to pick up what he needed from a sports shop there.

Once he thought that he had the basics of a plan started, he pulled up the file on Jacob Vance. He learned all about Jacob's family and their ties to the community. The best plan was for him to not let himself be seen in the community at all. He couldn't risk being seen by Jacob or his family, let alone Megan, or Mattie as she called herself these days. Bitch.

I'll teach her a lesson. She and her young new husband. The more he read, the more incensed he grew. *This guy is holding MY wife*, he thought. He was doing things with MY wife that he had no right to do. Who the hell did he think he was? Seeing my wife with no clothes on, touching her body. I own her. She was mine; he had no right to her.

He finished making notes on Jacob Vance and his family. He threw the pad and paper aside and picked up the picture of his wife, the way she looks now. He studied the picture in detail. She looked like a tramp with a short, dark hairstyle and tattoo. She was wearing earrings and makeup.

I would have to teach her more than one lesson, he thought. If she refused to learn, well he would deal with that too. He went from the thought of killing her outright to dragging her home where she belonged. He would make that final decision when he did some reconnaissance.

He grabbed his cell phone and made another call. "Yeah?" a voice on the other end said.

"I need the blueprints to a house in Moose Lake, Minnesota."

"By when?"

"Yesterday," Allen said. He gave him the address of Megan's house and hung up.

He put his stuff away, shutting everything off, to get some sleep. This time sleep didn't come as easily as it did the night before. Every time he closed his eyes, he had images of Megan in bed with Jacob. He got up, pacing the room. He thought about what he would do to Megan when he got her alone, away from her so-called husband.

He would take possession of her again, show her just who she belongs to.

He started imagining the things that he would do to her, to the body that belonged to him. He grabbed his jacket and headed out the door to the local bar.

He sat in a booth toward the back, where he could observe everyone in the bar. The waitress came over to him, taking his drink order. As she walked back to the bar to give his order to the bartender, he watched her. She brought his drink back. As she sat it down on the table, he said, "How about you join me, I'll buy you a drink."

"I'm off in an hour, how about then," She smiled at him.

"Sure," he said. He watched her wait on others, bringing him a couple more drinks while he waited. Finally, she got off work, sitting down with him. "I've never seen you here before," she said.

"Just passing through," he replied as they ordered some drinks. He was leaning back in his chair, "What's your name?"

"Mya," she said. "You?"

"Jacob," he said.

"Where ya headed?" she asked.

"Twin Cities. Visit a buddy up there." The waitress brought them their drinks.

"Do you always have drinks with complete strangers?" he asked.

She blushed, "No."

He looked at her, then pointedly looked at her breasts. It was obvious she had no bra on. He looked back at her eyes. She had watched his eyes roam, blushing even more. He slid around the booth to sit next to her. They were pretty much hidden from the rest of the bar. "Yeah?" he said. "Must be my lucky night."

He put his hand on her waist, running it up under her T-shirt to her breasts. He was watching her face. She closed her eyes, her breathing catching in her throat. He fondled her like that and then slid his hand down to her thigh and up under her short skirt. He slid his fingers into her panties and then inside of her. She groaned, putting her hand over his.

"Let's get out of here." He stood up, threw some money on the table, and headed to the door. He knew she was following him. They always did. They climbed into his car. He started the car and said, "Take your panties off."

She did; he slid his hand back up her skirt. She moaned, straining against his hand. When they parked at the hotel, he got out of the car leaving her behind. She got out, following him to his room. He locked the door behind her, came up behind her, pushed her over the side of the bed, and took her like that.

She spent the night with him. He got up early, leaving before she woke up. He felt better, having worked out some frustrations with the waitress. He had gotten a little rough with her, but not enough that he worried she would go to the cops. It was obvious that she enjoyed herself.

He made his stop in the Twin Cities, picking up the rest of the things he needed. He continued traveling north, stopping in Harris, Minnesota at a gas station to fill up. He knew he was about an hour away from Moose Lake. By the time he got there, it would be dark; it would be perfect to start the next leg of his journey. When he got close, he slowed down, looking for the turnoff to the boat ramp.

He found it easily, turning onto the gravel road from the highway. He shut his lights off, the moon was almost full, so he thought he could see the road without them. Pretty soon, he came up to the boat ramp. Continuing past it, he found the campground, closed at this time of the year, just as he had figured. Just past the campground, around the curve of the lake, the road was chained off with a no entrance sign on it.

Climbing out of his car, he unhooked the chain, drove in, then hooked the chain back up. A close look around showed that there was nothing around him. He drove slowly along the road that was turning into a two-lane path. The weeds were overgrown, showing that no one had traveled on this road for a long time, probably years. He found that he was able to follow it around to where he actually wanted to end up.

At the end, there was an old cabin. This was getting better and better. He pulled the car around the back of the cabin to hide it from view. He got out of the car and walked around to the trunk. Grabbing the night vision goggles and a flashlight, even though he didn't think he would need them, he walked around the side of the cabin to the front. He was in a heavily wooded area, but with the moonlight, he didn't need either the goggles or the flashlight.

The front door has an old, rusted padlock on the door. This was yet another huge break for him. He figured he would be using the tent he had packed, but if this cabin was in any shape at all it would offer a better shelter, especially since it could snow any day now. He went back to the car, grabbing a pry bar. He used it to pry the lock off the door, which wasn't too difficult.

The rust was just more evidence that no one had been here for years. Opening the cabin door slowly, he turned the flashlight on to make sure there were no wild animals in there. Not seeing or hearing any, he went inside. It was a one-room cabin, with a small fireplace on one end. Amazingly enough, there was little evidence that any animals, besides maybe a few mice, had been inside the cabin.

There was a small table with a stool which made up the only furniture in the room. On the wall opposite the fireplace was a platform built into the wall. He looked at it closer and realized it was a sleeping berth.

He tested it, but it still seemed pretty solid. This must have been a hunter's cabin years ago, exactly what he was going to use it for. He made a few trips out to the car to carry in his supplies. Placing his sleeping bag on the berth and his camping cookware on the shelf above the fireplace. He put his MREs up there also, along with his case holding the matches.

He took the flashlight, got down on his knees, looking up at the fireplace chimney. It looked like there was a nest of sorts up there. He went out and found a long skinny tree limb. This he put up the chimney until he was able to knock the old nest down. He checked the chimney again, satisfied it was clear, he went back outside to scrounge for enough wood to keep him warm for the night. Tomorrow during daylight, he would get some better firewood.

He built a fire using the old nest as tinder, soon he had a small blaze going. He took some old rags from the car, taping them over the windows to hide any light, even though the windows were small and wouldn't show much. After an MRE for supper, he took his phone and lay on the bed. He reviewed the email with the blueprints for Megan's house until he was positive, he could walk through there blindfolded.

He shut his phone off to save battery although he could charge it in his car when it got low. He didn't think he would need it much though.

Surveying the interior of the cabin, he couldn't believe his luck at finding it. This would serve him quite nicely, better than the tent he brought, even though he had a small propane heater that would have kept him warm in the tent. He could use the heater during the day in the cabin when he wanted to be careful of smoke from the fireplace. He changed his clothes and climbed into his sleeping bag.

Tomorrow, he would work on preparations for keeping himself alive this winter, if he had time, he would walk to the lake to start some reconnaissance.

He fell asleep in no time, sleeping soundly once again, only waking up a couple of times to check on the fire in the fireplace.

Chapter 24

Allen woke up at dawn out of habit. The fire was out in the fireplace, the cabin still seemed warm. He wanted to make sure that he didn't have a fire in the daytime, as the smoke might attract attention to the cabin. All the dirt and dust lying around was even more proof that no one had been here for years.

After he dressed, he grabbed his axe and then headed out for firewood. He found several downed trees; he worked on one that he was able to cut up into firewood. He was glad that he had more he could chop up if he needed it this winter. He stacked some firewood inside the cabin next to the fireplace, and some more outside the cabin, near the front door. He gathered a lot of tinder, stacking that next to the firewood inside the cabin.

Satisfied with the work he had accomplished so far that morning, he took his water system along with his binoculars, deciding to make his way to the lake. The road into the cabin had turned west at some point, away from the lake. When he stepped outside the cabin, he took a good look around, deciding that he was completely hidden, no one would be able to see him there. The only thing he really had to worry about would be smoke from the fireplace since there were no other cabins or homes on this side of the lake. It would be an obvious sign that someone was over here, someone would be sure to come look for the source.

Heading east to the lake, he examined the forest until he found what he thought was an overgrown path, so he decided to follow that. It was a bit of a hike through overgrown brush, but soon enough he found himself at the lake. There was quite a bit of brush at the shoreline, but he found a spot where he could build a sort of blind. Below that was an area where he could draw some water when needed. It was a place where the shore went out a little, if he cleared enough brush, he should be able to stay hidden as he filled his water jug. He would grab his machete later to clear the path a little to make it easier to travel back and forth, plus work on the blind.

He filled his water system from the lake, setting it aside. It would purify the water, but then he would also boil it that night to make it even safer to drink. He saved some bottles from his trip; he would reuse those to keep his water supply in. Clearing out some brush from below a tree, he sat down. He took out his binoculars, searching across the lake.

He started from the north end, counting houses until he settled in Megan's house. He noticed that there was a pier, a beach, and some open yard, leading up to a firepit area, then up to the back deck. He knew there was a walk-out basement, he was able to see the doors under the deck. He raised the binoculars, checking out the French doors over the deck. The side of the house had huge windows facing the lake. He would definitely be able to see inside the house if the curtains were open.

Following the house to the right or south, there were even more huge windows looking into what he knew was the master bedroom from his study of the blueprints. The house was dark, as he knew it would be. He still had a couple of days before the happy couple got home from their honeymoon. Tonight, he would check out the house, on the inside. He studied the houses on either side, not seeing much that concerned him. He thought he had seen enough for the time being, taking his water he headed back to the cabin.

After a quick lunch, he worked on clearing the path to make it easier and quicker to make the trip to and from the lake. He then packed a small backpack with things he would need that night. He packed his night vision goggles, a flashlight, his Bowie knife along with a smaller knife, and gloves, lying out the small Glock. He took the small two-person raft, getting it ready with the oar. He would inflate the raft at the water's edge. When he had made all the provisions for the night, he lay down to take a rest, knowing he would wake up at whatever time he told himself to.

Allen woke up well-rested, ready for his night-time excursion. He ate supper, tucked the pistol into his waistband on his back, threw the pack on, and then grabbed the raft and oar. He walked to the lake, pulled out the night vision goggles, and did a quick survey of the lake and shoreline. He didn't see anything worrisome, so he inflated the raft, putting it in the water.

Quietly, he started to paddle across the lake. He kept scanning the shoreline with the goggles, but he saw nothing. He made it across the lake in what seemed like no time at all. Pulling the raft up under the pier he tied it up. Using the goggles, he explored the backyard leading up to the house. He stealthily made his way up to the house, to the basement doors.

He looked the doors over well, noting that the bitch had a security system that was armed. He needed to figure out a way past that. He couldn't go in this door; he would have to be careful because it was hooked to a video system. If he went in this door, probably the front and the one on the deck, he would be caught on video. He would have to find a window that was not being monitored by the alarm system.

He crept around the side of the house, checking the windows as he went. The only one that seemed to not be monitored would be the hardest for him to climb in, the one over the kitchen sink. He examined the window closely. The window was a single-hung window. All he needed to do was to insert something between the sashes and open the latch. Then he should be able to open the window from the outside.

Pulling out his small knife, he popped the screen out, then slid the knife between the sashes. Very carefully, he slid the knife over to the latch, pushing until he finally was able to unlock the window. He then pushed up carefully on the window, sliding it open. He put his knife away, looking in the window. He would have to be careful climbing in.

He knelt down, taking off his shoes and socks. He didn't want to leave shoe marks on the outside of the house, his socks would not offer him any traction on the siding of the house. He put both in his backpack, then hoisted himself up into the window, being very careful not to scuff surfaces as he went. He crawled through the window, over the sink, then jumped down to the floor.

Once inside the house, he placed his backpack on the kitchen floor and listened for a few minutes. Hearing nothing, he turned to the basement door. He paused long enough to pull his socks on, leaving the shoes in his backpack, not wanting to leave footprints or shoeprints in the house. The moon was still bright, and with the amount of windows in the house, he felt he should be able to see fine without the goggles or the flashlight, but he did take them both with him. He opened the basement door, making his way down the stairs.

At the bottom of the stairs, he found himself in some kind of office. He walked over to a desk, sat down, opened drawers, and thumbed through the contents. He found nothing of interest. He turned his attention to the filing cabinet, trying the drawers. He found that they were all locked, and he hadn't seen any keys in any of the desk drawers. He could force the locks open easily enough, but he didn't want to leave any evidence that he was there. He would come back to this later if needed.

Looking around the rest of the basement, he noticed the other side of the basement looked like a child's playroom. That didn't make a lot of sense to him unless maybe she was running a small daycare. That definitely would make sense, she would have to make a living somehow. She certainly didn't have any useful skills or knowledge that would help her get a decent job outside the home.

Figuring that was probably what was going on down here, he turned his attention to the doors going outside, taking a closer look at the alarm system that she had hooked up to them. He was able to rewire her system so that these doors were no longer hooked to the alarm but would still appear to be. She could disarm and arm the alarm all she wanted, but this set of doors would remain unarmed at all times.

Pretty soon, Allen headed back up the stairs, closing the kitchen window, now that he would be able to go out the basement doors when he left. He went into the garage next, but looking around he didn't see much that alarmed him. There were only a few items that someone could grab as weapons, but he could take care of that when the time came. Going back into the house, he made his way through the living room, checking out the first door he came to, a bathroom. Walking past that, he looked into the smaller of the two bedrooms. This appeared to be a nursery, but he figured it was just part of her daycare, so he didn't give it a second thought.

He went into the master bedroom last of all. The first thing he saw was the king-sized bed. He was instantly enraged. This is where she betrays him with another man. Bitch! He took a few minutes to calm down, trying to keep his head about him.

Looking around, he decided there was really not much here of value. The only thing he did find was that the closet would offer a great hiding place should he need it. It was a walk-in closet, there was one corner where he could hide pretty easily, even if someone walked in. Upon opening a few drawers, he found himself getting enraged again at the sexy panties and bras he was finding. *Slut!* he thought.

He would teach her a lesson when he got his hands on her. Making his way back through the house, he did not find anything else of interest, so he concentrated on memorizing the layout of the furniture, so he could find his way around in the dark. Pretty soon, he grabbed his bag from the kitchen floor, took a look around to make sure that he didn't leave any evidence he had been there and then headed down to the basement. He walked out the basement door, shutting it behind him, stopping for a moment to put his shoes back on. He worked his way back around to the kitchen window that he had climbed in, replacing the screen that he had popped out. Looking over the window, he didn't see any evidence of his climb into the house.

Allen then headed back down to the pier. He climbed onto his raft and headed back across the lake. Making it to his takeout spot, he pulled his raft out, carrying it back to the cabin. He hung the raft on the side of the cabin, leaning the oar against the side of the cabin.

Once inside, he changed clothes and started a fire. Grabbing his notepad once the fire was going, he made notes while everything was still fresh in his mind. After finishing his notes, he lay down in bed, thinking about what his next step would be. He had a lot of plans to make.

***

Allen woke up the next morning, still trying to work out his plan in his head, he needed to get all the details figured out soon. Sitting up, he knew one thing that he needed to do for sure. He needed to be able to stop her or her husband from calling the cops if given a chance. He picked up his cell phone and made another call.

"Hello?" a man said.

"I need you to bring me something."

"What and where?" came the reply.

Allen told the man what exactly he needed, stating that he wanted it as soon as possible. The man on the other end stated he could actually meet him later that same day with the items he needed once he found out approximately where Allen was located. After setting the time and place, the call ended. Allen got up, warming up some water over what remained of his fire. He washed up and got dressed. The meeting place was a pretty good hike from where he was hiding out, so he got started as soon as he could.

Making it to the meeting place, a little before his contract was supposed to arrive, he surveyed the area to make sure they wouldn't be spotted. His contact was someone he helped escape arrest in Nevada, who had moved to Minnesota to hide out. Allen hid in the trees a few hundred feet from the actual meeting spot to wait for him to arrive.

When the contact arrived, Allen watched as he got out of the car, leaning against it while he lit a cigarette. Allen watched him for a few minutes from the trees, then made his way silently up to the man. Pulling out his pistol, another Glock but this time a .45 caliber, he placed the gun against the man's head. The man stiffened.

"Hey," Allen said. The man didn't say anything. "Did you bring what I needed?" The man nodded, motioning to the backseat. Allen glanced in the window, seeing a box sitting on the back seat. "Get it out for me, slowly." The man opened the back door to his car, pulling out the box. "Hand it to me." The man did, saying, "Listen, man, I don't have anything against you. Take the box and go. I won't say anything to anybody. I mean, what could I tell anyone?"

"You could tell them I am in the state," Allen replied.

"I wouldn't do that," the man whined. "I came here to start over. I am only here tonight because you asked me to."

"If you tell anyone I was here, I will kill you," Allen said.

The man continued to beg Allen, promising him he would never tell. Allen hit him in the back of the head with his pistol, knocking the man to the ground, unconscious. He couldn't risk the guy seeing which direction he headed. Allen felt for a pulse, making sure the man was still alive.

Grabbing the box, he took off to the trees, heading back to his hideout in the woods. He was pretty confident that the man would not reveal to anyone that Allen was in Minnesota. Once back to the cabin, he examined the package the man brought him. He found exactly what he needed in the package, making plans to go back to the house later the same night to put his plan into motion.

Following almost the same routine he had the night before, with the exception of going in through the basement door, instead of the kitchen window, Allen placed the devices from the package his contact had given him earlier throughout the house. He placed one device in the basement under the desk. The next one he placed in the living room behind the TV over the fireplace, the last one in the master bedroom on the back of the headboard. He ran a test of all three devices, pleased to find they worked perfectly.

Having finished what he needed to; he went back to the cabin. He was exhausted from the long day, soon falling asleep. The next few days Allen spent preparing for winter and Megan—or Mattie's—return. He checked over the outside of the cabin, looking for areas where the winter snow or wind would be able to invade the cabin or other possible problems. He made a few minor repairs, trying to winterize the cabin the best he could.

He knew the cabin wouldn't be an ideal home for the entire winter, but he didn't plan to be there that long. It just had to be livable for a couple of months, by then he would have his revenge on his wife. Allen also worked on a sort of blind by the lake, one that would offer some protection from the cold, but would also hide him from view. He needed to be able to observe Megan's house to learn everything he could about her daily routine. Then he should be able to pick the right time to make his move.

Chapter 25

We had a fantastic time on the cruise. Jacob was amazing, attentive, caring, and making sure that I got the rest I needed, but he also made sure that I got to see whales, dolphins, grizzly bears, and even a moose. As much fun as I had on the trip, it felt good to get back home. I was a little surprised to find out how much I really missed Lucky; he was happy to see us. Josh and Randy had been watching him for us, he never ran away once—until the day I got home. I found him sitting at the back door waiting to be let in the day we got back home.

"How does he know you're home?" Jacob asked, amazed. I couldn't explain it. I was just happy to see him again. Soon we fell back into our routine where he followed me everywhere I went. We came back home to see the first snow of the season; I thought it was beautiful.

I had never seen snow before, I loved it. Jacob was amused by my excitement over it, and we went for some walks in the snow. Lucky loved to romp and play in the snow too. Jacob warned me I would tire of it when there were a few feet of snow on the ground, but I didn't think I would.

We had the rest of the following week off to rest, needing to get a few things done before we went back to work. I worked on catching up on laundry while Jacob made sure the house was ready for the winter. We also started our Saturday night routine with Josh and Randy again, supper at one or the other's house, maybe playing a game or two or watching a movie, sometimes we would go out to eat and then catch a movie.

Soon enough, we were both back to work, Lucky keeping busy by following me around the house, keeping me company while I worked. Most mornings Randy would trek through the woods bringing Lady over to see Lucky. We would enjoy our morning coffee together, but instead of being out on the deck, we would sit at the table. Randy and Josh's wedding plans were coming along, and some mornings, Randy and I spent discussing choices for food or looking at dress choices.

On other mornings, we looked at cute baby clothes we found online, sometimes not being able to resist temptation, we would order an outfit or two. Then when they arrived, we would talk about how adorable they were. Jayden's closet was filling up with cute clothes of varying sizes. We were having a lot of fun shopping for the baby. I often kidded Randy that she and Josh needed to have a baby soon so that Jayden had a little playmate. It was obvious that Randy wanted to start a family soon.

***

My job was going really well, I really enjoyed the work that I was doing. Jacob's job was also going extremely well. In fact, Jacob was offered a promotion with a substantial raise. He was hesitant to accept it because it would require him to travel for training and conferences. We discussed the new opportunity for him at length, going back and forth over the pros and cons. "I don't know, Mattie," he said one night. "I have worked so hard for this promotion, but I'm not sure I want it now."

"Why not? You deserve this promotion; you should take it."

"If I take it, I have to travel even after the training is over and attend conferences. We just got married, I'm not sure I want to leave you alone. Especially once the baby is born."

"How long at a time would you be gone?" I asked.

"At the most, it would be two weeks," he replied.

"That's not very long at all. The baby and I will be fine. Josh and Randy are close, or at least Randy is when Josh is away. Your parents are close too. Maybe some trips we can go with you."

He got up and walked to the French doors and looked out. "I suppose you're right. It just doesn't feel right to just get married and then start traveling."

I walked up to him and put my arms around him. "This job means a lot to you. The baby and I are not going anywhere. We will be here every time you get back."

Jacob turned and took me in his arms. "I know. The job does mean a lot, I've wanted this for as long as I can remember. I've worked hard for it. Not only that, but the raise will be great for our family. You would be able to quit your job or cut back on hours if you decided you wanted to, not that I have a problem with your working, but it would be a possibility if you decided to."

"I like my job and would like to continue, at least for now. Who knows what I will want to do after the baby is born? But I don't care about the money, Jacob, I want you to take the promotion because you earned it because you want it."

"Are you sure?" he asked, looking at me intently.

"Yes, I am sure," I said.

He thought about it for a few minutes, then said, "I will take it on one condition."

"Oh? What's that?" I asked.

"I'll take it, but if you promise me that if my being gone is causing an issue with us—if you become unhappy with my being gone, you have to tell me. I'll make a change back or to a different position."

"I promise," I said. "But if you are happy, then I'll be happy."

"Then I'll do it. I'll tell them tomorrow."

"Perfect!" I said. "Let's celebrate!"

He smiled, "What do you have in mind?" I just smiled and kissed him.

***

Across the lake, Allen was sitting in his blind with his binoculars. He saw the dog, and that was unexpected. He would have never allowed Megan to have a dog. After watching the dog's behavior for a while, Allen decided he was not going to worry about it, it was more of a playful puppy than a guard dog. He could take care of it easily enough if he had to.

He watched Megan and her new husband go for walks in the snow hand-in-hand. The more he saw of them together, the more his rage grew. Oh, how he was going to make her pay for humiliating him, cheating on him. She was his, and he warned her what would happen if she ever tried to leave him. With the drapes open, he could see through the French doors into the house, could see them kissing, see them walk toward the bedroom.

He couldn't let his rage get the better of him. He needed to remain calm, so he could watch their routines. Once he had their daily routines down, then he could work out the remaining details of his plan on how to exact his revenge. He sat in the blind daily, there in the mornings before they woke up, staying until the lights went out at night. For a couple of nights, he stayed all night instead of during the day, watching to see if they let the dog out at night, which they did routinely twice a night like clockwork.

He made note of those times: what time her new husband left for work in the mornings and what time Megan got up. Every day she went downstairs, spending most of the day in the basement. The deck stairs and posts hindered his view of what she was doing down there, but he never saw any evidence of children running around. It was winter out, so maybe they stayed indoors. He wished he could see what she did down there.

He never saw her let in any kids upstairs so maybe she wasn't running a daycare after all. He needed to figure out what she did down there every day, but as long as she was alone it probably wouldn't make much difference. In fact, that might be the best place for his plan to be put into action. The basement was a walk-out with no windows except for the ones facing the lake. He remembered that there was a closet down there next to the small bathroom which would offer him perfect cover.

The main problem that he had was her so-called husband. He went to work every day but sometimes came home during the day for lunch or came home from work early. On other days, he worked late. It appeared that he really did not have any set hours. He was always dressed in some type of uniform too. He wasn't a police officer, it looked more like he was a game warden. That means he probably has a gun.

He would have looked for where he kept that when they were gone had he known. It was probably in the closet in the master bedroom. If Allen had the chance, he would make sure to find it, so he could take care of it before the husband could grab it for self-defense.

He also took notes of everything of importance about the Saturday night get-togethers they had with the other couple. Allen noted that the woman walked over a lot in the mornings, would have coffee with Megan then leave. He tracked her progress through the trees where he could and watched her head up to the house north of Megan's. Allen didn't think this would be too big of a problem for him, he could be in and out of Megan's house before the couple or the woman alone came back.

He also made notes about an older couple that stopped by often. Other than that, they didn't seem to get much company. That would be helpful for his planning. Megan seemed to have a pretty set schedule. It was the guy she was living with who was unpredictable, who might be the problem.

He had originally hoped to do this before the lake froze over, but he was beginning to think that would be possible. He would have to wait for the lake to freeze solid, then make his crossing over on the ice. That could create more problems for him, but he would deal with those when the time came.

Chapter 26

November went by quickly. Jacob took the promotion, with his training set to start in December. Even though I was not looking forward to his being away, I knew he was happy with the new position, so I encouraged him. My job was going well, I received my first raise. My supervisor commented on how impressed she was with my work that I seemed able to adapt to whatever they assigned me to work on.

Thanksgiving we spent the day at Nora and Donald's with the whole family. Nora prepared the turkey, and Randy, Janet, and I each prepared dishes and brought them over. The table had turkey, mashed potatoes, gravy, stuffing, sweet potatoes, green bean casseroles, a corn casserole, rolls, pumpkin pie, and pecan pie—so much food the men groaned about how much they ate but declared it one of the best Thanksgiving meals they ever had. Before we all sat down to enjoy our meal together though, we took the same meal including a whole turkey that we had fixed to the local homeless shelter. We had purposely doubled everything we cooked so the shelter could feed the homeless, this was a family tradition for Jacob's family, one that I was happy to assist with. The rest of the day was filled with good food, football, and card playing.

November was also when Randy and Josh finally set their wedding date, September 14th, so wedding plans were in full swing. Randy asked me to be her matron of honor, wanting Jayden to be her flower girl. After much discussion, they decided they wanted to get married on the family island.

Nora and Donald had been wanting to make improvements for a few years now on the island, in fact had some ideas on exactly what they wanted to do. Now was the perfect time to set those plans in motion. Josh and Jacob drew up plans for a large gazebo to place by the pond in the clearing. There were some other things that would need to be done, build a new pier on the island, make the path to the pond nicer, clean up the area, and do some landscaping.

Nora and Donald began looking for a contractor who could build a small cabin out there for them. They also purchased a pontoon that would arrive in the spring, they would use it for transporting building materials and then the wedding party. Donald had a good friend who was a contractor who would start the building off-site and then transport everything to the island to finish the building there.

It would be an off-grid home, with one bedroom with a small kitchen, a living area, and a loft area that would make up another sleeping area. It would be insulated with a fireplace, so it could be used even in the winter. A well would be drilled, so there would be running water. Donald kept the contractor on track, he would even go help him work on things on the weekends. The plans were coming along great, it looked like everything should be ready for the wedding in September.

December brought Jacob's first trip for training. He would be gone for a week. Josh did not travel much during the winter; he was working some jobs close to home. Jacob asked him to help clear any snow, and both Josh and Randy promised him they would be available should I need help with anything. Nora and Donald also promised him they would be happy to help out should I need anything. Even with all their encouragement, and mine, he was hesitant to go.

"I just hate the thought of leaving you here by yourself."

"Jacob," I said for about the tenth time that day. "I will be fine. You have everyone at my beck and call should I need them. Besides, we will talk every night and text throughout the day as able."

"I know," He sighed. He rubbed my enlarging belly, promptly being rewarded with a kick. He smiled. "See? She agrees," I laughed. "We will be fine."

"OK, OK. I'm going." Picking up his bag, he gave me a kiss and left.

I looked down at Lucky, "Well, Lucky," I said scratching behind his ears. "It's just you and me for a whole week." He barked, wagging his tail. "What should we do today?" He went to the kitchen and stood in front of the refrigerator, barking at me. Laughing, I walked into the kitchen. "You are just like Jacob, encouraging me to eat. You both take such good care of me." He barked again. "All right, all right! I'll eat some lunch." Making myself a sandwich, I sat on the couch to watch some TV.

***

From Allen's blind, he watched as Jacob walked out the door carrying what appeared to be a suitcase. This made him sit up straighter, wondering what was going on. Was lover boy going away on a trip? It appeared like he was, shutting the door leaving Megan alone. Allen wondered how long he would be gone if he should make his move now.

He looked at the lake, it wasn't completely frozen, still had open water. He thought he could cross it with his raft tonight after dark without much problem, check things out. He wasn't sure now was the right time, he needed more information. He wasn't quite ready to start his plan in action, but he was close. He felt like he needed a little more time, but if Megan's new guy was going to be gone, he could step things up.

He spent the day watching the house. Jacob did not return. Megan shut all the lights off and went to bed, alone. After waiting for a few hours, Allen took the raft and headed out across the lake. He had to break what ice there was as he went along, it was a little more difficult than he had anticipated, but he made it. This would definitely be the last time he crossed until there was ice.

This time, instead of heading to the pier, he landed on the south side of the beach near the trees. He didn't want to risk leaving footprints in the snow, so he went through the trees, which was rather difficult, there was no set trail to follow. When he finally made it even with the back of the house, he found a downed branch with some leaves still on it. Taking it with him, he snuck up to the house. He left the branch leaning up against the house, then bent down to untie his boots.

He quietly slid the sliding door open, stepping inside without his boots on. He slid the door closed behind him and stood silently, listening for a couple of minutes. He heard nothing. He activated the devices he had placed in the house with the remote he brought with him, checking his phone. It worked, blocking the signal to his cell phone. She wouldn't be able to call the police if she found him.

Walking over to her desk, he took out his flashlight and looked around. Laying on the desk was a manila folder with the name of a company on it. He took a picture of it, opened the folder, snapping pictures of all the papers inside. He put the folder back as he had found it, then started opening the drawers on the desk. In the middle of the desk, he found a planner with Megan's daily calendar in it.

He didn't risk reading it all, snapping pictures of the next couple of months instead and then put it back in the drawer. Looking around, he didn't see anything new that would be of interest to him. He wasn't going to risk going upstairs, he thought he had what he needed for now, even though it was hard to fight the temptation to go up and grab her. Allen deactivated the devices, allowing the cell phone to get a signal again. Heading back to the sliding door, he slid it open, he stepped back into his boots.

Sliding the door shut behind him, he grabbed the tree branch and used it to hide his tracks back to the trees. He glanced back over his tracks, deciding by morning she wouldn't be able to see them or any signs he had swept the path. Tossing the branch in the trees, he made his way back down to his raft and then back across the lake to the cabin.

***

As Allen was sliding open the sliding door to the basement downstairs, upstairs Lucky got up and walked to the kitchen. He went to the basement door, sitting a few feet away watching the door intently, growling softly in his throat. He stayed like that until he heard Allen leave, then went to the French doors, watching as Allen made his way through the trees, then back across the lake. Once Allen was out of sight, Lucky went back into the bedroom, lying back down near Mattie. He slept fitfully the rest of the night, keeping his ears tuned to the slightest noise.

In the morning, when Lucky was let outside, he went immediately down to the basement doors, then followed the path Allen had taken to the trees, down through the trees to the water. He followed the scent to the water's edge, looked out over the lake for a couple of minutes, and then went back up to the house. After Lucky was let back in the house, he walked to all the doors that led outside as if checking them to make sure they were locked.

I opened the basement door after I let Lucky back inside to go down to work but forgot my cell phone. I went back to the bedroom to get it, noticing that Lucky didn't follow me as usual. Lucky had run down the stairs to the basement the minute I opened the door. I didn't think much of it, he probably knew I would be down there soon. When I made it down there, Lucky was walking around my desk and sniffing at the floor. Then he went over to the door leading outside and sat there, looking out. All day while I worked, he sat or lay by those doors, facing outside.

223

"What's the matter, Lucky," I said, watching him spend his day looking out the door. "Are you sad the grass is gone for the winter?" Lucky came over to where I was sitting at my desk, lying his head on my leg. I scratched his ears for a couple of minutes while he wagged his tail, then went back over to lie down in front of the door again. I shrugged, thinking he was just having an off day, humans do so why can't a dog?

I finished my work for the day, so Lucky and I headed back up the stairs. I let him outside, watching as he ran straight into the trees. That was unusual for him, he usually romped in the snow for a little bit, then promptly came back in. Maybe he had been watching a squirrel all day and was now trying to find it. I wasn't worried about Lucky running away or getting lost. He always stayed within sight of me or the house.

I went to the kitchen, put on some soup for supper, then set the table with a bowl and spoon. Grabbing some crackers out of the pantry, I went back to the doors, watching Lucky come back up through the trees, up the stairs to the deck, coming to the door. He shook the snow off, and I let him back in.

Ladling up some soup, I sat down to eat. Lucky lay right at my feet. He seemed preoccupied; I really couldn't seem to figure out why. Maybe he missed Jacob and was waiting and watching for him to come home although why he would be watching the back door instead of the front is beyond me. Soon, Lucky got up and walked over to the basement door, and using his nose, he pushed the door until it was almost shut and then pushed it with his front paws to latch it.

Lucky sniffed at the door for a couple of seconds, then came back over to me, once again lying down at my feet again. I watched this with amusement, I normally shut the basement door when I was done down there for the day, but today, I hadn't. He was so smart to know something was out of place and then took care of it himself.

I washed up my supper dishes and then went to lie on the couch. My back was hurting a little bit tonight, so I grabbed a blanket, making myself comfortable. Lucky followed me, lying his head on my belly when I lay down. The baby seemed to respond with a kick, to which Lucky wagged his tail in response. I watched this in amazement.

Every time the baby moved, Lucky would react by wagging his tail or some noise in his throat. I started to believe that Lucky knew exactly what was going on, that there was a baby inside me. Pretty soon the baby quieted down, so

Lucky lay down on the floor next to me.

My cell phone rang about an hour later, I was happy to hear Jacob. "Hi, babe," he said.

"Hi back," I replied.

"How was your day," Jacob asked.

"It was good, work went well. Lucky has seemed off today though, probably just missing you," I replied.

"Off how? Is he sick or something?" Jacob sounded worried.

"No, he stared out the basement doors all day while I worked, then has been lying at my feet tonight. He even shut the basement door when I left it open after work."

"Well," Jacob said. "He has always stayed close to you, maybe with my being gone he is just being more protective."

"Yeah," I mused, "that could be. You should have seen him interacting with the baby tonight. It was extremely interesting."

"Interacting how?" he asked. I told Jacob about the episode when I lay down. "They say dogs are pretty smart and intuitive. He is probably aware that you are carrying a baby so feels protective of her also."

We talked for a while longer, discussing his training that he did that day. Pretty soon we got off the phone, both of us tired and needing to get some rest. I let Lucky outside again, watching as he went straight down to the water's edge, looking out over the lake, staring at some place across the lake that only he could see. I tried to see what he was looking at, maybe an eagle or something, but I saw nothing. Pretty soon Lucky came running back up to the house, so I let him in.

"What's going on Lucky? What did you see out there?" I asked him. He whined, sat down, looking at me. I looked back out across the lake. There seemed to be a quick glint of reflection, but it was gone before I could focus on it. Must have been seeing things. "Come on boy, let's get some sleep." I turned, walking into the bedroom with Lucky at my side.

***

Allen watched the lights go off in the house when Megan went to bed. He had watched the dog tracking his trail through the trees, then sitting at the shore looking across at him. Sure, the dog probably caught his scent, but there was no way the dog could possibly know where he was now. There must have been a reason the dog was staring over toward where Allen was hidden, some bird flying overhead or a deer moving close by.

Just a coincidence had to be. He would have to be careful because when he followed the dog back up to the house, he caught Megan staring across the lake also like she could see something. He knew that wasn't possible, but when he left the blind he checked it over, tightening up the coverings, adding some extra branches to make sure.

Heading back to the cabin, he lit the fire, grabbing something to eat. Sitting down while he ate, he pulled out his cell phone and looked at the pictures from Megan's desk. The folder contained information for a company that did legal transcription for clients. It appears that Megan is working at home for them, some online company.

He looked over all the material, finding nothing there that really interested him. He then looked at the pictures of the planner he had found. It looked like her so-called husband was due back on Saturday. She had a couple appointments the following week, but nothing too interesting.

Until he turned to January. It appeared that she was going to be alone again for a period of two weeks in January. She wrote on her calendar 'Jacob work conference' drawing an arrow covering two weeks.

She had noted his flight information, so Allen knew exactly when he was leaving and coming back. He started to smile. The lake would definitely be completely frozen by then, he had time to put the final touches to his plan. Laying down to sleep, he knew that he finally had a timeline to do things, so he needed to rest up. He wouldn't have to make a trip over to the house again until the day he put his plan into action. Until then, he had some things to do around here though to get ready for Megan. He fell asleep with the plan starting to come together finally.

Chapter 27

The week seemed to pass by slowly, but finally, Jacob came home. I was very glad to see him, I really did miss him while he was gone, but I made sure to downplay exactly how much, so he wouldn't feel guilty that he had gone. I had made lasagna for our supper on Saturday night; as a rule, our Saturday night get-togethers with Randy and Josh were off on a Saturday when one of the guys had been gone for a few days, so it was just Jacob and me. While we were eating, Jacob filled me in about all the training. He was so excited about what he was learning, about the chances his new position was going to give him. Jacob asked me questions about how things had gone around the house, including how my work went for the week.

I told him about Lucky's strange behavior when I let him outside. Lucky had continued running down to the beach every time, looking across the lake, almost like he was watching someone or something. "Probably found a deer trail in the trees, following the scent down to the water." Jacob shrugged. "Probably," I agreed. Lucky also continued his relationship with the baby. "Wait until after supper, I'll show you how Lucky interacts with the baby."

"He is still doing that?" Jacob raised his eyebrows.

I nodded, "He is. It is really cute. It is like they are communicating with each other." I smiled. "Interesting. I know some dogs are protective of babies after they are born, but I have never heard of a relationship like this before they are born." Jacob looked thoughtful. "Lucky must be more in tune with the baby because of his loyalty to you. He is a very smart dog."

I started cleaning up after supper. "He really is. You know, when I watched him sitting down looking across the lake, I swear for a moment or two…" I hesitated, then shook my head. "No, I must have imagined it."

Jacob brought some things off the table to the counter. "You swear what? Did you see anything?" He looked at me intently.

"Well, a couple of times I swear I caught a glint of like a reflection, you know like when the sun hits a window just right? The first time I just figured I imagined it, but I've seen it a couple of times. No one lives across the lake from us, right?"

Jacob shook his head, picked up some more dishes from the table, and carried them to the counter. "No, that side of the lake is all national forest land. Several years ago, they leased some of it out just for hunting, but they stopped that when there was a problem with poachers. I suppose there could be someone hunting illegally over there. Maybe I should check it out."

"I probably just imagined it. Maybe it was some icicle or something. I just thought it was odd it seemed to be exactly at the same time Lucky was staring across the lake."

We let the subject drop, settling down on the couch together. I lay down with my head on Jacob's lap. He watched as Lucky walked up to us, putting his head on my belly. Jacob laid his hand on my side to feel when the baby kicked. The baby would kick, and in return, it seemed, Lucky would wag his tail, making little noises in his throat. This continued until the baby settled down, and then Lucky lay on the floor next to the couch. I looked up at Jacob, he looked amazed. "I've never seen anything like that before. He is communicating with our daughter."

"I wonder if it has been the baby all along," I said.

"What do you mean? That instead of being loyal to you, it has been the baby? How could he have known about it before he could feel the baby kick?" Jacob asked.

"I don't know, but maybe he sensed I was pregnant and is protecting the baby instead of me," I replied.

"I think he would probably protect both of you should he have to. It will be interesting to see their interaction after Jayden is born."

"I agree," I said. "But right now, I have something else on my mind."

He looked down at me, "Oh? What would that be?" I sat up and started to kiss him. "Why Mrs. Vance, are you trying to seduce me?" He said smiling.

"Is it working?" I asked. His answer was to pull me onto his lap where I could tell for myself it was working. I looked at him all innocently, "Well, Mr. Vance, I hope you brought some protection, so I don't get pregnant." He looked at me, immediately starting to laugh. We got up, walking arm-in-arm to the bedroom.

***

Allen saw Megan greet Jacob when he got home from his trip, saw them sitting down to eat a meal together, and then worked together to clean up afterward. She must be getting lazy, he never helped her clean up, that was her job. Men should never do a woman's work. They aren't good for much else, let them do the things they were made for. He also saw the two of them going to bed early.

His rage came back with such intensity he almost lost control. Soon, he thought, very soon my darling Megan, we will be back together again. She would learn Allen was a man of his word, the hard way. He would have plenty of time to make sure she got the message. He went back to the cabin and started to work.

He worked most of the night and slept for a couple of hours. Then, in the morning, he went back to work. He would go to the blind later if he finished his work around the cabin in time, but he really needed to finalize his plan and work out all the exact details. He couldn't afford to make any mistakes. Going around behind the cabin, he checked on the car. It was well-hidden, the current snowfall was helping to hide it even better than he planned.

No one would be able to see it behind the cabin until they were right on it, even then they may not notice it unless they walked smack dab into it. If the snow kept up, it would make the car completely invisible. He went into the cabin, took off his coat, grabbing the shovel. He had some more digging to do. He made several trips from inside the cabin out to the trees, dumping buckets of dirt.

Once he finished with all the digging, he had a little construction work to do. He sawed and hammered the rest of the day, well into the night. Finally, hot and dirty, he surveyed what he had accomplished, immensely pleased with a job he felt was well done. He was exhausted but washed up, ate something, and then finally crawled into his sleeping bag, falling sound asleep within minutes.

In the morning, feeling a little stiff and sore from all the digging and construction he did the day prior, he made his way to his blind to see what the bitch was doing. She and her lover boy apparently slept in, he sat there for quite a while waiting for signs of life. Eventually, Allen could see them moving around. Megan went into the kitchen, appearing to make coffee while Jacob let the dog out.

The dog ran around a little bit then took up its spot on the snow-covered beach, staring across the lake. If Allen didn't know better, he would swear it seemed like the dog was looking right at him, but that was impossible. He didn't know much about dogs and had always hated the things himself, but he doubted a dog could see that far.

He raised the glasses to look in the house and saw the man staring right at him too. Probably just trying to see what the dog was staring at so intently. Allen moved a little bit, adjusting his position in the blind while he watched. It was at that point he saw Jacob raise his hand, shading his eyes, seeming to stare more intently in Allen's direction. Allen froze.

Megan joined him at the door, shading her eyes as well. They had to be looking at a deer or something. He was pretty sure he was well-hidden. He looked back down at the dog to see it turning to run back up to the house. They let it back in, Megan heading back to the kitchen, but her husband continued to stare in Allen's direction with the dog sitting by his side doing the same.

Allen almost wanted to get out of the blind to see if he could figure out what they were looking at, but he knew better. Even though he doubted they could see him if he was standing there, they might catch the motion. The last thing he wanted was to have them looking back in his direction with binoculars of their own.

Allen watched them throughout the day. They left for a couple hours, coming back with a Christmas tree. He could see them putting the tree up, decorating it together, laughing, and having a grand time. He sat out in the blind, barely keeping warm, while the bitch stayed nice and toasty next to a roaring fire drinking cocoa. He had all he could take for the day, so he went back to the cabin.

Digging to the bottom of his supplies, he found the bottle of whiskey he brought with him. Since he had all of his plans finalized, he could relax a little bit. It was too early to start a fire, his smoke would probably still be visible, so he poured a cup of whiskey, reviewing his plans. His plan would work. He had enough information gathered in his weeks of studying Megan and her habits he didn't see what could go wrong with his plan. He sat back, feeling smug, very confident, and proceeded to get drunk on the whiskey.

Chapter 28

Jacob and I decided to host Christmas for his family at our house. The next couple of weeks leading up to Christmas were spent decorating and shopping for gifts. I planned the menu for our Christmas dinner, making a huge trip to the store to buy groceries. We both had the week of Christmas and New Year's off, and then Jacob would have to leave for a conference. He would be flying to Wisconsin for two weeks.

We wanted to spend as much time together as we could before he left, so we took the days off that weren't part of our holiday time. The weekend before Christmas, I spent baking and getting as much prep work done for Christmas dinner as I could. Jacob tried to help, wanting to take some of the workload off of me, but I soon shooed him out of the kitchen and out of my way.

He laughed, "OK! I get it. I'm going to run over to Josh's house. He asked for some help with something." He gave me a kiss as he put his coat on and left. I finally finished all the baking and got everything cleaned up before Jacob was back. When he came in, I was resting on the couch. He was carrying a huge Christmas gift in his arms, setting it on the floor next to the tree. It was so big it wouldn't fit under the tree at all.

"Wow!" I said looking at it. "Someone has been good this year!" He put his coat and boots away and came back to sit by me.

"Smells really great in here," he said.

Motioning to the coffee table in front of us, "I figured you wouldn't be able to wait, so I made some extra for you."

"Mm mm, I love you," he said, through a mouthful of cookies.

I laughed, "So are you going to tell me?"

"Tell you what?" trying to appear innocent, reaching for another cookie.

"Who is the large gift for? Is it for your mom and dad?" I already had a gift under the tree from Jacob, so I really didn't think it would be for me.

"Possibly," he replied. "I'm not going to tell. It will be a surprise, you will have to wait for Christmas to get here, just like everyone else. And don't bother looking for a name tag on it, there isn't one. I'm pretty sure I will remember whose gift it is."

"I would certainly hope so," I said laughing, slapping his hand as he reached for a third cookie. "You are going to ruin your supper!" I exclaimed.

"Maybe, but it will be worth it," he stated as he reached again, leaning past me, managing to grab another one.

"No fair!" I cried. "You're taking advantage of the pregnant lady's inability to move very quickly or reach past her huge belly!"

Jacob laughed and looked at me with a mischievous glint in his eyes, "I'll take advantage of the pregnant lady after she feeds me. I'm starved."

I laughed. We went to the table to eat the soup and fresh bread I made for supper.

"That was fantastic. You could open your own restaurant, you know? You are a fantastic cook!" He leaned back in the chair, patting his stomach.

"You keep eating like you are your belly will be bigger than mine!" I laughed. I started to stand up to clean up after supper.

"Nope, not tonight. Tonight, you go relax on the couch; I will clean up. You look exhausted. I hope you didn't overdo it today." He looked at me with concern.

"Thanks, Hon," I replied. "I am a bit tired. Back is hurting a little bit today." I went over to the couch, lying down, pulling the blanket over me. Before I knew it, I was sound asleep. I woke up about an hour later, stretching. Jacob was sitting on the couch opposite me reading.

"Hey, sleepy," he said, smiling.

"I'm so sorry. I didn't realize how tired I was." I yawned.

"It looks like you are still tired."

Rubbing my eyes, "I'm fine."

He laughed. "Come on, let's tuck you in bed. We have a big day tomorrow." He got up, helping me stand up. After brushing my teeth, I changed into a T-shirt and then walked back into the bedroom. Jacob looked at me. "Oh man," he groaned.

"What?" I asked.

"How is it you make a T-shirt sexy?"

I looked in the mirror at my big belly, "Oh, I'm sexy all right."

"Hey," he said, coming over to me, "I've told you; you are extremely sexy to me." He kissed me. I responded by wrapping my arms around his neck, pulling him closer. "Oh no," he said, pushing me gently away. "As much as I would love to take you to bed right now, you are exhausted. We are going to have a houseful of people tomorrow. You need to get some sleep."

Now it was my turn to groan. He laughed but led me to bed, making sure that I was all tucked in. He leaned over and kissed me. "I love you, Mrs. Vance."

I was already falling asleep, "Love you too." I murmured. I was sound asleep before he got to the door. He shut the light off, glancing back. Lucky was lying at the foot of the bed. "Come on Lucky, let's go," Jacob whispered. Lucky looked at Jacob, then put his head down, staying where he was. Jacob watched Lucky for a little while. When I moved, Lucky moved. Jacob finally left the room, shaking his head in wonder, then went out to watch TV for a little bit.

***

The next morning, I rolled over in bed. Jacob was lying there sleeping. I climbed out of bed quietly; it seemed my new favorite thing to do was go to the bathroom. I headed out to the kitchen to start a pot of coffee. As I was passing the French doors I stopped, looking out.

There was fresh snow overnight, everything looked so pretty, perfect for Christmas Day. As I was looking out, something across the lake caught my eye. There it was again, the glint of reflection that Jacob and I have both seen multiple times. I wouldn't think anything of it, but it was always in one spot, I never saw anything like it from another spot around the lake. It could happen at any time of the day when the sun was out.

Maybe I'll have to ask Jacob if he has a pair of binoculars to check out what is over there. Maybe there is just something metal there that catches the sunlight. That didn't make a lot of sense though because the sun could be in different positions, and we could still see the glint. Shaking it off, I let Lucky out, continuing into the kitchen. I turned on the coffee, then pulled out the cinnamon rolls I made yesterday, putting them in the oven.

Walking back to the door, I looked out at Lucky. He was romping in the snow, but every so often he would stop, staring across the lake. The smell of coffee and cinnamon rolls started to fill the house; I heard Jacob stir in the bedroom. I stood there waiting for Lucky to stop playing around; pretty soon he was at the door, so I let him back in. Jacob came up behind me, putting his arms around me. "Have I told you how sexy you look in my T-shirt?" he asked.

"No, I don't think so," I said thoughtfully.

"Really?" he asked. "Well, how about I show you instead," he said hoarsely as he leaned down, kissing my neck.

I leaned back into him, both of us letting out groans. Turning toward him, I snaked my arms up around his neck. He pressed my back against the glass, I felt the cold against my back. He slipped his hands down, then up under the T-shirt. They roamed over my stomach, up to my breasts.

He slid the T-shirt off over my head, lowering his head to my nipples, teasing them with his teeth while his hands slid down, slipping my panties down my thighs. I stepped out of them, kicking them aside. I slid my hands down his back, pushing his underwear down his thighs also. Jacob knelt in front of me kissing my belly, sliding his hand between my thighs. I moaned loudly. Jacob pulled me down with him, lying on his back. Straddling him, I took him right there.

Afterward, we lay on the floor together, breathing hard and holding each other. "Merry Christmas," I whispered. "I love you."

"Merry Christmas, Mattie," Jacob replied hoarsely. "I love you too."

We continued to lay there like that for a few minutes until the timer went off in the oven. I stood up, throwing the T-shirt back on, ignoring my panties. Jacob rolled over on his side watching me. I pulled the rolls out of the oven, shutting it off. I set the table with plates and coffee cups. I got a platter out, scooped all the cinnamon rolls on it, and then set it on the table, and then I poured us both a cup of coffee. All this time, Jacob just lay there on the hard floor, following me with his eyes.

"What are you doing?" I asked him smiling.

"Enjoying the view," he said, smiling back. I looked at him questioning him with my eyes. His eyes went down the front of me. I followed his eyes but couldn't see past my belly. I ran my hands down the front of my belly, realizing that my big belly pulled the T-shirt up so that I was completely exposed. Laughing, I walked over, grabbing my panties.

I slipped them on, saying, "Come on, let's eat, I'm hungry."

It was at that point the doorbell rang. We looked at each other, both of us surprised that someone was here that early. Jacob quickly put his underwear on, wrapping a blanket from the couch around his waist. I grabbed the other one, wrapping it around me. The doorbell rang again, so Jacob walked over, pulling the door open.

"Merry Christmas!" I hear Josh and Randy yell. They walked past Jacob without noticing he was wrapped in a blanket.

"Wow," Josh said turning to Randy. "I told you she would have…" He stopped speaking as he realized our current state of dress.

Randy slapped Josh on the shoulder. "And I told YOU we shouldn't just show up uninvited!"

Jacob walked over to me, grinning. It was obviously a grin that told them exactly what we had been up to. Jacob points to the table, "Help yourselves. We will just go and, um… get dressed." He led me to the bedroom; we could hear Randy giving Josh the riot act for showing up unannounced. Closing the bedroom door behind us, we burst out laughing.

We quickly showered and dressed, then headed back out to the kitchen. We got ourselves fresh coffee, joining Josh and Randy at the table, where we hungrily grabbed ourselves some cinnamon rolls.

Randy looked at us and cleared her throat a little, "I'm sorry if we interrupted anything. I told him we shouldn't just show up like that."

Before I could reply, Jacob said, "Oh, don't worry about it. We finished about five minutes before you got here." I slapped him on the shoulder as Josh burst out laughing.

"I forget you two are still newlyweds," he laughs.

Jacob said, "Newlyweds has nothing to do with it. I would advise you never to come over unannounced because any chance I get…" He never finished the sentence because I cried out, "Jacob Lee Vance!" He grinned, and we all started laughing. At that moment, the doorbell rang again.

Jacob looked at me, "For crying out loud, has no one respect for the time of day."

Josh looked at Jacob with a wicked grin, "We can't help it if you are a horny bastard!" Randy looked at him in exasperation as we all laughed. Jacob went to the door, to let in Nora, Donald, Janet, and Jack. "What's so funny?" Donald asked when he walked in.

Josh smirked at his little brother, "It seems like Randy and I interrupted something when we got here." Jacob looked at Josh, "And I told you that you didn't interrupt anything."

Josh replied, "Oh, that's right, you had just finished…" He trailed off as his mom flicked him on the ear. "Ow, Mom!"

Jacob laughed, "Can we just stop talking about our sex life? Merry Christmas everyone." Everyone laughed.

Everyone had coffee and homemade cinnamon rolls. Turned out they all figured I would bake them for breakfast, so they invited themselves over. We all took our coffee to the couches and sat down. We sat around, discussing the usual things, the wedding, and everyone asking how I was feeling. At that point, Lucky walked up, placing his head on my belly.

Jacob said quietly, "Hey, watch Lucky." They all watch Lucky respond to the baby's movements until the baby stopped. Then Lucky went to lie down in his dog bed. The room was silent for a few minutes as everyone took in what they had just witnessed. We discussed how Lucky seemed to be really in touch with the baby and probably be the best protector of the baby.

I got up and put the ham I had prepared in the oven and also started the scalloped potatoes. I went back to the couch, and as I sat down, Jacob announced it was time we opened presents. He handed out the first round of gifts, made sure everyone had one, then we took turns guessing what they were and then opening them. Everyone had a great time; all the gifts were very thoughtful. I had given everyone handmade items along with something sentimental that made me think of them when I saw them.

Finally, the only gift left was the big box that Jacob had said would be a surprise. He looked at Josh, nodding at him. Josh stood up, helped Jacob pick up the big box, and then placed it in front of me. I looked at them in surprise. "What is this?" I asked.

Josh smiled, "This is all Jacob." He sat down by Randy again.

Jacob looked at me, "This is for you. Well, it is more for our daughter I should say." I looked at him, then started taking the paper off the box. Opening the top, I let out a gasp. I looked at Jacob, tears starting to stream out of my eyes. It seemed that only Josh knew what was in the box, he, again, helped Jacob pull the item out and move the box aside. They set the gift on the floor next to me where everyone could see it.

"It's beautiful," I cried. Everyone echoed my sentiments. "Did you make it?" I asked Jacob.

He nodded, "Yes, I made it by hand." Sitting on the floor in front of us was a beautiful handmade cradle. On each end was carved a puppy that looked a lot like Lucky. "I love it so much," I said, tears flowing.

I stood up, giving him a hug. "Jayden will love it."

"Oh, I love that name," Nora cried, tears in her eyes also.

Jacob smiled. "Yes, our daughter's name is Jayden Lee Vance."

"That is so perfect!" Randy said.

"How did you decide on the name?" Donald asked.

Jacob looked at me, "It was all Mia's idea."

I smiled at him. "I wanted something rather similar to Jacob, so Jayden seemed like a fit. Then I wanted to name her Lee after her daddy."

"That is so sweet," Janet said.

I left them to discuss the cradle along with our daughter's name while I checked on our dinner. I cleared off our breakfast dishes and loaded the dishwasher and started it. Lucky had followed me to the kitchen and was watching as I moved around the kitchen getting our dinner ready.

"Can I help?" Nora asked, walking into the kitchen.

"Can you set the table for me? Normally I would insist you sit and enjoy visiting with others, but I'm not moving as well as I normally do."

Walking up to me, she smiled, "Do you mind?" she asked, motioning to my belly.

"Not at all," I smiled. She reached out, placing her hand on my belly. Lucky watched closely, ready to jump to my aid should he sense danger.

"She is very active," Nora said, pulling her hand back.

"My insides are black and blue," I laughed. Nora set the table while I finished our dinner. We chatted about the new cradle; I said the blanket I had just recently finished for the baby would look cute in it. "Oh, can I see it?" she asked.

"Sure, it is back in the nursery, hanging over the rail to the crib."

She went back there, walking back out with it. "Oh, Mattie," she cried. "This is lovely!" She showed it around to everyone. "The nursery is adorable," Nora commented.

Everyone went back to see it while Jacob helped me finish up putting dinner on the table.

Later, after everyone had left, Jacob and I cleaned up the kitchen and dining area. I finished loading the dishwasher while he took the trash out to the garage. When the dishwasher was finally running, I went over and sat down on the couch next to the cradle. I ran my hands over it, feeling the smooth wood. I traced the carvings on the end of the puppy. Jacob came back in from the garage, washing his hands, he was watching me at the cradle.

He came over, sitting behind me, "Do you like it?" he asked.

"Oh, Jacob," I replied. "I love it! You did such amazing work. Have you carved anything like this before?"

"No," he replied. "I never felt like I could do this type of work. I can honestly say this was an act of love. I wanted to build something special for our daughter."

I turned to face him. "I don't know what to say, it is perfect."

"We need to get a mattress for it, but I thought we could put it next to our bed, for the first few weeks of her life."

"Yes, it will be nice to have the baby close to us, but yet sleeping in her own bed."

"I was going to carve her name on the ends," he said, reaching out, tracing the puppy with his finger.

"Why didn't you?" I asked.

"Well, I didn't think our son would want to sleep in a cradle with his sister's name on it." He said, smiling at me.

"Our son?"

"Yes, I am hoping to have lots of babies with you."

I laughed, "Lots? How many is that exactly?"

He thought for a moment, "I think five or six would be nice. Eight would be even better, we could have our own football team."

My eyes widened. "Do you mind if I deal with this pregnancy first, before we decide on the next baby?"

He leaned forward, kissing me. "On one condition," he stated.

"Oh?" I asked.

He kissed me again, "We continue to practice for the next one."

"Deal," I whispered.

Chapter 29

Allen spent Christmas Day in the blind, but now he was getting drunk again in the cabin. His rage was out of control tonight. He watched Megan have sex with her 'husband'. He witnessed him putting his hands all over her. He couldn't tear his eyes away from the scene.

He had wanted to charge over there, finish them both right then and there. The only thing that stopped him was the thought that all of his planning would be wasted. He had spent a lot of time getting his plan figured out, making all the arrangements.

He drank whiskey, pacing back and forth in the small cabin. That bitch has to pay. Maybe he would draw out his planned revenge a few days longer than initially expected. He stopped, yes, that is what he would do. He planned on just a day or two, but maybe he could make it last even longer.

She would be begging him to kill her by the time he was through with her. He could add some other forms of suffering to his plan. The thought of her crying, pleading with him excited him. Oh, she would definitely cry and plead. She would promise to do anything to get him to stop.

Without really thinking, he started a fire in the fireplace. Pouring another cup of whiskey, he continued to pace, trying to get the image of his wife on top of another man out of his head. He went outside, pacing around outside, relieved himself in the trees, and then drank even more whiskey. He decided that tonight he would check out the ice on the lake.

It should be solid enough for him to be able to cross the lake on it. He stopped pacing, looking around. His footprints were all over the place. Tomorrow he would find something that could sweep his prints out. Something he can take across the ice with him, help hide his prints leading to and from Megan's place.

He originally planned on using the raft, pulling it across the ice, but he realized that wouldn't work. The ice would tear it, deflating it. He would have to build some sort of sled. He had a few supplies left that he could figure out something with. If he built it right, it would cover any tracks as he pulled it behind him. It would have to be sturdy, yet lightweight, so that with Megan's weight on it he could still easily pull it. Hell, maybe he would make her pull it, like a dog.

He continued to drink, starting the pacing again as he designed the sled in his mind. He went back into the cabin, pouring himself another drink. This time, he took his boots off and lay down on his sleeping berth. He lay there drinking his whiskey, plotting and raging until he finally passed out.

Allen woke in the morning, feeling miserable with a hangover. Making a pot of coffee, he added whiskey to his cup when he drank it. He drew out his plans for the sled he would pull across the lake. Once he had it drawn out, he set off to build it. It didn't take him long to see his idea come to fruition.

It would leave a trail, but there are ice fisherman that will be out on the lake, so if he played it right, the trail he would leave would blend in with their tracks If he gets really lucky, it will be snowing the night he puts the plan into action. That way he could go straight across the lake. If not, he may have to figure out a different pathway. He would have to watch the lake during the day to watch the habits of any ice fisherman.

If he had to pass as one of them, he would have to get on and off at the same point that they did. That wouldn't make his plan impossible, just a little more complicated. He would figure it out. Just a week and a half to make sure that everything is set and ready.

***

Jacob and I had a fantastic time together after Christmas. I only had two more months to go until my due date, so we spent time finishing the nursery. We washed all the baby clothes and blankets; we hung the rest of the decor and the curtains. We put the cradle that Jacob built next to my side of our bed so that Jayden would be close to me. I washed all the bottles and stacked diapers in the cloth hanger.

Finally, we sat down and went through everything to see if there was something we had forgotten. The only thing left was to pack a bag for the hospital. That wouldn't take long, the diaper bag was already packed. I wouldn't need much, so I planned on packing that when Jacob left for the conference. Right now, I want to spend time with him.

We spent a lot of time just sitting together, talking about our future, about Jayden and the children we would like to have in the future. Josh and Randy came over a few times, always announcing when they would come over now. We spent time with them discussing their wedding and helping with plans. Jacob was the best man, I was the matron of honor, so we helped as much as we could. The building of the small cabin and the gazebo were well underway. Nora and Donald were working with a landscaper to make plans for the pond and the clearing around it.

One night when Josh and Randy came over to visit, we had something else to discuss with them. We all sat down on the couches, Jacob shutting the TV off. I looked at Randy and Josh, "We have something we would like to ask you both."

Randy and Josh looked at each other and then at us, the curiosity apparent on their faces. I glanced at Jacob, he smiled at me, encouraging me to continue. "We were hoping that you would be Jayden's godparents," I said.

Randy's eyes instantly teared up. She squealed, jumping up to hug us. "We would be honored," Randy said, as Josh nodded his agreement.

"I'm so thrilled," I said, hugging Randy, then Josh. "After Jacob, there is no one else I would want to take care of my baby if something happened to me." I caught Jacob glancing at me out of the corner of my eye. I hadn't told Jacob that I had seen a lawyer recently and had paperwork drawn up, including a will, to say that if Jacob was unable to raise Jayden, I wanted Josh and Randy, then Janet and Jack, then Nora and Donald after them to raise her. I knew his family already loved Jayden as a member of their family. They would take very good care of her, raising her as one of their own.

We sat, talking about Jayden and her future, having children in general, including the fact that Randy and Josh couldn't wait to start their own family. They were hoping to start one right away after they got married, wanting their first baby to be close in age to Jayden, so they could be close to each other.

We spent a lot of time with Josh and Randy, they were our best friends. We also spent a lot of time with Janet and Jack, even though they lived a little bit further away. Nora and Donald were great. Every weekend we could, we were at their house for a Sunday dinner. Our last Sunday before Jacob went to his conference we went to Nora and Donald's house as usual. After dinner, the guys cleaned up as had become the new tradition. We were sitting around when everything was cleaned up chatting when Donald looked at Nora. "I think now would be a good time to show Jacob and Mattie the project we have been working on."

Nora nodded, "I think so too." Jacob and I looked at each other, trying to figure out what they were talking about. Nora stood up and said, "Come on, follow me."

She led us upstairs to a bedroom that Jacob said used to be his as a kid. Nora motioned for Jacob to open the door. "Mom?" he said, turning to look at her.

She smiled, "Well, go on in." Jacob took my hand, leading me in. They had taken his old bedroom and converted it into a child's bedroom. I looked around amazed.

"I don't know what to say," I stammered.

"Well," Donald said. "We wanted our granddaughter to have her own place whenever she was here and…"

Looking at Nora, "we hoped that she could come to spend some nights here with us once in a while. We are so looking forward to our first grandbaby, we can't wait to spend as much time with her as you will allow."

I turned to them in tears. "I am thrilled that you love her so much already. I want you both to be a huge part of her life. She will love spending time with her grandpa and grandma and will probably want to spend as much time here as she can."

Nora threw her arms around me. I felt like such a part of this family. For the first time in my life, I felt like I really belonged. I just hoped that if my past came out someday, they would find it in their hearts to forgive me and understand.

That night, I drove Jacob to the airport. He was leaving for his conference. I had tears in my eyes as I kissed him goodbye. He looked at me, wiping away my tears. "Remember your promise, if you ever felt my traveling was an issue, you would say so."

I nodded, "It isn't an issue, but I can't help but miss you when you are gone. I love you so much."

He kissed me gently, saying, "I miss you too. I'll be home soon, I promise."

"I know," I said.

I stayed until he made it through security, then made my way back home. Lucky met me at the door. It seemed he could feel my sadness at Jacob's leaving for two weeks. He stayed at my side or at my feet no matter where I went or what I did. I went to soak in the tub for a little bit, then went to bed early. I fell asleep watching TV, with Lucky lying on his blanket on the bed next to me, which he only did when Jacob wasn't home.

***

Waking up in the morning, I got dressed and headed out to get my morning cup of coffee. I let Lucky out on my way to the kitchen and then went back to the doors to watch Lucky for a few minutes. Lucky romped around in the snow for a little bit, looking like he was having a good time. It amazed me how big he has gotten in just a few months. He ran down to the beach, standing there staring off at the other side of the lake again.

I looked over and saw the glint of something again. I went into the garage, getting Jacob's binoculars, using them to look across the lake where I saw the glint. Panning the shoreline of the opposite side of the lake, I caught the glint of light in the binoculars again, trying to focus on it. I thought I saw something move, but after looking for a few minutes I couldn't make out anything so gave up. Lucky wanted back in, I needed to get to work. Leaving the binoculars on the table, I went down to the office.

Lucky seemed nervous or upset today. He was in front of the doors watching outside, pacing back and forth all day. I tried to let him out a couple of times, but he refused. I continued to work, but his pacing unnerved me a little bit. After work, we went upstairs, Lucky pushing the door to the basement shut behind us. He then went to the French doors, staring out, pacing back and forth.

"What is wrong Lucky?" I asked, walking up to the doors.

Opening the door, he ran out this time, heading straight to the lake, even going out on the ice a little bit. He stood there, barking, looking at the opposite side of the lake. Pacing back and forth on the ice for a little bit, then running back to the house. I let him back in, but he spent the rest of the evening next to the doors, alternating between pacing and lying in front of the doors.

After a small supper, I was sitting on the couch, trying to watch TV. Something about Lucky's behavior that day had me on edge. When Jacob called that evening, he must have sensed my mood. After we shared our day's activities with each other, Jacob enjoying the conference so far, he asked how my day was otherwise. When I hesitated a bit before replying, he asked, "What's wrong, Mattie?"

"Nothing," I said. I didn't want to worry him over a feeling.

"I can tell something is bothering you, what is it?"

I hesitated a minute, then said, "It is probably nothing, but I feel on edge today."

"Did something happen?" he replied.

"No," I said. "Not really. Lucky has been pacing in front of the doors, staring out across the lake nonstop. When I let him out, he actually ran out on the ice, barking something across the lake from us. It is probably nothing, but he has continued to stay by the doors tonight."

There was a pause on Jacob's end, "Do you want me to come home?" he asked.

"Oh no, Jacob," I replied. "I'm fine. It just has me on edge, seeing him unsettled. I'm sure there is nothing to it."

"You could go stay with Josh and Randy, or have Randy come stay with you if it would make you feel better. I can call them if you want me to."

"No, Jacob," I said. "Don't do that. I'm fine. I can call them if I need to. Lucky is just nervous, it put me on edge. Maybe there is some animal around that has him on edge."

"Probably," Jacob said, obviously not quite convinced. "Call me anytime if you need me. I'll fly home on the next plane if needed."

"Enjoy the conference, Jacob. I'll be fine. I love you," I said.

We hung up the phone, deciding I was tired I went to take a bath to help me relax and then climbed into bed, Lucky lying on his blanket.

Chapter 30

Allen watched as Megan went through her morning routine, made coffee, and let the dog out. What was with that damn dog? This time it came out onto the ice, barking in his direction. He glanced back up at the doors with his field glasses and was surprised to see Megan looking back in his direction with what looked like a pair of binoculars. He backed away from the small opening in his blind that he used to look out of.

He put the glasses down, wondering if she could see him after all. He stayed hidden for about 20 minutes, then took a chance, deciding to look again. The dog must have run back up to the house, he didn't see the dog in the yard anymore. Megan was no longer standing at the door either, she had gone downstairs to start her workday. The deck hid her from view down there, but he could see there was a light on, so he knew she was at her desk.

Tonight was to be the night, but he needed to make sure she would be home alone. He decided he had some time, so he went back to the cabin, napping throughout the day. He waited until a few minutes before Megan usually ended her shift at work, then walked back to the blind. He had everything packed onto the sled that he thought he would need for the trip over to Megan's that night. He had heard snowmobiles on the lake during the day, it was a small lake, so there were not many, but a few were good.

He was hoping to be able to blend his tracks with theirs. There were two places he had observed the snowmobilers getting on and off the lake throughout the day, so he planned out the route he would have to take to hide his tracks with theirs. It looked like fate was on his side though, it started snowing about lunchtime and has been snowing all day. He hoped it would keep up through the night. He looked up the forecast on his phone and saw that the storm should last for at least 48 hours. That was perfect, it would make any search for Megan harder.

He tried looking across the lake, but the snow was making it difficult. He could make out lights, but other than that, visibility was not good. He would stay until the lights went out, then head back to his cabin to rest until about midnight, then he would start his trek across the lake. Thankfully, he didn't have long to wait, as she shut the lights off about 10 that night. He went back to the cabin, resting until midnight.

He checked his pack, to make sure it had what he needed. He checked his guns and put one around his ankle, the other in the back waistband of his fatigues. He didn't bother with the night goggles; the snowstorm would hinder his view. He would have to rely on his compass to keep him going in the right direction. He had a flashlight in his pocket, he put his Bowie knife in a sheath on his hip. Deciding he was ready, he left the cabin, got the sled, and headed down the path to the lake.

The trek across the lake was slow, but he was able to keep his direction easily. He could make out some of the landmarks he had gotten to know while watching Megan. Soon, he made it across the lake, working his way up the backyard to the house. He stayed close to the tree line but was not worried that Megan would spot him. He got up level with the house, pulling the sled over to the basement doors. He quietly slid the basement door open and stepping in, leaving his boots outside the door like he did before.

Shutting the door behind him, he slipped out of his parka, leaving it by the door. He took off his gloves, lying them on his parka. He took out a pair of sterile gloves from his pocket, slipping them on, so he didn't leave any fingerprints behind.

He listened carefully, and after not hearing anything, he headed to the stairs. Reaching into his pocket, he activated the devices, shutting off all cell phone access. He made his way up the stairs quietly, listening the whole time to make sure that Megan was still asleep. Pausing at the door to the kitchen, he listened again, after not hearing anything, he slowly pushed the door open. He stepped into the kitchen, making his way to the living room, leaving his backpack on the kitchen floor.

***

In the bedroom, Lucky perked his ears up, hearing something he stood up, growling. I heard him and woke up. Listening carefully, I didn't hear anything, but Lucky growled again, heading to the bedroom door. I climbed out of bed, trying to walk to the door. Lucky got in between me and the door, blocking my way.

I stopped, listening closely, but still didn't hear anything. I looked down at Lucky and saw that his hair was standing up on end. I debated what to do and then decided to go back to the bed stand where my cell phone was. Grabbing my cell phone, I tried to dial Josh's number, but there was nothing. Looking at the service bars, I noticed it showed nothing there, which was odd. We always had decent service here. Maybe it was the storm.

All of a sudden, I thought I heard a noise in the kitchen, maybe it was just the house settling in the cold weather. Lucky growled again, deep in his throat, suddenly I knew it wasn't the house. There was someone in the house. I moved to the hall, Lucky trying to block me from going that way.

Peering around the corner into the hall, I didn't see anything. I patted Lucky's head, moving around him into the hallway, but he stuck close to my side. I crept to the living room, looking around. Stepping out into the living area, I saw a figure next to the dining room table.

"Well, look who I found," Allen said. I recognized the voice, instantly terrified. Somehow, Allen had found me. "I knew you weren't dead," Allen's voice came out of the dark. Lucky was still by my side, growling. Allen suddenly flipped the light on, blinding me for a couple of seconds. "What the hell?"

Allen said, "You're fucking pregnant?" I didn't say anything, too scared to speak. "You slut. How long were you cheating on me?"

I just shook my head, I didn't know whether to tell him the baby was his or not, maybe he wouldn't kill me if he knew the baby was his. "Allen," I started.

"Shut up!" He yelled at me. Lucky growled again. "Walk this way bitch." I slowly walked into the living room.

"Allen, listen," I started again.

"Shut up!" He said again. "I told you what I would do if you ever cheated on me. You not only cheated on me, but you are pregnant with his baby."

"Please," I pleaded.

"Please? You have the nerve to beg me? Five years of marriage, and you leave me for another man? You fucking slut. You're coming with me. I'll teach you a lesson. Let's go." Allen motioned to the basement door.

"Where are we going?" I asked.

"Never mind," Allen replied. "Let's go." He waved a gun at me, and my heart about stopped.

"Allen," I tried again, "I'm not dressed to go outside. Please, I'll freeze."

Allen laughed, "Like I care. Let's go." I started walking toward him, trying to figure out how to get out of this. I looked around with my eyes, trying to figure out a weapon I could use. Lucky stuck to my side but was quiet.

"At least let me get a coat and something on my feet," I pleaded.

"Just get over here and shut the fuck up."

I walked closer to him. When I was within arm's length, I stopped. He looked at me. "What the hell did you do with your hair? That is going to have to go back to normal. You look awful." He reached out, stroking my face. When I flinched away from him, he backhanded me.

I didn't fall but stumbled a little. Lucky growled, but I put a hand on his head, restraining him. I looked at Allen. "I don't care what you think Allen. I left you. You don't own me."

Allen looked stunned; I had never spoken to him like that before. "The hell I don't, you are my wife."

Something gave me courage that I had never had before. "No, Allen, you don't own me. I have a new life now, a life that you are not part of."

"You bitch!" he exclaimed. This time it wasn't a backhand; it was a fist. I flew backward over the couch, ending up on the floor. Lucky ran to me, whining. I started to sit up, dazed.

"Get up slut!" Allen exclaimed. He pointed the gun at me. I slowly got up, feeling blood run down the side of my face from his punch. "Get over here," he growled at me.

"I'm not going anywhere with you!" I cried. Right at that moment, Lucky dove over the couch at Allen. The gun went off as Lucky hit Allen in the chest. The force of the leap threw Allen backward. He lost the gun; it flew into the kitchen. Lucky was on top of Allen, snapping at him, it was all Allen could do to hold him back. Allen put his hand up to Lucky's head, Lucky grabbed it fully in his mouth. Allen screamed as Lucky bit his hand, drawing blood.

I was thrown back when the gun went off. I had been hit in the chest by the bullet. I lay there for a few minutes, watching as Lucky hit Allen and the gun went flying. I saw the gun fly into the kitchen. I struggled to my feet, blood running out of the wound, stumbling toward the kitchen.

Lucky had Allen pinned and was not letting go of his hand at all. As I tried to pass Allen, he reached out, grabbed my ankle with his other hand, and tripped me. I went flying and landed hard on the kitchen floor. I had the wind knocked out of me; I lay there trying to catch my breath.

Lucky had released Allen's hand, going for his neck. I couldn't move, my sight dimmed, and I struggled to remain conscious. My chest was on fire, I knew the bullet missed my heart, but it was so painful to breathe I thought it hit my lung.

I heard Allen scream again and looked at him. Lucky had him by the neck, biting as hard as he could. Allen's hands were trying to push Lucky away. I looked for the gun and saw it a couple of feet away. I crawled over to the gun, feeling a hand grasp my ankle.

I looked back and saw Allen had grabbed my ankle. He twisted my ankle as hard as he could. I screamed as I felt the bone snap. In response to my scream, Lucky started biting Allen's neck even harder. Allen let go of my ankle, trying to push Lucky off of him.

I pulled myself across the floor, grabbing the gun. I heard Lucky scream and saw Allen with a knife in his hand, Lucky was lying beside him on the floor. "NO!" I cried.

Allen, bleeding heavily from the neck, rolled over, pushing himself up onto his hands and knees. He looked at me, starting to crawl toward me. "Fucking bitch," he spit out, blood pouring out of his throat.

Lucky had almost ripped his throat completely out.

I grabbed the gun in both hands, aiming it at Allen. He raised the knife, bringing it down to my thigh. I screamed, pulling the trigger. Allen's head flew backward, blood, and brain matter flying everywhere. Allen fell on my legs, and I dropped the gun.

I lay there breathing hard, unable to catch my breath. "Lucky," I whispered. I heard Lucky whimper. "I'm so sorry boy," I started crying.

A few moments later, Lucky was at my side, licking my face.

"Oh, Lucky," I said, hugging him. I looked at him, it appeared as if the stab wound was in his upper hind leg area. He limped, but he seemed OK otherwise. He was bleeding pretty well though. "We need help boy. Can you try to get help?" I scratched his head briefly, feeling really faint. I don't know what I expected, but as I started to fall into unconsciousness, I saw Lucky head to the basement door.

***

Lucky struggled as he nosed open the door, then went down the basement stairs. His back leg hurt, and he was bleeding, but he knew his human needed help. So he went down the stairs, heading to the basement doors. He pawed at the doors, Allen had left them open just a little, just enough that Lucky was able to work on getting his paw in between them. He kept struggling was finally able to fit out through the gap in between the doors.

He headed outside, into the storm. He knew he had to get help, or his person would die. Lucky went through the snow, managing to find the path that led to Randy and Josh's house. It seemed to Lucky to take forever, but he finally got to his destination. Making his way up the steps to the back door, he scratched at the door, letting out a couple of feeble barks, nothing happened at first, then Lady showed up at the door checking out what was going on.

When Lady realized it was Lucky at the door she started barking, running back to the bedroom and then back to the door. Lucky lay down in the snow on the deck, worn out by his efforts and the amount of blood he lost.

The lights came on in the house, and soon, the light on the back deck turned on. Josh opened the door, "Lucky?" he said. He picked Lucky up, carried him into the house, and lay him on the kitchen floor. Randy shut the door, following close behind. "Look," Josh said, pointing to his hind leg. "He has been injured."

"Another animal?" Randy asked.

"Doesn't look like it," Josh said. "It looks like a stab wound from a knife."

"What do you think happened?" Randy asked. Josh was already up and grabbing his coats and boots out of the front closet.

"I don't know," Josh said. "Looking at his mouth it looks like he attacked something too. Call the cops and the vet, I am going to check on Mattie."

Randy nodded but grabbed Josh's arm as he was headed out the door, "Be careful," she said. He gave her a quick kiss and ran out the door after grabbing his hunting rifle.

Josh ran out to his truck and climbed in, speeding over to his sister-in-law's house. In the house, Randy was calling the cops, sending them to Mattie's house, then calling the vet. After she made those two calls, she hesitated for only a moment, then called Jacob to tell him what was going on.

"Hello?" a sleepy voice said on the phone.

"Jacob, it's Randy," she said.

Jacob was instantly alert, "Randy, what's wrong?"

"I don't know for sure yet," she replied. "Josh and I were woken up by Lady barking. We found Lucky on our deck. It looks like he has been stabbed. Josh is on his way to check on Mattie. I called the cops and the vet."

"Oh my God," Jacob said. "Keep me posted, I'll be on the next flight home." He hung up, immediately calling the airport and making arrangements for the next flight. He got on the first flight out in the morning, then called his boss, explaining to him what was going on. His boss understood, telling Jacob to let him know if he needed anything.

"A ride from the airport," Jacob said.

"I'll be there," his boss said. Jacob packed his bags, calling for a taxi. He could have gone to sleep for a couple of hours, but he knew he wouldn't be able to. He went to the airport, waiting impatiently for the flight home.

Josh arrived at Mattie and Jacob's house and switched the lights off before getting clear up to the house. He had a flashlight and grabbed his gun out off the front seat. He stopped a little distance away from the house, hiked up to the front door, and grabbed the key out of his pocket. He unlocked the front door but didn't worry about the alarm, he wanted it to go off. He turned on his flashlight, first looking toward the dining area, seeing blood on the floor. He followed the path of the blood to the kitchen, what he saw there stopped him cold.

Some man was lying there with the back of his head obviously blown away. Josh couldn't see more than that, so he walked forward. Soon he saw that the man was lying on top of Mattie's legs. He ran to her, pushing the man off of her—he was obviously dead. "Mattie," Josh called to her. "Oh God, Mattie! Can you hear me?"

Mattie was unconscious. Josh felt for a pulse. He felt a very faint one, almost nonexistent. He turned on the flashlight and looked over her for wounds. The one in her leg was bleeding heavily, but so was the one in her chest. He looked around and saw that the guy was wearing a belt he took it off, putting it around Mattie's leg, in an attempt to stop the bleeding.

He grabbed the two kitchen towels hanging nearby, putting pressure on her chest. He was horrified by the scene and was having trouble taking it all in. He pulled out his cell phone but discovered he had no service. That was odd, he never had a problem with service here. He threw it aside, praying the police would be here soon.

Josh was putting pressure on Mattie's chest wound, watching her breathing. "Come on Mattie, hang in there. Don't leave us." He pleaded.

As he watched, Mattie all of a sudden took a long, deep shuddering breath, then stopped breathing. "No, Mattie," Josh cried, tears coming to his eyes. He started CPR, praying help would arrive soon. He kept up CPR and soon heard the sirens. Please, he begged, please hurry. Within minutes, the lights lit up the house.

He heard car doors opening and yelled, "Hurry! In here!" Cops came in the front door, taking in the scene by flashlight. "Please," Josh yelled. "She's dying! Please help me!" Two policemen relieved him of the CPR while a third called for EMTs. A fourth helped Josh up asking him what happened. "I don't know. Her dog showed up at my house, looking like he had been stabbed and like he attacked something—his mouth was all red from blood. I had my wife call 911 and a vet while I drove straight over here."

"I take it you know her then?" the cop asked.

"Yes, she is my sister-in-law. Please help her, she is pregnant!"

"I have a pulse!" the one cop stated. They stopped the CPR and monitored.

"Who is the man?" the policeman asked Josh.

"I don't know," he said. "I have never seen him before."

The EMTs arrived soon, taking over care of Mattie. They loaded her up in the ambulance, taking her to the city. The police asked Josh a lot of questions, but finally allowed him to go home. One policeman followed him home to check on Lucky. Josh walked through the door and Randy ran over to him. She hugged him, then looked at him. "What happened?" she asked, then saw the cop behind him. "Josh?"

"Mattie is hurt," he said.

"What? How?"

"It looks like she was stabbed and shot. This policeman wants to see Lucky. Has the vet been here?" Randy looked stunned. "Yes, he is still here, looking after Lucky's wound. Lucky was stabbed. He checked him out and said he would be just fine, stitched him up, and is bandaging him up now."

They led the cop into the living room where Lucky was lying in a dog bed by the fireplace, his sister, Lady, by his side. The cop got all the details about Lucky's injuries from talking to the vet. Once he felt like he got all the answers he needed he left. The vet stayed, finished dressing Lucky's wound, told Randy and Josh he would come back the following day to check on him, and then he also left. Randy closed the door behind him and went to Josh.

"How is Mattie?" she asked.

Josh shook his head, "Not good. I need to call Jacob." He pulled out his cell phone, noticed he had cell service here while he didn't at Mattie's house, then called Jacob.

"Josh," Jacob said upon answering the phone. "What's going on? Is Mattie OK?"

Josh closed his eyes. "No, Jacob, she is on her way to the hospital."

"Hospital!" Jacob cried. "What happened?"

"I'm not sure," replied Josh. "It appears she has been stabbed and shot."

There was silence, "What? Who did it?"

Josh rubbed his eyes, "I don't know Jacob. The guy is dead. It looks like Lucky attacked him, allowing Mattie to get the gun, and she shot him."

"Oh my God," Jacob said. "Tell me she will be OK Josh."

"I can't," Josh replied. "Her heart stopped when I was there. I had to do CPR." He heard Jacob sob on the phone.

"Is she… dead?" he asked.

"No," Josh said. "We got her heart beating again, but Jacob, it doesn't look good."

"I'm on the next flight home. My boss is picking me up. He will take me straight to the hospital." There was silence, and then Jacob said, "You said Lucky was hurt too?"

"Yes," Josh said. "I think he jumped the guy. He then came to our house to get help for Mattie."

"Take care of him, Josh," Jacob said.

***

Josh left Randy at home to care for Lucky, then drove to Nora and Donald's house. It was now around 2:00 am, but he didn't want them to hear about Mattie on the news. He knocked on the door continuously until Donald finally opened the door, Nora right behind him. Their eyes opened wide when they saw Josh.

"Josh, what's wrong?" Nora cried as he came into the house.

Josh told them what happened, once they got over their initial shock they ran upstairs and got dressed. They all got into the car, starting for the hospital. The trip there was quiet, except for the occasional question that no one seemed to be able to answer. They arrived at the hospital, running.

They rushed to the emergency desk where a nurse led them into a private consultation room. She told them a doctor would come to speak to them in a few minutes. None of them seemed to be able to sit, pacing back and forth. Finally, a lady walked in wearing a doctor's jacket.

"Hi," she said. "Are you Mattie's family?"

Nora spoke up, "Yes, I'm her mother-in-law. This is my husband Donald and our son Josh, Mattie's brother-in-law. Her husband is flying back from a conference as soon as possible."

The doctor nodded. "I'm Dr. Jackson," she said. "Mattie is in very serious condition. She has lost a lot of blood and, unfortunately, has gone into labor due to stress. I have to take her to surgery to repair her injuries from the gunshot and the stab wound. I have consulted with OB; they will perform a C-section to deliver the baby."

Nora was crying, "It's too soon for the baby."

"We know, but if we don't deliver now the baby won't make it. As it is, I'm not sure Mattie will make it. Her heart has stopped twice since she got here. I've got to go, now. I'll be back to update you as soon as I can." With that, she rushed out of the consultation room before anyone could ask any questions.

Nora sat down, holding her head in her hands. Donald sat down to comfort her while Josh pulled out his cell phone again. He called Jacob, filling him in on what was going on. He then called Randy to fill her in also. He told her to get some rest if she could, it was going to be a long night.

They waited in the consultation room, alternating between pacing and sitting. It was about four hours later that the doctor came back, this time dressed in scrubs. Everyone jumped up at her entrance. "Please," the doctor said, "sit down." She pointed at the chairs, taking the one nearest to the door as everyone sat down. The doctor sighed, running her fingers through her hair.

"Dr. Jackson," Nora said, "please tell us, how is Mattie doing?"

"I'm so sorry," Dr. Jackson replied. "Mattie lost a lot of blood. The bullet splintered when it hit her rib. A piece of it nicked a major artery, the rest of it went through a lung."

"What are you saying?" Donald asked.

"Mattie died on the operating table. We did everything we could, but there was too much damage and blood loss."

"Oh my God," Nora cried, weeping. Donald wrapped her in his arms, crying himself.

Josh had tears flowing too, but asked, "What about the baby?"

"The baby is fine," Dr. Jackson said. "She is premature, but she seems well-developed and doing well. She has been taken to the NICU where they are monitoring her."

"Can we see her?" Nora asked.

Dr. Jackson looked at them, "I will make arrangements for you all to see her, but it will have to be one at a time."

"Thank you, doctor," Donald said, as Dr. Jackson rose to leave.

She looked at them all, "I'm so sorry for your loss. I wish I could have done more." She walked out of the room, shutting the door behind her. Nora, Donald, and Josh all burst into tears.

Josh pulled himself together, calling Randy. "Josh?" Randy said. "How is Mattie?"

She heard Josh sob. Then he said, "She's gone, Randy. They couldn't save her."

Randy started crying, "Oh no. God no. What about the baby?"

"Jayden is alive. She is in the NICU and appears to be doing OK. They are monitoring her since she is premature."

Randy cried for a little bit, then asked, "Does Jacob know?"

"No, I haven't told him yet. I can't bring myself to call him to tell him over the phone."

Randy agreed, "I think you should wait; he will be so upset. Telling him over the phone before he flies here is not a good idea."

Josh looked at his watch. "His plane leaves in about 25 minutes. I will wait to tell him. He is going to be devastated."

"He is, but he has a daughter to think about. We will need to stress that to him."

Josh agreed, "We get to see Jayden soon. We can only go one at a time, she is in the NICU." Josh told Randy to try and get some sleep. "We are going to keep one of us at the hospital at all times for Jayden. We will need you to take over later."

"I'll be there," Randy said. They hung up, Randy went to Lucky, lying on the floor next to him. "I'm so sorry, Lucky," Lucky whined, it appeared to Randy like he understood, mourning the loss of Mattie as they all were.

Chapter 31

Jacob paced around the gate for his flight, waiting for news of Mattie and the baby. They soon called for people to board the plane. He grabbed his bag and made his way onto the plane. Once in his seat, he could barely contain himself as he waited for the plane to take off. He kept praying that Mattie and the baby would be OK. He couldn't live without her, didn't want to live without her.

Everyone around him seemed to fall asleep on the flight, but he was wide awake. He glanced at his watch, two hours until they landed. This flight was going to be unbearable. He stared out the window as they flew across the country. All he could do was pray his wife and daughter would be alive when he got there.

He called for the stewardess and explained to her his situation. She spoke to the captain who then called ahead to the airport. She soon came back, telling him they would get him off the plane first. There would be a customer transport waiting for him at the gate to take him to the exit. She also said there was a seat up front that they were going to move him to, so he could get off quickly.

They took his bag from overhead, moving it with him to the front of the plane. He expressed his gratitude, taking his new seat. He asked the stewardess if she thought they could find out the status of his wife and daughter for him. She told Jacob she would see what they could find out but did tell him that she wasn't sure they would be able to get too much information for him due to the privacy laws. The stewardess came back a few minutes later, stating that the captain was trying to arrange for him to get a phone call to the hospital. She came back soon and said they hadn't been successful in reaching the hospital, but that they would keep trying for him.

They kept trying to reach the hospital, to get information for Jacob, but were unable to. After what seemed like an eternity, they finally landed at the airport. The airline was true to their word, getting Jacob off first, then rushing him to the exit where he met his supervisor. They drove as fast as possible in the snow to the hospital, pulling up to the entrance where Jacob dove out, running in.

He ran up to the desk, asking where Mattie was. From a room off to one side, Josh stepped out and called for him. Jacob ran over, Josh pulled him into the room. Donald and Josh were both there, eyes red. "Where's Mattie?" Jacob asked.

Donald stood up, "I'm so sorry Jacob," he started to say.

"NO!" Jacob cried out.

Donald took his arms, "Mattie is gone. They tried to save her, but they couldn't."

Jacob fell into a chair, sobbing. "How?" he asked.

Josh replied, "She was stabbed in the leg, shot in the chest. The bullet hit a rib, a piece splintered off, then hit a main artery to the heart, the rest went into a lung. She lost too much blood. They tried to repair the artery, but it was too late."

"Stabbed? Shot? Who did it? Why? I don't understand." Jacob looked at his brother and father for answers.

Donald answered, "We don't know. Lucky attacked the guy, which apparently allowed Mattie, who had already been shot, to get the gun, then she shot the guy. That's all we know right now. The guy is dead."

"I need to see Mattie," Jacob said.

Donald nodded, "I'll go tell them."

Jacob walked to the window, looking out but not seeing anything. "Who would do this to Mattie?" He said aloud, not expecting an answer. He turned quickly, grabbing Josh's arm. "What about the baby? Is Jayden…" he couldn't bring himself to say it.

Josh shook his head, "Jayden is fine. They did a C-section; she is in the NICU. She is a little small, but she is doing great. Mom is with her right now."

"Thank God," Jacob said.

Donald came back in with a nurse. "Mr. Vance, if you come with me, I will take you to see your wife." Jacob followed the nurse down the hall. She took him to a room where Mattie was lying on a hospital bed, with a sheet pulled up to her chin, then left him alone. Jacob walked over to her, tears flowing. He reached out shakily, stroking her cheek. She was so cold. "Oh, Mattie." He moaned, sitting on the stool next to her bed. "How am I going to live without you?" He leaned his head down on the bed next to her head, crying. He heard

Mattie's voice in his head, heard their conversation about naming the baby. "Jayden Lee," Mattie had said.

Jacob looked at Mattie and tried it out himself. "Jayden Lee."

"I wanted to name her after you. Jayden is close to Jacob and, well…"

"Lee is my middle name. Are you sure?" he asked her.

"Only if you like it. If you don't, we can discuss some other names." Mattie said, watching him. "Jayden Lee Vance. I love it. I feel honored that you want her to be named after me."

"How could I not want to name her after you? You have accepted her as your own, you love her as your own. She should be named after her father."

"Jayden," Jacob had said. He looked at Mattie. "I'll take care of our baby girl, Mattie. I promise to be a good father to her, the best that I can." He stood up, kissed Mattie on the forehead for the last time, then walked out the door to go see his daughter.

Nora was back in the private waiting room with Donald and Josh. She ran over to hug Jacob; he hugged her back. "I'm so sorry honey," she said.

Jacob just nodded, then said, "I want to see my daughter."

Nora smiled through her tears. "She is beautiful Jacob. She is doing so well."

He smiled a little, then went out to the desk to ask to be taken to see her. They took him to the NICU, had him put on a gown, mask, and gloves, then took him in to see her. He expected her to be in an incubator, but she wasn't. She was in a bassinet, swaddled with a blanket and a warming light over her. A doctor walked up to him, "Mr. Vance?" he asked.

"Yes," Jacob replied.

"I'm Dr. Patel. I'm taking care of your daughter."

Jacob nodded at him, "She isn't in an incubator?"

Dr. Patel smiled and shook his head. "She is doing very well for her size and being born a few weeks early. I want to keep her here for a day or two, make sure she is eating well, and her vitals and lab work remain stable."

Jacob reached out and touched Jayden's hand. She is so small. She was beautiful. Jacob looked at Dr. Patel, "Can I hold her?"

The doctor nodded. "In fact, it is time for her feeding, would you like to give her a bottle?" Jacob nodded.

The doctor told Jacob the best way to pick her up, then led him over to the rocking chair. Jacob sat down, cradling his daughter in his arms. "I'll have the nurse bring a bottle. Here is the button, if you need anything, just push it."

Jacob nodded, but he couldn't take his eyes off his daughter. She looked like a miniature version of Mattie but with light blonde hair. He could see Mattie in the shape of her face, her eyes, her nose, and her mouth. Jayden opened her eyes, looking up at Jacob. She didn't cry, just looked up at him intently.

"Hey, little one," Jacob said. "I'm your daddy." He smiled down at her, a tear sliding down his cheek. The nurse brought him the bottle, instructing him on feeding and burping her. Jayden took the bottle eagerly, eating well. He burped her as instructed, and then Jayden nestled her head into his neck, falling asleep there. The nurse came back in, telling him he was a natural.

"I do need to take her through," she said. "The doctor wants to check some lab work." Jacob nodded, kissed his daughter on the head, then handed her back to the nurse.

Jacob left the NICU, taking off the gown, mask, and gloves. The doctor was standing at the nurse's station, so Jacob walked over to him. "When do you think I can take my daughter home?"

Dr. Patel looked at him, "She may be able to go home late tomorrow if she continues to do well, but it may be the following morning. We will know more tomorrow morning."

Jacob thanked him, heading back to where his family was waiting. They were all sitting there waiting for him. He walked in, sitting down, putting his head in his hands. His mom rubbed his back, asking "How was Jayden?"

He raised his head and smiled, "She is perfect. I fed her a bottle and talked to the doctor. I may be able to take her home tomorrow night or the following morning. We will know more tomorrow." He noticed that Randy wasn't there. "Where's Randy?" he asked.

Josh spoke up, "She is at home, taking care of Lucky."

"Lucky is alive?"

Josh nodded, "The vet came and saw him and said that he lost some blood and would be a little weak for a few days. He should be fine. There is a slight concern he may be a little lame on that back side where he was stabbed, but time will tell."

Jacob shook his head, "I just can't figure out what happened." There was a knock on the door just then, a man walked in.

"Mr. Jacob Vance?" He looked at the men in the room.

"I'm Jacob Vance," Jacob stood up.

"I'm Detective Ron Miller. I'm sorry for your loss, I hate to intrude, but I have some questions I need to ask all of you if that is OK." Jacob nodded, motioning to a chair. The detective shut the door behind him, sitting down.

"Do you know who the man was that killed Mattie, Detective Miller?" Jacob asked.

"Call me Ron. Not yet, but we are working on it. We should know soon," Ron said. "Has there been anything strange going on that you have been aware of? Any strangers in the neighborhood? Cars pulling in the driveway, then turning around? Catch anything on your video cameras?"

Jacob shook his head, "No, nothing out of the usual." He thought for a few minutes, "Well, there was something, but I don't know that it is of any importance."

"You never know," Ron said. "What is it?"

Jacob told him about the way Lucky had been acting, looking out over the lake, going into the trees on one side of the house to come out at the lake, his attitude toward Mattie, and shutting the basement door. This was all news to Josh, Nora, and Donald. They looked at Jacob in surprise. Ron took notes. "We just chalked it up to his being protective of Mattie and the baby. Then we would catch a glint of light, like a reflection across the lake in the area the Lucky was staring."

"Does anybody live over there?" Ron asked.

"No, that is all national forest grounds. We didn't think anything of it, but it kept happening at different times of day when the sun was out."

"You said that it was right across the lake from you?"

Jacob nodded, then asked, "Do you think that is important?"

Ron shrugged, "It could be. We will look into it."

"Detective? Ron," Jacob asked, "Can you tell me what happened? I just don't understand."

Ron nodded. "I can tell you what we know right now. It appears that this man entered through the basement doors. He snuck up the stairs, but I think your dog heard him. Mattie must have either heard the guy or heard Lucky get up and growl. They walked out of the bedroom and probably saw the man standing in the dining area."

"Somehow, probably by pointing the gun at her, he got her to walk toward him. We are not exactly sure what happened first, if he shot her first, or if Lucky attacked first, but the gun must have flown out of his hand. The man's hand was almost torn off, Lucky had a hold of him and apparently wouldn't let go, until he saw an opening and went for the man's throat. Mattie was able to get to the gun. The man stabbed Lucky, which made Lucky let go, and then Mattie shot him in the head, killing him instantly. He fell, landing on her legs."

"Truthfully, had Mattie not finished him with a bullet, he probably would have died from his throat wounds. Lucky did a hell of a job on him. We hope to learn more after the doctor's reports are done, it should tell us in what order things happened when we learn more about Mattie's injuries." Jacob looked at his family, they all seemed to be in shock.

"There are a couple of other things that we discovered," Ron said, opening his notebook. "First off, we realized that the no one was able to use their cell phones in your house. Upon a search, we found three devices that blocked cell phone services hidden, one under the desk in the basement, one behind the TV in the living room, and the third behind the headboard of the bed in the master."

"What?" Jacob said. "That means he had to be in our house at some point in the past. How could that be."

Ron shook his head, "We will know more when we find out who he is, I hope. Have you had any repairmen or delivery men come to the house in the last several months?"

Jacob shook his head, "No, Josh and I take care of all repairs that would need to be done. No delivery men at all." Ron made note of that.

Donald asked, "You said a couple of things, what else did you find."

Ron hesitated, then said, "It appears that this man intended to kidnap Mattie."

"What?" Jacob cried, "Why?"

Ron shook his head, "We don't know. Outside the basement door was a homemade sled. Inside the door, he left his snow boots, parka, and gloves. We found a backpack near the basement door. It was filled with rope, duct tape, a couple rags, needles, and a couple of vials of some drug. We have sent that in to be analyzed. Can you think of anyone that would want to harm Mattie?"

Jacob shook his head, "She did move here because of a bad relationship, but he ended it with her. He was married and had never told her that."

"Do you know his name?" Ron asked.

"No, she never said, and I never asked. It wasn't important to me; I didn't need or want to know the details."

Ron nodded. "OK, I'll look into that. You mentioned that Lucky followed a path through the trees down to the lake shore. That is how he got to your house. The snow covered a lot of his tracks, but in the trees, it didn't."

"Do you think he came across the lake? That he had been watching Mattie from there?" Josh asked.

"I think that is a good possibility. We will check into that. Is there anything else any of you can think of that might help?"

Jacob shook his head. "Mattie had a rough childhood and went from foster home to foster home. She told me about her past once, and then we never really talked about it again. She had worked hard to get over the past."

Ron nodded, put his notebook in his jacket pocket, and pulled out some business cards, "If you think of anything that might be helpful, no matter how small or insignificant it may seem, please call me." He gave a card to all of them. "I'll be in touch when I know more." He looked at Jacob, "Your house is an active crime scene, so you will need to stay somewhere for at least tonight. If you need to go pick something up, the cops on the scene will let you in. I would suggest that before you go home, you hire someone to clean up. You shouldn't have to see that. Again, I'm sorry for your loss."

They thanked him and the detective left the room. Jacob and his family sat there in stunned silence.

Finally, Josh spoke up, "Come on Jacob, you can stay with me. Lucky will be happy to see you." Jacob nodded. They all got up and left the room. Jacob left his contact information with the NICU, so they could reach him. He told them he would be back first thing in the morning, which truthfully was only a few hours away.

***

They walked into Josh's house and were met by Randy. She had been crying, immediately she wrapped Jacob in a hug. "Oh, Jacob, this is horrible."

263

Jacob hugged her, then pulled back. He had spotted Lucky over by the fireplace. He walked over, sitting on the floor next to the dog. Lucky put his head on Jacob's lap as Jacob leaned back against the wall next to him. "Hey, Lucky," Jacob said.

"He is a brave dog, a hero in a sense," Josh said.

Jacob looked up at him, "What do you mean?"

Randy said, "If Lucky hadn't found a way to get out of the house to make his way over, Josh would have never found Mattie."

"You found her?"

Josh nodded. "I knew Lucky was hurt. He would have never left Mattie unless something was wrong. I had Randy call the cops and the vet for Lucky; I went over to your place."

Jacob looked down at Lucky, stroking his head. He had never seen the dog look so sad. It was like he knew Mattie was gone. "What did you find at the house?" he asked Josh.

"Jacob," Josh said. "You don't need to have that image. Remember her as you last saw her before your trip."

Jacob nodded, tears edging down his cheek. "Did she say anything?" he asked.

"No," Josh said, "she was unconscious." He wouldn't tell him that she died while he was there, that he had to perform CPR on her. There were some things that he didn't need to know, having a visual picture of all the blood and Mattie lying there dying, was something Josh would never tell him. Josh couldn't get the image out of his head, that was bad enough. Jacob would be tortured by that image.

"I should have never left," Jacob said.

"Don't do that Jacob," Randy said. "You had no idea this was going to happen. None of us did. She wanted you to go. Remember that she encouraged you to pursue your dream job."

"She was my dream," Jacob said. Tears streamed down Randy's face as she watched the pain that Jacob was in.

"I know," she said. "That dream included that baby girl that survived. Jayden needs you, Jacob." Jacob let out a sob and drew in a huge breath. He nodded. He smiled up at Randy through his tears. "I need her too. I can't wait for you to see her Randy. She is beautiful. She looks just like Mattie." Randy smiled back, "I can't wait to meet her."

Josh spoke up, "Jacob, you should get some rest if you are going back to the hospital early. The spare room is all yours."

Jacob shook his head, "If you don't mind, I'd like to lay on the couch next to Lucky." Randy told him that was fine, going to get him a pillow and blanket.

Josh told Jacob that as soon as they were notified by the police that they could get into Jacob's house, he and Randy would arrange for someone to clean it for him. They would start calling around to find someone in the morning and have them on alert for when the house could be entered. Jacob nodded, staring down at Lucky, stroking his head. Randy and Josh left the room quietly and headed to their own bedroom, where Josh held Randy while she cried herself to sleep.

***

Jacob had a fitful night, sleeping very little. He finally gave up, going to take a shower. Josh had gotten his suitcase from Jacob's supervisor when he had dropped him off at the hospital. He tried to be as quiet as possible, so he wouldn't disturb Josh and Randy. He walked out of the bathroom to find them sitting at the table. "I'm sorry," Jacob said, "I didn't mean to wake you."

Josh shook his head, "We didn't sleep very well either."

Randy smiled at him, her eyes swollen and red. "Have a seat, I'll make you some breakfast."

Jacob scratched Lucky on the head, the dog wagged his tail weakly in return. Jacob turned to face Randy again, "No thanks, I'm really not hungry."

Josh looked at him, "At least have some toast and coffee. Jayden needs you to keep your strength up." Jacob knew he was right, so he sat down, ate a couple pieces of toast, and drank a cup of coffee. They ate in silence, none of them seemed super hungry so Randy just made everyone toast.

Finally, Randy asked, "When will you get to bring Jayden home?"

Jacob smiled at the thought of his daughter, "Dr. Patel said maybe tonight, if not then probably first thing tomorrow." Jacob's cell phone rang. He looked at it, it was early for a phone call. He answered the phone, and after a brief conversation, he hung up. "The police are done with the house. We can go in any time."

Josh nodded, "I will call for someone to clean it while you are at the hospital."

"I need my truck; I can't have you two driving me everywhere."

Josh looked at him, "I can take you to go get your truck, but I won't let you in the house until it gets cleaned."

"I don't want to go in to see it," Jacob replied. "I'll wait. I hope we can get it cleaned up soon, as I will need to get the car seat from the nursery for Jayden."

Josh nodded, "I'm sure I know someone who can take care of it this morning."

"Thank you, both," Jacob said, choking up a little bit. "I appreciate all you are doing for us."

Randy started tearing up again, "We loved Mattie too. We will be here for both you and Jayden, at any time. Please don't hesitate to lean on us or let us know if you need anything."

Jacob stood up and hugged her, then he and Josh headed out to the truck.

They pulled up to Jacob's house, and they both sat there staring at the house. Jacob knew he didn't have the strength to go in there until it was cleaned, he asked himself last night if he would even be able to ever go in there again. The happiest days of his life were spent in that house. They had decorated the nursery for Jayden together and fixed up the playroom in the basement together. Mia loved this house. This is the house he would bring their daughter home to. The house was full of her love for the baby she never got to meet.

"Jacob?" Josh asked quietly. "Stupid question, but are you OK?"

Jacob smiled, "You're right, it is a stupid question. Yeah, I was just thinking about bringing our daughter back to this house. Mia loved this place."

Josh nodded, "Do you think you can live here after what happened."

Jacob nodded, "Yes, I think so. She filled this house with love, and I believe that it is still full of love. I want our daughter to be here where Mia loved her so much." With that, Jacob got out and went to his truck, going to the hospital to see his daughter. Josh watched as he drove away, turned and looked at the house, then went home to make some calls.

Jacob got to the hospital early and went to the NICU. "Just in time, Mr. Vance," the nurse said when he came in, dressed in gown, mask, and gloves again. "She needs a diaper change and to be fed. Would you like to do the honors?" She smiled at him.

"I will if you walk me through it, I've never changed a diaper before," Jacob replied.

"Not a problem. Come on over." She let him change the diaper, instructing him on how to do it. He wrapped her in a blanket, swaddling her like the nurse instructed him to. The whole time, Jayden followed him with her eyes and never cried. "Your daughter is such a good baby. She rarely cries and when she does it is for a diaper change or to be fed. She consoles easily."

Jacob picked her up, "She seems really… laid back, calm."

The nurse agreed, "She doesn't seem to let much stress her out, that's for sure."

Jacob sat down in the rocking chair with her, putting his finger in her hand. She grasped it with her hand, holding on. "You are a strong little girl." She looked at him like she understood what he was saying.

"You're going to have to help me be strong too."

The nurse came in with a bottle and gave it to him. "Dr. Patel should be here soon to check on her. You are welcome to stay here as long as you want to."

He thanked her and started feeding Jayden. She took the bottle hungrily but soon was starting to doze off. He tickled her chin to wake her up, so she could finish eating. She soon finished, Jacob laid her on his shoulder, patting and rubbing her back. She let out a couple of belches, then tucked her face into his neck, falling asleep. He sat there rocking her, enjoying just holding this amazing little girl.

They stayed like that for over an hour when Dr. Patel showed up. "Well, good morning, Mr. Vance," Dr. Patel said.

"Jacob, please," he replied. "Morning doctor."

Dr. Patel nodded. "You seem perfectly at home holding her. She definitely feels comfortable with you."

Jacob smiled, "I hope so."

"Well, she wouldn't let anyone else hold her for any extended period of time. Just long enough to feed her and burp her, then she wanted to be laid back down. Only then would she sleep."

"Really?" Jacob looked down at her in amazement.

"Yep. She knows you are her dad; that is obvious. Unfortunately, I need to take her from you to give her a quick exam." Jacob nodded and handed Jayden to the doctor. Dr. Patel walked back over to the bassinet, telling Jacob he was welcome to come watch and ask questions if he had any.

Jacob watched as the doctor listened to her heart and lungs, then her abdomen. He checked her hip joints and reflexes, explaining why he was doing things as he did them. He finally pulled back, wrapped her back up in the blanket, and handed her back to Jacob.

"Well, doctor," Jacob asked, "how is she doing?"

"She is doing great. She has been eating well, sleeping well and made dirty and wet diapers. I want to check her bloodwork again early afternoon. If that is within normal limits, I would say you can take her home late afternoon today."

"So no problems related to…" he hesitated, "her mom's attack?"

Dr. Patel shook his head, "None whatsoever. She is perfectly healthy. A little small due to being a few weeks early, but she will catch up in no time."

"Thank you, Dr. Patel," Jacob said.

"Don't thank me. Someone was looking out for this little one. Now if you will excuse me, I need to go check on some other patients."

Jacob nodded, taking Jayden back over to the rocking chair. Jayden had woken up during the exam, seeming to watch both the doctor and Jacob intently while the exam took place and the two of them talked.

A nurse walked in after Jacob had been sitting for a few minutes. "Excuse me, Mr. Vance," she said. Jacob looked up at her. "There is a lady here, Randy, who would like to come in and see your daughter, is that OK?"

Jacob nodded, "That's fine. She can come anytime she wants to."

The nurse nodded and went back out. Soon Randy came in, all gowned up like Jacob. Jacob stood up, telling Randy to take the rocking chair. After she was seated, Jacob handed her Jayden. "Meet your goddaughter," he said, smiling.

Randy looked down at Jayden, Jacob heard her breath catch, "Oh, Jacob, she is perfect," Randy said.

Jacob sat on the stool next to the rocking chair. "Yes, she is." He agreed.

"Hello little girl," Randy said softly. "I'm Auntie Randy."

Jacob laughed, "Auntie Randy?"

Randy laughed, "Well, maybe not, but I'm sure she will come up with a name for me in time." Jayden looked at Randy just as intently as she had Jacob and the doctor. After a few minutes, she snuggled in, falling asleep.

Jacob smiled, "That means she likes you. I was told that she wouldn't fall asleep for anyone else. They had to put her back in the bassinet for her to fall asleep. She only falls asleep with people she seems to know are her family."

Randy smiled down at Jayden, "She is a smart girl. Have they said when she will get to go home?" Jacob nodded, "Dr. Patel wants to check another lab early afternoon. If it is good, then I can take her home shortly after that. Did Josh find someone to clean the house?"

"Yes," Randy replied. "They are actually there now. He called some friends of his. Josh is supposed to let me know when they are done."

"Great," Jacob said. "I need to go get the car seat and diaper bag from home, so I can have those here to take Jayden home."

"Josh said he could grab those for you if you would like, so you can spend the day here." Randy offered.

Jacob looked down at Jayden, "I think I will take him up on that offer."

Randy handed Jayden back to Jorden and traded him seats. She watched Jacob with Jayden and could see in his face how much he loved this little girl. It was then that she knew the two of them would be just fine. They sat there, talking quietly while Jayden slept. She got fussy after a bit, so Jacob took her over to change her diaper, while Randy watched, holding Jayden's hand. Jayden looked at both of them. When Jacob got the diaper changed, she kicked her feet.

"Oh my," Randy said, "look at those little feet."

Jacob swaddled her back up and looked at Randy, "You and Josh will make great parents. I hope you don't take too long to make me an uncle. Jayden wants a little cousin to play with."

Randy smiled, "I can't wait to be a mom," she said. The nurse came back in at that point.

"This is a popular little girl," she said. "Mr. Vance, your mom and dad are here."

"Can we all be in here together?" Jacob asked.

"Normally, we would only let two in at a time, but since she is the only baby in here, it will be fine. I'll send them in."

Randy slid the other couple of rocking chairs closer so Donald and Nora could sit down as well. Jacob picked up Jayden, waiting for his mom and dad to come in. They soon came in; Jacob motioned them to have a seat. He knew his mom had got to see Jayden last night, but his dad hadn't, so he took her and handed her to his dad. He motioned Randy to take the third rocker, while he sat on the stool, next to his dad. His dad handled her gently but like a pro.

"She is so tiny," he said, an obvious hitch in his voice.

"Tiny but perfectly healthy," Jacob said. Donald put his finger in Jayden's palm, and she closed her hand around it.

"Strong little one," Donald smiled at her. Nora was leaning over the side of his rocking chair, looking at Jayden with an adoring smile on her face. Jayden was looking up at Donald, then let out a little yawn. Nora looked up, tears in her eyes, "She looks just like Mattie." Jacob nodded. Pretty soon Josh joined them bringing the car seat and diaper bag, promptly taking Jayden away from Nora, who had taken her away from Donald as soon as she could.

"Let me see my niece," he said. Donald let him sit in the rocking chair and sat on another stool. "Well, thank goodness," Josh said.

"What?" Jacob said.

"Thank goodness, she doesn't look like you," Josh said, smiling at his brother. Everyone laughed.

The nurse came in a little while later. "The lab tech will be here in a few minutes to draw blood. I should take her for now. Why don't you all go find some lunch then come back?"

Jacob looked at his watch and was surprised to find it was after one in the afternoon. "I will give her a bath and get her dressed for when you come back. Dr. Patel is pretty sure she will be able to go home once the lab is back. Do you have an outfit in the diaper bag for her?"

Jacob nodded, and she smiled. "Perfect. Go eat and come back. Hopefully, we will have good news for you then."

They walked out of the NICU, taking the gowns and things off. Surprisingly, Jacob found that he was pretty hungry, so he agreed when his parents suggested some place better to eat than the hospital cafeteria. They went to a small restaurant close by, asking for a table in a quiet section of the dining room. They were taken to a table toward the back, where the other tables near them were empty. They sat down, giving their waitress their drink orders. She brought the drinks and then said she would be back in a few minutes for their food order.

As they were looking over the menu, Jacob's phone rang. "It's Detective Ron," he told the others. They all listened to Jacob's side of the conversation, heard him tell the detective where they were, and watched expectantly as he hung up. "He says he has news and wants to talk to us. He will be here in a few minutes."

While they waited, they placed their orders, even though now their appetite wavered due to the tension they all felt at what news the detective had for them. They received their food and started to eat. When the detective got there, he took a seat at the table. He ordered a coffee and slipped his coat off.

"I'm sorry to intrude on your meal, but I knew you would want to be updated," Ron said.

"It's really OK," Donald said. "Did you want to order something to eat?"

Ron shook his head, "I had a sandwich earlier, thanks. Please, eat, don't let me stop you." Ron looked at Jacob, "I wanted to ask you if the name Allen Davis meant anything to you?" Jacob shook his head, "Never heard the name before. Why?"

"He was the man that attacked your wife." Ron didn't offer any more but watched everyone around the table.

"Why?" Jacob asked. "Who was he?"

When Ron felt sure that nobody here knew the name, he told them what he knew. "Allen Davis is a homicide detective from Sparks, Nevada. He was married to a woman named Megan for five years."

"I don't understand, what does that have to do with Mattie?" Donald asked.

"Megan disappeared a few months ago. Her abandoned car was stolen by a thief and later went over the bank of a river. State police never found his body. They theorized that he had kidnapped Megan, and she was in the car with the thief when it went into the river. She was also thought to have been killed. Her body was never found either." They were all listening, intently.

Jacob said, "I still don't know what you are getting at Ron."

Ron opened a manila folder he had lay on the table in front of him, pulling out a picture. "This is Megan." He handed the picture to Jacob. Jacob stared at the picture.

"How can this be?" He looked at the detective.

"I don't know, we are still investigating."

"Jacob?" Nora asked. Jacob looked at her dazed, he handed her the picture. They all looked at it. It was a picture of Mattie, but a couple years younger with long blond hair. There was no mistaking her.

Ron said, "It appears she left her husband, let it seem like she was killed and started over here. She never said anything about a husband?"

Jacob shook his head. "No, she never mentioned one. Why would she do this?" Jacob was struggling to understand.

Ron said, "Usually the reason in a situation like this is he was abusive. She couldn't take it anymore, so she took off."

"You're saying this man, this homicide detective, beat Mattie?" Donald asked, looking furious.

"I don't have evidence of that yet, but that could be it. I should know more soon." His phone rang, "Excuse me for a minute," he said. He walked a little distance away and took the call.

Jacob was lost for words. He finally looked at his dad, "Why would she lie to me?" he asked.

Donald looked at him, "Listen, Jacob," he said. "If this man abused her, she must have felt her life was in danger. She started completely over from scratch, wanting a new, happy life. She found that with you."

Jacob heard his dad, thought about that. He sat back in silence, the thought of someone abusing Mia, his Mia Amata, for five years made him furious. He could never understand how someone could do that to a woman.

"Jacob," his mom said. He looked at her. "You need to forgive the lies. To you, to us, to Mattie herself—she was Mattie, not Megan. She escaped a lot of abuse and pain. Can you do that?"

"Yes, I think I can," Jacob said finally.

Detective Ron came back and sat down. "I'm sorry about that, I had some men searching the other side of the lake across from your house."

Jacob leaned forward, "Did they find anything?" he asked.

Ron nodded, "Quite a bit, I'd like to take you out there right now if you have time."

Jacob nodded, "I have to be at the hospital soon to pick up my daughter, hopefully take her home, but I can go." Josh said he was coming with them. He told Randy he would see her at home.

Jacob and Josh climbed into Jacob's truck, following the detective out to the lake. They followed the gravel road past the boat pier they both had used many times. The detective had stopped his car at the pier, Jacob pulled up behind him while Josh rolled down the window. He walked up to the window, "I was told not to try and drive my car past this point. They said a truck can make it though, I need to hop in with you if that is OK."

Jacob nodded, he climbed into the back seat. Jacob looked at him, "Where to?"

"Follow the road around." Jacob did, he and Josh had never been past this before as it was always marked as no entrance. The road turned into no more than paths for two tires. He glanced back at Ron who nodded. He followed it around the lake until they were about straight across from Jacob's house.

They pulled up behind a truck belonging to the sheriff's department and parked. As they climbed out, they were met by a sheriff's deputy. He shook Ron's hand, who introduced him to Jacob and Josh. He offered them his condolences, then turned to Ron. "You are not going to believe what we found here."

He led them in a little deeper until they came to an opening where a little cabin stood. He motioned to it, "I'll show you what we found there in a minute. Let's go this way first."

He started walking to the bushes, and they followed him. Pretty soon they came to the lakeshore. Jacob said, "That's our house!" as he pointed across the lake.

The deputy nodded. He showed them the blind that Allen had made. "We figure he sat in here, watching your house." They looked inside, seeing a pair of binoculars in there along with a couple of empty water bottles. The deputy showed them tracks leading down to the ice, "He must have crossed here." Jacob just shook his head in disbelief. "So we must have been getting reflection off his binoculars from time to time."

"I believe so," the deputy said. "Come on, let's head back to the cabin."

They made their way back to the cabin. "Follow me around back." He led them behind the cabin where they found a car. "The car was almost completely hidden under branches and snow. We had someone bring the keys from the guy's belongings that were found at the victim's house. We found this." He opened the trunk and showed them weapons, ammunition, a raft, and oar. "It seems he used the raft to paddle across before the ice cover."

Josh exclaimed, "He was here that long?"

"Yes, it seems that he got here in about late October, early November." He motioned them to follow him. He led them back around to the front of the cabin, opening the door. They all crowded in, there wasn't much room in there. "It appears this was an old hunting cabin he found. He made some repairs to it, using the fireplace for heat." He pointed to the packages of food on the shelf above the fireplace. "MREs?" Ron asked.

"Yep. He has plenty there to last another month or two." They looked around and Jacob noticed a pad of paper on the table that had writing on it, it was in an evidence bag. The deputy saw him look at it. "He had extensive notes on you, your wife, your daily activities. They haven't all been read through yet, but it appears he was watching you really close."

Jacob was furious at this invasion of their privacy. The deputy went on, "It seems he had some plan to kidnap your wife, bring her here, and torture her." Jacob felt sick to his stomach. He wanted to leave and get the hell out of here, but the deputy said, "There is one more thing to show you. If you gentlemen would step back, please."

They all did as he asked. He reached down, putting his index finger in a small hole, what looked initially like a knothole in the floorboard. They heard a click, then he pulled up. To their amazement, it revealed a small wooden enclosure.

"What the hell?" Jacob said.

"We found his drawings of this. He had tried to burn them, but we were able to get the idea." He pulled out his phone and showed them all a picture of a drawing they had rescued from the fireplace. It showed a hole in the floor with a woman lying in it. Jacob couldn't stand it anymore. He ran out the door, running to the trees, throwing up in the bushes. The others followed him out but respectfully waited until he could pull himself together again. Once he was able, he rejoined them.

"I'm sorry," he said.

Ron looked at him, "I would have reacted the same way, don't worry about it." Jacob gave him a nod of thanks.

The deputy said, "Well, that is all we have found. We are almost finished here, need to get all the evidence bagged up." He turned to Jacob, "I've been in touch with the government about this cabin and what happened here. They are going to send a group in to tear it down and burn it." Jacob nodded.

Ron said, "I'm going to stay here and help out, I think the deputy can give me a ride back to my car." The deputy nodded, "Happy to."

Jacob shook their hands, "Thank you."

The deputy shook his hand, but said, "I just wish we had caught him before this all happened."

Chapter 32

Josh and Jacob went back to the hospital. They pulled into the parking lot, parking next to Josh's pickup.

"You OK?" Josh asked.

"Again, with the stupid questions." Jacob smiled wryly. "No, but I have to be. I have a daughter to take care of. I can't let Mattie down there. Do me a favor?"

Josh nodded, "Name it."

"Can you tell Mom and Dad what the cops found across the lake? I just don't have it in me."

"Of course. I'll call them when I get home. Let me know if you are taking Jayden home tonight."

Now it was Jacob's turn to nod, "I will." They both climbed out of Jacob's truck and Josh gave Jacob a hug before climbing in his truck and driving away. Jacob made his way into the hospital, going straight to the NICU. Dr. Patel was just coming out, seeing Jacob putting a gown on he said, "No need for that, Jacob," Jacob must have looked panicked for a minute. "Oh no, no," Dr. Patel said holding up his hands.

"I'm sorry. I should have been more considerate of what you have been through. I just meant that your daughter is ready to go home. You don't need to gown up. The nurse is in there getting her dressed. She passed her hearing test, and the car seat test and her lab is looking really good. The nurse will show you how to use the car seat if you need her to and then you can take your beautiful baby girl home."

"Thank you, doctor," Jacob said, shaking his hand. "That is the best news I've had."

"No need to thank me. You have a strong little girl there. I've set up an appointment for her in a couple of days with the pediatrician on file for her. It is important she follow up then."

Jacob nodded, "I'll make sure she is there."

"The nurse has all the paperwork for you to sign, you should be able to leave soon." The doctor turned, starting to walk away, when he looked back and said, "Take care of yourself Jacob, and that little girl. If you ever need anything…" He trailed off, turned after a moment, and walked away.

Jacob smiled, Jayden seemed to have the doctor wrapped around her little finger, just like everyone else. He turned, entering the NICU for the last time. After some car seat training and signing a bunch of paperwork, he finally walked out of the hospital with his daughter.

The car ride home was uneventful. He kept looking back, seeing the car seat. He couldn't believe he had a daughter. *Oh, Mia Amata*, he thought. *I wish you were here to see how beautiful she is.*

He pulled up to the house, walked around to get Jayden out and also grabbed the diaper bag. They went into the house, where he sat her seat on the table. He was surprised to see that she was wide awake. They had told him when she would need her next bottle, and she was freshly changed before she left the hospital. She wasn't fussy, she was just awake. He unbuckled her, taking her out of the seat. He walked over to the couch with her, sitting down.

"Hey, baby girl," he said softly. "It's just you and I now." He unwrapped the blanket from her.

She stretched her little arms above her head. He examined her hands and fingers. She grasped his finger in hers, letting out a huge yawn. When she let go of his finger, he slipped off her little socks, examining her little feet and toes. *She was so perfect*, he thought.

He put her socks back on and realized that the newborn outfit was too big for her. He should probably get her a few preemie outfits since she was so small. The hospital sent home some smaller diapers for her, but they won't last him very long. He wrapped her back up in the blanket. She appeared sleepy, so he took her back, lying her in the crib.

She looked at him, then closed her eyes, falling to sleep. He stared at her for a while, watching her sleep, then remembered he needed to text Josh. He walked out, shutting the light off after making sure the monitor was on. He walked out to the living room, sat down, and turned on the baby monitor. He made sure to set it up where he could see Jayden.

Pulling out his cell phone, even though he was exhausted, he sent his family a text message, letting them know he was home. He called his supervisor who told him he could start his FMLA, after his bereavement time off. That meant he had several weeks at home with Jayden before he had to go back to work. He then sent Randy a text, asking her if she would possibly have time the following day to pick up some smaller outfits and diapers. She replied that she would be happy to, asking him if he wanted help tonight since it was his first night home with Jayden.

He thanked her, saying he thought they would be fine, but promised if he needed anything he would let them know. He invited them to come over in the morning, to bring Lucky home. He looked at the live video on the baby monitor, smiling as he watched his new daughter sleep. She was sleeping so peacefully. He decided he would try to nap while she did, she would want a bottle soon. He lay down on the couch, soon falling asleep watching his daughter as she slept in her crib.

Jacob woke up a couple of hours later to Jayden fussing in her crib. He got up and walked into the nursery, turning on a small lamp, so he could see. "Hey, baby girl," he said. "What's wrong?"

He picked her up, taking her to the changing table. He changed her diaper, swaddled her, then took her out with him to get a bottle. She stopped fussing but was trying to fit her fist into her mouth like she could eat that. "Hang on," He smiled at her, "I'm going as fast as I can!"

He followed the nurse's instructions, made a bottle, then walked to the couch and sat down. He gave her the bottle, and she ate hungrily. "Well, you take after your dad in one way at least! You have a good appetite. Your mom ate like a bird." His heart hurt when he mentioned Mia, but he was determined that their daughter would get to know her through him.

***

Jacob and Jayden survived their first night together without much trouble at all. He was able to get some sleep in between feedings and diaper changes. He was up the next morning, sitting at the table drinking coffee and eating toast when someone knocked at the door. He opened it, letting Randy and Josh in.

They brought Lucky with them. "Hey, Lucky," Jacob said, leaning down to scratch his head. He wagged his tail, then promptly went straight back to the nursery, limping on his sore leg. Everyone watched him go, then quietly followed him back to see what he was up to. They entered the nursery to see him with his paws on the rail, standing on his back legs, looking in the crib at Jayden.

Jacob started to say something, but Josh grabbed his arm, motioning for him to stay quiet. Lucky soon got down, lying down beside the crib, promptly falling asleep. They all backed out, heading back out to the table.

Josh spoke first, "Lucky is something else. He didn't sleep the best last night; we could hear him whining in the living room. Checked on him a couple of times but couldn't find any reason for it, he seemed fine. He was waiting at the garage door for us this morning, ready to come home. It's like he knew Jayden was home."

Randy said, "I noticed he didn't look for Mattie like he used to do."

Jacob nodded, "He is a smart dog. Mia and I came to the conclusion a few weeks ago that he was not her dog, he was Jayden's dog."

Josh and Randy agreed with that, there was too much they had witnessed not to believe it. They finished their coffee and left. Josh was taking Randy into town to pick up a few things for Jacob. Jacob had given her a small list of things he needed, along with his credit card.

About mid-morning, when Jacob had just put Jayden down after feeding her again, this time lying her in the cradle he brought out to the living room, his cell phone rang. "Hello?" he said. "Mr. Jacob Vance?" a man's voice asked.

"Yes," he replied.

"My name is Harry Wilkens. I was your wife's lawyer."

Jacob was surprised. "My wife's lawyer? I didn't know she had one."

"She came to see me right after the two of you married. I was sorry to hear of her death."

Jacob thanked him, then asked, "Why did she come see you?"

"To make a will. She asked that I get a hold of you right away after her death to read the will with you. I was wondering if I could swing by today? Maybe in about an hour?"

"Um, sure. I'll be here."

"Perfect. I will see you soon."

Jacob hung up, standing there pondering what the lawyer would tell him. Josh and Randy showed up, carrying in the sacks of things they had picked up. Seeing Jacob looking so intent, Josh asked him if something was wrong. Jacob shook his head, "I don't think so. I just had a strange phone call."

"From whom?" Randy asked. Jacob was putting away the groceries she picked up for him, while she was taking the clothes, she had bought for Jayden out of the bags, starting to take tags off. "Mattie's lawyer," Jacob said.

Josh and Randy both stopped and looked at him, "Her what?" Josh said.

"Her lawyer," Jacob said. "He is on his way over here to read her will."

"She had a will?" Randy said, as she went back to taking the tags off the clothes. "Apparently. I never knew anything about it," Jacob said.

"I guess it makes sense," Josh said.

Jacob looked at him, "How so?"

"Well, if she was running from an abusive husband like the detective said then she might have been worried about him finding her. She would have wanted to leave something for you and Jayden."

Jacob thought about it as he finished putting groceries away, stowing the sacks. "I guess. The problem with that is, if she left with only the clothes on her back, what could she possibly have to give us? I know she owns the house, so maybe that is it. I wonder now how she managed to be able to buy the house."

Randy took the baby clothes to the washer and put them in, starting it up. There came a knock at the door, Jacob said, "Well, I hope we get some answers from the lawyer." He opened the door and let him in.

Jacob introduced the lawyer to his brother and Randy asked if it was OK if they stayed. The lawyer smiled and said, "Mattie thought they might be here and said it would be fine for them to stay if you wanted them to." They started to take seats at the table when they heard a little fussing from the cradle.

"I'll get her," Randy said. She went to pick Jayden up, coming back to the table with her. She sat down, "I guess she just wanted to be included." Jayden was wide-eyed, looking up at Randy.

Harry looked at them, "Again, I am so sorry to hear about Mattie. She was a very special young woman, I only met with her a couple of times, but it was obvious how much she loved you all. This must be Jayden? Her daughter?"

Jacob nodded, "Our daughter."

Harry replied, "Of course. Shall we get to it?" Without waiting for a reply, he pulled a manila folder out of his briefcase. "Before the will, Maddie asked that I read you a letter." He opened the letter and started:

"My dearest Jacob, if Mr. Wilkens is reading this to you, then I assume that Allen has found me and killed me."

"You would also by now have learned that I was married to him. I am so sorry that I had to lie to you, but I was terrified. The five years that I spent married to Allen were a living hell. He controlled my life, flying off the handle for nothing. I was beaten on a daily basis, usually his punches were to areas that could be hidden by clothing. I can't tell you how many times I contemplated suicide just to end it all. I came to the conclusion that either he would kill me, or I would, until that last day."

"I woke up, after having had a severe beating the night before, the worst yet. In the shower, I grabbed the razor, almost slit my wrists, but something stopped me. Maybe I was too much of a coward. Allen dictated my entire world, from what I would wear to what I did with my time. He created what I see in my mind as 'THE LIST'."

"It dictated what I would be doing that day. Any detour from that list would result in a beating. This particular morning, he wanted me to go get groceries. He had the list and money waiting for me and told me which store to go to, how long it would take and what time I would get home. He laid my clothes out for me, even makeup which I never was allowed to wear, but this time he had lost control in the beating, so my face was all bruised up."

"I got to the store, but once I got out of the car, I found myself getting sick. I can't give you details, but two people came to my rescue. They knew by looking at me that I had been recently beaten. They took me away, helping me to escape."

"I need you to promise that you will not look for them, as it could put their lives in danger. They are in a similar situation as I was. I cannot tell you how I got the house or the job. I hope you can understand. There is a network of people that help others to escape situations like mine and by giving you details; I would endanger them all."

"I never expected to meet your family or you. I didn't expect to fall in love with you. I thought there was no such thing as love at first sight, my marriage to Allen almost made me believe that love didn't exist at all. Then I met Randy and Josh. They seemed so deeply in love my doubts were starting to go away."

"Randy became my sister by heart, Josh my brother, before I even met you. I love them both with all my heart. Then I met you. The moment I saw you on the path in the woods, I knew. I loved you then."

"I tried to deny it, tried to fight it. You helped me to realize that I never loved Allen at all. He was… a way to survive. I wanted to be loved by someone, having never been loved before. I was in love with the idea of being in love. The story of my childhood was not a lie. The only thing I kept from you was the fact that I was married. I thought Allen loved me. I was so wrong. I made another bad decision when I married him, I paid for it, dearly.”

“I found out I was pregnant just a couple days after I left him. When I saw the baby on the ultrasound, I knew I had to survive for her. I knew it was a girl from the start. I argued with myself about you, I wanted you to love me so badly because I loved you so much, but how fair was it to you that I couldn’t tell you the truth?”

“Several times, I thought I should let you go, so you could have a real marriage with a woman who was truly free. Then I started thinking that I was not Megan Davis anymore. Megan Davis died in a car accident when it went into a river. I could have the life I wanted with you that I dreamed of. I’m sorry if I wasn’t fair to you, but I hope I made you as happy as you made me.”

“I imagine Randy and Josh are with you as Harry reads this. I just want them to know I never took our friendship for granted. I love them so much. I hope they, as well as the rest of your family, can come to forgive me for my lies. Tell Nora and Donald, Janet and Jack that I love them all.”

“Jacob, I love you with everything in me. You gave me so much happiness and love, I never wanted anything. I hope that our daughter, Jayden Lee, is with you and that she survived whatever happened to me. I know that you will be the best father to her, that you will love her unconditionally. I hope that you can also forgive my lies and eventually tell Jayden about me. Let her know that I love her so much, that I am sorry I had to leave her when I did.”

Harry looked up, there was not a dry eye around the table, even his. “It is signed ‘All my love, now and forever, Mia Amata’.”

Jacob stood up, “I need a minute.” He went back into the bedroom, closing the door behind him. Those left at the table could hear him sobbing, crying out her name. Randy and Josh both had tears running down their faces, Josh got up, heading into the bathroom, washing his face. He came back out, taking Jayden from Randy. She then went and did the same, throwing water on her face. She came back to the table.

Harry stated, “I hope that this letter ultimately gives you all peace. I know it is hard to deal with the loss of a loved one.”

Randy spoke up, “It will. We all loved Mattie so much.”

A few minutes later, Jacob came out, red-eyed but under control. "I'm sorry," he said. "Please continue."

Harry pulled out the next paper. "This is Mattie's last will and testament. I will skip the usual sound mind and body legal jargon and get right to it. Let's see, I leave my husband, Jacob Lee Vance, my house and all my belongings, in the hope that he can raise our daughter there close to his family. I also leave Jacob the money that I have in my savings account, $10,000."

"I also make him benefactor to my life insurance. He is free to do what he wants with the money, but I hope that he will put some of it away to pay for college for our daughter, and any other children that we may have before my death." Harry read on, but the rest was mainly just legalities. He then pulled out the insurance policy. "Here is her life insurance." He handed it over to Jacob. Jacob looked at it, then looked back at Harry.

"Are you serious?"

Harry nodded. "I'll send it into the company along with a copy of Mattie's death certificate and your marriage certificate. You should receive a check within a month or two."

"But this is for a million dollars?"

Harry nodded again, "Mattie shopped around. She got the best deal she could for the largest amount she could. At first, it was to be put into a trust fund for her daughter, but after you married, she wanted you to be able to raise your daughter comfortably."

Jacob sat back, stunned. He looked at Josh and Randy, they were also stunned into silence. Jacob reached for Jayden, taking her from Josh and wrapping her in the blanket Mia had made for her. He looked down at her, her bright blue eyes looking back at him. After a few minutes of silence, Jacob looked at the lawyer, "I want half of it put into a trust for Jayden, can I do that?"

Harry nodded. "You can. It is yours to do whatever you want with. I'd be happy to handle all the paperwork for you if you would like."

Jacob nodded. "I would appreciate that. Maybe you could also help me draw up my will. I have a daughter to look out for now."